GET GRIBNITZ

HOWARD GIMPLE

There's a thin line between ad man and madman.
    Anonymous

CONTENTS

PART TWO
The Eastern Tip of Long Island

PART THREE
Back Home

PART ONE

Lower Madison Avenue, NYC, Circa 1988

CHAPTER ONE

Persons could have called the meeting at any time on any day in the last two weeks, but the scumbag made it at seven thirty on the day before Yom Kippur because he wanted to stick it to all the Jews in the department. That didn't bother me. The last time I set foot in a synagogue was my bar mitzvah. And that was under duress. Not only was I missing a Knicks game, but the rabbi's breath smelled like stale stuffed cabbage.

We're crammed into an empty office. Thirteen of us in a space designed for half that many. Plastic folding chairs are lined up in three rows of five, with a couple more against the back wall. I'm in the middle seat of the front row. Nicky's on my right. The rest of the row is empty. I guess they want to stay out of the line of fire.

Bart Vanzetti is sitting right behind Nicky, cackling, "Holy crap, holy crap. He's cleaning house. Last in, first out. I'm toast."

When Vanzetti first got here a couple of months ago, Nicky appointed himself the kid's rabbi, which in agency-speak is mentor, guru, sensei, and guide all rolled into one. He said Vanzetti reminds him of his younger self. Very talented with zero self-confidence and consumed by paranoia and anxiety. If he was really a Nicky clone he'd also have to be manic-depressive, obsessive-compulsive and semi-suicidal.

"Don't worry, Barto," Nicky says with pseudo sincerity. "Nothing's gonna happen. Stew talked to Barney. We're fine."

"So what does this mean?" He's waving the memo like kids do with those little flags at the Fourth of July parade.

CREATIVE STAFF MEETING

IMPORTANT PERSONNEL ISSUES

7:30 TONIGHT

MEETING ROOM B

ATTENDANCE IS MANDATORY

JAMES G. PERSONS, EXECUTIVE CREATIVE DIRECTOR

I say, "It means that Persons is doing what he should've done a couple of weeks ago. He's the creative director. Don't you think it's about time he meets the creatives he's supposed to direct."

Now everyone is shouting at me.

"You met with Barney?"

"What'd he say?"

"What's going on?"

This is one of those times I wish I could stick my fingers in my mouth and do one of those shrill whistles that you can hear for miles. But whenever I try it, nothing comes out but spit spray. I throw my hands up in the air and holler, "Shut the hell up, everyone!" Not as cool, but it gets the job done.

Now I have to say something. I don't want to tell them Barney confided that the agency almost went bust, so I say, "Barney loves us. He thinks we're a great creative department. He said he's super proud of the work we've done."

"So that's why he had his new creative director throw our great work in the trash?" This from Esther Goldfarb Emerson, Jewish American princess from one of the Five Towns on Long Island, I can never remember which one. Also the very talented lead writer on the Domino Sugar account.

"Barney didn't have anything to do with that," I tell her. "In fact, he was pretty pissed about it."

Somebody from the back shouted, "Are they gonna put them back up?"

"I wouldn't hold my breath."

I don't know if this calmed everybody down or stressed them out even more, but it quieted the room.

Seven thirty comes and goes, then seven thirty-five and seven forty. People are getting fidgety and the buzz of rampant paranoia is getting louder. At a quarter to eight Persons struts in like Leonard Bernstein making his way to the rostrum at Philharmonic Hall—that's if Leonard Bernstein weighed three hundred pounds and fell into a dumpster on his way to Lincoln Center.

He has a wild nest of curly black hair that looks like a family of small rodents set up housekeeping in it. His white button-down shirt has stains from his last dozen meals. It's tucked in just enough to cover his bulging gut. The ends of a skinny black tie dangle untied down the sides of his shirt. His shiny brown pants look like they were once part of a suit worn by a chimney sweep. His fly is hanging at three-quarters staff; a small tuft of yellow boxer shorts peeks out at the top.

He walks up to the front of the room, clears his throat, and says, "Hello, people."

He pauses for a few seconds, waiting for a response. Nobody says anything, so he continues. "I'm James Persons. I was brought in to bring this department to the next level. I've seen your work and it's good. Some of it is very good. But I think you can do a lot better. Some of you might find my methods a little unconventional, but I assure you they work."

He sneers down at me. "Mr. Gribnitz, it has come to my attention that you had a problem with my little demonstration yesterday."

I glare back at him. "Uh-huh."

"And why did you feel you had to go running to Mr. Boyce?"

I stand up. Now, instead of him looking down at me, I'm looking down at him. Me being six four to his five ten. I try not to gag at his skunky breath. I look back. Everybody's wide-eyed, like they're watching a horror movie.

I turn back to Persons. "The ads on that wall were the result of a lot of hard work. Not just by the creative staff but the whole agency. Barnett Boyce was a big part of that effort. Framing and hanging those ads was his idea. When you marched down the aisle, ripped them off the wall, and dumped them in a garbage bin, after I got over my initial urge to punch you in the eyeball, I wanted to see if Barney knew about your little stunt, because not only was it insulting to all of us, it was an insult to him too."

He looks out at the room. "Do all of you feel that way?"

No response. Most stare down at their knees.

"I'm sorry if I offended any of you," he says in a supercilious voice that lets you know he's not sorry at all. "But I was sending a message."

I don't know if it's what he said or the way he said it, but my blood, which was already simmering, is now at full boil.

Through clenched teeth, I say, "And you thought the best way to send a message to your new staff, most of whom you've never met, was to disrespect them and the work they were most proud of. Is that your idea of the best way to communicate with the people you're supposed to lead?"

He looks at me smugly and says, "Yes, it is."

I take a step closer.

"Let me explain to you the nuances of sending a message, Mr. Persons." I spit when I pronounce the *P*.

"If I wanted to send a message to you I could say something like, 'I don't know how it was in Harvey Nielsen's agency, but here at UPAN, even though we don't have a formal dress code and the creatives have wide latitude in the casualness of their attire, we really don't think it's a good reflection on the agency when our people, especially our senior executives, come in day after day looking like they've spent the night wallowing like a hippo in a particularly disgusting garbage dump. So, not every day if that's too much trouble, but at least two or three times a week, we'd appreciate it if you take a shower and perhaps change your clothes. A little deodorant and mouthwash wouldn't hurt either. It might erase that fetid stench that emanates from your presence.' That's one way of sending a message." I smile through clenched teeth. "Or I could do this."

I reach over, grab one of the dangling ends of his tie, and yank it hard off his neck. I scrunch it up in my hand, blow my nose in it, rub my armpits with it, and stick it down the back of my pants like I'm wiping my ass with it. Then I take the tie and throw it in his face. He catches it reflexively.

"But if I sent you a message that way," I scream, "I'd be a FUCKING ASSHOLE!"

Then I turn and stomp out of the room.

CHAPTER TWO

I head straight to Boyce's office. Karol's at her desk, looking at pictures of puppies.

"Is he in?"

"Yeah. You look a little weird. Is everything all right?"

"I'll tell you after I talk to Barney."

Boyce is at his desk reading the *Wall Street Journal*. He hears me come in. Looks up.

I stick out my hand. "Barney, I really enjoyed working here with you the last three years."

"What? You're quitting? I told you to sit tight and I would take care of things."

I'm feeling a little woozy, probably an adrenaline crash. I collapse on a chair. "I'm not quitting but I don't know if I'll be able to work here anymore."

"What the hell are you talking about?"

I tell him what happened. As I'm talking I'm getting pissed off all over again. When I finish, I figure he's gonna ream me out and fire my ass. If you're good enough, you can get away with being an insubordinate wiseass, but physically attacking your creative director is almost always followed by a boot out the door, usually while being escorted by security. I know this from experience.

I'm ready for him to start screaming at me, telling me what a stupid, irresponsible jackass I am. How I'm thirty-four years old and it's time for me to grow up. How he was the only one crazy enough to hire me when the rest of Madison Avenue wouldn't touch me with a ten-foot pool cue. He actually used that particular turn of phrase after I said something I probably shouldn't have during a new business presentation. The vice president of account services cut me off in mid-sentence and incorrectly corrected me during a pitch that was going well. It was at that point I told him that if I wanted to hear from an asshole I would have farted.

We lost the pitch, and I almost lost my job.

But Boyce doesn't say any of that. In fact, he doesn't say anything at all. What he does is let out a huge belly laugh and keeps laughing until he starts gagging and turns red. I'm sure he's gonna choke to death. He finally calms down, catches his breath and says, "Gribby, that's the funniest damn thing I ever heard."

"So I'm not gonna be fired?"

"Not if I can help it," he roars. "Remember, I still own 51 percent of the agency." He sits up and puffs his chest out. "The first time I saw Persons I wanted to spray him with Lysol. I swear to God, I don't know how someone can stand to be such a pig. Makes me sick to my stomach every time I get within ten feet of him." He furrows his brow. "Nielsen's going to be very upset. He seems to have a blind spot when it comes to Persons." His face tightens in concentration. He's doing mental calculations. "You may have cost me half a million dollars."

Now I'm confused. "How?"

"Nielsen's interested in buying the agency outright. I've been talking to some other people but he's the front-runner. Saving your hide is going to set back those negotiations." Then he breaks into a big grin. "But it's worth it." He looks at his watch. "It's late. Get the hell out of here. I'll deal with Nielsen. Be in my office tomorrow morning and I'll let you know where you stand."

CHAPTER THREE

Cookie sashays over to my table. She glances up at the Miller High Life clock and says, "You're early. Ya get fired again?"

"I'll let you know tomorrow."

"Guinness?"

"Yeah. And a shot of Jameson to keep it company."

I'm sitting in a corner booth at Raymondo's, a saloon masquerading as an Italian restaurant and not very good at either. The bar is nothing to write home about, six stools from beginning to end. There are a half dozen tables and a couple of booths with red Mystic tape over the rips in the red pleather seats. And it's never crowded. That's why we come here. Most bars and restaurants in Manhattan get really packed at the end of the day, first with happy hour then the dinner crowd. But most nights at Raymondo's, we're the only ones in the place. It's like our clubhouse.

Cookie is the other reason we come to Raymondo's. She knows us and what we drink. She's friendly without being overly familiar. She's Greek, with short jet-black hair and huge, dark brown, half-crossed eyes; one looks right at you while the other one looks in toward her nose. Her real name is Callidora Papageorgiou, which is why she goes with Cookie. Though she's probably around forty, she still looks great in the black minidress that Raymondo, the sleaze, makes all the waitresses wear.

She comes back with a bottle of Guinness and a tumbler of Irish whiskey. Two and a half shots and one cube, which she knows is the way I like it. "You wanna look at the paper?" she asks over her shoulder as she walks away.

"Nah, I don't think so."

So I'm staring into the whiskey, thinking about what I did. I don't regret it.

My father always said, "Don't take shit from nobody, 'cause once you do they'll always treat you like their toilet." The only worthwhile advice he ever gave me.

That advice worked on the streets and playgrounds of Flatbush a lot better than it does in the offices and boardrooms on Madison Avenue. Back then, the Irish and Italian kids from Holy Innocence, the local Catholic School, would come to Judea Center, where our parents forced us to go to afternoon Hebrew classes. The goyim thought it was big fun, or maybe God's will, to beat up the Jew boys.

Since I was the biggest in the class, I was close to six feet in the sixth grade, and also, to tell the truth, 'cause I sorta bullied them a little myself, maybe a little more than a little, I figured it was my duty to stand up for my classmates, defend my turf, so to speak.

One cold December evening, three of the Holy Indians (that's what we called them, but not to their faces) were waiting for us when we came out. The other kids cowered in the doorway. Usually these street fights between twelve-year-olds is just a lot of pushing and shoving. Not this time.

I walked toward them, trying to look tough. "Why don't you guys leave us alone."

The biggest one came at me. He had greasy blond hair and a little pig nose. A younger version of Joe Palooka, the comic book prizefighter. "You gonna make us? Jew bastard."

From the back, one of his pals yelled, "Christ killer."

Is that what they teach them in catechism?

He glared at me, spit at my shoe and swung at my jaw. I turned my head reflexively. The fake-fur collar of my winter jacket absorbed most of the blow. By the time it hit my cheek it was just a tap. But he didn't know that. As far as he knew I took his best shot and shrugged it off.

It was the first time I was ever hit in the face. Blind rage consumed me. I dived at him and tackled him to the ground, throwing wild punches. Most missed but one or two connected. That was enough.

After they realized their boy was getting the worst of it, his buddies pulled me off him. I stood there facing the three of them. The first kid's nose was bleeding. My fists were clenched at my side, waiting for them to jump me. I knew I had no shot, three against one. And I was sure none of my pansy-ass Hebrew school pals were going to pitch in. But I figured I'd at least get a couple of good shots in before I got massacred.

Nosebleed glowered at me and snorted. *Here it comes*, I thought. But instead of launching an attack, he turned to his friends and grumbled, "Fuck these kikes. Let's go."

That was the last time they came around the Hebrew school.

Every once in a while I'd see him around the neighborhood. He'd glare at me and I'd glare back. But it was a glare tinged with respect. I don't think Persons's disdain for us turned into respect, but I know he won't be throwing any more of our work in the garbage.

I'm sucking on my beer, considering my options, when the front door opens and in walks Terrance Asiago. He marches over to my table, stands over me, hands on hips, and shouts in his affected upper-crust Boston accent, "Are you out of your fucking mind!" Word is his family owned a couple of Italian bakeries in Boston's North End, which would make the top of the ciabatta the only real upper crust in his background.

He's wearing a gray pinstripe Brooks Brothers suit with a perfectly pressed powder-blue oxford shirt and a navy-blue tie with red and gold diagonal stripes. He's the first account guy I ever thought of as a friend. Of course, he spends most of his day kissing clients' asses like the rest of them, but he does have some respect for the creative product, which is more than most account pukes. And he'll go out of his way to sell the good stuff.

Once you get to know him, he's really not as much of an asshole as you'd think when you first meet him.

I look up. "So you heard about my little tantrum."

"Everyone in the agency heard about it. By now I'm sure half of Madison Avenue is talking about it. You know damn well what the New York advertising community is like. It's a small town filled with petty gossips who like nothing better than to spread lies and rumors about their competition at every opportunity.”

“So I really stepped in it this time, huh?”

He sits down opposite me and grins. “Actually, no.”

“No?”

“James Persons is one of the most reviled people in the industry. Right now, the word on the street is you’re a hero.”

“You’re kidding?”

“That’s what I’m hearing.”

“So I have nothing to worry about?”

“Not exactly. It seems that the only individual in our business who doesn’t think Persons is a vile snake is Harvey Nielsen. Fuming would be one way to describe how he reacted to what you did. When I left the office, Boyce was in a closed-door meeting with him. My guess is you’ll still have a job on Tuesday, but I can’t guarantee it. As you know, Nielsen bought himself a lot of clout at the agency.”

At that moment Nicky walks in with Jeannie, Terrance’s right-hand woman, along with Bart Vanzetti and Esther Emerson. A couple of minutes later the rest of the creative crew arrives.

Cookie comes over, but before she can ask anyone what they’re drinking, Terrance puts his arm around her and says, “My dear Callidora, today all drinks are courtesy of the Fiduciary Trust of New York. Make mine a Campari and soda.”

As the senior account manager, Terrance can charge almost anything to any of his accounts using the agency’s credit card and the client will get billed for it, usually with a 17.65 percent markup.

Cookie comes back with the drinks, then puts a bottle of Jameson on the table with a couple of clean glasses.

Cookie keeps the beer and booze coming. We’re all talking, laughing and telling advertising war stories. I’m about as shit-faced as I’ve ever been in my life, which is saying something. I have a vague recollection of saying goodbye to Terrance, Nicky and some other blurry faces.

Next thing I know, I’m in a back booth, curled up in Jeannie’s lap. The place is empty except for Cookie carting away dead soldiers and wiping off tables.

I open my eyes, see Jeannie looking down at me. "You're a real shmuck, you know that, don't you?"

"What are you talking about?" I slur. "I'm a hero. Everyone loves me. Didn't you get the memo?"

She shakes her head in exasperation. "They don't love you. They loved what you did because it's what they would love to do, except they're not self-destructive lunatics. They want to keep their jobs. Only Stewart Gribnitz is stupid enough or crazy enough or reckless enough to take what should be a brilliant career and flush it down the toilet just to be dramatic."

I look up at her and smile. "You think I'm brilliant?"

"Yes, you're brilliant." She yells like it's a curse. "You're also immature, irresponsible, irritating, idiotic and . . ."

Before she can finish her alliterative rant, I pull her down on top of me and kiss her hard on the lips. Soon we're making out like two high school kids on prom night.

After a while, I'm not sure how long, Cookie comes over and says, "I hate to break this up but I need to get home. I got cats to feed."

We both dart up. I mumble, "Sure, Cookie, sorry."

We straighten ourselves up. Jeannie says a quick "see you tomorrow" to me and sprints out of the place. By the time I stumble outside, she's gone. Probably grabbed a cab to her apartment. She lives somewhere uptown in the fifties.

I'm trying to calculate how much I'm gonna have to pay for a taxi to take me all the way to the ass end of Brooklyn, if I can get one to take me at all. Cabs never want to leave Manhattan. Most don't like to stray too far from Midtown. I only have twenty bucks in my wallet so if it's any more than that, I'm in for a long ride to the last stop on the L train. Out of nowhere a Lincoln Town Car pulls up. The driver sticks out his head. "You Stewart?" I nod. "Canarsie, right?"

"How'd you know?"

"Cookie gave me a call."

"How much?"

"She said to tell you it's on Terrance's tab."

This guy knows his way around Brooklyn. Most of these hack jockeys have no clue where they are once they cross the East River. One time, coming home from a longer than usual night at Raymondo's, I passed out in the back seat. When I woke up we were on a dead end and I was looking into the mouth of the Gowanus Canal, a cesspool of a waterway that smells like a dirty diaper floating in a clogged toilet. The driver starts yelling at me in some crazy language (Uzbekistanish? Azerbaijanish?) like it's my fault he nearly drove us into this sewer-swamp.

The whole ride I'm trying to get my head around what the hell happened in the last twelve hours. When I woke up this morning I had a good job at the agency and a good friend in Jeannie. Now I'm not sure I have either.

As far as my confrontation with Persons, I have no regrets. What a dick. I shoulda shoved that tie down his throat after I wiped my ass with it.

It's my impromptu make-out session with Jeannie that has my brain roiled. She's probably my closest friend after Nicky. She's my first real friend who is also a woman. I can talk to her about all kinds of stuff that I never talked about with a woman before, like how many dates do you have to go on before you can fart in front of the other one. She said at least four, but one has to be a sleepover. And she's great to work with too. She bailed my ass out of more slings than there are on the entire island of Singapore with her eagle-eye editing of my copy and the way she comes super prepared for meetings, including stuff I'm supposed to bring but forgot.

So is that all over? All we did was kiss. It was a great kiss. Actually, a shitload of great kisses. Does that tip the scale from friend to lover? I don't know. And my head is too spongy to think about it.

CHAPTER FOUR

The driver drops me off in front of my father's house in Canarsie. I've been here for almost four months. Ever since I split with the Orthodox Jewish Vampire Bride from Hell.

Whoever said opposites attract was either a moron or a sadist. It was New Year's Eve. I'd just moved into my new apartment in Park Slope and figured I'd throw a party. I invited everyone I knew and told them to invite everyone they knew. We were a bunch of ex-hippie dopers dressed in dungarees, flannel shirts and work boots. My pal Levine, who was one of Brooklyn's bigger quaalude dealers and used his pill-gotten gains to buy himself a deli in Sheepshead Bay, supplied all the food, which was set up on the ping-pong table that took up most of my living room.

We're all hanging out, smoking dope, drinking Remy out of the bottle, listening to the Stones and the Dead cranked all the way up, looking like we just got back from a Woodstock reunion, when in walks this woman in a full-length mink, clingy black dress and shiny red high heels, smoking a Virginia Slim. Talk about a barracuda out of water. I figure she was on her way to the Waldorf to ring in the new year with Guy Lombardo and got on the wrong train.

Ever the charming host, I walk up to her, look her up and down, and say, "Who the fuck are you?"

She smiles, says "Shoshana," drops her cigarette on the floor, crushes it with a spiked heel, then takes a step toward me, thrusts her hand between my legs, grabs my crotch and gives it a hefty squeeze. "Very pleased to make your acquaintance."

And so began my two-year odyssey through parve purgatory, which was as harrowing and torturous as the original *Odyssey*, but instead of winding up back in my kingdom with my ever-faithful wife, I ended up in my ever-feckless father Moish's basement in Canarsie, the neighborhood that time forgot.

Look at a picture of this block from 1952 and one from yesterday and you won't be able to tell the difference. Same redbrick one- and two-family houses with little, well-kept gardens in the front and garages on the side, filled with Monte Carlos, Mustangs and Buick Rivieras, all shined to a high gloss with custom whitewalls and glistening wheel covers. A lot of the cars are new, but you'll also see a lot of old beauties that look just as good or better than when they rolled off the showroom floor thirty years ago.

That time warp is why my parents wound up here. Time didn't stand still in Flatbush. Back when I was growing up, the neighborhood bookie hung out in front of OTB. The local pot dealer set up shop in front of the candy store across the street. So there's my father and his horse-playing cronies making bets on one corner and me and my hippie dope-fiend friends buying nickel bags on the other.

My mother treated us like her two wayward boys. Moish drove a cab on and off but more off than on. Sylvia was the major breadwinner. She loved our old neighborhood because the D train was right around the corner, so it was a little more than a half hour door-to-door to get to her bookkeeping job on Wall Street.

The old yentas sat on folding chairs in front of the building all day in the summer, gossiping and butting into everybody else's business, especially an eight-year-old kid who they thought needed a little extra watching since his mother shirked her parental duties and went back to work. Fat Lucille was the loudest and most annoying of the gaggle.

Every day as I ran the gossipmongers' gauntlet she would screech, "Stewee, did you do all your homework? Steweee, your face is dirty, go upstairs and wash up. Steweeee, tell your mother there's a good sale at Waldbaum's this week."

One warm May afternoon, just as I was leaving the building to meet my friends at the schoolyard, I noticed that Lucille's chair was empty. I was thrilled that I would have a kvetch-free passage. Joy turned to misery when I saw her about to plop her fat ass back down after grabbing a huge piece of coffee cake from one of the other old battle-axes. On pure instinct, I scooted behind her and yanked the chair away. She hit the sidewalk like a ton of rancid schmaltz, then bellowed like a wounded hippo. I ran like hell, covering my face, hoping no one would notice it was me. They noticed.

That night I got the two worst beatings of my life. First from my mother. Then from my father. My arms had red welts from trying to fend off my father's Garrison belt. One of the other mothers called my house after school the next day and asked my mother what kind of monster she was, beating her son like that. When my mother told her what I did and how she was humiliated in front of the whole building, the other mother, Ruthie, said she was right and they became good friends.

I moved out of my parents' house as soon as I started working and could afford to split Manhattan rent with some friends. Even before I left, Flatbush was starting to change complexion. Black families moved in, the Jews and Italians moved out. Except Moish and Sylvia Gribnitz.

"I have nothing against the coloreds," my father would say. "I had lots of colored friends in the army." Then my mother would chime in. "I don't know why everybody's running away. There's a colored woman who works in my office and she's very nice. And Dolly is like one of the family."

When my mother started working again, they hired Dolly Williams to come to the apartment once a week to clean. Thursday was her day. She was a saint, went to church every day before work. And she was beautiful, looked a little bit like Lena Horne, tall, slim with straight hair and chiseled features. But she was tough. She would always say to me, "Stew-heart, you watch yourself. Don't you be hanging around with any of that trash I see walking around this neighborhood. I see you doin' any of that mess I'll smack you with this broom handle." And she would have.

If I cut class, it would always be on Thursday. Once the school called to check up on me. "Oh, he's sick, all right, halfway to dyin'," she said. "But I'm sure he'll be better by tomorrow."

I loved Dolly.

But as more and more middle-class families left the neighborhood, including many of the original black families, welfare started moving people in and the place deteriorated. Even Dolly noticed. "They lettin' anybody move in here lately. They animals. I'd rather live with go-rillas."

One night my mother got mugged walking home from the subway. Two punks grabbed her handbag and pushed her to the ground. She didn't get hurt too badly, a couple of bumps and bruises is all. But that was the camel's back-breaking straw.

One of my father's street-corner cronies had found his way to Canarsie a couple of years back and convinced him that it was as close to the old neighborhood as you can get. For my father it was heaven. For my mother it was Siberia, cold, strange and foreboding. She didn't drive, there were no familiar faces and no stores within walking distance. What passed for a social life for my mother had been gossiping with the other women at Waldbaum's or the butcher's. That ended in Canarsie.

Now, her only friends were at her job. So every day, well into her seventies, she trudged to Steinberg and Gluck, a small brokerage firm at the southern tip of Manhattan. But what used to be a forty-five-minute commute from Flatbush now took the better part of two hours from the new neighborhood, deep in the ass end of Brooklyn.

Summer and winter, rain or shine, she got up at six, walked the two long blocks to the bus stop, rode for fifteen minutes to the Kings Highway station, and waited in the rain, wind, snow and cold on the outdoor platform for the D train. Then she transferred to the IRT local at Atlantic Avenue, got off at Wall Street and walked to her office on Trinity Place. Coming home, she reversed the process, except she had to stand for most of the trip.

One cold, dreary November evening, waiting for the bus at Kings Highway, she crumpled to the ground. The doctors said it was massive heart failure due to severe cardiac calcification. Her heart, literally, turned to stone, which is ironic because she had the softest heart of anyone I've ever known. They said it was a condition that she probably had since she was a kid. But I know it was Canarsie that killed her.

CHAPTER FIVE

I've become my father's father. Payback really is a bitch.

Around nine thirty every night since I've been here, he falls asleep on the La-Z-Boy in front of the TV, drops the *Post* on the floor, gets up to pee around eleven and shuffles off to bed, usually leaving a half-smoked Garcia y Vega smoldering in the ashtray.

But tonight when I walk in, the TV's off, the *Post* is lying unread on the coffee table and the ashtray is empty.

I yell, "Pop! Pop!" No answer.

I look in the bathroom. Maybe he fell asleep on the toilet. (Did I mention he's constipated?) Not there. The bedroom's empty too.

I check the closet, though why he'd be in the closet I have no idea. I try the basement. He's not there either.

I'm starting to panic. He's old. He's already had a heart attack. His mind isn't as sharp as it used to be, and let's face it, in his prime he was no Einstein. He could be lying dead in the street somewhere. Or wandering aimlessly around the neighborhood. Or lying in the ER after getting hit by a bus.

I search the house again, as if I might have missed him the first time. Where the hell can he be? I'm trying to think of who to call. I know the names of a couple of his buddies from the old neighborhood. Shifty

Shapiro, Bummy Loberfeld, Willie Levine. I have no idea if he hangs out with them anymore. Or even if they're dead or alive.

I slump down on the recliner, exhausted, when the front door flies open and in struts Moish, all smiles.

I jump up and scream, "Where the hell were you?"

He shoots me a smirk. "Out."

"That's all you have to say?"

"What do you want me to say? I went out. I came back. Now I'm tired so I'll say good night."

"I was worried sick. I get home, it's past midnight and you're not here. No note. No nothing. For all I know you could've dropped dead and been carted away to the morgue."

"All right, I'm sorry. Next time I'll leave you a note. I didn't realize I wasn't allowed to go out without your permission."

I was about to say that it wasn't about permission, it was about consideration. Then I remember that we had this exact same argument twenty years ago, except it was me who came home late and he was doing the yelling.

CHAPTER SIX

Manhattan is a different city at six in the morning. This is Woody Allen's Manhattan, not mine. My city is crowded, dirty and full of women who wouldn't give me the time of day if I presented them with a diamond-encrusted Rolex. Woody's is filled with long-limbed, flaxen-maned shiksa goddesses who can't wait to jump into bed with a short, balding Jewish nebbish.

What the hell am I doing here at sunrise, you might ask. As would everyone at the agency, most of whom have never seen my face before nine thirty. The trifecta of what happened with Persons, what happened with Jeannie and what happened with Moish, on top of an alcohol-induced migraine, meant that sleep wasn't even a pipe dream. So instead of lying in bed feeling sorry for myself, waiting for Moish to wake up so we can have another fight, I decided to get the hell out of the house. There sure as hell wasn't anything to do in Canarsie at five o'clock in the morning, so I headed for the subway to take the L train to the city.

The pinks and purples of the morning sun reflecting off the glass and steel of the high-rises is a light show that the Fillmore would be jealous of. The only people on the street are porters in spiffy uniforms cleaning glass doors, polishing brass handles and sweeping the sidewalks in front of the gleaming glass and chrome office towers where the buttoned-down titans of finance, commerce and advertising come every day to perpetrate yet another scam on the American consumer. Not that I have a problem with that; if it wasn't for the stupid, greedy and gullible, I'd be selling ladies' pumps in my uncle Benny's shoe store on Flatbush Avenue.

Most people, when they think about Madison Avenue ad agencies, imagine opulent offices with spectacular views of the Manhattan skyline, original oil paintings on the walls, and sharp, sophisticated hotshots in Calvin Klein suits shooting glitzy TV commercials and making multimillion-dollar deals. That's advertising's major league, about fifty agencies and their subsidiaries, where Fortune 500 companies spend hundreds of millions of dollars trying to eke out a few extra percentage points of market share.

That's not where I work. I spent most of my career in advertising's nether regions. Schlock shops that spend their days hawking brochures, posters, newspaper ads and the occasional local radio or TV spot to clients who don't have a clue.

Underhill, Prescott, Anderson and Nelson is somewhere in the middle. It was established at the turn of the century, about the same time as Grey and Thompson and McCann. But unlike those guys, who grew to become Madison Avenue titans, UPAN stagnated. It wasn't the bottom of the barrel, more like the bunghole.

When Barney bought the agency he decided to move the offices from downtown to Madison Avenue, figuring the change of address would put him on the same level as the big boys. But the only space available for the price he could afford was a festering wart on the ass end of advertising's main street: a six-story rundown runt of a building fronted by a Korean deli that used to be a pizzeria and before that was a crêperie. Our offices are on the fifth floor, which wouldn't be so bad if the goddamn elevator didn't conk out every other week.

I check my Seiko. It's a little before seven; if the door's locked I'm out of luck. I was issued a key when I first got here but I have no clue where it is since I never needed it until now.

I try the door. It opens. I look around to make sure Persons isn't walking around the office. Supposedly he's always in early, another reason to despise him. But the only ones here are a couple of junior account execs trying to earn brownie points.

I need to talk to Nicky. When I first met him I thought he was a moron. One of our clients was Fiduciary Trust. When he asked me how to spell it, I started, "F-I-D-U . . ." but he stopped me. He didn't know how to spell *Trust*. Then I found out he has severe dyslexia. He has a hard time reading and he spells like a second grader. Other than that he's one of the smartest people I know. And I'm betting that his problem with letters is what makes him an artistic genius. Sorta like Ray Charles and Stevie Wonder being brilliant musicians even though they're blind.

Our old creative director, Dick, hired us within days of each other. He must be an *Odd Couple* fan, 'cause we make Felix and Oscar look like twins. Nicky's fastidious. Painfully thin with longish, perfectly coiffed hair. He could pass for one of the Ramones after a *GQ* makeover. He buys his clothes at Barneys and Saks and has everything custom tailored. My haberdasher of choice is the Army-Navy store. Somehow, Dick knew we'd work well together. He also figured we'd shake things up. Bull's-eye on both.

Nicky's the most talented art director I've ever worked with. And I've worked with a lot, one of the advantages of my inability to hang on to a job. We function like two sides of the same brain. Nicky's a totally visual being. Words to him are like grown-ups' dialogue in *Peanuts* cartoons, all mwa-mwa-mwa. And as for my artistic ability, compared to me, Stevie Wonder is Rembrandt.

We spend eight hours a day (most days more) within three feet of each other, working, fighting, yelling and cursing. Somewhere in the middle of all that, an ad or a commercial is born. After a couple of years, the guy sitting across from you is either your brother from another mother or just a mutha.

I park myself in the barber's chair in Nicky's office.

Nicky's grandfather Rocco had a three-chair barber shop in Astoria. He gave each of his grandsons a chair when he turned in his barber's pole after sixty-five years of pompadours and flattops. Nicky thought it would be a cool chair to work in, but after half a day he realized that though it was great for sitting in when you're having a shave and a haircut, it was torture to work at a computer on it. Now Grandpa Rocco's chair is Nicky's guest chair, which makes it basically my chair.

Nicky usually gets in early, not because he's the most industrious worker bee in the UPAN hive but because he sees a shrink up on Park Avenue from six thirty to seven thirty, four mornings a week. That gets him to the office around eight.

He walks in at five after, sees me, does an exaggerated double take, runs over and puts a hand on my forehead. "No fever. Pulse normal. Are you all right?"

"I'm fine. Ask me again at five o'clock."

"What are you doing here?"

"I work here, remember?"

"You've been working here almost three years and I've never seen you in at eight o'clock. Or nine o'clock, for that matter."

"I couldn't sleep."

"You mean that thing with Persons?"

"That's part of it."

"There's more! I would think wiping your ass with your new creative director's tie would be enough for one day."

"What can I tell you, I'm a multitasker."

"What else happened?"

"Last night at Raymondo's after everybody left . . ."

"Don't tell me you made it with Cookie."

I shake my head. "That wouldn't have been so bad."

His eyes bulged. "You went to Persons's house and beat the crap out of him?"

I shake my head. "That's what I shoulda done."

"What did you do?"

"I made out with Jeannie."

"Made out?" He scrunches up his face. "What are you, in high school? What base did you get to?"

"What can I tell you, we were in the booth in the corner and all of a sudden we were in a clinch, swallowing each other's tongues."

"How'd it happen?"

I shrug.

"Something made you do it. Maybe it was your subconscious."

"My subconscious is a shmuck. Every time I listen to it I get screwed."

I see that look. The lecture's about to start. "It couldn't be any worse than your conscious mind, which is telling you to do things like wipe your ass with Persons's tie."

"Yeah, yeah, I know. I'm working on it. In the meantime, what do I do about Jeannie?"

"You like her, don't you?"

"Of course."

"You should go out with her."

I shake my head so hard my neck hurts. "Absolutely not."

"Why not? You guys get along great. She's really nice looking. I know you're a boob man and she's got lemons, not melons, but so what. All those big-titted women wound up making you miserable."

"I know, I know. She's smart, funny, and I can talk to her about anything."

"So what's the problem?"

"That's the problem."

Nicky looks at me cockeyed. "You're not making any sense."

"All those things make her a great friend. I don't want to lose that."

"Who said you have to lose it?"

"Every relationship I've ever had has been a total clusterfuck. The last thing I want to do is kill a great friendship by turning it into another horrible relationship."

"How do you know it'll be horrible?"

"Because when it comes to relationships, I have the Midas touch. Everything I touch turns into a broken muffler."

"So if you don't want to go out with her, what are you gonna do?"

"I'm thinking of acting like it never happened."

"But it *did* happen. You can't unkiss her."

"What do you suggest?"

"Talk to her."

"And say what? I get along better with you than with any woman I've ever known. You're smart, funny and cute as a button, so of course there's no way I could ever date you. Sorry I kissed you. It won't happen again."

"That's probably not the way to go but you better think of something. She's walking down the hall."

I jerk my head around and here she comes, eyes bright, a bounce in her step, that pixieish grin. I'm usually pretty good at shaking off the effects of a night of booze and debauchery but she has me beat. She pokes her head in and says, "Hi, guys, can't talk now, got an eight-thirty status meeting." And she's off around the corner.

Nicky says, "She seems just like always. Are you sure you didn't hallucinate the whole thing?"

"Maybe I did. Right now I'm not sure about anything. Including whether or not I still have a job. Speaking of that, where is Persons? Isn't this the time you usually see him?"

"Yeah, he goes for coffee every day at around eight fifteen. The first morning I said hello when he walked by. He didn't even turn his head. After that, fuck him."

I look at my watch. "It's twenty after. Where is he?"

"Why? You wanna kiss and make up."

"Absolutely not. As far as I'm concerned, he owes us an apology."

"Yeah, good luck with that. You're gonna have to figure some way to get along with him."

"Maybe I'll just shoot him."

"Stop saying that," Nicky yells at me. "Somebody's gonna think you're serious."

I stand up, finger guns at my sides. Then I point them at Nicky. "That's me, Six-gun Stew, the baddest hombre west of the Waldorf. Arrrgh."

Nicky shakes his head. "Arrrgh is pirate talk. You wanna talk like a cowboy, it's yippie-ki-yay."

"I didn't know you were such an expert. Anyway, unless Persons turns up dead, I have nothing to worry about."

"You gotta worry about saving your job and how you wanna handle your make-out session with Jeannie."

"And one more thing I'm worried about."

"How many worries do you need?"

"I think my father's losing his mind."

"What are you talking about?"

"He wasn't there when I got home last night. When he finally showed up, I asked him where he'd been and all he said was 'out.' When I pressed him he got defensive. I don't know if he's playing me or if he lost a couple of cards out of his pinochle deck."

"How old is he?"

"Seventy-something."

"Let's see how good your memory is in forty years."

Nicky's phone rings. He grabs it. "Hello. Yeah, he's right here." He hands me the phone. "It's Karol. She wants to speak to you."

"Hey, Karol. How'd you know I was here?"

"After yesterday, you're hot news in this office. All anybody's talking about is your little stunt with Persons. When people saw you in Nicky's at eight thirty this morning, they got worried."

"I'm at Nicky's every morning."

"Never before ten."

"Good point. By the way, I still have a job here, don't I?"

"As of this moment. But Boyce wants you in his office. I can't make any guarantees after that."

"Is there an office pool yet?"

"Of course. The smart money is saying you'll be out by lunchtime."

"Can I get in on that? I got a feeling I'm gonna need the extra cash."

CHAPTER SEVEN

When I get to Boyce's office Karol is looking at pictures of kittens on her computer.

"What happened to the puppies?"

"I decided to broaden my horizons."

"Good for you. Is he in?"

She looks up. "He's waiting."

"Does he have blood in his eyes?"

"Yeah. But that might be from too many martinis last night after he left Nielsen."

"He was with Nielsen last night?"

She nods ominously.

"Into the valley of death . . ." I walk in.

Boyce shakes his head and glares at me. It's the same scowl I've been getting from teachers, principals, coaches and bosses since sixth grade.

"Stewart." Always a bad sign when they start using your full first name. At least he didn't say Stewart Arnold; that's what my father would call me right before laying a beating on me.

Boyce clears his throat. "You're a very talented writer. The best I've ever worked with." This isn't as impressive as it sounds. Before he bought the agency seven years ago, he was a banker for twenty-odd years.

Last time I looked, there aren't a lot of great writers working in banks. "You're also a huge pain in the ass. When the pain outweighs the gain, and it's getting close to that point, that will be the end of you working here."

"But we haven't reached that point yet?" I say with more hope than conviction.

"Have you spent any time with Harvey Nielsen?"

"Not really. I ran into him once getting coffee downstairs. He made a big deal about remembering my name. He informed me that Gribnitz was a high-cholesterol Jewish snack made from chicken skin fried in chicken fat. He asked me if I ever tried it. I said no and he lost interest and walked away."

"I had to spend three hours with him at my club last night and we didn't talk about chicken fat, though that would have been an improvement. Mostly he talked about the many and impressive accomplishments of Harvey W. Nielsen." He rolls his eyes. "It was not an enjoyable experience." He stops for a second to give me the stink eye.

"Then he started about you." I feel a chill going up my spine. "He said, and these are his words exactly, that the kind of reckless behavior you exhibited can be a cancer to UPAN's reputation. That if we want to be known as the kind of agency that companies can trust with millions of dollars of their business, we have to excise the malignancy before it becomes fatal."

I cringe, try to think of something pithy to say, but all that comes out is, "What did you say?"

"I told him that you were the most creative guy in the agency. That half our clients are here because of you."

"That's not true."

"It's not like you to be modest."

I smirk. "I'm not. I'd say it was more like three-quarters." He shakes his head and gives me one of those "why do I even bother?" looks. "Sorry, sometimes I just can't help myself."

Finally, he cracks a smile. "That's exactly what I told him. So for now, you're safe."

"You told him I couldn't help myself?"

"In a manner of speaking."

"What exactly did you tell him?"

"I convinced him that you were mentally ill, that both you and Nicky are under a psychiatrist's care. I said if we let you go we'd have to deal with the ADA and a lot of discrimination crap that would make us look bad, especially to our clients."

"He bought that?"

He grins. "Let's face it, Gribby, convincing him you're sane would be a much harder assignment than making him believe you're a psycho."

I shrug. "I don't care if you told him I was a homicidal, cross-dressing Trappist monk, as long as it keeps me my job. For some strange reason, I enjoy working for you."

"Same here. And I don't understand it either."

I stand up. "If there's nothing else, I'll go back to work."

"There's one more thing."

There always is. "Yes?"

"He wants you to apologize to Persons."

Fuck! I was almost home free. Now the rage is firing up all over again. I bite my lip and force a smile. "Sure, as soon as he apologizes to me and the rest of the department whom he insulted and humiliated with that unprofessional and reckless stunt that he pulled." I'm pleased with myself for using Nielsen's own words against him.

Boyce isn't pleased. He's squeezing the life out of the poor pencil that he always holds between his fingers since he stopped smoking.

"Don't make this harder than it has to be. Persons is a prick. Every-body knows it. I'm sure deep down even Nielsen knows it. But for some reason, Persons is his guy. I don't know why, and I don't care. I do know that I don't want to spend another tedious evening with that pompous blowhard saving your ass."

He wags a finger at me. "Go to Persons's office and say 'I'm sorry.' It shouldn't be hard for you, you bullshit clients all the time. It's your specialty. You don't even have to lay on that phony sincerity you're so good at. Just walk in, apologize and walk out."

"But Barney . . ."

He bangs his fist on the desk, breaking the pencil. "No buts, just do it. Now!"

Before I can reply, Karol opens the door. She's standing next to another woman. I've never seen her before 'cause if I did I would have remembered. Mid-thirties with the austere beauty of a Bond villainess. Long and lean. Ice-blue eyes. Straight nose. Thin, severe mouth. Deep red hair, cut short.

Boyce glares up at Karol. He hates to be interrupted when he's reaming someone out.

Karol says, "I'm sorry for barging in, but I thought you'd want to know this immediately. This is Detective Grodotzke. She has some very disturbing news."

Karol shuffles quickly out of the office, closing the door behind her. The redhead walks in, exuding a callous confidence. There's an empty chair next to me but she doesn't sit. She stands with her feet apart, hands clasped behind her back, like somebody said "at ease." She looks over at Boyce then at me. It's a look of utter contempt. I've gotten that look before, but never from someone I never met.

She says, "James Persons was found dead early this morning."

It's like somebody just dumped a bucket of ice on my head. Boyce's mouth gapes open. I'm sure mine did too.

Boyce gathers himself and says, "It's not possible. He was here yesterday. He was fine."

She doesn't respond, just gives Boyce a sympathetic nod.

I say, "What happened? How'd he die?"

She turns away from Boyce and gives me the death stare. "He was murdered. Beaten and strangled with his necktie. The same one you attacked him with."

Boyce shrieks, "Oh my God!"

I say nothing. I'm feeling my skin get clammy as it hits me. She thinks I did it.

Without taking her eyes off me she says, "I've already spoken to several people in this office about your altercation with Mr. Persons."

I'm trying to think of something to say, but I got nothing. I just sit gaping at her with my mouth open like a world-class douchebag.

"You were also heard threatening his life."

"That's a lie."

She pulls out a small notebook and reads, "'I'm gonna kill him. I'm gonna murder that fat fuck.'" She looks back at me. "Do you deny you said that?"

Before I can get a word out, Boyce bellows, "This is ridiculous. Gribby didn't kill anybody. That's just the way he talks. He wasn't serious." I coulda kissed the guy.

She stares him down. "A man was murdered last night, Mr. Boyce. That's extremely serious." She turns back to me. "If you don't mind, Mr. . . ." She glances quickly down at her notebook. "Griberniz, I'd like you to come with me so we can get a complete statement."

I wanna say "Of course I mind," but all I do is nod.

Boyce stands up and shakes his finger at her, his bluster making a full recovery. "You're making a big mistake, young lady. Stew Gribnitz is a lot of things, but he's no murderer. I have friends in the mayor's office who will hear about this."

She nods serenely at him and begins to speak in the slow, measured tone that you usually use with a young kid or a senile old geezer. "I understand your feelings, Mr. Boyce. Mr. Gribnitz isn't under arrest, but he is a person of interest and we do need to talk with him in more detail about his involvement, if any, in this unfortunate situation. I imagine I could do that here but I wouldn't want to disrupt your business any more than necessary."

He snorts and growls, "Don't take too long. My creative department's already one man short. I can't afford to lose two."

She gives him the slightest of nods then turns back to me. "Come with me." She grabs my arm and perp-walks me out of the office.

Everybody's out in the corridor. Jeannie and Nicky are looking very concerned. What really hurts is that a lot of the others are shaking their heads as I walk by. These are people that know me and work with me. And they believe I'm a murderer.

CHAPTER EIGHT

The ten-minute drive to the 13th Precinct, not my lucky number, was the longest ride of my life. This could be the end of my life as I know it. I bet there are hundreds of guys rotting in jail, convicted with less evidence than they have on me. Grodotzke doesn't say much. When I ask questions like what was the time of death or were there any witnesses she grunts and says, "You'll find out."

When we get there a mob of reporters, photographers and cameramen surround the car. As I'm getting out, flashbulbs blind me. Someone sticks a microphone in my face. "Why'd you kill him?" "Was he your lover?" "Did you act alone?"

As we're pushing through, I say to Grodotzke, "What the hell is all this?"

She shrugs, grabs my elbow and hustles me in.

Everybody in the squad room is staring at us. One of the other detectives shouts, "Hey, Maureen, who ya got there? We haven't had this kinda media circus since the preppie killer."

"He's nobody," she says without breaking stride.

I don't know whether to be insulted or relieved.

She leads me into a room with a table and a couple of chairs, tells me to sit down, then leaves. I guess to let me stew about my situation and maybe confess. But all that happens is I'm getting less depressed and more pissed off. Who the hell are they to treat me like I'm the scum of the earth? I read about the city's budget cuts in the paper. They probably called all those reporters and told them they solved a big murder case to make themselves look good for the politicians.

Grodotzke walks in with another cop. She sits across from me. He stands against the back wall, giving me an angry glare. He's built like a dishwasher, short and thick, with curly black hair that looks like it was dyed with tar and a sharkskin suit that's bulging at the arms and shoulders. I'm guessing he's around forty.

She looks at me with an expression somewhere between disgust and contempt. I'm used to that look. It's the same one I got from my ex-wife every night for the last six months of our fifty-one-week marriage. If she's trying to intimidate me, she's nothing compared to the Orthodox Jewish Vampire Bride from Hell.

She studies a notebook on the table in front of her then looks up at me. "How well did you know James Persons?"

"I hardly knew him at all."

"Yet you attacked him and threatened his life."

"I never threatened his life," I yell.

I take a breath, trying to calm myself down. "And I didn't attack him. It was more of a demonstration."

She glances quickly down at her notes. "You tried to choke him with his own tie."

"Absolutely not!" I scream. Then I jump off my seat. "Whoever told you that is a goddamn liar!"

The guy at the wall takes a couple of steps toward me.

Grodotzke calmly says, "Please sit down."

The voice in my head tells me I'm not doing myself any good acting like an out-of-control maniac. I sit. "You've received bad information," I say calmly. "There were a dozen people in that room who'll tell you that all I did was pull his tie off his neck. And it was untied, so there was no chance of choking him."

She leans in. "All right, tell me exactly what happened."

I give her the whole story, starting with him trashing our ads and ending with me calling him a fucking asshole. Then I say, "There are dozens of guys up and down Madison Avenue who he screwed worse than me and would love to see him dead. I'm just the latest in a long line of possible suspects. I hope you put all of them through the media gauntlet that you just dragged me through."

Dishwasher-boy struts to the table, leans over, and yells in my face, "What are you, a fucking smart guy, telling us how to do our job? We know it was you. You don't think anybody saw you?"

"I'm sure nobody saw me 'cause I wasn't there, wherever there is. I don't even know where he lives."

He ignores this. "They're gonna love you in Attica. Fresh white meat. You won't last a year." He shoves a yellow pad and pen across the table at me. "Write down what you did and we can help you. You'll go to a place like Fishkill. You'll stand half a chance of surviving there."

I push the pad away. "Fuck you. I didn't do anything. And between you and me, a little Listerine would be a good idea."

Now we're nose to nose. I think he's gonna yell at me or curse me out but no—he slaps the side of my face. Hard.

I yelp, jerk back. "What the . . ."

He slaps me again.

I push my chair back, out of his reach. "You can't do that."

He smirks. "Call a cop." He gets up. "Think about what I said, white meat." He turns to Grodotzke. "C'mon."

She follows him out the door.

I'm reeling. He hit me right at the point where my jaw connects to my head. It's throbbing.

You see that "good cop, bad cop" thing on TV all the time and think, *How can anybody fall for that?* But when it's you and you're scared shitless and it's not "good cop, bad cop" but "bad cop, worse cop," and the worse cop is slapping you around, yelling that you're gonna spend the rest of your life getting fucked up the ass by some four-hundred-pound rapist-murderer–child molester, all of a sudden confessing, even to something you didn't do, to avoid a bad blind date in the prison shower, doesn't seem so unreasonable.

They leave me in there for a good while. I spend most of the time feeling sorry for myself, but then it hits me: I can account for every minute of my whereabouts from when I left the agency to when I got to

Canarsie. From Cookie to the cabbie to Moish, I have witnesses for the entire time.

Grodotzke comes in alone. I'm writing on the pad.

"Is that your confession?"

I shake my head. "It's the name and location of the restaurant I was in at the time when Persons was killed."

"We never told you the time of death."

I grin. "It doesn't matter. I was there from a little before five in the afternoon until about eleven that night. Then I took a car service to Canarsie. Go to Raymondo's on Madison and Thirty-Third. Ask for Cookie. She can tell you the name of the car service."

I push the notebook across the table.

"Does this Cookie have a last name?"

"It's some unpronounceable Greek name. Just go to Raymondo's any time after three, she'll be there."

"And the name of the cab company?"

I shrug. "No clue. Like I said, she can probably tell you. But if she can't, go back to UPAN and ask Terrance Asiago or Jeannie Higbie. They'll know."

"Did anyone see you once you arrived in Canarsie?"

"My father. I'm living with him temporarily."

"Oh. I see." Now she's looking at me differently. Not like I'm a potential murderer but a pathetic loser. A guy in his mid-thirties who still lives at home with his daddy.

"We're done here," she says abruptly. "You're free to go."

As I'm getting up to leave I say, "Can I ask you a question?"

"What?"

"Why'd you call all those reporters when you brought me in?"

"It wasn't us."

"Who was it?"

She shrugs.

"Does that kind of thing happen a lot?"

"No. Never."

She closes her notebook and stands up. I'm waiting for an "I'm sorry for any inconvenience" or "I apologize that my partner slapped you across the face," but all I get is a scowl.

On my way out the press corps is gone, except for one guy. He looks more like an overage hippy than a news hack. He's wearing John Lennon glasses, a worn-out dungaree shirt, faded jeans, boat shoes and no socks. And his hair, which is black with streaks of gray, is tied in a short ponytail.

He walks over to me and hands me a business card. "Mr. Gribnitz, Joe Glennum, *East Hampton Eagle*. Give me a call if you want to tell your side of the story."

I shove the card in my pocket and start walking.

What now? I'm not sure what the protocol is after you've been escorted out of the office by police. Especially if the charge is murdering your boss.

Might as well find out.

CHAPTER NINE

Helen Cinzano runs out from behind the reception desk, throws her arms around me, and hugs me like I was her son just home from the war. "Stew, honey. Are you all right? You look pale. What did they do to you?"

The funny thing about Helen is that she doesn't really need to work. Jeannie tells me her handbag costs more than my car—that is, when I still had a car. She has a three-bedroom co-op on Central Park West that, if she wanted to sell it, is probably worth more than the whole agency. Her husband was some big Wall Street honcho who died and left her a pile of money. She got bored of being a rich stay-at-home widow and called Boyce, who was pals with her husband from his old banking days, to see if she could do something at the agency. He wanted to make her an account exec so she could hit up her rich friends who own businesses. But she didn't want the stress or the responsibility. Boyce stuck her at the front desk, figuring she'd quit in a few days and he would have done his duty. Instead she's been here for two years, ecstatic as an oyster, which I believe is a notch higher than a happy clam in the bivalve mollusk happiness hierarchy.

She lets me go, takes a step back and says, "When I saw that police-woman drag you out of here, I didn't know what to think. Then I heard

Persons was murdered and you were arrested. I thought I'd never see you again."

As she walks back behind her desk I wink and say, "I figured you'd be thrilled to be rid of me."

She shrieks, "Never!"

I pick up the wooden egg on her desk with Mary and Jesus painted on it, toss it up and catch it a couple of times. "What about when I tell you there's no God, and even if there is, he's an asshole?"

She gives me a big grin. "That's what gives my life purpose, to save your godforsaken soul. Besides, you make me laugh." She gestures at the door to the main offices. "The jamokes in there take themselves way too seriously. If I had to listen to them all day without any comic relief I'd stick my head in the microwave and throw away the key."

"The microwave doesn't have a key."

"See, that's why I need you around, to keep me on my toes. Go ahead in, your friends are all worried sick about you."

I scoot around the desk, give her a quick smooch on the cheek and head inside. There's a whole crowd of people waiting for me as soon as I turn the corner. Nicky grabs me by the shoulders. "Are you all right?"

"Yeah, fine."

Jeannie's standing next to him not saying anything but looking pleased to see me. The rest of the crowd starts closing in, peppering me with questions.

"What happened to Persons?"

"Do they know who did it?"

"Will you have to go back to jail?"

I throw up my hands and yell, "Whoa."

After they quiet down I say, "Everything's fine. I guess you all heard that Persons was found dead last night. The police think it was murder. Somehow they heard about our little, uh . . . disagreement, and I shot to number one on their prime suspect list. Lucky for me, it happened while I was with you guys in Raymondo's. So you're my airtight alibi."

After another minute or two of schmoozing and more questions they amble back to their offices.

I go over to Nicky's. Jeannie's there and punches me in the shoulder.

"Oww! That really hurt."

"Don't ever do that again, ya big lummox!" she yells. "I had diarrhea because of you."

"At least I know you give a shit."

"Not funny." She hits me again in the same spot. "I'll talk to you later. I have a meeting." She leaves.

Nicky, looking very serious, says, "Can I ask you something?"

"Of course."

I'm figuring he's gonna ask me if I'm really okay, or how was it in police custody, or something like that, but instead he says, "Did that policewoman say anything about me?"

"You? Why would she think you had anything to do with Persons's murder?"

He shakes his head. "I didn't mean about that. I mean, ya know, just in general."

"What the hell are you talking about? Why should she be asking anything about you?"

His eyes widen. "She's so hot. When she walked by with you our eyes met. I really think there was a connection. A little electricity, you know. Are you sure she didn't mention me at all?"

"Are you out of your mind!" I scream. "She wasn't here looking for a date, she was here to lock me up and throw away the fucking key."

"I know, I know, I'm sorry. But it's been three months since I broke up with Mikaela and you know I have a thing for redheads."

"I'm sorry, Nicky. While she was dragging me out of here and I was contemplating spending the rest of my life behind bars, I forgot to consider how it might affect your sex life. How about this: I'll confess to killing Persons. That way you can see her when you visit me in stir."

He looks contrite and I think I'm done with this ridiculous conversation, but then he says, "Now that everything's okay and you're not gonna be arrested, you think I could call her?"

"Sure. Call her. Marry her and have six redheaded kids. Do whatever the hell you want."

"I just don't want to do anything that would make you uncomfortable."

"Right now, your breathing is making me uncomfortable."

He breaks into a big grin. "All right! That's the Stew I've been waiting for. It's been ten minutes and you haven't abused, insulted, or humiliated me. I thought something was really wrong."

Nicky's phone rings. He picks it up.

It's Karol. "Barney wants you."

"I guess he heard I'm back. Tell her I'll be right in."

"I bet he asks you to be creative director."

"What are you talking about? A couple of hours ago half the agency had me down as a cold-blooded, homicidal maniac."

"Now that you're in the clear and the agency needs a creative director, you're the logical choice."

That never occurred to me, but I guess it's possible. I think about it for a few seconds then shake my head. "No way. I don't want to manage other people, especially creatives. Most of them are cocky, wiseass, shit-for-brains prima donnas who think they know all the answers."

"You mean like Stew Gribnitz?"

"That's exactly what I mean. The only creative director I ever got along with was Dick. And he got fired for being too nice a guy. No way I want to deal with a Stew Gribnitz clone, or worse yet, a whole department full of them."

"But suppose Barney does offer you the job, what are you gonna do?"

"I'll drop back fifteen and punt." I have no idea what that means in this context but I've used it a couple of times when I have no clue what I'm talking about and it always seems to work.

Nicky nods and says, "Okay."

I head to Boyce's office.

On my way over I'm trying to figure out how to turn down being offered the CD gig without making myself look bad. Knowing him, he probably thinks that putting me in a position of authority will be just the thing I need to make me grow up. I'll just tell him that I'm flattered but I'm not ready yet.

I get to his office and Karol nods at the door. "He's waiting for you."

Boyce is looking very serious. "Sit down, Stew." I sit.

He's staring nervously down at his hands clasped in front of him, the way he does before a big client presentation. Now I'm pretty sure he's gonna pop the CD question. Why else would he be so tense?

"You know I think you're a terrific writer."

I nod. "Thank you."

"And I've told you that I don't think the agency would be anywhere near as successful as it is without you and the great work you've done."

Here it comes. I don't say anything, just smile humbly. I'm thinking maybe I will take the job. How bad can it be?

He looks up, his bloodhound jowls dangling below his chin. "That's why it really pains me to have to let you go."

I double over then shake my head like my ears are clogged. "You're kidding, right? You didn't really just fire me, did you?"

"Technically we're laying you off."

"I don't understand."

"I'm sorry, Stew, but we have our clients to consider. A lot of them believe we're putting their business in the hands of a murderer."

I feel like I got drop-kicked in the cookies by Garo Yepremian. I jump up, start yelling, "What are you talking about? Who said I was a murderer?"

"They did." He reaches into his desk and pulls out copies of the *News* and the *Post* and puts them on his desk. My snarling face is on the front page of both papers, two different close-ups of me perp-walking into the police station with Grodotzke. The headline on the *News* reads, "Madison Avenue Murderer." The *Post* says, "Death in Advertising."

"It's on the radio too. I've already gotten calls from Suntory, Chase and Rolling Rock. They love your work but don't want to be associated with a mad-dog killer."

I'm trying to calm down but it's not working. "But I'm not a killer. I was totally exonerated. It was all bullshit. Just tell them that."

He shakes his head forlornly and says, "I wish it were that easy. You, of all people, know that perception is everything. Especially in this business." He glances down at the papers on his desk. "Unless you can get them to run a big headline that says 'Gribnitz Didn't Do It,' you're guilty in the eyes of the public."

I'm starting to throw up in my mouth. "What do you want me to do?"

"Just hang in there. This thing will blow over in a couple of months, maybe sooner. They'll find whoever killed Persons and everything will be back to normal. You'll get your old job back." He winks at me. "Maybe even a raise and a promotion. In the meantime . . ." He reaches over the desk and hands me a check. "A month's severance."

I peek at the number. It's for $7,000. "Thanks, Barney. That's very generous."

"You earned it." He points to the door at the rear of his office. "Could you do me a favor and take the back elevator down."

"The trash elevator? You're putting me out with the garbage?"

"C'mon, Stew. You know it's not like that."

"So what is it like?" I say through clenched teeth.

"The past few days were chaotic enough. You walking through the agency announcing that you were let go would cause another firestorm. That's the last thing we need."

"Who's we?"

"Nielsen and me."

"So now you're best buds?"

He sighs. "He's my business partner, and in agency matters, I have to listen to him. But in this case I gotta say he's right. I love you, Gribby, but when the clients start walking, it's time to shit or cut bait. And unfortunately, you're the bait."

I want to say that that makes him the shit, but I don't, I just stand there, gaping.

"I know this is tough for you. It's hard for me too. Don't make it any worse."

"I don't even get to say goodbye to my friends?"

"Nicky's on his way to a photo shoot and Jeannie and Terrance are with a client."

"That's pretty convenient. Who arranged that? Let me guess. Your Machiavellian partner."

He nods. "He thought it would be better this way."

"Don't you see what a sneaky sleazebag he is? He concocted this whole scheme so I would quietly disappear. He'll do the same to you if he gets a chance."

"You're wrong, Stew. Nielsen doesn't have a problem with you. He said your work was first rate. When he heard what Persons did, pulling those ads off the wall, he was just as angry as I was. In fact, it was his idea to give you the severance money."

"Yeah, he's my number-one fan." I stand up. "I'll see you later."

"Don't worry, Gribby. It's really going to be all right."

He looks beaten, like he was just fired. I'd feel sorry for him if I wasn't too busy feeling sorry for myself. I put out my hand. He grabs it tight and shakes it hard and keeps shaking. "Trust me. It'll work out."

"Yeah, whatever." I yank my paw out of his death grip and head for the back elevator. It's full of big, black, stench-ridden sacks of garbage.

CHAPTER TEN

"What'd you do, break outta jail?" Cookie says when she sees me walk through the door.

"You saw the paper, huh?"

"Everybody walking past a newsstand saw it. What happened?"

I sit down at my usual table. Cookie comes with a Bass Ale. Since there's nobody else in the place, she sits down. I tell her the whole story, and when I'm finished, she shakes her head and says, "You know what my old man woulda called this?"

"Tell me."

"A freakin' snafu."

"Your father was Greek, right?"

"With a name like Papageorgiou, what do you think?"

"I didn't realize *snafu* was a Greek word. I always thought it was Chinese or Vietnamese, like *kung fu* or *Dien Bien Phu*."

"No. It's neither of those and it's not Greek either. It's army talk. My father was a master sergeant. It was his favorite word. It means 'situation normal, all fucked up.'"

"The story of my life. From now on you can call me Snafu Stew."

"Okay, Snafu, what are you gonna do now?"

I shrug. "No clue. Everybody in the city thinks I'm a murderer. That kinda puts a crimp in my job hunt. And besides, Barney sorta promised me he'd hire me back when all this blows over."

"So what are you gonna do in the meantime?"

"I really have no idea. I was an English major. Maybe I'll read all those books I was supposed to have read in college when I was too busy smoking dope."

"Well, I'm glad you're not in jail."

"Me too."

I'm staring into the amber foam, hoping it'll give me a clue about how to unscrew up my life. It's unresponsive so I slug it down instead.

When I look up, there's Jeannie standing next to the table. "You just gonna sit there and drink away your troubles?"

"If you have any better ideas, I'm up for suggestions."

"Can't think of any right now. When I do, I'll let you know." She sits down. Cookie ambles over. They exchange greetings and Jeannie orders a white wine spritzer.

"How'd they announce my unceremonious departure?"

"We got a memo from Nielsen." She reaches into her bag and hands me a sheet of paper. "Here, take a look."

It's mostly about James Persons's untimely death and a list of his credentials and accomplishments, which aren't many. I'm disappointed to see that "world-class asshole" isn't among them. It doesn't say that he was murdered, only that there is no memorial service or funeral scheduled at this time. Of course, that's because the medical examiner is still chopping him up.

I'm almost down to the bottom of the page and there's still nothing about my layoff. I'm thinking maybe Jeannie gave me the wrong memo and there's another one about me. Then I come to it, the last line: "Stewart Gribnitz of our creative department has taken an indefinite leave of absence in order to take care of some personal issues."

I slam the memo down on the table and scream, "That sonuvabitch! I didn't take any stinking leave of absence. He ran me outta there like I had the fucking plague. Anyone who reads that will think I've fled the country or I'm in rehab. He made it sound like I'm either a criminal or an alcoholic."

She gently eases her hand over mine. "Calm down. You're fine. Everybody in the agency knows what the story is. Nobody thinks you're a criminal. As far as alcoholic." She glares at the empty bottle. "That's up for debate."

As if on cue, Cookie arrives with Jeannie's spritzer and another Bass for me. She looks at me, cocks her head, and says, "Is everything all right? You seem a little agitated."

"I'm fine. Just blowing off a little steam."

"I can't have you frightening the customers."

I look around. "What customers?"

"See." She gestures around the empty room. "You scared them all off." She gives me a playful smirk and walks away.

Jeannie looks around and says, "How do these people stay in business? Half the time, we're the only ones in the place."

"You're wrong."

She looks around at the empty bar, arches her eyebrows, and gestures at the empty tables.

"It's more like three-quarters of the time."

"All kidding aside, what are you gonna do?"

"About what?"

"About the fact that anyone who's seen the front page of today's paper thinks you're the Madison Avenue Murderer."

"What can I do?"

"I dunno, sue them for libel."

"I checked that out. It's not libel. They never said I did it or even that I was accused of killing Persons. They said I was brought in for questioning, which is true."

"What about splashing your picture all over the front pages?"

I shrug. "Celebrities get their photos in the paper all the time. They can't do anything about it. I don't think I can either."

She gets in my face and yells, "There must be something! What happened to the guy who fights with everybody over the most ridiculous crap? Now that you really have something to fight for, you mope around and suck on a beer. I don't get it."

I shout back. "Who do you want me to fight with? Nielsen? The police? The press? Tell me who and I'll go and punch him in the face."

"I don't want you to punch anybody. But seeing you sit there feeling sorry for yourself is making me sick."

"Okay, I'll stand up."

"No, I will." She stands. "You think this is all a big joke. Well, it's not funny. I already lived through seeing somebody I care about destroy himself. I promised myself I'd never do it again." She turns to leave.

As she walks by, I grab her arm. "Okay, okay. Sit back down. Please." She does. "Who was this guy?"

"His name was Robby."

"How come I never heard you mention him?"

"It was a long time ago. Before I came to the agency."

"How did you know him?"

"He was my fiancé."

"What?" I do a reverse spit take while I'm taking a sip of beer, miss my mouth, and splash it all over my face. "I didn't know you were ever married."

She shakes her head dolefully. "We never made it that far."

"What happened?"

"He was a great guy. Smart. Funny. He treated me like a goddess. Even my screwed-up family liked him."

"Sounds perfect."

"It was. Except for the pills."

"What kind?"

"Quaaludes. Reds. Any kind of downs."

"You couldn't get him to quit?"

"I tried. I threatened to break up with him if he didn't stop."

"That didn't work?"

"It did for a while. Then he started sneaking it, thinking I wouldn't notice. How could you not notice somebody slurring his words and walking into the furniture. I kept trying but he was addicted." She brushes away a tear. "Saying goodbye to him was the hardest thing I ever did."

"What finally happened? He OD'd?"

She shakes her head sadly. "Worse. He got really strung out. He had to take more and more pills to get high. Handfuls. It destroyed him. A total body meltdown. Liver, kidneys, heart, they were all shot. Septicemia was the official cause of death."

"You never went to see him?"

Her eyes well up. "I couldn't even bring myself to go to the funeral."

"I'm so sorry. I had no idea."

"How could you?"

"I promise that won't happen to me."

She shakes her head again. "No. Your problem isn't what goes into your mouth, it's what comes out of it. If you could keep that piehole of yours shut, you might make it to forty."

I shrug. "You're right. I've just never been any good at taking shit."

"Taking shit is a big part of the advertising business. And life."

"I know. Did you notice I'm not doing too well at either."

"If you don't learn, you'll destroy what's left of your career, then what? Drink yourself to death? I'm not gonna hang around to watch that one either."

I reach across the table, take her hand. "Thanks, Jeannie. I needed to hear that." I fish around in my pocket, pull out the hippie reporter's card and hand it to her. "I got this from a guy who said he wanted to hear my side of the story."

She gives it a quick look and says, "Did Persons have a place in the Hamptons?"

"What does that have to do with anything?"

"You never even looked at this card, did you?"

"Nah. I wasn't gonna call him. I've had it with fucking reporters. As far as I'm concerned, they all suck. The only reason I still had his card is I never got around to emptying my pockets."

She gives it back to me. "Read it."

"*Joe Glennum, Editor/Publisher, The East Hampton Eagle.* Ever hear of it?"

"Nope."

"Me neither." I put the card back in my pocket. "Great. The only reporter who might be on my side works for a newspaper a hundred miles from here that nobody's heard of."

"Are you gonna call him?"

I shrug. "When you ain't got nuthin, you got nuthin to lose."

"Good. I gotta get back to the office. What should I tell Nicky when I see him?"

"Tell him I'll call him when I can. And everything's gonna be fine."

She shakes her head. "You believe that?"

"Not even a little."

CHAPTER ELEVEN

The good news is, the subway car is only half full. The bad news is, everybody in here is reading the paper and every paper has my snarling mug on the front page under blaring headlines about me being "New York's Most Wanted." People around me are sneaking nervous glances in my direction then turning quickly away. A few get up and move to the next car. I don't know who was more relieved when I got off, me or everyone else.

On my way to the house I'm hoping Moish isn't home. But as soon as I walk in there he is, standing in the living room, holding the *Post* in one hand and the *News* in the other.

I gird myself for what's coming. "So I guess you read about me in the paper."

His smile gets broader. "You bet I did."

"It was all a huge misunderstanding. Believe it or not, you're my alibi. I was here with you last night when it happened."

He sticks his thumb in the air. "Of course you were. I'll back you up a hundred percent. Just tell me what time I was supposed to be here and I'll swear on a pile of Bibles." He winks at me. "Old Testament, of course."

"No, really."

He shakes his head. "This is better. We were here together all night, playing pinochle. Wait a minute, you never learned to play pinochle. How about gin rummy? You know how to play gin rummy. Of course you do. Any moron can play gin rummy."

"Pop, listen to me. We don't have to make up a story. If it ever comes up, just tell the truth."

"Okay, son," he says, still grinning. "Whatever you say. But I still think the gin rummy routine is the way to go."

Son? He never calls me son. Putz, schmendrick or shmuck with earlaps, which for my father is the absolute worst thing you can be, are his usual terms of endearment for me, but son? Never.

Since my mother died, giving me a hard time has become my father's favorite pastime. Even more than playing cards or going to the track. After forty-five years of arguing with her, he needed someone else to yell at. Not that he didn't yell at me when she was alive, it's just that she was his number-one target. She told me that he never means anything by it. She used to say, "When he gets quiet, that's when you have to worry. As long as he's yelling, everything's fine."

That's why I'm so confused. Here's the perfect chance for him to tell me what a shmuck I am for getting myself into this mess, instead he's kvelling like I just won the Nobel Prize.

"You did see the paper, didn't you?"

"Of course. I bought extra copies. I'm gonna hand them out to everyone at the track."

"And you're not upset?"

"Upset?" He puffs out his chest. "I've never been prouder."

"But everyone thinks I'm a cold-blooded murderer."

"I know." There's that grin again. "It's terrific."

"I don't get it."

"What's to get? You finally made a name for yourself. Made it to the front page. The page that's usually reserved for presidents, governors and generals. And now my boy is right up there with them."

"They made me look like a homicidal maniac. It's not the same."

"You're right. It's better."

At this point I don't know what to say, so I just stand there with my mouth open.

"You know where I grew up, right?"

I nod. "Yeah. Brownsville. Chester Street, right?"

"You know my mother had a chicken market around the corner on Dumont Avenue?"

"Of course. You told me that story a hundred times. They called her the Chicken Lady. She made you get up at five in the morning to pluck chickens before you went to school. Made you come back before you went to bed to sweep up."

"She was a hard woman, my mother. She had to be. After that goddamn flu killed my father, she had three babies to feed. But that doesn't matter now." His eyes start to twinkle. And Moish wasn't usually a twinkler. "Do you know what was down the street from my mother's store?"

I shrug.

"Rosie Gold's candy store."

"Okaaaaay?"

"You know who hung around Rosie's?"

"Not a clue."

He puffs out his chest. I'm thinking it's gonna be some old-time Jewish sports hero like Kingfish Levinsky or Slapsie Maxie Rosenbloom.

"Murder, Incorporated. That's who. The toughest SOBs in the country. And they were all Jews. Louis Lepke, Abe Reles, Buggsy Gold-stein. Killers, every one of them. Everybody feared them. The Italians, the Irish, the coloreds. They had class too. Money, women, fancy cars, you name it. When I was a kid, twelve or thirteen, I'd sneak out of my mother's shop and hang around outside Rosie's. Those guys loved me. They treated me like I was their little mascot. Their good-luck charm. I'd run errands for them. Bring them cigarettes, drinks, the paper. What-ever they wanted. And they'd throw me a twenty-dollar tip like it was a nickel. You know what that's worth today? Five hundred dollars. I was a snot-nosed pisher with more money in my pocket than most of the grown men in the neighborhood. In a couple of years I coulda been one of them."

I don't know whether to be impressed or aghast. "So what happened?"

He shrugs. "This and that. Reles turned rat. Then he fell out of a hotel window. Pretty soon they were all dead or in jail. The Depression hit. The war happened. I spent five years in the Philippines shooting Japs. And when I came home I married your mother."

I'm a little taken aback that he puts marrying my mother in the same category as the Second World War and the Great Depression.

"Besides, when your grandmother found out what I was doing, she beat the living crap outta me. Told me if she ever caught me hanging around with those bums again she'd pluck me like one of her chickens."

"Let me get this straight, your childhood dream was to be a gangster?"

"It was different then, not like the scum-bums you see now. Back then, if you were in the rackets you were somebody, a big shot, a mensch."

"So seeing my commercials on TV and the awards I won, that all means nothing to you, but having everybody in New York think I'm the Jewish Dillinger, that you're proud of?"

"It's not like you're a senator or governor, but it's something."

"I'm sorry to disappoint you but I really didn't do it."

"Whatever you say." He pauses for a second. "Listen, do you know Shifty, the bookie from back in our old neighborhood?"

"Yeah, sure."

"He's been giving me a hard time. He says I owe him some money but he's fulla shit."

"How much money?"

"I dunno, two . . . three hundred."

"Dollars?"

"No, kishkes. Of course dollars."

"And you're sure you don't owe him the money?"

"Of course I'm sure. You think I wouldn't remember something like that?"

I don't say anything.

"He says he's gonna come over here with some leg breakers and take it if I don't give it to him. How about you pay him a little visit and convince him to lay off?" He holds up the paper and grins. "He'll listen to you."

"Listen, Pop. I'm not a thug. I don't even play one on TV. There's no way I'm gonna threaten your bookie or anybody else."

He shoots me a scornful smirk. "I shoulda known you didn't have the guts." He walks to the bathroom. Before he shuts the door he looks at me with disgust and shouts, "Putz!"

I pull Glennum's card out of my pocket, go to the phone. I get his answering machine. "It's Stew Gribnitz. If you still want to talk to me, I'll be at Raymondo's on Madison and Thirty-Third tomorrow around two."

I go for a walk. Maybe I'll frighten a couple of old ladies and make my father proud.

CHAPTER TWELVE

Raymondo's is deserted except for Cookie, who's behind the bar polishing beer mugs and glasses with a white towel. "This is the third afternoon in a row you've been in. You looking to work here or you just got the hots for me?"

"Both. I always had the hots for you, and it just so happens that right now I'm between gigs. Got any openings?"

"Got any skills?"

"If I had any skills I'd still be working."

"Good point." She grins. "What can I get you?"

"How about a Guinness in one of those mugs you just cleaned?"

"I hate to waste a clean glass on an out-of-work bum like you." She winks. "How about I just bring the bottle."

"Sounds good."

I'm sitting in our usual booth over in the far corner sucking on my second beer when in walks the hippie reporter. He's wearing the same outfit as yesterday. Cookie keeps the place pretty dark in the afternoon and he doesn't spot me. He checks a slip of paper with a puzzled look on his face like maybe he's in the wrong place. He looks around again. I stand and give him the high sign. He ambles over.

"I didn't think you'd call."

"Me neither."

Cookie glides over to the table like she's on ice skates. I wonder if she was a dancer back in the day. She sure moves like one. I'll have to ask her sometime. "What can I get for you?"

He glances at my bottle of Guinness. "Same as him."

"You need a glass?"

"The bottle's fine."

I look up. "Bring me another one while you're at it?"

She nods and is gone.

"So what made you change your mind?"

"Let's see . . . I got fired from my job. The whole city, including my father, thinks I'm a psycho killer. Women look at me like I have congenital genital leprosy."

He sits up with a start. "That's very poetic."

"I'm an advertising copywriter, words are my tools."

He points to himself with both thumbs. "Newspaperman. Words are my tools too, but I don't talk in rhyming couplets."

"I guess we hucksters are more erudite than you hacks." I take a slurp of beer and make a show out of clearing my throat. "As I was saying, right now I'm in the middle of a head-first cyclonic swirly down the existential toilet bowl of life." I give him a wink. "That was blank verse. Any better?"

"Actually, it was free verse, but either way, it was a little forced."

"That's what I get for talking to another lit major. Anyway, to get back to why I called you, I figured what do I have to lose? It was news jockeys who dragged my name through the manure. Maybe one of you can clean it up."

"Not so fast. I checked up on you a little. You did a pretty good job of shitting on your own reputation." He checks his notebook. "Three arrests. One for disorderly conduct. One for indecent exposure. And here's a good one: assault with a deadly weapon."

"Did you also notice that none of those ever went to trial. The disorderly conduct was when I was still in school. I went to a Richard Nixon campaign rally in downtown Brooklyn with a couple of my pals. We made signs that said, 'You Can't Lick Our Dick.' The Kings County Republican Club didn't think it was funny."

He grins broadly. "I do."

"The indecent exposure was me and some friends, actually the same friends from the Nixon rally, mooning a bunch of fraternity douchebags during Brooklyn College Greek night. We figured showing our asses was a very Greek thing to do."

"All right. You were a college prankster. I get it. But assault with a deadly weapon, that's no prank."

"You're right. It wasn't a prank, but it wasn't assault either."

"What was it?"

"There was an early-morning meeting at one of my former ad agencies. They had a breakfast spread on the conference table. Bagels, Danish, coffee. During the meeting, this little prick of a junior account exec figured he could make a name for himself by giving me a hard time in front of his bosses. I was trying to ignore him but he got right in my grill. I was in the middle of putting cream cheese on a bagel. I took the knife full of cream cheese and smooshed it all over his face. He went batshit. Screaming like a banshee on crack. Yelling that I attacked him with a knife. Some idiot called the police. When they showed up, they saw it was nothing, but they said they had to file a report."

All this time, Cookie's standing behind me with more drinks. She's shaking her head and chuckling. She puts two fresh bottles down, grabs the empties and says, "You're too much." And glides away.

I turn to Glennum. "That's my story. What's yours?" I pull out his crumpled business card. "It says you're the editor and publisher of the *East Hampton Eagle*. I never heard of the *Eagle* and the only Hampton I'm familiar with is Lionel. So why are you interested in me?"

"To tell you the truth, I'm not interested in you. It's Persons. I wanted to make sure the sonuvabitch was really dead."

I bolt upright like there's a blast of electricity shooting up my ass. "You hated Persons too?"

"Hate's a strong word." He smiles. "But it's not strong enough. Despise. Loathe. Detest. Abhor. Put them all together and it's still not enough. If I wasn't three hours away, I probably would have been arrested instead of you."

"I wasn't arrested. That's what's so fucked up. I was brought in for questioning because of a little run-in I had with him the day before.

That's why I can't understand the media frenzy waiting for me at the police station."

He shrugs. "The newswire said it was a grisly murder and the cops had the guy who did it dead to rights."

"That's crazy. How often does something like that happen, where they get it so screwed up?"

"Never. It's usually very reliable. What did you do to make you a suspect?"

I tell him the whole wiping-my-ass-with-Persons's-tie story.

"That's the best thing I ever heard."

"Except now I'm totally screwed."

"Why? You have an alibi."

"I do, but it doesn't matter. My clients saw the headlines. Now they all think I'm the Madison Avenue Murderer. My boss said it was either cut me loose or say goodbye to a lot of business. Guess which one he chose."

"As soon as they find out you're innocent you'll probably get your job back."

"Advertising is a cutthroat business. I'm sure other agencies are calling my old clients right now, telling them that murder is the least of my transgressions."

His eyes flash. I can see the proverbial lightbulb going off in his head. "That's it! I have my story."

"What? That I lost my job, and my former clients, who used to think I was the Bard of Flatbush, now think I'm Attila the Hebrew. Sorry, but that doesn't sound like Pulitzer material to me."

"It won't be about you. It'll be about how feckless reporting ruins innocent lives. I'll use what happened to you as my lead. Talk about how you were just brought in for questioning and the tabloids already had you tried and convicted. I'll compare it to Richard Jewell, another innocent man whose life was ruined when he was vilified by the media after the Atlanta Olympics bombing. Then next to it, I'll write Persons's obituary. I'll try not to make it too cheerful."

"So people in the Hamptons will know I'm not guilty, but that won't help me here."

"I'll send you reprints to send to your clients. Sometimes my pieces get picked up by the New York papers."

I shoot him a thumbs-up. "So tell me, what the hell did Persons do to you?"

Cookie comes with two more beers, which gives him time to collect his thoughts.

"He has a house in East Hampton, a converted barn. He thought it would be cute to have chickens running around his front lawn. He said it was a health issue, that chickens eat ticks. His neighbors didn't care; they hit him with a nuisance suit. Then the village officials slapped him with a summons. He went to the steps of town hall and set it on fire."

"I guess he always liked those dramatic gestures. What happened after that?"

He shakes his head. "The sonuvabitch ran for mayor. He thought he could pit the old money against the new. And the thing is, he grew up in East Hampton. On the poor side."

"I didn't know there was a poor side."

"Of course there is. The year-rounders, the municipal workers, the locals who serve the summer people, where do you think they live?"

"I dunno. I never thought about it."

"Persons was one of those people. Then he came back with money in his pocket. He couldn't wait to stick it to the upper crust. The people who treated him like a lower form of life when he was a kid."

"I'm still not getting what this has to do with you?"

"When he first decided to run, I was all for him. Local boy does good. Comes home to serve the community. It's a nice story." Glennum takes a long swig of his beer. "Then he demanded I print a guest editorial by him saying that the entire administration was a gang of fascists. That their policies were anti-American and unconstitutional. Then it went on to personally attack the mayor and everyone on the village council in the most vile and nasty language you could imagine.

"I couldn't run a piece like that. These were the most powerful people in town. I'd be sued, ostracized, boycotted and probably tarred and feathered. When I refused, he was livid. He said he expected that kind of treatment from the right-wing rags but not from the only progressive newspaper on the East End. He called me a traitor, a lackey, a stooge and a scumbag. He lost by a landslide and blamed me. He actually hired an investigator to dig up dirt on me.”

“Did they find anything?”

“Nothing that the world doesn't already know. I got busted for a joint when I was sixteen. A drunk and disorderly a few years later. Some asshole groped my girlfriend in a bar so I clocked him.”

“I like your style.”

“I'm not finished. He called the IRS to try to have me audited. That didn't work either. A few weeks later my office was vandalized. I can't prove it, but I know it was him . . . or somebody he hired.”

“God! If he did all that shit to me, I *would* have murdered him.”

“Yeah. Like I said, it's a good thing I was three hours away when it happened.”

I look up and Cookie's standing by the table. “You guys want another beer?”

Glennum says, “I'll tell you what, how about another round of Guinness and a shot of whiskey to go with it?”

“Don't you have to drive back to the Hamptons?”

“I'll spend tonight in the city. The paper rents space down in the Twenties. It's a small room in a lawyer's office with a computer, a phone and a sofa bed.”

I wink at Cookie. “Make it Jameson and put it on my tab.”

She scowls. “You don't have a tab.”

I nod at Glennum. “All right, put it on his tab.”

“He doesn't have one either.”

He smiles, pulls out his wallet and hands her an American Express card. “Now I do.”

She takes it and walks away.

I raise my glass. “You're all right.”

“I thought you didn't like reporters.”

“I don't. It was the drunk and disorderly that won me over.”

Two minutes later she's back with the beer and booze.

CHAPTER THIRTEEN

It's 8:00 p.m. Do you know where your crazy, senile, pain-in-the-ass father is? Neither do I. And right now I don't give a shit. I have a jackhammer inside my head that's trying to drill a hole through my eyeballs.

There's a note sitting on the recliner. "Going out now. Be back later. P.S. Your friend Nicky the Nudnik called. Ten times!"

I've been avoiding him and I'm not sure why. I grab the phone.

"Yo, Nick."

"You're a fucking hump!"

"What? Why?"

"I get back to the agency and you're gone. Fired. Then I don't hear from you for a whole day. No call. No note. Nothing."

"I was freaked out. I wasn't just fired. I was fired because all our clients think I'm a murderer. That kind of thing has a way of messing up your head. Boyce made me go down the freight elevator. He threw me out with the goddamn garbage. I didn't speak to anybody."

"You spoke to Jeannie."

"She followed me to Raymondo's. What do you want me to do? Throw her out?"

"I don't care, you should've called me."

"You're right. I should have. I'm sorry."

"So where the hell have you been?"

"Raymondo's."

"Whaddaya do, sleep there?"

"No. I slept at Moish's and went back."

"So now that's your new office?"

"I had to meet someone. I figured Raymondo's was as good a place as any."

"Who'd ya meet?"

"A newspaper guy."

"I hope you punched him in the face."

"Not this guy. He's the one reporter on my side."

"So they're printing a reduction?"

"Close. It's retraction. But no."

"So why'd you meet him?"

"He works at a paper out in the Hamptons. He hated Persons as much as we did."

"Why does this reporter from way out there give a shit about you?"

"He doesn't. He just wants to write bad stuff about Persons and he's using me as an excuse."

"Oh." I hear Nicky talking to someone. "That was Esther. She says get your ass back in here. She says she doesn't want to get stuck with your crappy accounts."

"Tell her our accounts are the best accounts in the agency."

I hear some more muffled conversation, then Nicky says, "She said no account is worth having to deal with Terrance."

"Tell her he's not so bad once you get used to the sarcasm, put-downs and unreasonable demands."

"Yeah, cute. You're still a fucking mook."

"I thought I was a hump."

"That too. You're lucky I'm even talking to you."

"Yeah, right. I'm outta work, got no place to live, and the whole city thinks I'm a mad-dog killer. Not to mention, I haven't gotten laid in a year and a half. If I get any luckier, I'll slip on a banana peel and get crushed by a garbage truck."

"Maybe your luck is changing. Barney wants to see you."

"Maybe I don't want to see him."

"Can you try to not be a complete shit-for-brains for at least a minute? Barney asking for you is good. Maybe he changed his mind."

"So you think he's gonna apologize and give me back my old job with a hefty raise?"

"Maybe. He didn't say."

"What did he say?"

"He asked me if I heard from you, and I said not since he fired you. He said you weren't fired, just laid off. And if I spoke to you I should tell you to call his office first thing in the morning."

"Did he say why?"

"No. But whatever it is, it beats sitting in Raymondo's all day."

"I'm not so sure." I hang up, stumble to my bed, and pass out.

I wake up to Mick Jagger whining that he can't get no satisfaction. Hey, Mick, wanna trade places? After three swipes I manage to shut Mick up, at least for five minutes, 'cause I'm not sure if I hit the "OFF" button or the "SNOOZE" button.

I look over at the clock; it's a little after seven. The house is strangely still. Every day when I wake up I hear Moish clomping around. This morning, nothing. I'm betting I find him on the couch, still dressed, mouth open, making that half-snore, half-gurgle noise that he usually does between the sports and the weather during the eleven o'clock news.

When I walk upstairs from my basement hovel, he's not on the couch, not in his bedroom. Nowhere. I look outside, the car's not there either. Fuck!

I walk from room to room looking for who knows what, trying to think. If he was in an accident the police would have called. Same if he had another heart attack. I dial 911.

"What is your emergency?"

"My father's missing?"

"For how long?"

"Since last night."

"Is he ill?"

"No."

"Has he been diagnosed with dementia?"

"Not exactly. But he's pretty ditzy."

"There's not much we can do right now. If he's not home by tomorrow, call back."

I dial Nicky's number. "Hey, Nick."

"You getting ready for your big meeting with Barney?"

"Oh yeah. No. Something came up."

"What's more important than getting your job back?"

"My father's missing."

"Whaddaya mean, missing?"

"He's not here. I don't know where he is."

"Was he there last night?"

"No. He left me a note."

"Where did he go?"

"I don't know."

"Whaddaya mean, you don't know. What did the note say?"

I'm starting to yell. "It just said he was going out."

"What are you gonna do?"

"I don't know."

"Where do you think he might be?"

"He could be anywhere, in a ditch, wrapped around a telephone pole."

"Did I ever tell you about my Uncle Vito? He was about your father's age."

"I thought your uncle's name was Johnny."

"This is another uncle. On my father's side."

"How many goddam uncles do you have?"

"A lot. Now shut up and let me tell you about Vito. He had a 1960 candy-apple-red Thunderbird that he kept mint. He simonized it every week. Polished the wheels with a toothbrush and a Q-tip. He took it out a couple of times a week, just to drive around the neighborhood, pick up the paper and come home. One morning he went out and nobody heard from him for a couple of days. My Aunt Lorraine got a call from the police somewhere in the middle of Pennsylvania. I think it was Altoona. He rear-ended a school bus."

"Ah, shit."

"At least nobody was hurt."

I yell into the phone. "Is that supposed to make me feel better?"

He yells back. "Don't holler at me. I'm trying to help you."

"Well, you're not."

"Fuck you."

"I'm sorry, Nicky. With everything that's happening, I'm a little edgy."

"Don't worry about it."

"So what happened to Uncle Vito?"

"The Altoona cops put him on a bus to New York. My Aunt Lorraine was waiting for him at the Port Authority. When she asked him what the hell happened, he told her he went for a spin."

"What happened to the car?"

"My cousin Robert sold it to some guy in Florida for five thousand bucks. He gave the money to Lorraine."

"How did your uncle take it?"

"Bad. He sorta went off the deep end. He accused Robert of stealing it. Then he said gangsters were after him. Then it was Russian spies. All kinds of paranoid shit. When my aunt tried to tell him what really happened, he started yelling and screaming at her, saying she was screwing one of the Russians. He stopped eating because he thought everyone was trying to poison him. He died six months later."

"Shoot me now."

"That doesn't mean that Moish'll be the same way."

"But it could."

"My advice would be that when he comes home . . ."

"You mean *if* he comes home."

He makes like he didn't hear me. "*When* he comes home, don't confront him. Don't ask him where he went. If he says he was on a rocket to the moon, you smile and say, 'That's nice.'"

"And what if he doesn't come home?"

"As Barney would say, we'll jump off that bridge when we come to it. Speaking of Barney, you might as well come into the office and talk to him. There's nothing you can do about your father right now."

"I guess you're right."

CHAPTER FOURTEEN

I walk into the agency and it's like nothing ever happened. Helen looks up and says, "Hi, honey," just like she does every morning. I get the usual nods and waves from the people I pass. My cubicle is just how I left it, papers and random crap all over the desk, no decorations, tchotchkes or photos. The walls are bare. I've learned to be ready to get the hell out of an agency in a hurry and not have too much stuff to carry with me. That's what happens after you've been fired as many times as I have. I throw my bag and jacket on my chair and head for Nicky's office.

He looks up from his sketch pad. "Welcome back."

"Yeah, thanks. Nobody seems that excited to see me."

"Nobody's ever excited to see you."

"Yeah, but that's most days. I thought maybe today would be different."

"Most of them don't know you were gone."

"I guess that's a good thing."

He shrugs. "Any word on Moish?"

"No. I'm getting ready to panic."

"I've been panicked since I was nine years old. You get used to it after a while."

"Somehow that doesn't comfort me."

"If anything terrible happened, you'd have heard by now. He probably got tired, pulled over, and is sleeping on the side of a road somewhere."

"Great. He'll probably get rear-ended by a semi."

"Way to be positive." Nicky's phone rings. He grabs it. "He's right here. Do you wanna talk to him." I reach over for the phone but he hangs up. "He's ready to see you."

When I get there Karol looks up from her computer and gives me a wink. "They're waiting for you."

"They?"

She shrugs.

I walk through the door and Barney's not at his desk. I'm about to go back out and ask what the hell is going on when I hear, "Over here." Barney's sitting at the conference table at the other end of his ballroom-sized office. Nielsen is next to him. There's a pile of magazines in front of him.

I walk over and Nielsen says, "Sit." He still looks like the marine captain he used to be. Every strand of his silver-gray hair is exactly in place. His Brooks Brothers suit is pressed and creased. His $500 shoes don't just shine, they sheen. Why he liked or even tolerated that walking vomit bag Persons is beyond my comprehension.

He gives me the same stare-down I'm sure he gave his junior officers when they screwed up a bivouac or muster or whatever the hell marines do. "Do you have any idea what Barney and I have been doing the last two days?"

I give him a dumbass look and say, "Uh . . . no."

"We've been reassuring our clients that we don't run a criminal organization or an insane asylum."

I have no clue how to respond so I just sit there with my mouth open and my eyes blank like a prize yutz.

"In my forty years in this business I thought I'd seen it all, but I never thought I'd have to explain why my agency's best writer is the prime suspect in my creative director's murder."

"I'm sorry, sir, that was a total screwup."

"You're damn right it was!" Now he's screaming. "Wiping your behind with James's tie? Calling him a fucking asshole? And yelling at the top of your lungs that you'd like to murder him?"

Nicky was wrong. Looks like they wanted me to come in so Nielsen could ream me out and fire me face-to-face.

If I'm gonna get shitcanned anyway I might as well say my piece.

"What about the shit that he pulled?" I yell back. "Throwing our best work into the garbage. Locking himself in his office and never saying jack shit to the people he's supposed to lead. Not to mention coming into the office looking like he spends every night in the Grand Central Station dumpster."

He lowers his voice to a dull roar. "I'm not excusing what James did. Trashing your work was unprofessional and insensitive. But your response was totally beyond the pale. Within an hour the incident was all over the street. And you can be sure every one of our clients heard about it, if not from their own people, from our competitors."

I slump down in my chair.

"If that was the worst of it, we could deal with it. But then the next day poor James turns up dead and every newspaper in town has your face on the front page screaming *murderer*."

"That was bullshit. I was totally exonerated."

"It doesn't matter. The damage is done."

"Do you want me to call the clients?"

He's screaming again. "I don't want you anywhere near our clients."

"Then why the hell am I here? You already fired me. If you just dragged me in here to yell at me, mission accomplished." I stand up.

"Sit the hell down!" He slams his fist on the table. "We're not finished. If it were up to me, I'd see to it that you never work in this city again, on Madison Avenue or anywhere else." He nods over at Barney, who is squirming in his chair, looking like he's trying to hide in the space between the backrest and the seat. "But he thinks you deserve another chance."

I turn and look hopefully at Barney. "So I'm getting my old job back?"

He sits up and clears his throat. "Not exactly."

"I don't get it. Either I'm working or I'm fired."

"We have a conflict issue with one of our clients and one of Harvey's."

"I don't want to sound dense, but what does that have to do with me?"

Barney's about to say something when Nielsen glares at me and yells, "Shut the hell up and you'll find out." He nods over at Barney.

"We've had the *Savvy Investor* account for about five years."

"That's Esther's account." Another glower from Nielsen. I jerk back contritely, lips sealed.

Barney looks over at Nielsen then back to me. "Harvey was the agency of record for Rivette Publications. It's flagship magazine, the *Capitalist Rag*, is a direct SI competitor. Since we can't keep both accounts and SI bills twice as much, the *Rag* would be the one to go."

"I don't want that to happen," Nielsen says before Barney can finish. "The *Capitalist Rag* was one of my first accounts. I've been friends with Edward Rivette, the publisher, since college."

"Wow! *The* Ed Rivette, the Prince of Page Six."

Nielsen grunts. "As I was saying, the *Capitalist Rag* has special significance to me. I'd hate to give it up. Barney has come up with a brilliant solution that could save both accounts and give you a chance to redeem yourself."

"You take on the *Rag* as a freelance client," Barney says, beaming. "Rivette will pay you what you were making here, maybe even a little more. You can even work in your old office here at the agency. Nobody has to know anything's different."

"What about my other accounts?"

Nielsen says, "The day-to-day creative will be reassigned. You might have to step in for a meeting or special projects. You'll just bill us like any other freelancer."

Barney winks at me. "I'm telling you, Stew, you're going to make out with this arrangement."

"What am I going to do for an art director?"

"You'll work with Nicky, of course. There's no reason why you can't have your usual team on this."

"Terrance and Jeannie too?"

Nielsen cuts in. "You probably won't need much in the way of account management. As far as media plans and marketing strategies, there's no reason to change what we did at Nielsen and Company." He gathers up some of the magazines on the table and pushes them over in front of me.

I leaf through them. In addition to a few copies of the *Capitalist Rag* there are a couple of other titles.

"What's with the *Hampton Howler* and *Greenwich Growler*"

Nielsen glares at me. "Don't worry about them. Those titles have no ad budget."

"I think Ed does those just so he can write off his homes in Greenwich and East Hampton," Barney says with a chortle.

Nielsen clearly isn't amused. "Read through these. Concentrate on the tone as well as the content. When you're done, give them to Nicky."

"Nicky doesn't read."

He glared at me. "What do you mean he can't read?"

"Not can't, doesn't. He has dyslexia. To him words on a page look like ants crawling around on a piece of paper. It would take him a whole day to get through one article."

"How does he deal with the paperwork? Memos, creative briefs, marketing plans and the like?"

"He doesn't, I do. I read and write. He draws and designs. It works."

Barney perks up. "Sure does. We have the awards to prove it. Last thing we want to do is change a winning game plan."

Nielsen stands up, shaking his head and scowling. "Whatever. Remember, this is your last chance, Gribnitz. Screw it up and you'll be driving a cab. In Guam!"

Before I could say anything, he does an about-face and marches out the door, slamming it behind him.

When I'm pretty sure he's out of earshot I say, "What a prick! It's too bad I'm not really a murderer. He'd be next on my hit list."

Barney wags his finger at me. "Keep your mouth shut, will you? It's talk like that that got you into trouble in the first place."

"Sorry."

"Listen, Gribby, this really is your last chance. You don't know what

I had to go through to get you this deal. Screw it up and I can't help you."

"I appreciate that."

"Good."

"What now?"

"I'll call Rivette and set up a meeting."

"Can I tell Nick?"

"Of course. And I'll speak with Terrance."

"I thought he isn't going to be involved."

He shoots me a conspiratorial grin. "As far as Nielsen is concerned, he isn't."

"Got it." I stand up to leave.

"Make this work. Jobs depend on it. More than just yours."

I try to look a lot more confident than I feel. "Have I ever let you down?"

He shakes his head and smiles ruefully. "Dozens of times. Just don't make it one more."

I head straight for Nicky's office. Terrance is there, pacing back and forth near the door. He glares at me, arms folded in front of him. "So?"

Nicky's panting like a puppy waiting for a Milk-Bone. "Is everything back to normal?"

"Not exactly."

Terrance beams his laser eyes at me. "What does that mean, not exactly?"

"Nielsen was there with Barney. He told me if it was up to him, he'd can my ass and make sure I never work in advertising again."

Nicky jumps up. "He fired you?"

Terrance shouts, "That's insane! Barney told me everything was going to be fine." He takes a stride toward the door. "You stay right here. We'll see who's fired."

I grab his sleeve. "Hold on. I didn't say I was fired."

Nicky looks confused. "If you're not fired and you didn't get your job back, don't tell me he made you creative director."

"Not hardly." Then I tell them the whole deal with the *Capitalist Rag*.

Terrance says, "I've heard of this Rivette. He's supposed to be some kind of wild man."

Nicky brightens. "Might be fun."

Terrance knits his thick mohair brows. "We'll see."

CHAPTER FIFTEEN

The hour-long subway ride to Canarsie gave me plenty of time to obsess about the multiple dumpster fires that comprise my life. There's my screaming match with Nielsen, Moish's disappearance, my smooch-fest with Jeannie and the fact that everyone in the tristate area thinks I'm a murderer.

I'm more worried about my father than the other stuff.

Working with Rivette could be fun if he's half as wild as the gossip columns say. And if Boyce wasn't full of shit, which is always possible, I might even get more money, which is all good. Jeannie seems to have blown off our little make-out session. And, hopefully, the whole Madison Avenue Murderer mess will die down.

It's the Moish situation that's making me crazy.

Walking back to the house, I'm trying to remember if he has any kind of address book lying around with the names and numbers of his OTB buddies or anyone else who might have a clue where to find him. I have no idea where his Canarsie hangout is or if he even has one. In Flatbush it was either Garfield's Cafeteria or the candy store outside the Church Avenue subway station.

I saw a movie once where this old Hollywood actor with memory problems got on a bus and went back to his hometown in Iowa or Idaho or some other godforsaken dirt pile in the middle of the country. I guess Flatbush is as close to a hometown as Moish gets. I'll try there. I have to find his Medicare card in case he's in a hospital somewhere. I don't want to think about what happens if he turns up dead.

I open the door and there he is—sitting on the living room couch in his underwear, drinking coffee and reading the *Daily News*. He looks up at me and yells, "You called the police on me!"

I shout back, "I had no idea where you were. For all I know, you coulda been wrapped around a tree somewhere."

He slams the paper down on the table. "What, I forgot how to drive? Let me tell you something, I'm still a better driver than you."

"I never said you were a bad driver."

"So good drivers go crashing into trees?"

The man is fucking impossible! "This has nothing to do with your driving," I scream.

"Then what the hell are you talking about?" he yells back.

"I was worried about you. I didn't know what to do so I called the cops. Sue me for caring about you."

"You're a putz!" he screams.

That's the way my father ends every argument. He knows he's wrong, he won't admit it, so he curses you out. I used to fall into the trap of cursing him back. That's what he wants. He's not getting it from me.

"I'm sorry. I'll never call the police again, even if you're missing for a month."

He smirks. "Good."

"If you don't want to tell me where you were, that's fine. It's none of my business."

"You're goddamn right it's none of your business. I coulda been playing cards all night. I coulda gone to Atlantic City. I coulda been with a lady."

"You spending the night with a woman? C'mon."

"Yes, a woman. As a matter of fact, that's where I was. I had a date. Now you know."

I can't decide whether he's really delusional or if he's saying it just to egg me on. I'm about to press him on it when I flash on Nicky's Uncle

Vito and how confronting him made his condition worse. I force myself to smile and say, "That's great, Moish. At least one of us is getting laid."

He glares at me and shouts, "Show some respect, goddamn it! Can't a man keep company with a lady without you turning it into something dirty? Is that the way you thought of your mother too?"

"No. Of course not. I'm sorry. I was just trying . . ."

"I don't care what you were trying. How about trying to be a mensch for once in your life."

"You're right. I'm sorry." I gotta admit, in his own peculiar way, my father is brilliant. He's the one who didn't call and had me beside myself with worry and the next thing I know I'm apologizing to him. "Does this lady have a name?" I say, trying to bring the conversation back to some semblance of normalcy.

He scowls. "Everybody has a name."

I stand. "Listen, I've had a really bad couple of days. If you're just gonna give me a hard time no matter what I say, there's no reason for us to talk." I take a few steps toward the basement door to my hopefully soon-to-be ex-room.

"It's Ruth."

"I'm sure she's a very nice lady." I keep walking.

"You should be sure. You've known her since you were six years old."

"What?" I stop with a jolt. "Are you talking about Ruthie Berns?"

He smirks. "That's right."

"I didn't even think you liked her."

"Who said I didn't like her?"

"You never went over to her house with Mom. You guys never went out together."

"It was that phony husband of hers I couldn't stand."

"Harold?"

"Yeah, Harold Bernstein. A pisher of a bookkeeper. Told everybody he was an accountant. Changed his name to Berns. Wanted people to call him Hal. Didn't want anybody to know he was Jewish. With a schnoz like that he coulda changed his name to Roosevelt and it wouldn't matter."

"They moved out way before you did, somewhere on Long Island, wasn't it?"

"Valley Stream. The first time they saw a black face in the neighborhood, they were gone. Your mother took it hard. Ruthie was a good friend."

"But that was, like, fifteen years ago. Don't tell me you kept in contact all that time."

"After they left, your mother would talk to Ruthie on the phone, first a couple of times a week, then once a week, and pretty soon nothing. You know how it is."

"So how did you and Ruthie reconnect."

"That thing you wrote in the paper about your mother after she died. She saw it and called me."

A lot of newspapers sell space on their obituary page for paid death notices. It's a huge rip-off. They make the grieving family pay the same rates as major advertisers, then tack on an extra fee to rewrite it into English. Terrance arranged to have a few papers publish a two-column obit I wrote for my mother in exchange for an extra placement or two.

"What about Harold?" I ask.

"Her husband? He dropped dead a couple of years ago. Stroke." Moish spit as he said it.

"So, is it serious between you and Ruthie?"

"Serious? War is serious. A heart attack is serious. A man and a woman keeping company, that's not serious. It's something to do."

CHAPTER SIXTEEN

We're standing at the entrance of the Union League Club, an austere limestone and brick building with strange flags flying in front like it's the embassy of some exotic foreign country, which to me it is.

Nicky's looking at me with fascinated repulsion, like he's examining an exotically shaped turd. "You look like a garbageman at a wedding."

He, on the other hand, looks impeccable in a black Armani suit, black Gucci loafers, a light gray shirt and a charcoal gray tie. For a straight guy, Nicky's much too much into fashion.

"I'll have you know, this was the best suit on the Sears clearance rack," I say with pride. "At least it was five years ago when I bought it."

He shakes his head in disgust. "I didn't think anyone under seventy even owned a brown suit. And that tie, it looks like something they give you when the guy at the county fair can't guess your weight. It's a good thing your creative sense is better than your fashion sense."

Barney comes strutting down the street like he's leading a parade that disappeared behind him.

"Hello, boys." He looks Nicky over and grins contentedly, like a priest checking out a new alter boy. "Nick, you look perfect." He turns to me and crinkles his nose. "Gribby, try not to do anything to embarrass me. I've been a member of this club for over forty years. I'd like to remain one."

"I'll make sure not to fart or pick my nose, at least not at the same time."

He scowls. "Get it all out now."

We walk into a grand ballroom of polished marble floors, mahogany walls and huge columns that might have been stolen from the Lincoln Memorial. "Am I the first Jew ever to set foot in this gold-plated mausoleum?"

"I think Justice Brandeis had dinner here once." Barney grins. "He didn't have the pork chops."

He leads us up a circular marble staircase, past a grandiose ballroom, and down a narrow corridor with four doors. Each has a gold plaque emblazoned with the name of a legendary club member. John Jacob Astor, E. H. Harriman, J. P. Morgan. We are ushered into the Cornelius Vanderbilt room. About the size of a master bedroom, I'm guessing it's a private dining room. There's a round table with four place settings in the middle of the room, a filled crystal water goblet in front of each. A burled wood credenza is against the white wood-paneled wall. Everything is polished and pristine to the point of sterility. A youngish waiter is standing at attention next to the credenza, black vest, white shirt, black pants. As we walk to the table he quicksteps ahead of us and pulls out a chair for Boyce, who says, "Thank you, Bernard."

Nicky and I, not being used to such white-glove treatment, sit down without any help.

I have the same feeling of impending doom as when I was waiting outside the principal's office at P.S. 181 after I pulled up Nora Braverman's skirt on the way out of second grade assembly. I got my ass reamed out, but a few years later she was the first girl I ever kissed. She wound up marrying a dentist from Tuckahoe.

Barney smiles benevolently at me. "Relax, Gribby, you're gonna love Ed Rivette. He's as crazy as you are."

The door opens and in walks a guy who looks like a young, emaciated Winston Churchill, with a touch of Ichabod Crane. He walks rigidly over to the table and stands next to his chair, waiting as the waiter pulls it out. He sits down, ramrod straight, so as not to dislodge the pole that was obviously shoved up his ass at birth. If this is Barney's idea of a maniac, I'd hate to see who he thinks is a stiff.

Barney leans over to shake his hand. "Hello, Urban. Meet my team." He looks over at Nicky. "Nick Coletti, one of New York's top art directors." Then turns to me. "And this is Stewart Gribnitz, our award-winning copywriter."

The stiff looks us up and down, like he's examining breeding stock at a thoroughbred auction. I'm waiting for him to check my teeth.

Barney says, "This is Urban Sangster. He's the marketing director at Rivette Publications."

Sangster stares straight ahead, his eyes blank. Then, as if awakened from a hypnotic trance, he bolts up, thrusts out his hand and grumbles, "Umm, yes. Pleased to meet you." He gives Nicky's hand a quick shake, then mine. It's not quite a dead fish, but it's on its last fins. After we're all settled in our seats he says, "Edward will be here shortly." Then he goes back into his trance.

I take a drink of water, Nicky's doing something with his napkin and Barney's glaring at his pocket watch. After two agonizingly awkward minutes, Edward Rivette throws open the door and struts into the room. "Sorry I'm late, gentlemen," he says with absolutely no sincerity. He's a big man, Oliver Hardy to Sangster's Stan Laurel. He glides gracefully over to Barney, saying, "So good of you to come, old friend. It's been too long." Barney stands and extends his hand, which Rivette engulfs in both of his, shaking it vigorously, like he's mixing James Bond a martini. He turns and extends both arms toward me and Nicky. "And these must be the creative geniuses I've heard so much about."

Barney beams like a proud papa. "Nick Coletti and Stew Gribnitz, the agency's best creative team."

"Gentlemen, your reputation precedes you," Rivette says as he sits in the seat being held by the hwaiter. "I very much look forward to working with you. I have no doubt that this will be a long and rewarding relationship for all concerned." He turns to the waiter, who's back at his post next to the credenza, and bellows, "Edward, drinks all around. A Tanqueray martini for Mr. Boyce, Campari and soda for Mr. Coletti." He smiles warmly at me. "Stewart, I hear you are, like myself, a single malt aficionado."

"When I can afford it."

"They have a thirty-year-old Talisker that I'm sure you'll appreciate."

"I appreciate the ten-year-old. I grovel at the feet of the thirty."

He shoots me a quick nod and a tiny smile. It's gone by the time he turns to Sangster. "And for my friend Urban, iced tea with lemon."

Bernard nods crisply and is off for our drinks.

Nicky says, "How'd you know all our drinks?"

Rivette grins with self-satisfaction. "I do my homework. It's the only way to survive."

Barney says, "Then I'm sure you know that the advertising for the *Capitalist Rag* is in the best possible hands. These boys have won awards."

"Quite right. Three Effies, two Clios and a One Show. Am I correct?"

"Right on the money." Then, as usual, instead of dropping the pitch once he made the sale, Barney keeps pushing. "I know you were very close with James Persons."

"I knew James for a very long time. His death came as quite a shock." He turns to me. "I heard about the unfortunate contretemps between you and the police. I hope everything was resolved."

Before I could say anything Barney blurts out, "That was all a big clusterdump. Stew's no murderer. The only thing he'd kill is a bottle of Scotch or maybe a bad headline." He laughs and claps me on the back. "The dumbass police got it all wrong and this poor guy got branded as public enemy number one all over town until it got cleared up."

I look over at Nicky who's sighing silently and shaking his head. Sangster's still in his trance. I figure the best thing I can do is change the subject. "I think '*Rag* to Riches,' the tagline you're using now, works well with your demographic. I see no reason to change it moving forward."

He waves his hand dismissively. "Yes, that's fine. There's no need to screw around with the *Rag*'s ad campaign, a trained monkey could do it. That's not the campaign I wanted to talk with you about."

What the fuck? We're his new creative team. If he doesn't want to talk about his ad campaign, why the hell are we here? I look over at

Nicky. I can tell he's seething. He sees advertising as high art. I'm sure the trained monkey comment didn't sit too well with him.

"If you don't want to talk about advertising, what *do* you want to talk about?" Leave it to Barney to state the obvious.

"My political campaign." Rivette puffs out his chest. "I'm the new Republican candidate for governor of Connecticut."

Barney, who lives in Greenwich, bolts forward in his chair. "You're what? Governor? Seriously?"

"Why would I kid about something like that?"

"Well, uh, of course you wouldn't," he says, not wanting to piss off a new client. "I was just surprised. I belong to the Greenwich Republican Roundtable and no one mentioned anything about your candidacy."

"Negotiations were handled in secret at the highest level to avoid any petty gossip." Rivette's voice was tinged with disdain. "None of the local clubs were read in."

For a blue blood, Barney always came off as a pretty regular guy. But there was always a slight whiff of class superiority about him. It's fascinating to see him smelling it on someone else.

"Of course, of course," Barney says heartily. "Just curious how it came to pass."

Rivette sighs. "After poor Chuck Whittaker lost his life in that horrific car crash, the party was in a bind. With only a little more than a month until the election and very little money left in the coffers, none of the obvious candidates was willing to have a go. It looked as though Neil Monahan would run unopposed." Rivette cringes like he just swallowed a roach. "There was no way I could let that happen. The man is an out-and-out criminal. So I volunteered to run against him and fund the campaign out of my own pocket. They were more than happy to accept my offer."

Nicky, ever the idealist, says, "That doesn't seem right."

Barney, seeing tens of thousands of dollars in billings flying out the window, says, "He doesn't mean it's not right, just that it's a little out of the ordinary."

"Nicky happens to be correct," Rivette says. "It isn't right. But that's the way it is. They don't want to spend any money on a race they think they can't win. They think I'm doing it because I have a huge ego and want to see my name splashed all over the media for the next month. And, of course, that the publicity will do wonders for my brand."

He takes a sip of water and smiles conspiratorially. What they don't realize is that I intend to win. And you two," he gestures grandly at me and Nicky, "are going to help me do it."

Boyce says, "This is a huge departure from what we had planned for the *Capitalist Rag*." I can see the cash register in his head ka-chinging. "We'll have to assign a management team, create a new media plan and come up with an ad campaign, a revised budget."

Another dismissive wave from Rivette. "Of course. After we finish lunch, why don't you and Urban go back to your office and hash out all the logistical and financial details. Stew, Nick and I will remain here and toss around some creative ideas."

As if on cue, Bernard is back with our drinks.

Barney raises his glass. "To the next governor of the great state of Connecticut. You've got my vote."

Rivette drains his Scotch in a single gulp. I don't want him to think I'm a wuss, so I do the same. The Talisker feels warm and smoky going down. He holds up his glass. "Bernard, two more, please."

CHAPTER SEVENTEEN

It's morning. I think. I haven't been this fucked up from alcohol since I strong-armed all the other twelve-year-olds into giving me their Manis-chewitz at the Judea Center bar mitzvah boy seder. The rabbi had to call my mother to come pick me up. He told her I had a bad reaction to my sip of wine. He was semi-right. I had a bad reaction to eighteen sips of wine. I threw up all over the afikomen and wound up in a fetal ball on the cantor's couch, moaning and crying while the room spun around me.

Over time my capacity for booze has increased to the point where I can put away half a bottle of eighty-proof whiskey with a couple of beers and still be in fairly good shape. In fact, for the last couple of years, I felt it was my duty to end the perception that Jews can't hold their liquor. I drank a lot of guys under the table. But not Ed Rivette.

I'm staring up at a ceiling fan. A ceiling fan I don't recognize. I sit up a little too quickly, taste some bile, lie back down. I start the process over, only this time in slow motion.

I'm on a strange couch in a strange room in my underwear. A blanket's wrapped around me. I look around. There are a couple of comfort-able-looking chairs, a TV, a stereo and stuff like that. The furniture isn't museum quality but it ain't Goodwill either. I'm guessing Crate & Barrel.

The time on the VCR says 7:52.

I yell, "Hellooo."

Jeannie comes walking in from around a corner, arms folded, looking at me crossways. "You're back among the living." She's wearing a light blue terry cloth robe. A towel is wrapped around her head. She's foaming at the mouth. I think maybe I'm hallucinating, then I realize she's holding a toothbrush.

"I know this might seem like a stupid question, but what am I doing here?"

She sits down. "How much of yesterday do you remember?"

"I was in the club with Nicky, Barney, Rivette and that other Lurch-looking guy."

"Urban Sangster."

"Yeah. Barney and Lurch left after lunch. We talked a little about Rivette's campaign. The waiter kept filling my glass. I sorta remember Nicky helping me stumble back to the agency. Not much after that."

While I'm talking she gets up, goes back around to where I imagine the bathroom is. A few seconds later, she's back. No toothbrush, no foam. She sits down.

"According to Nicky, you and Rivette finished a whole bottle of Scotch and made a good dent in a second. He checked the bottle. It was more than ninety proof. He basically had to carry you back to the agency."

"What happened after that? Did I puke?"

She shakes her head. "Maybe you should have. There was a lot of moaning and retching but no chunks. You passed out on Terrance's couch."

"So how'd I get here?" I look around the room. "Nice place, by the way."

"Thanks." She pauses for a few seconds. "We decided that leaving you in the agency alone in the dark all night was a bad idea. Nicky thought you might wake up in the middle of the night, freak out, and jump out a window or something. Terrance was afraid you'd throw up all over his Michael Amini sofa."

"So how'd I get here?"

"Since my apartment is closest to the office, Nicky and Terrance managed to stuff you into a cab and the three of us got you up here."

"So I guess we can kiss the Rivette account goodbye."

She puts on this dejected look. "That's what we all thought." My heart sinks.

Then she grins. "But that's not what happened. According to Nicky, Rivette loved you. He thought you had great ideas. It seems that while you were getting shit-faced you came up with an advertising strategy that Rivette totally bought into."

"Too bad I can't remember it."

"Not to worry. Nicky brought that little tape recorder of yours, the one you usually bring to meetings because you're too lazy to take notes."

"It's not laziness. I like to concentrate on understanding what the client is saying. I can't do that if I'm busy scribbling on a piece of paper."

She shakes her head. "Save it for somebody who doesn't know you're full of shit." She grins. "Anyway, Nicky figured you'd forget it so he went to your office and quick grabbed the recorder."

"He got the whole meeting on tape?"

"Not only that." She looks up and shakes her head. "He recorded the last half hour of you and Rivette singing Motown songs at the top of your lungs. 'My Girl' was my particular favorite." Then she smiles. "But Nicky says Rivette was grinning from ear to ear when he staggered into his limo. Nicky thought he was in worse shape than you."

"I knew all those years of drunken debauchery would pay off sooner or later."

She chucks a throw pillow at me. "You're just lucky that Rivette is as big a degenerate as you are. Except there's one huge difference. He has a couple of billion in the bank, which makes him quirky and eccentric. In your situation, you're just a dirtbag."

"At least now I'm a dirtbag with a client. What happens now, with the account, I mean?"

"While you were getting drunk with your new best buddy, Barney called Terrance and me into his office to meet with Sangster."

"Does he have any idea what he's doing?"

She rolled her eyes. "Not much. But he agreed with everything Terrance said, including a million-dollar budget, over and above anything we do for the magazine."

"For a month's work? How the hell did he pull that off?"

"Terrance convinced Sangster that we needed total market saturation to make any kind of a dent. Connecticut is the most expensive media market in the country. You have to buy local media plus New York and Boston if you want to have total coverage. And the prices double during election season."

"One more question."

She raises a quizzical eyebrow. "Yeeessss?"

"What did you do with my pants?"

She points to a door. "I put all your stuff in the closet over there."

"Are you the one who undressed me?"

She shakes her head. "Nicky did. When I take off a man's clothes I like him to be conscious." She points to another door. "There's a new toothbrush in the bathroom. It's still in the wrapper. I don't have a fresh razor. You can use the one I shave my legs with if you want."

"Nah. But thanks for the offer."

She shrugs. "I'll be out of here soon, then you can take a shower and do whatever else you need to do. There's a meeting about next steps with the Rivette account at ten o'clock. Do you think you can make it?"

"Sure. That gives me a couple of hours. I'd have to be a real putz to need more time than that."

"No comment." She gives me her patented sneer and heads back to her bedroom.

She's out in less than five minutes. And she looks great. Wavy light brown hair almost to her shoulders. Just enough makeup to highlight those green eyes. Navy-blue pantsuit that's all business but still stylish. For a Queens kid who worked her way up from the traffic department to account executive, she has more on the ball than any of those snot-nosed MBAs that Barney likes to hire.

She points to the kitchen area. "There's orange juice in the fridge and bread for toast if you want it."

I grab my head, which is still pounding. "You got anything for a hangover?"

She shakes her head. "Sorry."

"How can that be? You're Irish, aren't you?"

"Just on my father's side. He left when I was ten. My mother is half Italian and half Jewish."

"That explains a lot."

She gives me the stink eye. "What?"

"Nothing. Never mind." Let's see if I can say something without pissing her off. I try to muster a smile. "Listen, thanks for everything. For putting up with me and letting me crash here. Let me take you out to dinner tonight. It's the least I can do."

"I can't. I'm busy."

"Have a date?"

"As a matter of fact, I do." She looks pissed off again. "Why do you look surprised?"

"I'm not surprised, it's just that . . ."

"What?"

"Nothing. Forget it. Who's the lucky guy?"

She scowls. "That's none of your business."

"I'm happy for you. There's no reason you can't tell me."

Quietly, she says, "It's someone from work."

"Somebody I know?"

"Of course. You know everybody at the agency."

"Yeah, that's true. If you don't want to tell me, don't tell me. Whoever it is, he better treat you right or he'll have to answer to me."

She smiles a little, shuffles her feet. "It's Ari."

"Ari? That's not who I would have guessed." I shake my head. "I don't see you two together."

"Why?" The anger's back. "Don't you think I'm good enough for him?"

"Just the opposite. I think you're too good for him."

She glares at me. "What's wrong with Ari?"

"Nothing. It's just that I'm not a big fan of account pukes in general, except Terrance, and he's an acquired taste. I always found Ari to be smug, arrogant, self-important—you know, a typical account person, and even worse, a typical Israeli."

"You don't like Israelis either?"

I shake my head. "Not much. I'm sure there are some good ones, just none I've ever met. All the Israelis I know, they come here, tell everyone how fucked up America is and how wonderful it is back there. Let them go back to the fucking desert and suck sand."

She looks taken aback. "I didn't realize you were such a racist."

Now I'm getting annoyed. "How is that racist? I'm Jewish. They're Jewish. You can't be a racist against your own race."

"Whatever it is, it's not very nice."

I try to backtrack. "Listen, have a great time with Ari. I'm sure he's a really nice guy out of the office."

"He's a nice guy in the office," she says belligerently.

Fuck it. I'm not gonna play nice when she's being so pissy. "Yeah. I guess all the screaming and cursing he does at our meetings, like when he called Nicky a no-talent shit, that's just his way of being nice."

She glares at me, grabs her bag. "Close the door behind you when you leave. It locks automatically."

She walks out and slams the door.

CHAPTER EIGHTEEN

Helen glances down at her watch as I walk in. "You're keeping them waiting in the small conference room."

The clock on the wall says 10:02.

"You're killing me over two minutes?"

"Don't look at me. Terrance called three times already, asking for you. To him, ten minutes early equals on time."

"Tell him I'm on my way."

When I get there Nicky, Jeannie and Barbara (aka the shiksa goddess) are sitting at the conference table. Terrance is standing in front of a white screen, scowling at me, like the Manhattan College marketing professor he used to be. "You're supposed to be leading this project. The least you can do is be on time."

"You're wrong. I can do a lot less than that."

He gives me a scornful sneer.

"And besides," I keep going, "most airlines consider five minutes late as being on time. And I was only three minutes late, so that makes me two minutes early."

"And you've just wasted those minutes with idiotic banter." He glares at me through his round tortoiseshell spectacles. "Now sit down, shut up and listen." He looks toward the back of the room. Bart

Vanzetti is standing behind a slide projector. "Bart, switch off the lights and begin."

The room gets darker. A publicity still of Ed Rivette appears on the screen.

"I'm sure you've all read about Mr. Rivette in one of the many gossip columns that feature him on a regular basis. Billionaire bon vivant. Successful magazine publisher. Married and divorced four times." Four glitzy wedding photos come up in quick succession. Rivette looked slightly older in each one and the various brides got progressively younger.

"He has a passion for vintage Americana. He drives a perfectly restored 1935 Duesenberg." Up pops a gleaming black convertible with glistening chrome trim. Visions of *The Great Gatsby* dance through my head.

"Rides a 1940 Indian Chief motorcycle." A hefty bike with blood-red teardrop front and rear fenders and fuel tank and a fringed leather seat.

"He was an accomplished pilot, flying a 1942 Cessna T-50." The screen fills with a bright yellow plane with twin propellers. Looks like a flying banana. "But since undergoing valve replacement surgery he's relegated to passenger status."

Now we're looking at a yellowed picture of the front page of an old newspaper, what I imagine the *New York Times* looked like a hundred years ago but not as flashy. The masthead says, "*Capitalist Review.*" "Rivette inherited his father's investor-oriented broadsheet, the *Capitalist Review*, when it was on the verge of bankruptcy." The ancient newspaper dissolves into the cover of a magazine that at first glance could be *Esquire* or *GQ*, with a handsome guy in a handsomer suit standing in front of a shiny, new Bentley. "And transformed it into the *Capitalist Rag*, the best-selling lifestyle, business and finance magazine that's half *Forbes*, half *Playboy*, with more subscribers than either.

"Using the same format—giving C-suite executives of major corporations the celebrity treatment usually reserved for supermodels, rock stars and screen idols—he created the niche publications *Hampton Howler, Greenwich Growler* and *Sutton Place Squealer*, all locations where he maintains a residence." Quick shots of the magazines flash on and off.

Terrance aims his laser stare at me. "Here's what you don't know. Peel away the devil-may-care veneer and you'll find a vicious gutter fighter. A ruthless businessman with a genius-level IQ. He's a former air force intelligence officer and was the captain of the Princeton wrestling team."

I shout out, "What's the matter, Terrance, you afraid he's gonna beat us up if he doesn't win the election?"

"Just you."

Nicky says, "I'd pay to see that."

Terrance smiles. "We all would."

"Jeez, rough crowd." I turn around to see the three women nodding, though surprisingly, Barbara's smiling in my direction. And I thought she couldn't stand me.

Terrance glares us all to silence. "You want rough? Try Neil Monahan, Rivette's Democrat opponent." Monahan's picture pops up. About the same age as Rivette, he's on the thin side with a salt-and-pepper crew cut and dark mustache. "He is the former special agent in charge at the New Haven FBI division and the current US attorney for the District of Connecticut."

Terrance takes a deep breath. "Monahan made his reputation by taking on drug lords, Cosa Nostra capos and hedge fund swindlers. I'm sure he doesn't see Edward Rivette as much of a threat."

I blurt, "He busted Boesky, right?"

"So, Stewart, you really do read something other than the sports pages."

Nicky perks up. "Isn't he related to Red Monahan?"

"I thought you might ask about that." The next face on the screen looks a little like Neil. The face is pockmarked and puffy with bloodshot green eyes and long auburn hair pulled back in a ponytail. "Robert 'Red' Monahan is Neil's half brother. He is the product of an affair between Neil's father, Hugh, a tavern owner, and one of his waitresses. It wasn't until Hugh's wife died and both boys were in their twenties that he acknowledged Robert, which by all accounts was too late. He was in and out of juvenile court as a teenager. As he got older he became involved with a Bridgeport narcotics gang. He's now an enforcer for the East Haven Vine Street mob, an offshoot of the New England Patricio crime family."

"From what I hear, the law won't touch Red because of his brother." Nicky's usually pretty quiet in these meetings, but he's a crazy Mafia addict. He must have seen *The Godfather* and *The Godfather Part II* fifty times each, *Goodfellas* the same. Any movie or TV show about mobsters, he's seen it. If he wasn't the most talented artist I've ever seen, he'd either be a G-man or a made man.

Terrance says, "There's never been any proven connection between the two. In fact, Neil once took Red into custody."

"Word is, that was just for show," Nicky shot back.

Terrance hits him with the same scowl he usually reserves for me. "Enough gangster trivia. Let's get back on task."

Nicky shrivels in his seat. "Sorry."

Terrance gives Bart the "cut" sign. The screen goes blank and the lights come on. "Monahan and Rivette are alpha males. They play to win and will trample anyone in their way."

Nicky perks up. "Like King Kong versus Godzilla." As soon as he says it he shrinks back into his seat, expecting to get his head bit off. Instead Terrance smiles and says, "Exactly. And right now Godzilla is winning. We're twenty points behind in the polls. The fact that Rivette is a quasi celebrity works in our favor. Name recognition shouldn't be a problem. But that doesn't always translate into votes." He scrunches up his face and glares at each of us. "We all have a lot of work to do and not a lot of time to do it. Any questions?"

Barbara says, "When do you want to see a finished media plan?"

"My usual answer is 'as soon as possible,' but in this case I'll need it sooner. Monahan's been on the air for several months already."

He turns to me and Nicky. "As soon as we have creative, it goes live." He actually favors me with a rare grin. "The good news is that Stew already has buy-in from the client on a strategy."

I whisper to Nicky, "It would be even better if I could remember what the hell it was."

Nicky pulls the mini recorder out of his shirt pocket and places it gently on the table in front of me. He smiles smugly. "You're welcome."

Terrance says, "That's all for now. I'll meet with each of you separately about next steps."

On the way out I walk over to Barbara. Lean and lanky, with sculpted cheekbones, chestnut hair, blue-gray crystalline eyes and skin as soft and sweet as the creme inside a Twinkie. If it wasn't for a little bump in the middle of her nose, she could easily be a Wilhelmina Model.

The first time I saw her walking down our corridor I turned to Nicky and whispered, "Who's that shiksa goddess?" Somehow the name stuck, at least with me and my pals.

Then about a week ago, when I thought she was at an all-day meeting, I grabbed Nicky and Bart and dragged them over to media planning. I walked over to her chair, got down on my knees, bowed my head, and said, "I worship at the alter of the shiksa goddess." Then, for good measure, I kissed her seat. I figured it would give the guys a good chuckle in the middle of a boring day.

Of course, she walked in just as I was doing it. I mumbled a stupid apology and got out of there as fast as I could, banging into a desk and nearly knocking over a lamp.

Nicky and Bart got more than a chuckle. They laughed so hard they almost shit in their pants.

I haven't spoken to her since that little escapade, so now, face to angelic face, I say, "I want to apologize for that stupid stunt I pulled a while ago. I was trying to be funny and, as usual, I failed miserably."

But instead of scowling at me and telling me what an immature bozo I am, she smiles and says, "Jeannie filled me in on your crazy sense of humor. Now that we'll be working together, I guess I'll just have to get used to it." She turns and leaves.

Terrance and Nicky are fussing around the room pushing chairs under tables and tossing coffee containers in the trash. How I got hooked up with not one but two compulsive neat freaks is beyond me.

They're finished in a few minutes and we're getting ready to leave when I say to Terrance, "You've been holding out on us about Ari."

He stiffens. "How do you know about that?"

"Jeannie told me."

"Jeannie? I don't believe it. She was sworn to secrecy."

"I don't get it. Why should her dating Ari be so top secret?"

"Ari's dating Jeannie? I had no idea."

"What do you mean? That's what I thought we were talking about."

"You weren't talking about the ESOP?"

Nicky says, "You mean the guy who wrote the fables?"

"That's Aesop, you twit." He shakes his head in disgust. "An ESOP is an employee stock ownership plan." He motions us back toward the conference table. "Sit down."

Nicky and I sit. Terrance comes over and stands between us. He puts an arm around each of us and in a hushed voice says, "Ari and I are negotiating with Barney about buying the agency."

"Whoa!" I yell. "Are you serious?"

He puts a finger to his lips and whispers, "Keep your voice down." He looks around the room as if to check for spies or bugs. "Of course I'm serious."

"I thought Nielsen was buying the agency," I say sotto voce. "Are you in with him?"

"Absolutely not!" he says louder than he wanted to. "I wouldn't be partners with him on a lottery ticket."

Nicky says, "I thought it was a done deal with Nielsen buying the agency."

"Not if we make a better offer."

"Does Nielsen know?"

"Not yet."

"You're sure you can trust Ari?"

"There's no reason not to."

"Suppose Nielsen makes him a better offer?"

Terrance shakes his head. "Ari's weak spot is his ego. I had a marble plaque made up. 'Nadler & Asiago Advertising' in embossed gold letters. I think he had an orgasm."

"Nielsen could do the same thing."

"He'd never put Ari's name on the door."

Nicky frowns. "Who designed it?"

Terrance says, "I did. It's three words and an ampersand. That much I can handle."

"What font?"

"Baskerville. I thought it looked classy."

Nicky nods. "It's okay. Bodoni would have been more elegant."

I say, "That's our Nicky, full of Bodoni."

Terrance shakes his head.

"So what's gonna happen to me and Nicky after all this boloney hits the fan?"

"You'll be fine."

"Are you sure? Ari's never been our biggest fan."

"Believe me. There's nothing for you to worry about."

"Where does Jeannie fit it, now that she's Ari's main squeeze?"

Terrance lets out a small sad sigh. "We'll have to wait and see. I haven't heard great things about the way Ari treats women. The word is he can get physical."

Nicky says, "You mean like beating them up?"

Terrance nods.

I say, "He lays a hand on Jeannie and he'll have to deal with me."

Nicky says, "You mean us."

Terrance holds up a conciliatory hand. "Calm down, you two. Ari knows how we feel about her. I'm sure he'll be on his best behavior."

"He better be," Nicky says and storms out of the room.

Terrance says, "Is he interested in Jeannie? I didn't think she was his type."

"He likes her a lot . . . as a friend. And he despises Ari."

"Go settle him down. We have a lot of work to do. I need you both to be focused. You can tangle with Ari afterward, though I warn you, the word is he was in the Israeli special forces."

"My money's on Nicky. He's been doing karate since he was a kid. Says it calms his nerves."

"Obviously not enough."

I go right to Nicky's office.

"We gotta tell Jeannie," he says as soon as he sees me at the door.

"I don't think so."

"Why not? You heard what Terrance said."

"But you didn't hear what Jeannie said."

"She hardly said anything."

"I don't mean at the meeting. This morning when I was at her house."

"What did she say?"

"Basically, she said if she wants to go out with Ari, she will. And she doesn't need my approval. In other words, butt the hell out."

"Sounds like she was pissed."

"She was. Big time."

"Why?"

"I guess she thought I was being possessive . . . jealous."

He gives me a sideways look. "Are you?"

"Absolutely not!" I yell.

Nicky puts a finger to his lips. "Keep it down. We don't need the whole office to know our business." He shakes his head. "You'd never make it as a Sicilian."

"I'm hardly making it as a Jew."

"You really have no interest in going out with Jeannie?"

"No. I thought about it a lot," I whisper. "She's a great pal and I love working with her. But that's as far as it goes."

A smirk. "You make out with all your pals? Maybe I need to worry."

"You're not my type."

"So what did you say to her this morning that pissed her off?"

"I told her I don't like account execs and I can't stand Israelis and that Ari epitomizes everything I hate about both."

"So she won't pay any attention to anything we say about him."

"Basically."

"What do we do?"

"Be there for her if she needs us." I pause for a second. "And beat the shit out of Ari if he steps out of line."

He breaks into a broad grin. "Yeah."

Karol's at Nicky's door, holding a couple of folders. "Barney just got off the phone with Rivette. He wants to have a meeting."

I look up. "Tell Barney we'll be right there."

"Not Barney. Rivette. He wants you guys to come out to his bungalow in the Hamptons."

We both say, "When?"

"Tomorrow."

I look over at Nicky waiting for the explosion. I'm a seat-of-the-pants kinda guy. But he's the opposite. He over-prepares. He makes lists for everything. His lists have lists. Springing a meeting on him, especially with a new client, is guaranteed to make him crazier than he already is.

"No! Impossible!" he screams. "We hardly talked about it. We don't have anything to show. We're not even close to being ready."

"That's what Barney said you'd say." She says it like she's talking to a three-year-old having a tantrum. "It's not a presentation meeting. It's what Rivette called an idea-group meeting. It's how he deals with writers and designers at his magazines."

Nicky's still crazed, teeth clenched, eyes bugged out. I'd be laughing if it didn't annoy me too. "This ain't no magazine," he yells. "It's advertising! Something he knows nothing about."

"Barney said to inform you that the agency is billing this account at max rate and to remind you that Stew's entire salary is being paid out of it. Plus, you get to spend a day out of the office in the glamorous Hamptons."

Nicky's not appeased. "It's a fucking bungalow, how glamorous can it be?"

She shrugs. Drops the folders on Nicky's desk.

"What's this?" he asks.

"The transcript of your meeting with Rivette. Have fun, guys." She smiles and walks out.

Nicky's still fuming, shaking his head, glaring up at the ceiling for what, divine intervention? I'm betting God's not hanging out in the air-conditioning vent.

"I wish I was dead," he screams.

Only the second time this week for that. He's making progress. Maybe all that therapy is starting to work.

"Of course you do. In the meantime, talk to me about what I said to Rivette that made him go gaga."

He thinks for a minute. "Something about red. I remember picturing red type on a white background."

"I was thinking more about the concept, not the color scheme."

"That was the concept."

"Red was the concept he thought was the best thing since night baseball? That makes no sense."

"You were totally bombed. Falling out of your chair. Of course you didn't make sense."

"But Rivette thought I was brilliant."

"He was in worse shape than you."

"Maybe we'll find something in here."

I start leafing through the transcript. It's about fifty pages long. Most of it is Rivette talking about himself. His cars, his motorcycles, his plane that he's not allowed to fly anymore. My end of the conversation consists of me laughing like a jackass on crack and saying stuff like *really*, *no shit*, or *that's fucking awesome!*

The last thing you need when you're shit-faced is to have somebody record everything you say and then write it down. Really bad for the self-image.

At around page thirty we start talking about his gubernatorial campaign. Rivette figures he can go after Monahan as a tax-and-spend liberal. He more than doubled his operating budget when he was federal prosecutor. And we'll position Rivette as a cost-cutting business innovator who took a failing magazine from the brink of bankruptcy to become one of the most successful players in the publishing industry. And a big Connecticut job creator. That's a big edge for us.

Monahan's claim to fame is that he's a gang-busting crusader, somebody with the guts and the know-how to take on crime and corruption at the highest levels. Captain America in a three-piece suit. That image made him a legend in Connecticut. Rivette wants to connect him with his mobster half brother. When Nicky mentions that from everything he's seen they have nothing to do with each other, Rivette says, "I know that and you know that, but if we can get the voters to believe something different, we'll win."

From there we started talking about general advertising strategies and marketing schemes. Then taglines. Out of the blue I blurt, "How about, 'Better Ed than Red'?"

There's silence for about ten seconds. Then he bangs the table and shouts, "Absolutely brilliant! It gets at the fiscal and the criminal in one elegant line and seeds my name in the bargain. It also subtly implies that he has Communist leanings. All in four words. Barney was right. You are the best copywriter in New York."

According to the transcript, I say something unintelligible and the conversation degenerates, aided by several more shots of thirty-year-old ninety-plus-proof single malt whisky, into slurred, self-aggrandizing bullshit.

I look up and see Nicky's head buried in *Communication Arts* magazine. "I found the line."

He stares at me for a couple of seconds. "Well, are you gonna tell me or do I have to guess?"

"Better Ed than Red."

"Yeah, I told you."

"All you said was 'red.'"

"That's what it is."

"No, it's not. Red is just a color. This is a theme line, a marketing concept, an ingenious juxtaposition of image and metaphor."

"Yeah." He sneers. "Red."

CHAPTER NINETEEN

I'm feeling pretty good about myself for the whole limo ride to Canarsie. Now that I'm gainfully employed again, I can charge it to the client. If Moish isn't asleep when I come in, I'll tell him the good news about my new gig with Rivette. I doubt that he'll be proud of me. I'd have to shoot Rivette for that to happen.

We'll never know. 'Cause when I walk in, there's Moish and Shifty Shapiro, my father's bookie from the old neighborhood, cursing, grunting and grappling on the living room floor. Moish has Shifty in some kind of headlock while the bookie is pounding my father's back with his gnarled knuckles.

How do you react to two alter cockers rolling around like a couple of geriatric mud wrestlers? It would be hilarious if there wasn't a good chance they'd both wind up in the ER. Or the cemetery.

"What the . . . !" Then I scream, "Break it up!" I grab each of them by the back of their shirt and hoist them up. This isn't the herculean feat it sounds like. They're both pushing eighty—Moish has a potbelly but he's got a slender frame, and Shifty has the body of a Holocaust victim on a diet.

They're doubled over, faces red, gulping air. It occurs to me that if either of them has a heart attack I'll be busted for manslaughter. Thankfully, neither one looks like they're ready to check out just yet.

They're glaring at each other. Moish bares his teeth and growls, "Now you're in for it, you sonuvabitch." A little spittle drips off his lip. "That's my son. Maybe you read about him in the paper. He killed his boss on Madison Avenue. Now he's gonna kill you."

"Liar!" Shifty breaks out of my grip and lunges at Moish.

Now I'm pissed. I grab him by both arms, lift him about six inches off the floor. I stick my face nose to nose with his and scream, "I don't know what's going on between you two but it ends now."

He looks at me with petrified eyes and croaks, "Yeah, yeah. Okay. Whatever you say." I put him down on a chair.

In the meantime, Moish finds the newspaper with me on the cover and shoves it in Shifty's face. "Now you believe me?"

Shifty stands up slowly, his entire body quaking. He stares at the paper. His sickly gray complexion turns a couple of shades whiter. He looks like a Yiddish grim reaper in a brown polyester suit a couple of sizes too big. His thin mousy gray hair is combed over his sweaty scalp. One look at his eyes and you know how he got his nickname.

He gapes at me with awe and fear. "You really are the killer from the newspaper."

Before I can answer, Moish says, "He sure is. A one-man Murder, Incorporated. Now you get the hell outta here while you still can."

Shifty looks at me beseechingly. "B-but he owes me $300."

"Bullshit!" Moish shouts. "I paid you. We're all square."

"You never settled up for the last time."

"That's it." Moish takes a step toward the bedroom. "I'm getting the gun."

Shifty grabs his coat and half runs, half stumbles to the door. Before he leaves he turns and growls, "This ain't over, Gribnitz."

Moish is doubled over laughing. "That was the best thing I ever saw." He shuffles over to me, puts his arms around me, and kisses me square on the lips. "Thank you. Thank you. You're the best. The best son in the world."

In thirty-four years, that was the most affection he's ever shown me.

I'm not sure if he really thinks I'm a homicidal maniac or if he just likes that I stood up for him. I hug him back. "You're not so bad yourself, Pop."

CHAPTER TWENTY

We're crawling along at twenty miles an hour. What do you expect from the morning rush on the Long Island Expressway? We could have been in a nice, comfortable Lincoln Town Car with Terrance and Jeannie, drinking coffee, munching on the picnic-basket breakfast that Jeannie packed. Bagels, muffins, croissants and fresh-brewed Colombian coffee. But nooo, Nicky can't ride in a car he's not driving; he gets carsick. So we're stuck in his ten-year-old Honda Prelude with a couple of stale donuts and Taster's Choice.

Nicky looks over at me anxiously. "I shouldn't have eaten."

"Why? So besides being uncomfortable you can be hungry too?"

"Any more than a couple of hours without going to the bathroom, nasty things happen in my intestines."

"You gotta go now?"

"I'm fine at the moment. But I never know when it'll hit. And when it does, kaboom! It's Mount Vesuvius in my sphincter."

"Let me know when it's ready to blow. Maybe traffic'll ease up and we'll get there before the chocolate lava starts to flow." I turn on the radio. Instead of the traffic eye in the sky, I hear a familiar voice.

"Connecticut is awash in red. Red ink in the budget after eight years of wasteful spending on misguided Democrat programs. And red blood in the streets from drug dealers, street gangs and mobsters. What is our state's highest law enforcement official doing about it? He's going after honest businessmen who create jobs and boost the economy while he treats criminals like family. That's because one of Connecticut's most notorious gangsters is his family. Neil Monahan's brother, the notorious Robert "Red" Monahan, is wanted in connection with armed robbery, extortion, racketeering and murder. Yes, murder. But he's running free on the streets of Connecticut. Why? Ask Neil Monahan. Then ask yourself which candidate will keep our great state safe and prosperous. I believe the answer is clear. Better Ed than Red."

The announcer intones, "That was the new Republican gubernatorial candidate Edward Rivette at a kickoff rally last night at his Greenwich headquarters. He might be entering the game in the ninth inning, but it looks like he doing a full-court press to the finish line with a no-holds-barred blitz. Which reminds me, stay tuned for sports."

I turn off the radio. Mixing cliché metaphors from four different sports all in one sentence is too much, even for me.

I look over at Nicky. "Well, Watson, the game's afoot."

He glares at me. "Who's Watson? What foot? I swear to God, three-quarters of the time I don't know what the hell you're talking about."

"It's a classic line from Sherlock Holmes. I know you don't read but I figured you must have seen Basil Rathbone or one of the other Sherlocks."

He shakes his head disdainfully. "I can't watch it. I hate that ridiculous hat he wears."

Traffic eases up and we're on a one-lane road in a cute little village that a hand-painted wooden sign tells me is Wainscottt. The map on my lap says the next town is East Hampton.

Nicky's squirming. "I don't know how much longer I can hold it."

"According to this we're almost there."

"That's what you said twenty minutes ago."

"We passed a couple of gas stations. Next one, we stop. You hit the can."

He scrunches his face like he just ate a bug. "Are you out of your mind. I'd rather stick my ass down a sewer than sit on one of those disgusting things."

"So, what do you want to do?"

"I can hang on if we're really close." He lets out a sigh. "You know what I'm dealing with."

"Crohn's, irritable bowel, hemorrhoids. Any rectal issues of yours that I forgot?"

"An asshole for a partner."

I nod. "Good line." I appreciate a snappy comeback, even when I'm the butt of it. I double-check the map. "Hey, we're almost there."

"You sure?"

"Positive. It's the next right."

I've never been in the Hamptons before, but I thought there were supposed to be all these unbelievable mansions and estates. And there may be, but all you can see from the road we're on is a continuous thicket of trees and shrubs. I guess these gazillionaires like to keep themselves insulated from the riffraff and this petrified forest is the best they can do since their property isn't zoned for moats.

We turn down Cowbell Path, a long and winding road that Paul McCartney would be proud of. According to Jeannie's directions we should be here. But I don't see anything except more foliage. Then I notice a tiny sign about four feet off the ground. In faded painted letters it says "102," with an arrow pointing down a gravel drive. More twists and turns. All of a sudden we're in front of the biggest house I've ever seen up close. If this is Rivette's bungalow, what the hell does his mansion look like?

Before we get to the front door, Rivette throws it open. "Welcome, gentlemen," he says, brandishing a huge unlit cigar like a drum major's baton. "I'm very glad you could make it."

As if we had any choice.

Nicky rushes past him. Without breaking stride, he says, "Where's the bathroom?"

Rivette hollers, "Ms. Lepro, please show our friend the WC."

A tall, dour woman lumbers into the room. Her close-cropped hair is a dull orange and thick like a whisk broom. Her face is flat and plain, with no makeup and a permanent scowl. She reminds me of the detention lady at P.S. 181, except for her arms. I've never seen muscles like that on a woman. I'm not sure I've ever seen them on a man who wasn't in a pro football uniform.

She glares at Nicky. "Follow me," she says in a voice that would make Frau Blücher sound like Mary Poppins. She does an about-face and marches into the house. He hustles along behind, thighs pressed together, his face strained.

"Your friends and Bitsie are in the great room." Rivette starts walking. "This way."

I look sideways at Rivette. "Bitsie?"

He smiles wryly. "Back in Princeton everyone had a nickname. I was Swanee, as in Swanee River, from Rivette."

"That makes sense. But how does Urban Sangster become Bitsie?"

"Urban became Urb. Then, thanks to his dour demeanor, we started calling him Bitter Urb. That evolved into Bitsie."

We enter a room that's the size of my high school gym. One wall is all windows with a panoramic view of fine white sand and translucent blue water. The rest of the room is all wood and leather. There are two huge red leather sofas on either side of a mahogany coffee table and two white leather club chairs catty-corner to the sofas. Terrance and Jeannie are on one of the sofas. Sangster is sitting stiffly on one of the white chairs. Rivette leads me to the empty sofa, then sits on the other chair.

Lepro walks in with Nicky, seats him next to me, then marches to a corner of the room and stands, her python arms folded in front of her, like King Tut's tomb statue.

Rivette leans back, plops his size twelves on the coffee table, boots and all, and says, "Did any of you see my interview last night?"

I was about to say that we heard a replay of it on the way here when Terrance says, "Yes. I was surprised to hear you speak before we had the opportunity to discuss marketing strategy."

"We did discuss it." He looks over at me. "Back at the club. When Stewart came up with the brilliant 'Better Ed than Red' strategy."

"That's a theme line, not a strategy," Terrance says.

Rivette looks over at the corner. "How rude of me! I didn't introduce my invaluable executive assistant, Sharon Lepro. It was Sharon's idea to incorporate Stewart's concept into my first speech. And it made quite an impression. The phones at my campaign headquarters back in

Greenwich are ringing off the hook. Linking Monahan to his hoodlum half brother was a stroke of genius."

"Thank you," Terrance says, as if he had anything to do with it (typical account exec move, take credit for the stuff that works, blame everyone else when things go south). "Now that we know the creative is solid, we have to decide on media strategy." He pulls a few folders out of his briefcase. "We have several media plans based on very cursory demographics that we'd like to show you."

Rivette waves his hand, still holding the cigar, in the air. "We'll go with whichever one you think is best."

"I appreciate the vote of confidence but I'd feel much more comfortable if we could spend a few minutes going over them."

"All right." He looks over at me and Nicky. "There's no reason why we have to bore our creative geniuses with mundanities." Ms. Lepro and I will hear the media proposals. He turns to Sangster. "Bitsie, show Stew and Nick the rest of the house."

Terrance looks taken aback. "I would think you'd want your marketing director to be involved in this discussion."

"Sharon will take notes."

Sangster lurches up, says, "Follow me," and walks out of the room, the pole up his ass still firmly in place.

Nicky and I are right behind him. We go from one room to another, they all look pretty much the same to me, except the kitchen, where instead of dark wood and leather, it's light wood and marble.

Nicky, though, is in his glory. He loves this kind of shit. He's got all kinds of questions about the paintings on the walls, which Sangster informs us are from the Hudson River School. Nicky sticks his nose right up to the canvases. All he has to do is sneeze and he'll ruin a million-dollar piece of art.

But it doesn't stop with the paintings. He wants to know about the plaster curlicues on the ceiling, where the oriental rugs came from, and what kind of wood the tables are made out of. Sangster is, if nothing else, a very good tour guide. He answers every question and even has a few stories about how some of the pieces found their way here.

After twenty minutes, we come to the final room on the grand tour and it's my turn to get excited. It's about the size of the UPAN large conference room. There's a bar against one wall stacked with top-of-the-top-shelf liquor. But that's not why I'm jazzed. Right in the middle of the room is the most beautiful pool table I've ever seen. The wood, I'm guessing mahogany, is polished to a high sheen. The felt is deep burgundy. And the diamonds, those are the markings on the side of the table, look like real diamonds, inlaid into the mahogany. The balls are racked up and there's a cue stick on the table. I'm salivating like a dog in front of a steak.

Sangster says, "Do you play?"

Before I answer, Nicky says, "He's been telling me he's the second coming of Fast Eddie Felson since I met him.

At first Sangster looks puzzled, then he brightens. "Ah, from the Paul Newman film." To me he says, "Would you like to try a few shots?"

"Can I?"

"Of course."

"I haven't played for a while so don't expect too much."

Back in high school, I spent a lot of Friday and Saturday nights in Spinelli's on Flatbush Avenue, along with the other losers who had nowhere else to go on date nights. There were a couple of pro-style tables up front, new felt, tight rails, cushioned chairs all around so people could watch. That's where the really good players played. Players with their own fancy two-piece cue sticks that they carried in long skinny pseudo-leather cases. Also, every once in a while, when the pros came to do exhibitions, pool-playing legends like Willie Mosconi, Lou "Machine Gun" Butera and Steve Mizerak, they used those tables.

Me and my friends, we were relegated to the back tables, where the felt was threadbare and the rails were mush. We played with house sticks, which were so warped that if you tied a string to each end you could use them to shoot arrows. Even so, after a while we got pretty good. One night, after making a fourteen-ball run (still my personal best), my swagger was at an all-time high. My friends were in awe and I was thinking maybe I'm too good for these guys. After they went home I was still feeling it. I walked over to the front tables and asked one of the guys if he wanted to shoot some nine-ball.

He snickered, looked me up and down like a lion sizing up a herd of wildebeests, deciding which one he wants for dinner. "Sure, kid. Fifteen bucks a game."

I had seventy-five dollars in my pocket from my job stocking shelves in the dairy department at Waldbaum's. I figured maybe I'd lose fifteen or twenty bucks.

A couple of his friends moved their chairs over to watch. I went to grab a cue stick off the rack on the wall and dropped it. Derisive laughter stung my ears.

"You break," he said with a sinister smile.

The pool table looked like a football field. My hand was shaking and my stomach was churning. I miscued the break shot. More snide giggles. Helen Keller would've beat me. Less than an hour later I was tapped out. All seventy-five dollars gone. As I walked dejectedly out, one of them shouted, "Keep practicing, kid. Your money's good here anytime."

I don't know why but standing in front of this jewel-encrusted shrine to the billiard gods, I'm feeling like I did that night at Spinelli's. I lift a cue off the table. It's a Balabushka, the Mercedes-Benz of pool sticks. At least I hit a clean break shot. The balls are pretty well scattered. I'm thinking maybe I still got it. I take my first shot. Not even close. The next few are even worse.

Nicky shouts, "You're no Fast Eddie, more like Slow Stewie."

Sangster lifts an eyebrow and says, "You *have* played before, have you not?"

That's it! Now I'm getting snarky comments from Ichabod Crane. All the anger and frustration from my nine-ball humiliation comes roaring back. I tighten my grip and send a couple of balls screaming around the table, bouncing off the rails, nowhere near the pockets. One jumps over the cushion and clunks to the floor, a few inches from Sangster's shoe. He scoops it up gingerly, like it's a wounded bird, and places it gently back on the felt. "May I have a go?"

I hand the cue stick to him. To Nicky I whisper, "This should be good."

He bends over the table and calmly and confidently sinks his first ball, a cut shot into the corner. Then he strokes a delicate angle into the side pocket, followed by a bank shot to the opposite corner. He's controlling the cue ball like it's on a string—draw, follow, reverse

English—the works. I sit there with my mouth open as he runs the table, hands me back the stick, and says, "Thank you, Mr. Gribnitz."

I was so engrossed in Sangster's billiard wizardry that I didn't hear Rivette walk in.

"Bitsie's been our club champion six years running." He puts his arm around him. "There's talk of renaming the billiards trophy the Sangster Cup." He glances at his watch. "If you're done, there's lunch in the dining room."

After filet mignon and garlic mashed potatoes, we get a little pep talk from Rivette about how we're going to surprise all the pundits and pull off the greatest political shocker since Truman beat Dewey.

We're back in the great room for coffee and dessert. After the crème brûlée it's Baileys for Terrance, Nicky and Jeannie and Martell Cordon Bleu for me and Rivette. Sangster had tea and Lepro was gone. Off on what Rivette described as strategic reconnaissance.

Rivette says to me, "I heard you're a man who enjoys a good cigar." He pulls two Cohiba Esplendidos out of his pocket and hands me one. I'm expecting him to pull out a fancy cigar cutter but he just bites off the end and spits it in an ashtray. I do the same. He pulls out an antique Zippo, lights mine then his.

I love this guy.

The room is blissfully quiet. I'm just about to take my first puff of my first Cuban when the peace is shattered by a loud crash. Jeannie screams, the rest of us jump.

The floor is covered with glass shards. There's a gaping hole in one of the floor-to-ceiling windows. What looks like a brick wrapped in newspaper is sitting in the middle of the mess on the floor. Sangster's shaking, Jeannie's crying, Terrance and Nicky are sitting with their mouths open. Rivette looks intrigued.

Since nobody else is doing anything, I go get the brick and hand it to Rivette. He unwraps it and holds up the newspaper so we all can see it.

The headline says, "Rivette Links Monahan to Mob." He turns it over, and scrawled in thick, red Magic Marker it says, "WATCH YOUR FUCKING MOUTH."

He smiles and says, "As I said, we made an impression."

CHAPTER TWENTY-ONE

We're driving on a deserted patch of a one-lane country road somewhere between East Hampton and Southampton. We're both a little freaked out. It's not every day you're sitting in a billionaire's living room and a threat brick comes crashing through the window.

Nicky's been staring up at the rearview mirror more than he's looking at the road. "Somebody's following us."

"It's your imagination. Except for the people we just left, nobody knows we're here."

"A big black pickup truck has been tailgating us for the last five minutes."

"This is the only road out here, of course he's tailgating us. There's nowhere else for him to go."

"A mile back he coulda passed me but he never did. When I slowed down he slowed down. When I accelerated he stayed right on my ass."

"I'll tell you what. We're coming to a long straightaway. Slow down and move over to the right."

"Where? Into the ditch?"

"It's not a ditch, it's a dip."

"Whatever you call it, I'm not driving my car in there. It's ten years old. The shocks are shot. If I drive in there it'll damage the under-carriage."

I have no idea what the hell he's talking about. I couldn't tell you the difference between an undercarriage and a baby carriage. Guys like Nicky grow up working on cars with their fathers, doing tune-ups, changing the oil, stuff like that. Moish doesn't know how to check the oil, much less change it. I say, "Move over as far as you can. He'll pass us."

"I'm telling you he won't. He had his chance and he didn't."

"I'll bet you a dinner he does."

"You're on."

We pull to the right and slow to about twenty. The pickup comes up next to us. It's not exactly a monster truck but close. Not King Kong but Mighty Joe Young. Instead of zooming by he slams into the side of the Prelude and knocks us off the road into the dip or ditch or whatever you want to call it. The car bucks and spins. Rocks fly. There's a loud clunk. I guess that's the undercarriage that Nicky was so worried about.

The truck screeches to a stop. The windows are tinted black so it's impossible to see who the hell just ran us off the road.

The door opens. Out steps a husky guy with a red watch cap pulled down almost over his black aviator sunglasses. There's an ugly red scar on his cheek. He's wearing a black long-sleeve T-shirt, black jeans and black motorcycle boots.

If he thinks he can intimidate us, he's dead right.

He points a black-gloved finger at us, with his thumb straight up like a gun. He cocks his thumb and finger-shoots. First at me, then at Nicky. He brings two fingers up to his eyes then points them at us. The "I'm watching you" sign. Then he walks back to the truck and peels out.

We just stand there, speechless, gaping at each other.

Nicky says, "Did you see who that was?"

"Yeah, some demented, crazy-ass, Mad Max–looking asshole."

"That was Red Monahan."

"You're crazy. With that hat and those glasses you couldn't see his face at all. There's no way you could tell if it was Red Monahan or Red Skelton."

"*You* can't tell. You're a writer. You look but you don't see. I'm an artist. My eyes see what yours don't. It was Red fucking Monahan. I could tell by his jawline."

"C'mon. No one could identify someone just by his jawline."

"You'll see. I'm right."

"Even if you are, if Red is pissed off at anyone, it should be Rivette. How would he even know who we are?"

"The Monahans probably have Rivette's phone tapped. Neil Monahan was in the FBI; they do that all the time."

"Even if that's true, why go after us?"

"We in the enemy camp."

"Great."

"And by the way . . ."

"What?"

"You owe me dinner, hump."

CHAPTER TWENTY-TWO

"You pissant, no-talent pieces of shit, I've been wiping my ass with dickweeds like you two before either one of you even had an ass to wipe. You'll regret the day you thought you could take me on."

When I first open the door to Terrance's office I assume Nielsen's screaming at me and Nicky. Then I realize he doesn't even know we're here.

Nielsen and Ari are glowering at each other, fists clenched at their sides, like Ali and Frazier doing the pre-match stare-down. Terrance is at his desk, his hands clasped in front of him, with an amused look on his face.

"We'll come back," I say to no one in particular.

"Don't go anywhere. We're done here," Nielsen barks, his shark eyes oozing with rage. He turns and storms past us as Nicky executes a nifty matador pirouette to avoid being knocked over.

"Ari, you can remain if you like," Terrance says, as calm as can be. "We're going to discuss the Rivette campaign."

The veins on Ari's neck are bulging. His face is borscht red. "I have things I must do." He stomps out.

Terrance leans casually back in his chair, clasping his hands behind his head. "That could have gone a little better."

"Yuh think?" I look over at Nicky, who's shaky and a little short of breath. Confrontation, along with about a million other things, trigger his panic attacks. And after yesterday, he's been all panic all the time. "So who let the proverbial feline out of the proverbial satchel?"

A wry smile from Terrance. "That would be our fearless leader."

"You mean Boris and Natasha's boss?" I wink at Nicky. Strangely, this calms him down. He's a huge fan of cartoons in general and Jay Ward's particular brand of animation in particular. His whole body seems to loosen.

Terrance says, "If that's the case, who's Rocky and who's Bullwinkle?"

Nicky points at me. "He's definitely Bullwinkle, a big moose. That would make me Rocky." He turns to Terrance. "And you." He grins. "You're Dudley Do-Right."

"Okay, Dudley," I say to Terrance. "Now that this civil war is out in the open, where does that leave us? I don't think there are too many creative jobs available in Frostbite Falls."

Nicky shoots me a thumbs-up. He's impressed that I know Rocky and Bullwinkle's hometown. I could really wow him and say we could get jobs teaching at Wossamotta U, but Terrance's hairy eyeball signals he's had enough of the Bullwinkle show.

"As far as the agency's concerned, it's business as usual."

Nicky's agitated again. "How can it be business as usual with you and Ari in a blood feud with Nielsen?"

"The last thing anyone wants is to let the succession situation affect our business. The agency won't be worth anything to any of us if we drive away our clients."

"You didn't answer my question. What happens to me and Nicky after the bloodletting?"

"Don't worry. I'll take care of you."

"Suppose you lose?"

"How long have you worked with me?"

I'm about to say too long, but I figure now's not the time, so I say, "I dunno, three years give or take. But I don't see what that has to do with anything."

"Have you ever known me not to have a contingency plan . . . or two?"

"I'm sure *you* have a plan. How does that help us?"

"Wherever I go my team comes with me."

Nicky looks troubled. "Who's on your team?"

"Who do you think? The same people who've been with me for the last three years—you two, Jeannie. Though, from what you told me, she might want to stay with Ari, if we go our separate ways."

Nicky's not appeased. "What if you and Ari stay together? I don't want to work anywhere near that asshole."

"Nothing will be different than it is now. You'll work with me. Ari'll work with his people. You won't have to have anything to do with him."

Nicky says, "This isn't his agency. Things might be different when his name's on the door."

"My name will also be on the door," Terrance says sternly. "You have absolutely nothing to be concerned about."

"Forget about that," I say. "I'm more worried about what happened yesterday."

"What happened yesterday?" Terrance looks as if he's really at a loss.

Nicky screams, "Remember that brick that came crashing through Rivette's window? That was only the beginning. After we left, Red Monahan ran us off the road."

Terrance looks over at me. "Is this true?"

"Someone ran us off the road. Nicky thinks it was Red. All I know is he was one badass motherfucker."

Nicky glares at me. "It *was* Red. This time he shot us with his finger. Next time it'll be a Glock. Or an Uzi."

Terrance shakes his head. "You've been watching too many gangster movies."

"What happened yesterday was no fucking movie," Nicky yells. "It was real. Very real. I got a $1,500 auto body estimate to prove it."

Terrance holds out his hand. "Give it to me. That's a work-related expense. The agency will cover it."

"Well, uh, thanks, Terrance," Nicky stammers. "That's great. I don't have it on me. I'll give it to you tomorrow."

"Good. Is anything else troubling you?"

"I still think it was Red who did it."

Terrance shakes his head. "If it really was Red Monahan, why would he drive three hours to East Hampton when Rivette's Greenwich estate is twenty minutes from his home base in Bridgeport."

"'Cause nobody knows him out there. In Connecticut he'd be recognized."

Terrance shakes his head. "You're a very creative person, Nicky. But this time you've created something that doesn't exist."

"If it wasn't Red, who was it?"

Terrance shrugs. "It could have been anyone. The *Capitalist Rag* is the *National Enquirer* of the moneyed class. Rivette printed countless stories that have made a lot of people very angry, quite a few who have homes in the Hamptons. One of them probably paid a kid fifty dollars to toss that brick. I doubt anything more'll come of it."

"What about the guy who ran us into a ditch?"

"It could have been the same person who threw the brick or it could be road rage. Maybe you were driving too slowly and whoever was in the truck lost his temper."

"Nicky was driving pretty slow," I chime in.

"See," Terrance says smugly. "There you have it."

Nicky says, "I hope you're right. I'm not ready to have my kneecaps busted."

"Your knees will be fine," Terrance says. "You'll need them for the TV spot you're shooting next week."

"What?" We both scream.

"I told Rivette you'd have five storyboards ready to present to Sangster on Friday."

"Today's Wednesday," I yell. "You're giving us one day to come up with five concepts. Who do you think I am, Superman?"

He smiles. "You once told me you had powers and abilities far beyond those of mortal men."

"I've told you a lot of things, including to go fuck yourself. I don't see you doing that."

"The client didn't ask for that. He did ask for a commercial on air by the middle of next week."

"And if we can't do it?"

"Right now, Rivette is paying your entire salary. If he decides you're not up to the job . . ."

CHAPTER TWENTY-THREE

I've been at it for a couple of hours, trying to come up with ideas for the spot. Nicky's doing the same in his office. Then we'll meet and hash it all out, which involves discussing, cursing, yelling, cajoling, more yelling, and, finally, coming up with concepts that neither one of us would've thought of without the other.

Once we have the rough storyboards, that's when the real work starts. The approval process. You gotta present your boards to the account shmucks and hope they get what you're trying to do. Terrance gets it, of course, but you know he's gonna be a pain in the ass and reject one or two anyway, just to show who's in charge. We call it leg lifting, when account execs piss on your work just to mark their territory.

When you get it down to three, it's time to show the client. The problem is, the account team is looking for the easiest concept to sell and the creatives want a spot that they can put on their reel, even though neither of those choices might be what's best for the product. Even if there's a concept that everyone agrees on, you can't go in with only one board. You need at least three to justify the exorbitant agency fee. But if you throw a couple of clunkers in just to round out the field, you can be sure that the shit-for-brains client will choose the worst one and you'll be stuck with a piece of crap that won't work and isn't worth putting on your reel. That's when the finger-pointing begins. Best-case scenario, you learn from your mistakes and get it right the next time. Worst case (and this is what usually happens), the agency loses the business and you're out on the street.

That's why I'm so pissed off at myself for doing my usual "ready, fire, aim" routine with Rivette. I should know better. I have the scars to prove it. The first things that pop into your mind are never good, except as a jumping-off point at a brainstorming session. Now we're stuck with this ridiculous "Better Ed than Red" concept. What am I talking about? It's not even a concept. Nicky's right, it's a fucking color. I can blame it on the fact that I was drunk as a skunk. (Do skunks drink? I never saw one at a bar, though I have smelled some.) The truth is I'm a show-off and a blabbermouth and no matter how many times I wind up kicking myself in the ass, I keep doing it.

So here I sit, with a yellow pad in front of me, scribbling anything that I can think of that makes any kind of sense. Also, it has to be fairly low budget because we need the money for the media buy.

Nothing is making me too excited, but here's what I got so far . . .

"Red Marks on a Report Card." We can mock one up for Monahan and give him failing grades while Rivette gets straight A's.

"Red Herring." Bogie-lookalike detective talks about all the false clues Monahan's giving and uncovers the real facts.

"Red Light." Use as a metaphor to stop crime and rampant spending.

"Red Sea." Rivette is Moses. Monahan is Pharaoh. CT is drowning in a sea of red: blood, ink, etc.

"Red Hot off the Presses." We get all the footage and still shots of Red Monahan, plus newspaper clippings about him, and use a Walter Winchell–type voice to talk about all the bad shit he's done and how you don't want that in the governor's mansion.

They all work with the "Better Ed than Red" line . . . more or less. I like the last one a little. Sure, it's corny but it might be fun. What the hell do you expect with a one-day turnaround?

While I'm in my creative trance, oblivious to anything going on around me, I hear a noise and look up. There's Ari, standing next to my desk, glaring down at me.

"I'm sorry you had to see that display in Terrance's office."

"I've seen a lot worse."

"I'm sure he told you what's going on with the agency." I nod. "I want you to know, in case you were concerned, that when Terrance and I take over, your job will be secure. In fact, there have been discussions about promoting you to creative director, copy."

"What about Nicky?"

He stiffens. "We'll see."

"Terrance told us that we have nothing to worry about."

"You don't." He turns and walks out, almost banging into Nicky who's on his way in.

Nicky jumps out of the way and glares at Ari's back as he walks down the hall. "What did that scumbag want?"

"He said that when he and Terrance run the agency we shouldn't worry."

"You believe him?"

"About as far as I can piss into a tornado."

Nicky sits down in my one guest chair. "I had a visitor too."

After about five seconds of him staring into space, I say, "Are you gonna tell me or do I have to guess?"

"Nielsen."

"What did he want?"

"To tell me that he thought I was an outstanding art director and that when it's his agency I'll be a valued member of the creative department."

"So why do you look like you just got a prostate exam from Johnny Bench while he's wearing his catcher's mitt?"

"Who cares if that prick thinks I'm a great art director? Fuck him. I don't need him to tell me that. I don't want to work for him anyway. Or Ari." He looks up at the ceiling and shakes his head glumly. "I wish I was dead."

"Of course you do."

"You think I should be happy that for the first time in my career I have a writer I can work with and now that's going away?"

"Nothing's going away. Nielsen thinks you're a great art director, and Terrance said we have nothing to worry about. So whoever wins, you'll be fine."

"Not if you're not here."

"Who said I won't be here?"

"Nielsen said he thinks I would grow creatively working with different writers. I took that to mean not you."

"And you said, 'Fuck you! Me and Stew are a team. Batman and Robin, the Lone Ranger and Tonto, Abbott and Costello. Coletti and Gribnitz is like love and marriage, you can't have one without the other.'"

"Yeah, that's just what I said. Then I told him to bite me."

"What did you really say?"

"I didn't say anything. Maybe I mumbled 'thank you.'"

"We'll just have to make sure that Terrance wins."

"Then Ari'll win too. I hate him more than I hate Nielsen."

"We won't have to have anything to do with Ari. He has his own team. We're with Terrance. That won't change."

"You don't think Ari'll start throwing his weight around once he's an owner?"

"Terrance'll have our backs."

Another glum look. "I love Terrance. He's a great guy. But he's still an account exec. He's always gonna back another account exec over a creative. You know it's true. And that'll be it." He sighs. "I'm definitely gonna kill myself."

"Let's finish these storyboards first, okay? If they don't work, maybe I'll join you."

CHAPTER TWENTY-FOUR

I should be ecstatic. I spent last night with the shiksa goddess, so why do I have this feeling of dread? Barbara Hendrickson was everything I hoped she'd be and then some. Bright, beautiful, playful, sexy without being slutty, and funnier than any woman that gorgeous has a right to be. So why does it feel like there's a festering turd churning in my stomach? I guess it's because for the last decade my track record with women has been a soul-crushing death spiral of disasters, catastrophes and calamities culminating in my apocalyptic marriage to the Orthodox Jewish Vampire Bride from Hell. So now, after a shockingly wonderful evening, instead of getting ready for my pool hall performance with Ichabod Sangster, I'm steeling myself for the inevitable emotional pie in the face.

Still, I'm stunned that it happened at all. I was positive that the most intimate I would ever get with Barbara was when I kissed her chair. Turns out she thought it was very amusing. Seems she has a thing for funny Jewish New York guys. Mel Brooks, Woody Allen, Elliot Gould, George Segal—she's seen every movie that each of them ever made, most more than once. Who'd a thunk a girl from Manitowoc, Wisconsin, would develop a taste for kosher baloney.

Last night, I was at the agency until almost midnight, working with

Nicky on the storyboards. It was Terrance's brilliant idea that I meet Sangster at Bizarro Billiards, a nouveau-hipster bar-restaurant-poolroom in SoHo, and present all five boards to him there. His theory is that after Sangster humiliates me at the pool table, he'll be in a positive frame of mind and more likely to approve one.

We're talking five storyboards with six frames apiece—that's thirty miniature illustrations. A lot of art directors would scribble some stick figures and call it a day. Not Nicky, he's a perfectionist. He drew every person, every tree, every background and painstakingly colored them all in. By the time he was finished his fingers were ready to fall off, his eyes were glassy, and he was mumbling stuff like, "What's the use, we're all gonna die anyway." I told him that I'd lock up and he should go home and take a Xanax or twelve.

Almost every night, someone's here late. That's just the way the ad business is. We all know the drill, last one to go home turns off the lights, sets the alarm, locks the back door and double-locks the front door. First you gotta make sure no one else is still here. One time a junior AE was in the back making copies for a presentation the next day and some shmuck locked him in. He had to sit there in the pitch black for eight hours. When they found him the next morning he was three quarters of the way to a nervous breakdown. I got my ass reamed out royally for that one. Did I forget to mention that the shmuck was me?

I packed the boards up and was doing my office walkabout, shouting an occasional "Anyone still here?" when I heard a faint, "I'm here. Don't lock up."

I made my way to the voice, and it was Barbara, huddled over her desk. "What are you still doing here?"

"Terrance wanted to have a couple of contingency media strategies with various budgets so we would have some leeway with the production costs."

"Of course he did. Terrance's motto is 'No sacrifice is too great,' especially when someone else is doing the sacrificing."

She chuckled. "Can I ask you for a favor?"

"Of course."

"I'll be finished in a few minutes. Would you mind waiting so we can walk out together? I'm a little nervous about being here all alone."

"Sure. No problem."

"If you're exhausted, I understand."

"Not at all. In fact, I'm always wired after these marathon creative sessions. I was thinking of stopping in at Raymondo's before I went home. You up for it?"

She smiled. "Only on one condition."

"What's that?"

"That you let me pay for the drinks."

I made a show out of ruminating for a couple of seconds. "It's a deal."

Twenty minutes later we were in the same booth I was in with Jeannie a couple of days earlier. Cookie came over for our drink order. I had my usual Guinness. Barbara asked for a Heineken. I don't know what Cookie put in her beer, but for the next hour and a half, she talked nonstop about her life, her passions, her hopes and dreams. She loves the Green Bay Packers, Broadway musicals and Kurt Vonnegut. She was a dance major at the University of Wisconsin, Green Bay and came to New York hoping to dance in the chorus line of a Broadway show. I told her I'd write a musical for her, *Slaughterhouse Eleven*, where the Packers travel back in time, tackle the Nazis and save the world. For the finale, the kick line would kick footballs into the audience. She laughed hysterically, thought it was destined to be a smash hit, "Springtime for Hitler" meets the Super Bowl. That's when she started talking about Mel Brooks and her love for Jewish funnymen.

I asked her how she got from Broadway to Madison Avenue.

"I walked. It's only four blocks." (Everybody's a comedian.) Then she explained that while she was auditioning for hoofer gigs, she took a series of temp jobs to pay the bills. One was as the assistant to the media director at Benton and Bowles. After two weeks he offered her a full-time position. After some soul-searching she realized that life on the chorus line is a lot less glamorous in real life than it is in the movies. And to her surprise, she liked working at an ad agency. So she traded in her Capezios for Kate Spade pumps.

She approached media planning as if it was choreography but instead of dance steps and body dynamics her tools were CPMs, demographics, reach and frequency. In a little less than two years she jetéd from administrative assistant to senior planner.

Two hours and five drinks later, Cookie started wiping tables and cleaning glasses. That's her not-so-subtle way of telling us it's time to go.

"Let me get you a cab," I said as we left the bar.

"I'm feeling a little tipsy, I think I'll walk. The fresh air might clear my head."

"Are you sure?"

"I do it all the time. It's only fifteen minutes."

"But it's late and it's dark. If anything happened to you, I'd never forgive myself. At least let me walk you."

"It's way out of your way."

"Since my divorce, I've been crashing in my father's basement in the bowels of Canarsie. Everything's out of my way."

She looked at me like I was a puppy shivering in the rain. "Your ex-wife really took you to the cleaners?"

"Oh yeah. She got the apartment, the car, everything but my baseball glove and my autographed Doors LP."

She beamed. "I love the Doors. I had a major crush on Jim Morrison."

"I'm on one of their albums, you know."

"No you're not."

"Really. Do you know *Absolutely Live*?"

"Of course."

"You know the part in 'When the Music's Over' and it's supposed to be real quiet but some bozo in the audience won't stop his loud blabbing and finally Morrison yells, 'Shut up!' at the top of his lungs?"

"Of course."

"That was me."

Her eyes widen. Her mouth opens. "Really?"

"It's the truth. I don't only piss off creative directors and account execs. I piss off music legends too."

"That's so cool!" she screams.

"So I'm walking you home. Right?"

She winks. "Sure. It's not every day a girl gets to walk home with a rock star."

We walk down to Twenty-Second Street and across to Eighth Avenue. She has an apartment on the top floor of a brownstone in the middle of the block. When we got there she says, "The least I can do is invite you up for a drink."

"I think I've had enough. I have to present tomorrow, remember?"

"Coffee, then."

"That sounds great."

As soon as we get up to her apartment, she leads me to the couch and sits next to me. It's not long before we make our way to the bedroom. We never got around to the coffee.

CHAPTER TWENTY-FIVE

I never dropped acid in Spinelli's poolroom, but if I did I'm betting it would hallucinate into Bizarro Billiards. This place looks like it was designed by Peter Max and furnished by Timothy Leary with a little help from Willy Wonka. It's dark with shimmery waves of light pulsating from neon tubes that curl up the wall and slither across the ceiling. A long glass bar cuts the room in half. On one side are a dozen chrome and glass restaurant tables. The other side has eight pool tables tricked out in candy colors. Bubblegum pink, taffy green, jelly bean blue and creamsicle orange. I'm getting a sugar rush just sitting here.

It's a quarter after eleven. The only people in the place besides me are the bartender and a couple of waitresses, dressed right out of *A Clockwork Orange*, white jumpsuits with black boots, suspenders and derby hats.

I'm at a table getting a little practice in before Sangster shows up. I know Terrance thinks the best thing that could happen would be for Sangster to wipe the table with me, but I intend to try to salvage whatever scintilla of self-respect I have left by giving him a game.

A waitress sashays over to see if I want a drink. I ask for a Diet Coke. While she's standing there I sink four balls in a row and look up to see if she's impressed. No reaction. Then I miss three hangers. She smirks.

It's almost noon and I can hear Jeannie's voice in my head: "You have a presentation that your job depends on and all you're worried about is your stupid pool game—what's the matter with you?"

I put down the cue and pull the six boards out of a big, black portfolio case. The agency has about six of them in various sizes that we use to lug stuff to clients. Usually the account execs schlep them around, it's the least they can do for the exorbitant salaries they make, but since I'm here on my own I get to be the schlepper.

Nicky and I went over all the spots with Terrance and Jeannie early this morning so I'm pretty clear on what I'm going to say. I still like the "Red Hot off the Presses" campaign, but as long as he buys one, my job is safe.

I hear someone coming. I look up to see if it's Sangster but it's a couple of bruisers in crew cuts, dark gray suits, tight in the arms and shoulders, and rubber-soled black shoes. I'm guessing cops or maybe ex–college football players who weren't good enough to make it in the pros so they got jobs selling insurance to alumni.

Sangster is behind them, walking slowly and stiffly, like the robot in *The Day the Earth Stood Still*. I give him a quick wave. He raises an eyebrow and shuffles over. But instead of saying, "*Klaatu barada nikto,*" he scowls at me angrily and shakes his fists. He's turning crimson. I'm afraid he's having a seizure. Then he says, "You are never to talk about me at the club. Never! Is that understood?"

"What club? What are you talking about?"

"Last night at dinner, someone mentioned that Stewart thought I looked a little peaked." He glares at me. "How dare you!"

"Urban, you can't be serious. I'm a Jewish street kid from the gutters of Flatbush. I couldn't get a job in the Union League Club sweeping the floors, much less become a member. The only time I've ever been inside that place was at our meeting with you and Rivette."

He leans back, processing what I just said. Then, after about five seconds, he says in that throaty, lockjaw voice of his, "Must have been Stewart Peterson."

"The hedge fund guy?"

"Yes. Sorry for the confusion." Then his demeanor totally changes.

He's back to being his usual stiff-ass self, but at least he's not glaring daggers at me. He grabs a cue stick. "Shall we play?"

I rack up the balls. "Straight pool, rack of twenty-five?"

"Good."

"I'll break."

He nods.

In a lot of pool games, like eight-ball, nine-ball and Chicago, you blast the rack as hard as you can, hoping you sink one. But not in straight pool. The idea is to play a safety, which means you don't give the other guy a clean shot. There are specific rules for playing a safety. You have to hit one of the colored balls with the cue ball and one of them, either the cue ball or the object ball, has to hit a rail. On a break it's different. Two balls plus the cue ball have to hit the rail.

I play a pretty good safety, but not good enough. Sangster has a long but makeable shot, which he sinks dead center. He hits two more, then tries a crazy combination to break up the pack and misses. He leaves me a couple of easy shots, which I make. Then I miss a cut shot into the side.

He runs the table and leaves himself a break shot.

In straight pool, the final ball stays on the table and you rack the other fourteen. Then the shooter tries to pocket the ball left over from the last rack and break up the pack with the cue ball so he can keep shooting. That's how you can get runs of more than fourteen. Willie Mosconi, the best pool player who ever lived, once ran 526.

Sangster misses the break shot and leaves some balls close to the pockets. I, miraculously, run four, then play a safety. He misses and I run a few more.

The waitress brings me another Diet Coke. Sangster orders a tonic water with lime. No wonder he always has that sour look on his face.

He wins twenty-five to fourteen. I still lost, but at least I wasn't humiliated.

"Wanna play one more before we get down to business?"

He nods.

"You break this time."

While I'm racking up, two more guys walk in and take the table next to ours. They're a little older than the first pair and even rougher around the edges. They're both overweight. One maybe twenty pounds, the other closer to fifty. They're both wearing black leather jackets. The thinner one has black wavy hair and a black mustache. He's wearing a black T-shirt, black jeans and black Doc Martens. The fat one is bald. He has on a white T-shirt, tan pants like the kind Indiana Jones wore and work boots. He puts a pack of Lucky Strikes on the pool table.

Sangster is still in his seat. He's staring at them trepidatiously. His hand quivers as he sips his tonic.

"Urban, are you okay?"

"Yes, of course," he mumbles. He walks up to the table.

All of a sudden, he can't make a shot. He's spraying balls all over the place, and I'm picking them off three and four at a time. I'm lining up the ball that'll win me the game, almost the length of the table at a tricky angle. Then I remember that the plan was for Sangster to win so he's in a good mood when he looks at the boards. I make sure to miss. I probably wouldn't have made it anyway. He has a fairly easy shot but his ball hangs on the lip. What can I do? Ray Charles couldn't miss this. I sink it and turn to Sangster. He's shaking and grinding his teeth. I can't tell if he's pissed or petrified. I guess he doesn't take losing very well.

"We're all tied at one apiece," I say. "Wanna play a rubber game?"

He shakes his head vehemently. "No. I have to leave."

"But you haven't seen the storyboards."

"Choose whichever one you think is best."

"Are you sure? Won't Rivette want your recommendation?"

"That *is* my recommendation." He stands up and marches out.

CHAPTER TWENTY-SIX

Back at the agency, Terrance lifts his glasses and shoots one of his patented laser-eye glares at me. "How did it go?"

"It was a push."

He crinkles his forehead. "Push? What are you talking about?"

"He won the first game. I won the second. We didn't play a third so it was one–one, a tie. In Vegas, that's what's called a push."

He shakes his head. "You are *such* an ass. I don't give a damn about your stupid pool game. How did the presentation go? Did he buy any of the boards?"

"I never showed them to him."

He stands up and yells, "Why the hell not?"

"We never got that far."

Louder. "What do you mean, you never got that far? That was the whole purpose of your meeting."

"Calm down. We're gonna do the 'Red Hot' spot."

He eases back into his chair. "So you did present the boards?"

I shake my head. "Sangster didn't want to see them. He said whatever we think is the best one we should run with. And we like 'Red Hot,' right?"

"Of course. It's effective, inexpensive and easy to produce—no shooting, only editing. It's also a perfect building block for our brand architecture." Terrance can't help spouting marketing-speak, even though he knows that I know it's bullshit.

"Yeah. That's why I wrote it that way."

"But I'm still not clear on exactly what happened. You did have the boards with you, didn't you?"

"No. I threw them in a dumpster." For half a second he looks horrified. "Of course I had them. I was all ready to present but first we played some pool, like you suggested. He was his usual dead-eye self in the first game. Couldn't miss."

"I don't need an entire play-by-play. Just tell me what happened."

"That's what I'm doing."

I get the glare of exasperation. "All right. Go ahead."

"We were just starting the second game when these two guys walk in and start playing at the table next to us. All of a sudden, Sangster's shaking and squirming. Next thing I know he's running out of the place like it's on fire and telling me that whatever spot we want is fine with him."

"Did they say anything to him?"

"They didn't even look our way."

"Who were they?"

"No clue."

"And Sangster didn't say anything about them?"

"Not a word."

"Very strange. You're sure we have his approval to move ahead?"

"I'm positive."

"Good." He hands me a video cassette. "While you were fooling around in the poolroom, Jeannie was looking at footage. She pared it down to about a half hour's worth. I want you and Nicky to select the pieces you think work best and get it over to Bryan's studio for a rough cut. I told him you two will be there first thing tomorrow morning. Sangster is scheduled to arrive around lunch."

"What about Rivette?"

"Of course, nothing can happen without his approval but I think Sangster will be the tougher nut."

"I can handle Sangster."

"You'd better." He points to the door. "On your way to the video room, stop in and tell Jeannie what's going on. She needs to be kept in the loop."

When I get to her office, she's not there so I grab a chair. There's a big pile of magazines on her desk, the ones our clients run ads in. I grab a two-week-old *Newsweek*. I'm just starting to read about what a crazy bitch Leona Helmsley is when I hear, "Oh, hello." Her voice is cool, like she's talking to a neighbor she doesn't really like.

I look up and she's standing in front of me. There's a big bandage over her right eye. My rage gauge is redlining. "That fucking sonuvabitch hit you!"

Now she's glaring at me like *I'm* the woman beater. "What are you talking about?"

"That fucking Ari!" I scream. "I'm gonna hit him in the fucking head and see how he likes it." I start for the door.

"Stop!" she yells. "Nobody hit me. A pile of brochures fell off the shelf in the storage room on me."

"Bullshit! Terrance warned me that the fucking Israeli bastard abuses women. Now I'm gonna abuse him."

I storm out and head for his office. His door's closed; I throw it open. He's eating a falafel at his desk.

"You beat up the wrong woman," I scream.

"Wha . . ." Bits of deep-fired chickpeas fly out of his mouth. He swallows, stands up. "What the hell are you talking about?"

"You'll find out, you fucking sonuva . . ." I lunge at him over his desk. Next thing I know I'm on the floor, curled up, moaning. I feel like I've been kicked in the balls by Pelé. I must have passed out for a couple of seconds, 'cause when I look up Ari's standing over me. Terrance and Jeannie are running in.

She's shaking her head in disgust. "You're a total out-of-control lunatic."

"Wha happened?" I croak.

"You jumped into Ari's desk safe. Solid steel," Terrance says matter-of-factly. "Landed right on the family jewels."

Barney is now in the room. He's looking down at me disdainfully. "What's this all about?"

Jeannie was about to say something when Terrance cuts her off. "It's nothing. An accident."

"Stew looks hurt. Does he need to go to the ER?"

"I'm fine," I rasp, and struggle to my feet.

"You don't look fine." Barney's shaking his head. "But if you say you're all right . . ." He walks out.

Ari looks totally confused. "Will someone tell me what the hell is going on?"

"Forget it," Terrance says. "It's a colossal misunderstanding. Stewart has been working nonstop on the Rivette spot and was hit with a bout of temporary insanity."

Jeannie hits me with a glare of utter contempt. "I wouldn't be surprised if you did kill Persons." She turns and marches out.

"Come." Terrance grabs my wrist and yanks me out of the office.

As soon as we're out of Ari's earshot, Terrance says, "What the hell is the matter with you? Are you out of your mind?"

"He beat Jeannie up."

"He didn't do anything to Jeannie. A pile of posters fell on her."

"That's bullshit."

"Karol was there. She's the one who put the Band-Aid on her head."

"I thought . . ."

He glares at me. "No, you didn't. You didn't think at all."

"But you said . . ."

"I know what I said. If it ever gets back to Ari that I said it, I'll kill you myself."

"But . . ."

"No buts." He points to the door. "Go. I don't want to see you until the Rivette spot is in the can."

Feeling like a first-class, blue-ribbon, grade-A shmuck with earlaps, I skulk out of his office. First thing I do when I get to mine is call Jeannie. It's a short conversation. "Jeannie, I'm sor . . ." Click.

I'm sitting in my office rubbing my lucky turd. The way things have been going lately, I need all the help I can get.

It was a gift from my ex-stepdaughter, Rachel, great kid. I got along with her a lot better than with her mother. Did I mention that Shoshana, the Orthodox Jewish Vampire Bride from Hell, was ten years older than me and had a fourteen-year-old daughter from her first husband, whom she dumped while he was in the hospital recovering from a horrific car crash that resulted in having his left leg amputated below the knee? Once I heard that story I should have run for the hills and never looked back. But the little head between my legs overrode the big one between my shoulders.

About two weeks into the marriage I came home from work and heard screams and shrieks coming from Rachel's bedroom. I ran in there, thinking maybe an intruder broke in and was raping her or some boy from school had her pinned on the bed. What I never expected to see was Shoshana beating the crap out of Rachel with a wood hanger. I grabbed her by both arms while the poor kid cowered in a corner.

"What the hell are you doing?" I screamed.

"I'm disciplining my daughter," she yelled back.

"That's not discipline, it's child abuse!"

She turned and snarled at me, baring her teeth like a wild dog. "How dare you lecture me on how to treat my child! Now let me go."

"Swear that you won't hit her again."

"Fuck you, Stewart. You have no idea what it's like to be a parent."

"You're right, I don't. But I do know what it's like to be beaten by a parent. And as long as I'm here that's not going to happen to Rachel."

That was the first time I got the glare of death. But it sure as hell wasn't the last. Then she harrumphed and stormed out of the room.

Rachel was still on the floor, quivering. I helped her up. "Are you okay?"

She nodded and whispered, "Thank you."

After that, we were best pals. When Shoshana had to stay late at the school where she taught, for some cockamamie meeting or conference or (as I found out later) to fuck the vice principal (a rabbi, no less), Rachel and I would go out for pizza and sometimes a movie.

One day, about a month after I split up with her mother, the kid showed up at my office. She was in the city for a field trip to the Museum of Natural History. She saw this fossilized dinosaur turd in the gift shop and bought it for me. "Something to remember my mother by."

I kept it, not to remember Shoshana (though she does have a lot in common with a craggy old piece of petrified shit) but to remember Rachel, the only good memory I have from my fifty-one weeks of hell.

I'm thinking this turd isn't any luckier for me than it was for the dinosaur who squeezed it out sixty-five million years ago when Barbara comes flying into my cubicle looking all concerned.

"What happened? I heard you got hurt in Ari's office."

Maybe the damn shit-rock works after all. "It's nothing. I leaned over to talk to him and got crunched in the crotch by his stupid desk safe."

She puts her hand over her mouth. I'm not sure if she's stifling a grimace or a giggle. "Are you all right?"

"I'm fine. My pride hurts more than anything else."

She smiles and sits. "Good. I wanted to make sure to see you before I left."

I smile back. "I'm glad you did. I wanted to let you know that last night was one of the best experiences of my life."

"I enjoyed it too. You're really very sweet. I'm even starting to appreciate all those wisecracks and silly jokes." She reaches across my desk and squeezes my hand, the one holding the turd.

"Great. Are you doing anything after work? How about we have some dinner? I know a great little Japanese restaurant in Gramercy Park, hidden in the basement of a brownstone."

"I'd love to but I can't. I'm leaving."

"It's late. We're all leaving."

"You don't understand. I'm leaving the agency."

"Wait. What? Don't tell me Terrance fired you. He can't do that." I jump out of my chair. "I'm going into his office right now to make him take you back."

She grabs my arm. "Terrance didn't fire me."

"Who did? That sonuvabitch Ari? I'll finish what I started with him."

She shakes her head. "Stew, you don't understand. Nobody fired me. I got a fabulous offer from a hot new shop."

"Oh. That's great. I hope you got a big fat bump in salary. You deserve it. You're the best."

She smiles. "Thank you."

"But just 'cause you'll be at another agency, that doesn't mean we can't see each other."

"I'm afraid that's exactly what it means."

"That's crazy," I yell. "No agency can stop you from dating whoever you want. It's not fair. I don't even think it's legal. I loved being with you last night. If you didn't feel nauseous after spending time with me, there's no good reason we can't keep seeing each other."

She looks soulfully into my eyes. "I'm afraid there is."

"What? You're secretly married? You're an undercover nun? I know for a fact you're not a drag queen." This gets a little smile. "Tell me one legitimate reason you moving to another agency prevents us from seeing each other."

"The agency is in Green Bay."

I feel like I just got a mule kick to the cookies. "Green Bay? You mean like Wisconsin?" No, Gribnitz, you dumb shit, Green Bay, New Jersey. Of course Wisconsin! I smile and make believe I'm happy for her. "Congratulations. Are you sure that's what you want?"

She beams with excitement. "Oh yes. It's a half hour from where I grew up in Manitowoc. I'll be able to see my parents more than at Thanksgiving and Easter, and reconnect with my old friends. And they have some wonderful accounts, including the Packers. Karma, that's the name of the agency, has a suite at Lambeau Field. I can go to any game I want. I might even get to meet some of the players."

I say, "They have some nerve doing advertising in Green Bay. How would they like it if we started making cheese on Madison Avenue?"

She smiles. "I thought you'd say something like that."

"When you get there, see if they need a hotshot New York copywriter."

This makes her giggle. "Oh, Stewart, I can't imagine you living anywhere but New York."

"Why not?"

"It's who you are. You're a New Yorker through and through."

"Let me a least take you out for a bon voyage drink."

"That's very sweet. But I'm on my way to the airport right now. I have a seven-thirty flight out of LaGuardia."

"Tonight?"

She nods, a little forlornly.

"Then I guess this really is goodbye." I give her a hug and go to give her a little kiss on the forehead.

She pulls me toward her, opens her mouth, and plants a kiss that rattles my wisdom teeth. "I really like you, Stew. I wish we could have spent more time together."

"Yeah, me too."

She peeks at her watch. "I really have to get going. I'd hate to miss my plane." She pecks me another quick kiss, gives my shoulder a tender squeeze, then turns and glides out.

I sit there gaping at the door for a few seconds, trying to make sense out of what just happened. Then I realize that I'm still holding the lucky turd. Lucky, my ass! That thing has brought nothing but misery. Mass extinction for its original owner and massive heartache for me. I toss it in the trash.

CHAPTER TWENTY-SEVEN

Editing is far and away my favorite part of the process of making a TV spot. It's the only time when the writer isn't a vestigial organ. In the world of commercials, the director is king. Then comes the producer, cameraman, lighting guy, script girl, down to the gaffer and key grip. The agency creative team is their client. And they treat us like we treat our clients, with disdain masquerading as deference. They make believe they're listening, smile and nod at our suggestions, then do whatever the hell they want.

It's the same with movies. Screenwriters are the Rodney Danger-fields of Hollywood. No respect. Hitchcock, Kubrick, Scorsese, do you know who wrote any of their great films? Of course not. Neither does anyone else. There's even a Hollywood joke, "Didja hear the one about the Polish starlet? She fucked the writer." But this time it's different. No director, no producer, nobody but the editor and the creative team. And we're in control. So I should be in a pretty good mood. But with everything that's happened in the past couple of days, shit warmed over would be a major attitude upgrade.

Nicky and Bryan are already there, sitting at the control board. They look like Sulu and Chekov at the bridge of the *Starship Enterprise*. The story is that the producers of the original TV series had a limited budget so they made a few cosmetic changes to a spare video editing board. Voila! There's your bridge.

They're looking at a huge TV monitor, but it's not a Klingon battle cruiser. It's the rough cut of our commercial. There's an extra chair at the board but I go right to the couch at the rear of the studio, usually reserved for account people, clients and anyone else who doesn't really have a say in what's going on.

Nicky turns around, looks me up and down. "What the hell's the matter with you?"

I shake my head. "Nothing. How are we doing with the spot?"

Bryan says, "What, no hello? That's not the Gribmeister we know and love."

"Sorry. How are you, Bryan?"

"I'm absolutely fabulous. But why so glum? The last time I saw a face that long was in the paddock at Belmont."

Bryan O'Brien is a part-time actor, occasional stand-up comedian, former Division III second-team all-American lacrosse player, and, for my money, the best film editor in New York. At six six, 250, if he wasn't such a sweetheart, he could be a leg-breaker for the mob.

"I just found out that the girl of my dreams is moving to Wisconsin."

"What?" Nicky almost falls out of his chair. "Jeannie's moving to Wisconsin?"

"Not Jeannie. Barbara."

Nicky does a double take. "Barbara's the girl of your dreams, since when?"

"Since I went home with her the other night."

"Last I heard, Barbara was pissed off at you for that seat-kissing stunt."

"That's what I thought. Then she walks into my office last night after you left and starts talking to me. She said that Jeannie told her I was a great guy once you get past all the stupid shit."

Bryan says, "I've known you for years and haven't got past the stupid shit yet."

Then Nicky: "What Jeannie didn't tell her is that with Stew it's all stupid shit."

I give them the double stink eye.

Nicky sighs. "All right, tell us. I know you're dying to. How did you do it?"

"I know this is hard to believe, but *she* seduced *me*."

"Not hard," Nicky says. "Impossible."

"I couldn't believe it either but that's what happened. She asked me to walk her home, invited me up and . . ."

Bryan cuts me off. "No need to elaborate, Grib-man. We can imagine the rest."

"No, you can't. It was incredible. And it's not even that she's drop-dead gorgeous and the sex was fantastic. Her skin is soft and smooth as a rose petal and it smells even better. And she's great to be with—funny, smart, nice, the whole fucking package wrapped up with a beautiful bow. So I'm thinking, this never happens to me. Maybe it was an acid flashback."

They're both staring at me wide-eyed.

Nicky says, "You should be ecstatic not suicidal."

I throw up a hand. "I was . . . until about seven last night. I'm getting ready to leave the office and she walks in, takes my hand in both of hers, looks lovingly into my eyes . . ."

They're sitting at the edge of their seats, leaning forward.

"She says she had a fantastic time with me and thinks I'm great. I'm ready to propose on the spot. Why not? I'm never gonna do any better than her. Then, wham! She tells me she's going back to Green Bay."

"Green Bay?" Nicky seems genuinely pissed. "What the hell's in Green Bay?"

"Her family, for one. And the Packers, of course."

"She's leaving because of a fucking football team?"

I shake my head. "She loves the Packers, but that's not why she's leaving. She got a job at this hot Wisconsin ad agency."

Bryan twirls his handlebar mustache. "I believe 'hot Wisconsin ad agency' is an oxymoron."

"Of course it is, but that doesn't help me." They both seem genuinely sad for me, which makes me feel even more like a loser. I walk over to the third chair at the board. "All right, Stewie's pity party is over. What's going on with the spot?"

"How tough do you want it to be?" Bryan asks with a gleam in his eye.

"As tough as we can get away with."

"We have tons of Red Monahan footage. Going into jail. Coming out of jail. News footage of his victims crying. Shots of dead bodies attributed to him." He winks. "He's a very, very bad person."

"What about brother Neil?"

Bryan shakes his head slowly. "Seems to be a fairly straight shooter."

"When they ask him about Red, what does he say?"

"He says Red's family and he's recused himself from anything to do with his cases."

"That's it?"

"A lot of 'no comment,' 'I'm not at liberty to talk' . . . things like that."

"You mean he never tries to defend him? Or say he's not guilty? Or that the charges are politically motivated? Anything like that?"

Bryan shrugs. "I couldn't find anything. He just pretty much refuses to talk about him."

"So, where does that leave us?"

He hits a button and we see grainy news footage of Red Monahan walking next to another guy through a throng of reporters. Red is dapper in a blue pinstripe suit, white shirt and blue tie. His trademark auburn hair is slicked back. He could be a small-town banker or insurance broker except for the deep scar over his right eyebrow and perpetual sneer. His partner in crime—literally—is about a hundred pounds heavier, wearing a sharkskin suit that maybe fit him in high school, looking like five pounds of Genoa salami stuffed into a three-pound bag. The newscaster voice-over says, "Leaving the courtroom after the hung jury verdict are Dominic Zito, reputed head of the Louisa crime family of Bridgeport, and Robert 'Red' Monahan, said to be a key associate and enforcer for Mr. Zito. Both men were charged with multiple counts of kidnapping, extortion and murder."

Cut to Neil Monahan, several mics thrust in his face. "No comment."

Cut to another newscast. In this one, a grim-faced newsman is in the backyard of a modest brick house. Behind him, a small front-end loader is digging up the lawn. "We're at the home of alleged mob hitman Red Monahan. Behind me, FBI crews are searching for the remains of several of his victims, said to be buried here."

Back to Neil, same shot as before. "No comment."

Cut to an FBI "Most Wanted" poster of Robert "Red" Monahan. An off-camera voice asks, "How do you feel about your brother being added to the FBI's 'Most Wanted' list?"

"No comment."

Cut to a photo of the Connecticut state house with prison bars over it. The voice-over says: "Crime families belong in a jailhouse, not the state house. Vote for Ed Rivette for governor. It would be a crime not to."

At the bottom, "BETTER ED" in big black type pops on the screen. After a beat, "THAN RED" appears underneath. This time the letters are red, with blood dripping from them.

Bryan and Nicky look at me, expectantly. I don't react for a couple of seconds, then shake my head slowly, looking glum. I bet Bryan was up most of last night working on this. He looks like he's ready to cry. I break into a big smile. "I love it!"

Bryan exhales. "Not too over the top?"

"Not at all. The graininess of the footage is perfect. The graphics were right on."

Nicky says, "You don't think the bleeding type was too much?"

"Rivette hired us to shake things up. If this doesn't get people's attention, nothing will."

We're all feeling pretty good about ourselves, talking about small tweaks we can do to make the spot a little tighter, what the next one will look like, stuff like that. Then I remember. "We still gotta get the okay from the client."

Nicky smiles. "Rivette thinks you're a genius. There's no way he'll shitcan the spot."

"It's not Rivette I'm worried about. Sangster's gonna be here any minute. If he doesn't like it, Rivette never sees it."

As if on cue, Bryan's phone rings. He listens for a few seconds. "Send him in."

A minute later, Sangster lurches in. His eyes dart around the room like a chicken on speed. He's wearing the same clothes he had on the other day. A soot-gray suit that has been to the cleaners too many times, white shirt, skinny black tie and Buster Brown–looking shoes.

As the de facto account guy, I stand up, give him a big smile and extend my hand. "Hi, Urban, thanks for coming. We think Mr. Rivette's gonna be really happy with this spot. It's just what he asked for."

I give his hand a shake. It's sweaty and limp, a dead, wet flounder. I try not to look too grossed out as I walk him over to the couch. "This is Bryan, our editor. You already know Nicky." They turn and smile. Sangster nods imperceptibly. "You remember we decided to link Neil Monahan with his gangster half brother, Red. We do it with actual footage so no one can say we're stretching the truth."

Sangster doesn't say anything, he just sits there stiffly, hands clenched in his lap, staring at the blank monitor. He's shivering.

I nod at Bryan. "Why don't we run the spot."

After it's over, Sangster's expression doesn't change. In fact, if his eyes weren't open, I'd swear he was asleep.

"Well, what do you think?"

Nothing for a few more seconds, then, "It's extremely provocative."

"That's exactly what we're going for. I'm glad you like it."

He scowls. "I didn't say I liked it."

"Oh." I feign surprise. "What didn't you like about it?"

"It's inflammatory. It will infuriate Monahan's people."

"Who gives a shit about Monahan's people. It's the voters we care about. If the spot hurts Monahan, it's good for us. We're twenty points behind in the polls with only weeks till Election Day. We can't afford to play nice."

He seems confused for a few seconds, then says, "Can I speak to you in private?"

I glance over at Bryan, who points. "My office. Through that door."

I gesture to him and Nicky. "C'mon, guys."

Sangster shakes his head. "Just you."

"The spot was a team effort. You should tell all of us what your issues are with it."

"It's not really about the ad." He points to the door. "Please."

I follow him in. It's like walking through a time portal. About the size of a big walk-in closet, Bryan's office has two old wooden kitchen chairs, a small school desk, a rotary phone and a Smith Corona typewriter. Bryan obviously spent all his money on state-of-the-art editing equipment and got his office furniture at Goodwill.

Sangster closes the door. He looks nervously around—for what, I have no idea.

I sit while he paces. He stops in front of me and glares down.

"Give me your word that you will repeat this to no one."

"Of course."

"Say it."

"I give you my word."

He nods. "Good." And whispers, "We have received threats."

"Threats? What kind of threats?"

"Death threats. More than one."

"From who?"

"Monahan's people, of course."

"You're sure?"

"He didn't send them on his letterhead, if that's what you mean. But who else could it be?"

I promised Terrance I wouldn't mention anything about our close encounter with Red on the road in the Hamptons, so I just say, "What does Mr. Rivette think?"

He shakes his head sadly. "He thinks they're a so-called dirty trick. An attempt to divert our attention from the campaign."

"Did you report these threats to the police?"

"Edward forbade it. He said not to talk about it with anyone. He said that would only play into Monahan's hands."

"I'm sure he's right." I muster a smile. "Do me a favor, run the spot by him. If he thinks it's too provocative, we'll tone it down. But I really believe it's exactly what we need if we want to have any chance of winning. You do want to win, don't you?"

"Yes, of course."

"Then you'll show it to Mr. Rivette?"

He thinks for a second. "All right."

"Great."

We walk back into the studio. Bryan and Nicky are looking grim. I flash them a quick thumbs-up behind Sangster's back.

"Bryan, make Urban a half-inch cassette. He's gonna show it to Mr. Rivette."

He says, "Already boxed and labeled." Then hands it to Sangster who grunts and walks out.

Bryan exhales deeply. "You had us worried for a while there, sport."

"It was never in doubt," Nicky says. "Nobody bullshits clients like Stew. He shoulda been an account exec."

"Jeez, you don't have to insult me."

Back at the agency we show the spot to Terrance and Jeannie.

Terrance loves it. Jeannie's shaking her head.

"Do we know for sure that Neil Monahan is in cahoots with his half brother?"

Before I can answer, Terrance says, "If there was any real proof, he wouldn't be a viable candidate."

She points a finger, like it was a dagger, right at my Adam's apple. "So you're accusing this man, a man with an impeccable record who spent his life serving and protecting the public, of being involved with a criminal and murderer?"

"That criminal and murderer happens to be Neil Monahan's brother. It's not that big a stretch to think they're in cahoots with each other."

Jeannie glares at me. "It's his half brother. We spent hours looking at all kinds of documents and couldn't find anything to substantiate any of those accusations."

"What accusations? We're not accusing anyone of anything. We're just showing legitimate news stories about Red and playing Neil's actual quotes."

She's turning red. "That's bullshit and you know it."

"All I know is that Red Monahan is a thug and very likely a murderer. You don't think that's true?"

"Of course it's true. It's what you said about Neil Monahan that's a big, fat lie."

"We didn't say anything about him."

"What about the end?"

"We didn't mention Monahan. We said crime families don't belong in government. You think they do?"

"You know that's not what I meant. You used dirty tricks and distortions to make it look like Monahan is a criminal. Or worse."

"Maybe he is a criminal."

"And maybe you're a murderer," she screams. "That's what it said on the front page of the paper."

"If that's the way you feel, there's no reason for us to work together anymore."

She gets all red and says, "No, there isn't!" Then she storms out of the room and slams the door.

Nicky glares at me. "What the fuck is the matter with you?"

"What's the matter with *me*? What are you talking about? She attacked us. Our work. I defended it. What did you want me to do, tell her she's right? That we're sleazy, dishonest dirtbags that represent everything that's wrong with American politics?"

"No. But you didn't have to go after her the way you did. She's our friend. Our teammate. You verbally beat her up."

"C'mon. She's a tough kid. She can take it."

Terrance, who all this time is just standing there with his arms folded, says, "Did you know that she has a close relative, I think her uncle, who was in law enforcement?"

Nicky says, "Yeah. I think he was a state trooper."

"So?"

Terrance says, "He was involved in some sort of scandal. I'm not sure of the details. Either he or his partner shot someone under questionable circumstances. The victim's family sued, and her uncle was thrown off the force in disgrace."

I'm starting to feel like a real shit-heel. "I had no idea."

"He died a few months later. Jeannie is convinced it was because of the scandal. You can see that this is a very sensitive subject for her."

"Should we kill the spot and try another approach?"

"Absolutely not. It's just what Rivette wants."

"What about Jeannie?"

"I'll talk to her." He peeks at his Patek Philippe and shoots us a sadistic grin. "It's after six. Go home. Enjoy the weekend. The torture starts all over on Monday."

CHAPTER TWENTY-EIGHT

I throw open Moish's door and yell, "I'm home." I flick the light. It looks like the living room puked all over itself. Shards of broken glass litter the floor. Tables and chairs are toppled over. Lamps, tchotchkes, picture frames and glasses are in pieces.

"Moish, where are you?" I yell.

I hear a faint, throaty, "In here."

I'm walking in circles. "Where's here?"

"The bedroom."

I run over and he's sitting on the edge of the bed, hunched over, shaking. He never looked as old to me as he does this minute. He looks up at me pathetically. "I'm sorry, son."

I take his quivering hands in both of mine. "There's nothing to be sorry about, Pop. I'm worried about you. Are you all right?"

He nods. "Yuh. I'm okay." His usual stentorian voice is a throaty rasp.

"Can I get you a glass of water?"

"Some water would be good."

I run to the kitchen, grab a glass out of the cabinet, fill it from the tap, and hustle back, trying not to trip on the scattered debris that's all over the floor.

He grabs the glass with both hands, dribbling half the water down his white T-shirt as he drinks.

After his drink he looks a little calmer. I ask, "Who did this?"

"Two big bulvons."

"Who were they? Where did they come from?"

He sits up. "How should I know?"

"You never saw them before?"

"Never."

"What did they say?"

His color's coming back. "Nothing. Not one word." His voice is now tinged with indignation.

"They didn't say who sent them?"

He slams the now empty water glass onto the bedside table and yells, "They didn't have to say. I know who sent them. That stinking Shifty Shapiro."

"The bookie? Are you sure?"

"Of course I'm sure. Who else would do this?"

Now I'm starting to get angry. "How dare that senile old bastard send his thugs to wreck our house! Is he still in the old neighborhood?"

"No, he moved . . . Brighton Beach, I think."

"Where in Brighton Beach? What's his address?"

"I dunno."

"You gotta have it written down somewhere."

"What do you need to have his address for? You wanna send him a postcard?"

"Just tell me where he lives. I'm gonna pay him a little visit."

"Visit? What are you talking about?"

"I'm gonna make sure he never does this again."

"What are you gonna do?"

"I'll know when I get there."

"I'm going with you."

"Absolutely not. I don't want you getting hurt."

"I'm already hurt."

"No."

He stands and smirks. "Then no address."

Now we're glaring at each other.

After a few seconds, I say, "All right, you can come. Now what's his address?"

He smiles smugly, then opens the drawer of his nightstand and pulls out something that was probably an address book forty years ago. Its yellowed pages are held together by a rubber band. Strips of torn paper protrude from every angle, with names and phone numbers written on them in my father's surprisingly elegant hand. He carefully removes the rubber band, pulls out a tattered piece of paper, and holds it up. I can just about make out *Shifty S.* before he puts it in his pocket.

"You're not gonna give me the address?"

"I'll give it to you when we're in the car."

"I said I would take you and I'll take you."

Another sly smile. "Insurance."

"Let's go."

"Hold your horses." He goes to the phone and dials a number. "Shifty, you sonuvabitch," he yells. "We're coming for you, you rat bastard. Me and my boy, the killer from the paper." He slams the phone down.

"Why the hell did you do that for? Now he knows we're coming."

"Good. I hope he craps in his pants and there's shit all over the floor when we get there."

I've never seen Moish so amped up. He's staring straight ahead, rubbing his hands together. "We'll show that sonuvabitch that he screwed with the wrong Gribnitz."

The Brighton Beach exit is about fifteen minutes away on the Belt Parkway.

Moish is getting more and more agitated the closer we get. Me, I'm starting to cool down. While Moish is enumerating all the different ways he can torture Shifty, I'm thinking of the potential shitstorm that I'm driving into. Suppose the old bookie has a heart condition and drops dead. The police already have me pegged as a potential murderer; this time they'll throw away the key. Next thing you know I'm getting gang-raped in the shower at the Tombs.

"You know him a long time, don't you?"

"Who?"

"Shifty."

"Forty years, maybe more."

"I thought you guys were friends."

"Used to be. Then he turned into the gonif he is now, trying to swindle me out of $300."

"You're sure he sent those men?"

"Who else could it be?"

I'm thinking the same guy who ran me and Nicky off the road, but I don't say that.

"You're sure you paid him the money you owe him?"

"What are you, taking his side? I don't owe him a dime. Period!"

"I just want to make sure he's the right guy."

"He's the guy. Absolutely." He bangs his fist on the dashboard. If you're chickening out, drop me off and I'll do it myself."

"I'm not chickening out. I just want to be 100 percent positive."

"I'm 10,000 percent positive."

That makes one of us.

We're at the Brighton Beach exit. That was the beach we all went to as teenagers. It was twenty minutes on the D train or a half-hour bike ride. Coney Island was for tourists and New Yorkers who didn't know better. Sure it was fun with the rides, the arcades and Nathan's (everybody talks about the hot dogs, which are okay but not spectacular, but their french fries, the best!). You went to Coney Island for that stuff but never to the beach.

Brighton was where everyone went. (Everyone our age, that is.) It was *The Lords of Flatbush* meets *Beach Blanket Bingo*. There were the hitters with their slicked-back hair and cigarette packs tucked into their black T-shirt sleeves. Hitter chicks hung on their well-muscled arms, in heavy makeup, big hair and skintight bikinis. There was the cool crowd who never went into the water and languished on their beach chairs and chaises longues, looking like they were posing for a Macy's swimsuit layout. There were the nebbishes, who the hitters picked on and the cool guys made fun of. Then there were me and my friends, somewhere in the lower middle of the high school hierarchy. We were the invisibles.

Not cool enough to talk to, not dorky enough to pick on. So they just ignored us like we didn't exist.

Then all of a sudden the Russians took over. Ever hear of the movie *The Russians Are Coming, the Russians Are Coming*? Brighton Beach is where they came. Russian stores, Russian restaurants and Russian mobsters, the toughest SOBs around. We're talking ex-KGB, highly trained, ruthless, professional killers. Even the Mafia is scared shitless of them.

"Hey, Moish," I say, trying to sound calm. "Those guys who messed up the house, they weren't Russian, were they?"

"What? You think they showed me a passport?"

"Did they talk with an accent?"

He glares at me. "They didn't talk. They smashed. They broke. They destroyed. What they didn't do was converse. Why do you ask?"

"I was just curious."

Shifty's front hallway smells like a combination of old paper, stagnant water and fried shoe leather. The name on the mailbox says "Murray Shapiro."

"Is this him? His real name is Murray?"

"You think his mama named him Shifty? I think it's Murray."

"You think? You better be sure. If it's the wrong guy we're both in big trouble."

"It's him."

Murray or Shifty, take your pick, lives on the third floor, over a Russian (what else?) deli, in the shadow of the elevated subway tracks on Brighton Beach Avenue. We walk two flights up a dark stairway. I'm looking for KGB assassins lurking in every dark corner. Shifty's apartment is at the end of a dimly lit hall. Moish runs past me and pummels the door with both fists.

"Let us in, you farshtinkener sonuvabitch!"

The door opens a crack. A chain lock holds it in place. Shifty yells, "Gribnitz, you're a crazy man. Mashugana!"

Moish screams back, "You send hoodlums to wreck my house. You bet I'm crazy. Let me in and I'll show you how crazy I am."

"What hoodlums? I don't know what you're talking about?"

"Don't lie in my face, you rat bastard. You think my house wrecked itself?"

"I don't know anything about it."

"You're full of shit!" He's shaking. His face is red.

I put a hand on his shoulder. "All right, calm down. I don't want you getting another heart attack."

Moish turns and glares at me. "All of a sudden, you care?"

"What does that mean? Of course I care. Why do you think I came here with you?"

"How the hell should I know? Back at the house, you were a big shtarker. Now you're Mahatma Ghandi. Some killer." He glares with the same scornful disgust as he did when I got three automatic failures on my road test. "You wouldn't last ten minutes in Murder Incorporated."

What the hell am I doing, refereeing a fight between two crazy old Jews? "Let's just go. Coming here was a bad idea."

From the other side of the door, I hear, "He's a smart boy. Listen to him."

"You shut da hell up," he screams. He turns and glares at me, still yelling. "You wanna go. Go! Get the hell out of here. You never were any . . ." Next thing I know, his eyes get glassy, his face turns red, and he slumps and falls back into me, gasping for air.

I yell, "Let us in. My father's sick. He needs to sit down."

"He has to promise he won't be a lunatic."

"I promise for him. Please. Open the door."

He unhooks the chain. I have a grip on Moish's arm as I lead him inside. The place is furnished in early *Honeymooners*. The rug and upholstery haven't been changed since the fifties. It's a good bet they haven't been vacuumed since the sixties. There's an old table radio and a TV set that looks like the one Norton watched *Captain Video* on.

I ease Moish onto a chair. Shifty is huddled in a corner, not sure if Moish is faking or if he really has a problem. "Mr. Shapiro, can you get some water?"

Shifty shuffles off to the kitchen and comes back with two glasses. He hands me one and puts the other one on the table next to Moish.

"Thanks, Shifty. Or should I call you Murray?"

"Murray is good."

I take a sip of water. Moish sits there, scowling. "Take a drink, Dad."

"How do I know it's not poison?"

"Just have some water."

He drinks. Murray's on the couch, facing him. I'm pacing back and forth between them. I stop in front of Murray. "You really didn't send those guys?"

"What guys? You think I'm Meyer Lansky with my own army? I'm a poor shmuck who takes a couple of bets on the side to make ends meet. Look around. Is this the home of a major operator? Besides, your father doesn't owe me any money. I made a mistake."

Moish perks up, wags a finger in the air. "I knew it."

Now I'm confused. "I don't understand."

Murray digs into a drawer and pulls out one of those marble notebooks that kids use in school. He opens to a page with a column of names and numbers.

"It's Mendy Grossman who owes me. He's right under your father. See?" He shoves the book in my face, points to a line. "My hand shakes a little." He runs a quivering finger across the page. "I connected the wrong name to the wrong number." He looks supplicatingly at me. "I'm very sorry."

Moish jumps up, suddenly fully recovered. "What are you telling him for? It's me you should be apologizing to."

"You're right. I'm very sorry, Moish. Forgive me?" He extends his hand.

Moish walks over and grabs Murray's hand in both of his. "What are you talking about? Of course. I was never really mad anyway."

"I'm so glad to hear it. Do you want some tea? I got coffee cake. Entenmann's."

I can't believe what I'm hearing. I know it's a good thing that these geriatric nutjobs aren't at each other's throats, but why couldn't they figure this out before they gave me a triple migraine?

"I hate to break up this happy reconciliation, fellas, but if you don't mind, maybe you guys can do this some other time. I really need to get home and get some sleep."

"These kids today." Moish winks at Murray. "They're not as tough as when we were young, up all night, dancing till dawn with the tsatskeles."

Murray looks relieved. "Okay, Moish, I'll see you around." He looks at me. "Good night, boy."

"Good night."

As soon as we're in the car, Moish is snoring.

I'm starting to calm down when it hits me. If Murray didn't send those guys, who did?

It's nine o'clock Monday morning and I'm sitting in the barber's chair, gulping my third cup of coffee. Nicky is sipping mint tea. I can't imagine him on coffee. It would be like the Tasmanian Devil had a love child with Woody Woodpecker.

"If it wasn't the old bookie, who was it?"

I shrug. "I dunno. Maybe the same guy who ran us off the road."

"Aren't you worried?"

"I'm fucking petrified. But what can I do? Rivette basically said that if anybody on the campaign calls the cops they're out."

"And Sangster said he's been getting death threats?"

"Him and Rivette."

"And Rivette's not doing anything about it?"

I shake my head. "He thinks Monahan's people are trying to rattle us. And, you know what, they're doing a pretty good job."

"What about Sangster? Does he also think there's nothing to worry about?"

"Are you kidding? He's stressed out of his mind. He even lost to me at pool."

"I don't blame him. Red Monahan is nobody to fuck with. He'll stab you in the throat with his left hand while he's patting you on the back with his right."

"You watch too many gangster movies."

"Maybe, but those movies are based on real life."

"Let's say it is Red, it still doesn't explain who those bastards were who came to Moish's."

"Red coulda sent them."

"To do what, scare the shit out of a seventy-eight-year-old ex-cabbie who couldn't pick either Rivette of Monahan out of a lineup?"

"Maybe they were sending you a message. Did they tell him to tell you to lay off Monahan?"

"According to Moish, they didn't say anything."

"What did they look like? Did they look like mobsters?"

"No, they looked like Girl Scouts."

"C'mon, this is serious. If it was Red's gang, we gotta do something."

"What?"

"I dunno, call the police."

"Okay. Let's make believe I don't care about losing my job and going broke, so I call them. What do I tell them? That we heard third-hand that Ed Rivette is getting death threats from who knows who but he's not taking them seriously. And, by the way, somebody ransacked my old man's house and we think it might be the same guys."

Nicky looks confused, upset and stressed out all at once. "All right, we don't call the police. We gotta do something."

"That's all I've been thinking about for two days. If I could think of something that might work, don't you think I'd do it? Maybe the bookie hired some thugs to mess up Moish's house, then he had a change of heart and lied about it when we showed up. Maybe some friends of Persons didn't get the message that I didn't kill him and were out for revenge. Maybe it was a total fuckup and they trashed the wrong house. Whatever the reason, I say we just keep going on like nothing happened. If Rivette's not worried, why should we be?"

"You don't really want me to answer that, do you?"

CHAPTER THIRTY

We've been flooding the airwaves with "Better Ed" commercials nonstop for the last couple of weeks, and to everyone's surprise it's working. Election Day is almost here, and what started as a Greenwich no contest is now a horse race. One poll has us in a statistical dead heat.

Nicky and I have spent almost every day in Bryan O'Brien's studio. I've been crashing on his couch most nights. I went back to Canarsie only once, to get a change of underwear and a toothbrush.

We probably looked at a hundred hours of news footage, staring at Red Monahan's snarly mug, trying to find the perfect ten-second news clip to have his half brother say "no comment" to. After a couple of fourteen-hour days, Red's scarred, pockmarked face is permanently seared into my brain. He even invaded my dreams. Not only is this job destroying any semblance of an actual sex life I might have, it's even killing my fantasy sex life.

When there's a lull in the editing, we work on the radio, print and direct mail. Why we lovingly refer to it as dreck mail should be obvious to anyone with any creative judgement.

There are more than enough radio sound bites to do an audio version of the TV spots; we now have three running concurrently. For the print, we go with mug shots and grainy newspaper photos of Red for our artwork. We put "Crime Families Belong in the Jailhouse, Not the State House" as the headline and "Better Ed than Red" as the tagline.

On one ad we changed the format and put Neil's face on the FBI "Most Wanted" poster in place of Red's. The headline read "Not Wanted" with the subhead "By the Citizens of Connecticut." That's my particular favorite.

This morning we're in Nicky's Prelude, heading out to East Hampton for a meeting with Rivette. Mostly I've been dealing with Sangster, who, weird and Lurch-like though he is, I've developed an affection for. He's like the broken toy that you still played with when you were a kid.

To his credit, Rivette's pushing himself even harder than he's pushing us. He's been running around Connecticut hitting every bagel store, pizzeria, diner, deli and car wash in the state, not to mention all those ridiculous so-called civic organizations that people in places like Connecticut feel compelled to join. Rotary Clubs, Kiwanis, Elks, Lions, Moose, Knights of Columbus, Knights of Pythias and every other club, lodge, or fraternal group in the state except maybe the Ku Klux Klan and the American Association for Nude Recreation, and I'm not sure he didn't hit those too.

And he's not pulling any punches. He's hitting Monahan hard, making speeches saying Red Monahan is somewhere between Genghis Khan and Adolph Hitler on the all-time supervillain list. And his brother Neil is his consiglieri.

Which brings us to today. We're on our way to East Hampton for an emergency meeting with Rivette, which is a real pain in the ass. It's a two-and-a-half-hour ride when the traffic is good, which is never. His place in Greenwich is less than an hour from Midtown but we never go there. For someone who wants to be the governor of that state, he doesn't seem to want to spend any more time there than he has to.

Nicky doesn't like to talk when he's behind the wheel (driving is one of the ten million things that triggers his anxiety) so we spend most of the ride listening to the Stones and Led Zeppelin cranked up loud. Luckily, he installed a new kick-ass stereo system.

About two hours in, he lowers the volume. "What's this meeting about?"

"Not sure."

"They didn't tell you?"

"No. I got the memo, same as you. I figure they're gonna nominate us for sainthood, or maybe Jesushood, after raising Rivette from the dead. They guy supposedly is pretty generous with bonuses when his employees do a good job."

"I'm not holding my breath." Then, after a few seconds. "Who's gonna be there?"

"No clue."

"For a guy who's supposed to be the account exec on this account, you don't know much about what's going on."

"How can I? I'm spending every waking minute with you doing the creative."

"So who's doing the account work?"

"Terrance, I guess."

"Have you spoken to Jeannie?"

"In the last month I've spoken to you, Bryan, Terrance and Sangster. That's it."

"Is she still pissed at you?"

"You tell me. You talk to her a lot more than I do."

"We don't talk about you."

"Why the hell not? What else do you two have to talk about?"

"Fuck you, hump." He cranks the music back up. For the next twenty minutes, the only voice I hear is Robert Plant's.

When we get to Rivette's place, he answers the door himself. "Hello, fellows. Follow me."

He leads us into the great room, the room we were in the last time we were here. I expect to see Terrance, Jeannie, Sangster, and maybe Boyce. But the only one sitting on the gigantic red leather sofa is Harvey Nielsen, with his perfectly coiffed silver mane, thousand-dollar suit and aquiline nose that you could cut glass with.

Rivette sits next to him. Nicky and I plop ourselves on the couch on the other side of the glass-top mahogany coffee table, facing them.

Neither one of them look happy. Nielsen's permanent scowl is even more severe than usual. And Rivette's bluff-Ed-McMahon-style joviality is AWOL.

I don't get it. We made a nice piece of change for the agency, half of which goes into Nielsen's pocket, and resuscitated Rivette's drowned political hopes. They should be welcoming us with a fucking brass band, not glaring at us like we were a couple of bead-bedecked hippies at an ROTC meeting.

After a few awkward seconds, Rivette gives us a sickly smile and says, "This is one of those good news-bad news situations." He pauses for a minute, waiting for someone to say something. Nobody does, so he keeps going. "I, frankly, had serious doubts that anything would come of your efforts for my campaign, other than some publicity for my magazines. But here we sit, with Election Day looming and the governor's office a very real possibility. Tomorrow Bitsie and I will be flying back to Connecticut for the final full-court press down the homestretch."

What is it with these people who obviously know nothing about sports, mangling sports metaphors? I'm surprised he didn't say it's the two-minute warning in the bottom of the ninth of the fifteenth round. But I digress.

He beams at me. "Stewart, none of this could have happened without you. My arrangement with the agency was to cover your fee. You more than earned it." He leans over and hands me an envelope. "This is for all your hard work." He turns to Nicky. "Nick, I didn't forget you. A small bonus for all you've done." Another envelope.

He nods toward Nielsen, who's been sitting erect and stone-faced, like an eagle-beaked sphinx. "As you know, Harvey and I go back a very long time, more years than either of us care to enumerate. I trust his judgement implicitly." He takes a long breath, almost a sigh. "Which is why I'm putting the remainder of my campaign's marketing efforts in his hands."

"I'm confused," I say. "Do you mean we have to report directly to him and not Terrance?"

"No. Harvey will take over the entire account. Including creative."

It takes me a minute to process what just happened. "You're firing us?"

Rivette nods somberly.

"Nielsen's a suit. He can't do what we do."

He glowers at me. "I've got news for you, Gribnitz. I've been running successful ad campaigns since you were a juvenile delinquent stealing hubcaps back in Brooklyn."

This bastard's still technically my boss so I try to smooth things over. "I'm not saying you're not a great adman, it's just that we've been totally involved in the day-to-day of the campaign. You have enough on your hands running the agency."

He looks at me like I'm a turd on his Ferragamo shoe. "I guess you haven't heard."

"Heard what?"

"You know what's been going on at the agency between your friends Terrance and Ari and myself."

We both nod.

"Boyce made his decision last night." He sneers. "In typical fashion, he got it wrong. Your pals are in and I'm out. Of course, I'm taking my accounts with me. Including this one."

"Just for the record," I say, "Ari Nadler is no friend of ours."

Nicky perks up. "Yeah. We hate his fucking guts."

This brings a smile to Rivette's face but Nielsen isn't moved. "It doesn't matter. You two are finished."

I look over at Rivette. "After everything we've done for you, this is how you thank us?"

Rivette looks like he's ready to cry. "I'm sorry, boys. As I'm sure you can imagine, it was a very difficult decision."

"Is it because of the death threats? Were the ads too tough?"

"Not at all. They were right on the money." He chuckles. "In my business, if you don't get two or three death threats a year, you're not doing your job."

Nielsen's smug veneer is cracking. "Death threats. No one told me about any death threats." He turns to me. "Where did you hear about them?"

"From Sangster. He doesn't think they're so funny."

Rivette shakes his head. "Bitsie was a coddled child with a nervous disposition and has been fearful of everyone and everything ever since. I did my best to toughen him up when we were teenagers, but the damage had already been done."

Nielsen says, "Are you sure there's nothing to be concerned about?"

Rivette waves a dismissive hand. "Safe as houses." He turns to us and stands. "Thanks again, boys. I'm sorry it had to end this way but in time you'll see it's all for the best."

That's our cue to get out. I get up and extend my hand to Rivette who shakes it warmly. "Thank you, sir. It's been a pleasure." Why burn bridges. I figure once Nielsen screws up, which I'm sure he will, maybe Rivette will bring us back in.

Nicky stands, shakes hands and says, "Good luck in the election, sir."

Rivette smiles warmly. "Godspeed to you both. I'm sure we'll see each other in the future."

Nielsen says, "Ed doesn't speak for me. As far as I'm concerned, I never want to see you two clowns again, especially you, Gribnitz." He shakes a fist at me. "You're coarse and unprofessional, a disgrace to the advertising profession. I still think you have James Persons's blood on your hands."

It takes everything I have not to put a dent in that eagle beak of his.

I scream, "Fuck you, Nielsen! You over-the-hill has-been!" Then I turn to Rivette. "You're making a colossal mistake. You're a great man. You deserve to win. I hope this washed-up old empty suit doesn't cost you the election." I grab Nicky's arm. "C'mon."

We storm out.

Driving back, I'm still livid. Shaking, grumbling, cursing, stomping. Nicky's concentrating on the road, trying very hard to make believe I'm not here. Finally, he says, "Nielsen won, you know. You gave him just what he wanted."

"How did he win? He lost the agency. And in a few weeks, the election will be over and he won't have Rivette's business either."

"He'll still have the magazine. That's about a million in billing."

"Yeah, what can you do?"

"Now that Rivette has seen what real advertising can do, Nielsen's probably scared he'll lose the account to us. That's why he wanted to make you look bad."

"You're right. Talk about going from the penthouse to the shit-house. The last thing I thought would happen today is us getting shitcanned."

"It's not like we got fired from the agency. We're just off this account."

"I've already been fired by the agency. I was working directly for Rivette, remember? As of now, I'm on the street."

"Don't be stupid. Terrance isn't going to let that happen."

"It's also Ari's agency. The last time he saw me I was lunging at his throat."

Nicky stifles a giggle. "No, the last time he saw you was when you were on the floor, clutching your balls."

"Thanks for reminding me."

"At least you got a nice payday out of it. What was your deal with Rivette?"

That brings a smile to my face. "Five thousand a week."

"Wow. That's a lot more than Boyce was paying you. For six weeks, that's what?"

"Thirty thousand dollars."

"Holy shit! That's like $250,00 a year."

"But I don't have a year. Or even a day. This is my last check." I pull out the envelope and rip it open. "Oh my God!"

"What's the matter? He gypped you?"

"Here, look." I put the check in front of his eyes, blinding him. He almost swerves off the road.

He screams, "Are you trying to get us both killed?"

"Sorry."

"Just tell me how much."

"Fifty thousand."

"Dollars?"

"No, knishes."

"Holy Christ, that's like what, twenty thousand more?" He pulls onto the shoulder and stops the car.

"What are you doing?"

"I wanna see how much he gave me." He rips open the envelope, frowns and nods his head noncommittally.

"Well, how much?"

"Not as much as you," he says, like a jealous little brother.

"He's not supposed to give you anything. You get paid by the agency."

"I woulda been better off getting fired like you."

"When the money runs out I'll be on my ass. You'll still have a job."

He shrugs. "Whatever."

"So how much is it?"

"Five thousand."

"That's pretty good."

"Yeah, but it's not fifty." He cranks up the radio, his signal that he's through talking. But the scowl on his face signals that he's not through being pissed off.

For about forty-five minutes nobody says anything. As usual, traffic is stupid on the LIE. Fine for a couple of exits, then for no reason, it slows to a crawl, no accident or construction or anything that might cause a problem, then suddenly the jam magically disappears and you're back to normal. This happens two or three times. During one of these lulls, Nicky lowers the volume and says, "There's something I forgot to tell you."

"So tell me now." It's probably something about the new setup at the agency. I bet Terrance promised to make him creative director. Now I'll have to suck up to him to get my job back.

"I've been sorta seeing Jeannie."

"What? You mean like going out with her?"

"Uh-huh."

"And sleeping with her?"

"Well, yeah. That's what people who date each other do."

"And you forgot to tell me? It just slipped your mind?"

"We thought it might get you upset . . . with everything else going on."

I scream, "You're fucking right, I'm upset!"

"But you said you didn't want to go out with her. Right now you're not even talking to each other. So why can't I see her?"

"I'm not pissed 'cause you're going out with her. You can go out with whoever you fucking please. So can she. I'm pissed because my two best friends went behind my back and lied to my face."

"We didn't lie. We just didn't tell you."

"Same difference." I reach over and blast the radio. Neither one of us says another word.

CHAPTER THIRTY-ONE

I exited most of my former agencies the same way card cheats exited saloons in the Old West—kicked out through the swinging door face-first into the mud, then getting my saddlebags, or in my case my back-pack, thrown on top of me.

I'm gathering up a couple of things I want to keep—my mini tape recorder, my Rolodex and my Art Shamsky autographed baseball—when Terrance walks in. His arms are folded across his chest. "What do you think you're doing?"

"Packing up. I don't work here anymore, remember?"

"Don't be an ass."

"Nielsen took over the Rivette account and shitcanned us. I don't have any other accounts. I'm not on the agency's payroll. So, from where I sit, I'm out."

"If you saw Nielsen then you know the situation. There are still a couple of legal issues that have to be worked out, but for all intents and purposes, we own the agency, Ari and I."

"Yeah. Congratulations."

"Obviously there's no reason for you to leave if I'm running the agency."

"You and Ari. I'm betting he's not too hot to have me around."

"Ari's not a problem. All you have to do is apologize."

"Apologize for what?" I yell. "As I remember, I was the one in a fetal position on the floor in his office, writhing in pain."

"That's only because you decided to attack his desk safe with your balls," he says breezily.

"You want me to apologize to his safe?"

He does his special version of the stink eye, where he tilts his glasses forward and glares over the top of them. "Ari knows you were trying to defend Jeannie's honor. He's not angry. In fact, he thought your misguided chivalry was quaint."

"Fuck him!" I scream. "I'll show him quaint."

Terrance shouts back, "Grow the fuck up!" (He pronounces it FAHK.) He's the only guy I know who can sound genteel while he's cursing you out. "This isn't the schoolyard and you're not the class clown." He points to the door. "Go tell Ari you're sorry then come back here. I have some things I want to go over with you, Nicky and Jeannie."

"Forget it. I'm not working with them."

A deep sigh. "What happened now?"

"Do you know they're seeing each other?"

"Yes, they told me. But so what? You're not involved with her. In fact, you made it a point to tell Nicky and me, and half the agency, that you had no interest in her romantically."

"That's not the point. They're supposed to be my friends. Friends confide in each other. Then I find out that they're seeing each other and everyone knows. Everyone but me. What the fuck is that? Whatever it is, it's not friendship."

"And that's why you're leaving the agency?"

"I don't work with people who screw me."

"What will you do for money?"

"I got a nice little severance package from Rivette. That should hold me for a while."

"If this is really what you want to do, I can't stop you."

"You're damn right, you can't."

"Then there's nothing more to say." He shakes his head sadly. "You're an extremely talented man but, unfortunately, a total buffoon. Good luck." He walks out.

I give him a couple of minutes to get back to his office. Then I head for the rear staircase.

When I get outside, I feel liberated. Even the air smells like freedom, though the back door opens into an alley filled with a dozen overflowing garbage cans. I guess freedom really is another word for having nothing left to lose, except maybe your sense of smell.

CHAPTER THIRTY-TWO

"Hey, Moish," I yell as I open the door. "I'm back." I flip on a light. No sign of the old guy. But at least the place hasn't been ransacked. I figure he's over at Ruthie's, doing whatever it is old people do on dates. I don't want to think too hard about it.

I'm pacing back and forth wearing a hole, make that another hole, in the living room rug. I guess after working twelve hours a day, seven days a week, for the better part of a month, it's hard to come down. This is probably what it feels like being in combat, though thanks to either unbelievably good luck or a colossal clerical fuckup, I'll never know for sure.

I stayed in college a whole extra year, hoping Nixon would end the war in Vietnam like he said he would. No such luck. Then they came up with the draft lottery. If you got a high number, you were safe. The cutoff my year was 125. I was number 71. Right after I graduated I got a love letter from my draft board telling me I was reclassified from 2-S, the student deferment, to the dreaded 1-A, fresh meat. The next letter would be to tell me where to report for my physical. It was time to pack my bags. To Vietnam or Canada—that was the question. Could I really leave everything and run away to the frozen north? There were a lot of anti-war activists willing to help you along the way in those days, but still, the idea of being a fugitive in a strange place seemed pretty scary. Then again, the idea of being a soldier in a stranger place, and getting my ass shot up in a rice paddy by a bunch of midgets in black pajamas, sounded even less appealing.

A few weeks later, it came. My hand shook as I held the envelope. As I slowly tore it open I could taste the bile in my mouth. My heart was blasting inside my chest. I thought, this could be a good thing, maybe I'll get a heart attack. If I don't die, it'll be my ticket out.

Then blackness turned to light. Instead of telling me to report to Fort Hamilton for my government-sponsored ass probing, it said that I was reclassified 1-H. I had no idea what that meant so I looked it up. It said, "Registrant not currently subject to processing for induction." I had no idea why and the last thing I wanted to do was to call my draft board to ask. That would be like asking the teacher if she really didn't want to give the class any homework. If it was a bureaucratic fuckup (that's my guess) I had no intention of correcting it.

Rivette's fuckup is a different story. I honestly believe he made a huge mistake firing me and Nicky and going with his old college pal. Nielsen's a washed-up, arrogant has-been. He might have been a decent advertising guy back when radio was king, but now I bet he couldn't tell a good TV spot from a bad liver spot. It would be like hiring Joe DiMaggio today to be the Yankees center fielder. And, on a personal note, I'm gonna miss Rivette. He's the cool father I wish I had. I decide to call Sangster and see if he can get me back onto Team Rivette. I actually think he considers me a friend, as much as he can be friends with anyone.

I dial the number. "Hey, Urban, it's Stew."

"Uh . . . yes . . . hello." He sounds even more disjointed than usual.

"I guess you heard I won't be working with you anymore."

There's a long pause, then, "Yes."

"Is there anything you can do to get me reinstated? I know Nielsen's not my biggest fan, but I thought we were a great team. And the results speak for themselves."

Again he doesn't answer for several seconds, like he's processing this information. "Uh . . . um . . . we're scheduled to fly to Connecticut tomorrow."

What that has to do with anything I have no idea. "Maybe you can talk to Mr. Rivette on the plane."

Dead air for about twenty seconds. I think maybe I lost the connection or he hung up on me. Then he says, his voice quivering, "Stewart, I don't know what to do."

"Just ask if I can come back and work with you. Maybe we don't even have to tell Nielsen."

"Not about that."

"Then what?"

"I received another threat. Worse than the others. Much worse."

"Rivette's positive it's Monahan's people just trying to rattle you."

Another very long pause. "Do you own a firearm?"

Whoa! I didn't see that coming. "You mean like a gun? What makes you think I'd have a gun?"

"I just thought . . . you just seem like a person who might own one, being from Brooklyn and all."

"I never fired a gun in my life," I scream. "I've never even held one in my hand."

"I don't suppose you'd know where I can obtain one."

"Not off the top of my head, but if you're really serious I guess I can ask around. I'll let you know in a couple of days."

"I need it tonight."

"I can't just pick up the phone and order up a gun like it was a pizza and have it delivered in half an hour."

"Can you order a pizza that way? I had no idea."

"Urban, get a grip!" I yell. "Forget about pizza. Why the hell would you want a gun?"

"The voice on the phone, it was so threatening, so trenchant."

Trenchant. Who uses words like that? "What did he say?"

"He said if Edward doesn't drop out of the race immediately, we'd be shot. I think his exact words were, 'There's a bullet with Rivette's name on it. And one for you too.'"

"Sounds a little melodramatic. You sure you didn't confuse it with something you saw in a Humphrey Bogart movie?"

"I'm happy you find this amusing. I do not."

"Listen, Urban, if you think these threats are real, call the police."

"Edward absolutely forbade it. He said that's exactly what the other side wants us to do. That it would portray him as weak."

"I don't know what to tell you. What time do you leave tomorrow?"

"We're scheduled to depart at 6:30 a.m., but I'm contemplating not going. This entire situation has made me ill. I haven't eaten or slept. I have a constant headache. In fact, I'm seriously considering leaving the campaign."

Shit! If Urban drops out of the campaign, it reduces my chances of getting back on Team Rivette to zero.

"C'mon, Urban, that's exactly what the bastards want you to do. The threats are bogus. Edward's sure of it and so am I. He told me you're the one person he can't do without. You're his right-hand man. The Robin to his Batman, the Abbott to his Costello. Didn't you tell me that Rivette was like a big brother to you—that when you were kids he always stood up for you? Now it's your chance to stand up for him. He needs you, Urban. You can't desert him now."

Silence. Finally he says, "You're correct, of course."

"All right, then."

"I would still be grateful if you could provide me with a handgun."

"I can't do anything tonight. But I'll ask around and see if I can find you one."

He hangs up, no goodbye.

CHAPTER THIRTY-THREE

It's nine in the morning and still no Moish. I'm pretty sure he's at Ruthie's. Where else could he be? But suppose he didn't go there. I just assumed. And you know what happens when you assume. Okay, now I'm getting worried. The downside of having a creative mind is that at times like this you create all kinds of doomsday scenarios. He could've had a heart attack. He could've been mugged. He could've crashed his car into a telephone pole. I know I've been through this before but that doesn't mean that this time it's not true. I gotta call Ruthie or I'll drive myself crazy.

Where the hell is that decrepit old phone book of his? The one with Shifty's number. I go into his bedroom and start rummaging through the drawers. It's a total mishmash. Socks, underwear, pajamas all mixed together in every drawer, along with toothpicks, matchbooks, medicine bottles, an unopened half-pint of peppermint schnapps and dozens of losing tickets from every racetrack within a hundred-mile radius. Everything but my father's dilapidated little black book. Fuck it, I dial Long Island information.

The information operator gives me Ruth Berns's number in Valley Stream. I dial it.

"Hello, Ruth, it's Stew Gribnitz."

She sounds wary. "Stewart, dear, how are you? It's been such a long time since I heard your voice. Is everything all right?"

"Everything's fine. I was just wondering if my father is there."

"Your father? Moish?" she says, taken aback. "I haven't seen Moish since poor Sylvia's funeral. What makes you think he would be here?"

Whoa! What the fuck? "Well, uh . . . I uh . . . I was under the impression that you and Moish had gotten reacquainted. That you were seeing each other."

"We most certainly are *not*!" Confusion morphed into indignation. "And even if we were, he would hardly be spending the night under any circumstances."

"Oh, uh . . . I'm very sorry to have bothered you, Ruth. I'll say goodbye now."

"Goodbye, Stewart." I hear a click but I bet on her side it was more of a slam.

What the hell's going on? I don't know whether to be worried or pissed off. Either he's a total fucking liar or he's totally bonkers. I'm trying to figure it out when the phone rings. Maybe it's Moish.

"Hello."

"It's awful. I can't believe it." It's Nicky.

"What?"

"You haven't heard about the crash?"

I shriek, "Oh my God! I knew it. I should have done something."

"There's nothing you could have done. It was just a terrible accident."

"Who called? The police? Did they try to find me at the office?"

"No, I heard it on the radio."

"The radio? What the fuck? They should have called me first."

"Why should they call you? They probably called the next of kin."

"I *am* the next of kin."

"How the hell are you Rivette's next of kin?"

"Rivette? I thought you were talking about Moish."

"Who said anything about Moish?"

"Rivette? Holy shit! What exactly did you hear?"

"There was a plane crash this morning. Three people. Two passengers and the pilot. No survivors."

"Are they sure it was them? People are flying in and out of East Hampton airport all the time."

"The radio said the plane was registered to Edward Rivette."

I'm trying to wrap my brain around all this. "It's my fault he's dead."

"What are you talking about?"

"Sangster called me last night, scared shitless. He didn't want to go. I hounded him into it."

"Whoa. Back up. What was he afraid of?"

"Death threats."

"You mean like the rock through the window?"

"No, worse. Much worse. A voice on the phone said if Rivette didn't drop out of the race neither one of them would live to see the end of the week."

"He thought they were serious?"

"Dead serious. Then he asked me if I could get him a gun."

"What did you tell him?"

"I said I had no clue where to get a gun, but I was sure he had nothing to worry about. Rivette was adamant that the threats were bogus. Just Monahan's people trying to derail the campaign."

"Rivette did say that. I heard him myself."

"We all heard him. But Sangster didn't buy it. Not after this last call. There was no way he was getting on that plane. Until I badgered him into it."

"What did you say?"

"I kept telling him everything was fine. I played on his guilt. I said he owes Rivette. And now he needed him more than ever. That if he didn't go he was being disloyal to his lifelong best friend. That Rivette had his back since they were kids and he couldn't leave him in the lurch now."

He stifles a laugh. "You really said 'lurch,' like in the Addams Family?"

"I don't remember what I said. All I know is I said it for the wrong reasons. Sure, I like Rivette and I want to see him win, but that's not why I bullied Sangster into it. It was totally selfish. I wanted my job back and I thought he could help me. If I would've kept my big fucking mouth shut, he never would have set foot on that plane.

Maybe Rivette wouldn't have either. Now they're both dead and it's my fault."

"That's ridiculous. The radio said it was an accident."

"Bullshit. Monahan did it. I don't know how, but he did."

"Then you gotta tell the police."

"Tell them what? That I heard that Urban Sangster and Edward Rivette were getting anonymous death threats and I'm sure it was Neil Monahan. The same Neil Monahan who is the Connecticut federal prosecutor, former FBI bigwig and current Democratic candidate for governor. By the way, the only two people who can verify my story are dead and I was recently in police custody on suspicion of murder."

"When you put it that way, I have a hard time believing you."

"Tell me about it."

"So what are you gonna do?"

"I dunno, but I have to do something. Urban was as weird as they come, but I liked him. And Rivette, he was my fucking idol. I'm not gonna let the Monahans get away with it. I'll figure out what to do as soon as I find Moish."

"He's missing again?"

"He wasn't here when I got in last night and he's still not here."

"I wouldn't worry about it. He's probably with his new girlfriend that you told me about."

"That's what I thought, so I called her. She said she hasn't seen him since my mother's funeral."

"That was a couple of years ago, right?"

"Yeah, three and change."

"Maybe she's lying."

"Why would she lie?"

"If you were a going out with Moish, wouldn't you lie?"

He has a point but I'm not buying it. "She sounded pretty serious. She seemed insulted that I would even think that she was seeing my father socially."

He doesn't say anything for about ten seconds. "I wouldn't worry about it. He's been missing before and he's always been fine."

"But what about lying about Ruthie? Maybe his mind is going."

"I think it's your mind. Subconsciously you want your father dead. It's an Oedipus thing."

"Thank you, Sigmund Coletti."

"After twenty-five years of psychoanalysis I know a little something about it."

"All right, forget about Moish? You're probably right. Not about that psychological mumbo jumbo but that he'll show up when he's good and ready."

"Good."

"But I'm not letting go of this other thing. I know Monahan is somehow behind that plane crash and I'm gonna prove it."

He doesn't say anything for a few seconds, then, "Don't you have a friend who lives out there in the Hamptons? A newspaper guy?"

"Joe Glennum. What about him?"

"You should call him. He might have some more information about what happened."

"That's actually not the worst idea I've heard. I'm calling him as soon as I hang up."

"Good. I gotta go anyway. Keep me posted."

"One more thing."

"Yeah?"

"I'm sorry I went crazy about you and Jeannie. It just took me by surprise. She's a great kid. I just thought she had better taste than to be attracted to a mook like you."

"Fuck you, hump." Click.

I hunt around for Glennum's business card. I finally find it in the back pocket of dungarees I threw in the hamper.

"Hullo." The voice sounds like a mummy with a migraine.

"Joe Glennum, please."

"This is Glennum."

"Joe, it's Stew Gribnitz. You sound like shit."

"Thanks for the kind words. But for the record, I feel worse."

"You sick or something?"

"I'm exhausted. I haven't slept more than an hour any night in the past two weeks."

"What's going on?"

"Somebody's trying to put me out of business."

"Who?"

"The new owner of the *Southampton Sun* hired my entire staff away from me: two reporters, my graphics guy, my typesetter, the sales gal, even the guy who makes my deliveries. Offered each of them a 25 percent bump in salary and a $1,000 signing bonus."

"And you have no idea who it is?"

"I have a hunch."

"What are you gonna do?"

"I'm trying to hang on."

"How?"

"I spoke to everyone I know in the business. Out here, in the city, even my old pal Patrick who's at a paper in Sedona, Arizona. I might get a couple of people to come here in a week or two. In the meantime, I'm working twenty hours a day, writing, editing, laying out the paper, begging my advertisers not to leave. Then, once a week at three thirty in the morning, I drive over to the printers in Riverhead, pick up the new edition, and drop off the bundles at every godforsaken deli and convenience store on the East End. I just got back."

"No wonder you sound like shit." Should I even mention the death threats? One more thing on his plate and the guy will probably keel over and have a heart attack. Then I figure . . . what the fuck. "Did you hear about the plane crash?"

"Are you kidding? Of course. When you're a newspaperman and a plane goes down in your backyard you hear about it. Especially if a guy like Rivette was on it."

"Any news?"

"The plane crashed into the Sound five minutes after it took off. It'll take a while to haul out what's left of it. We probably won't know anything more until tomorrow at the earliest. From my experience with the NTSB, it'll be a week, maybe more."

"Any chance of survivors?"

"I doubt it. From what I hear, it exploded on impact."

Here it comes. "Did you know Rivette was getting death threats?"

Nothing for a few seconds. Then, in as excited a voice as a half-dead man can muster, "I had no idea."

"He got one last night. It said if he didn't drop out of the race he'd never live to see the end of the week, much less Election Day."

"Who else besides you knows about this?"

"Just Rivette and Sangster. Sangster was panic-stricken. Rivette brushed it off. He thought it was Monahan's people trying to throw him off his game."

"I guess he was wrong." There's a slight chuckle.

"If you don't mind my saying so, you don't seem too broken up."

"I think Rivette was the one trying to put me out of business. Still, if I break the death threat story it'll put the *Eagle* on the map. Rivette would do a 360 in his watery grave if he knew his death saved my paper."

"So do it. Nobody else knows about it."

"A piece like that needs a full-time reporter to do the legwork, talk to everyone involved, double-check the facts. Days of work. Right now I don't have time to take a leak, much less take on a major story with national implications."

I get a brain flash. "I'll do it."

"You already have a job."

"Actually, I don't. I'd been working freelance on the Rivette campaign but I got let go a couple of days ago."

"What about the agency?"

"They shitcanned me right after my bogus arrest for Persons's murder. Bad for business to have a suspected killer on staff."

"But you were never charged."

"Doesn't matter. In advertising, the truth is something you work around. Once clients saw my snarling face on the front pages of the *Post* and *News*, I was toast. The fact that I had nothing to do with it is inconsequential."

"That's just not fair."

"Fairness is right up there with truth on the list of things that don't matter in advertising."

"Jeez. Makes the newspaper business look good."

"What can I say?"

"If you really want to come out here and give me a hand, I could sure use the help."

"Just remember, I'm an ad guy. I don't know anything about being a reporter."

"You know how to write. You'll figure out the reporting part. Besides, Woodward and Bernstein aren't available. All I can pay you is $200 a week."

"Sold. It's more than I'm making now. I'll need a place to crash. Is there a cot in the newspaper office?"

"I can get you a room in my friend's motel for fifty bucks a week. Can you handle that?"

"When do I start?"

"How soon can you get here?"

"I can leave today. I need to pack some stuff then get to Penn Station."

He pauses for a few seconds. "You don't have a car?"

"Is that a problem?"

More dead air. I'm thinking maybe he fell asleep. "There's not a lot of public transportation out here. You can use my delivery van. There's a train that leaves Penn around two o'clock. If you make it you'll be here a little after five. Don't miss it. The next train is three hours later."

"I'll be on it. Don't worry."

CHAPTER THIRTY-FOUR

How hard can it be to be a reporter? It's the same as writing advertising copy but you can actually tell the truth. That should make it easier. Writing always came easy to me. In the sixth grade I wrote a story about George Washington that won a Best of Brooklyn award. In high school I wrote a love poem to Sherry Herbert comparing her green eyes to shimmering emerald pools. That was the first time I got laid. My first two years in college, the only thing that kept me off probation was the fact that I kept getting A's in English to offset my dismal performance in every other subject. I just never thought that writing was actually something you could do to earn a living.

Everyone told me that science and math were the classes to take if you wanted to earn the big bucks. After I screwed those up, just barely eking out D's, I tried psychology, sociology and anthropology. I managed to get C's in those. My academic advisor sat me down and told me that if I didn't switch my major to English I'd flunk out.

Hemingway is my favorite writer and he started as a journalist. I always wanted to follow in his footsteps. File stories from war-torn Europe, carouse around in Paris bistros and scribble iconic novels on bar napkins. But I never worked on the school paper or even took a journalism class, so I figured the news biz wasn't in the cards. I did spend a huge amount of time in front of the TV, which means I watched a shitload of commercials. So I figured I'd be a natural at writing ads.

My mother's friend's nephew Morty was a media buyer at Scali and he got me a part-time job as a messenger there. A young hotshot copywriter took me under his wing after he found out that my best friend was one of the biggest pot dealers in Brooklyn. I got him great weed and he taught me how to write advertising copy. It was a good deal all around.

So now maybe I'll get to live out my Hemingway fantasies after all, not that the chichi Hamptons will remind anyone of war-torn Europe, but it's something. I'm just about finished packing my duffle bag when the doorbell rings, which is weird because nobody ever visits here unannounced. In fact, nobody ever visits announced. I'm thinking Jehovah's Witnesses. I used to love to try to convince them that God didn't exist. "Then how did all this happen?" they'd ask earnestly. "The sky, the ocean, the mountains, you, me?" I'd shrug my shoulders and say, "I have no idea, but that doesn't prove there's a God. It just proves we don't know." I'd point to the TV. "I can push a button and suddenly pictures and voices come out of that box. Seems like a miracle to me. Maybe we should all pray to Sony."

I open the door. The two guys on the other side of the threshold look more like linebackers than Jehovah's Witnesses. They're both about my height but twice as wide. One's black, the other's white. The white guy's about my age, mid-thirties. His head's shaved, probably trying to hide that he's going bald. His nose looks like it's been broken, maybe more than once. His gut is hanging just a little over his belt. I'm betting the sneer is a more or less permanent fixture. The black guy could be the stand-in for a young Muhammad Ali, a little shorter and stockier but with the same pretty toughness.

"You Gribnitz?" the white one says.

"Yeah. Who are you?"

"FBI. Pristera and Raines." They flick their IDs at me then put them away before I can see anything. Nicky could make better fake IDs than those in about a half hour.

I look from one to the other. "What's going on?"

Pristera ignores this. "What's your relationship with Urban Sangster?"

"He was a business associate and a friend."

"You work on the Rivette campaign, right?"

"Used to. I've been relieved of my responsibilities."

"So you got a grudge against Ed Rivette?"

"Not really. We got along well."

"So why'd he fire you?"

"He didn't."

"Who did?"

I'm starting to get pissed. "What's it to you?"

He looks over my shoulder at the duffle bag on the floor. "Going somewhere?"

"Are you an FBI agent or a travel agent? Where I'm going is none of your fucking business. Now, what the hell do you want?"

"Ed Rivette's plane crashed this morning. Rivette and Sangster were killed."

"I heard. What does that have to do with me?"

"A note was found among Sangster's effects. All it said was 'Gribnitz gun.' What do you know about that?"

"He called me last night, wanted to know where he could get a gun."

"What for?"

"To protect himself. He obviously didn't trust you law enforcement types to keep him safe. Looks like he was right."

The black one, Raines, gives me the stink eye. "What are you trying to say?"

"Neil Monahan was a big shot in the FBI. Now he's the federal prosecutor for Connecticut. That makes him your boss. He's also the person who benefits most from Rivette being out of the picture. Sangster probably thought that you spend so much time covering Monahan's crooked ass that you wouldn't have much room left for the non-felons in the race. Maybe if you were watching out for them instead of hassling me, they'd still be alive."

Pristera grits his teeth and glares. "You think you're real smart, don't you?"

"Not really. I don't have to be that smart to be smarter than you."

He tenses, takes a step toward me. His partner grabs his arm. "Forget it. He's just a wiseass punk."

Pristera thinks about it and backs off. "That's the second suspicious death that has your stench on it, Gribnitz. One could be a coincidence. Two makes you a suspect."

"You don't know what you're talking about. The Persons thing was bullshit. I was nowhere near his place when he got killed. And if you think I could've got to the Hamptons, figured out how to crash the plane, and got back here to deal with you two bozos, you're even dumber than you look."

Pristera grinds his teeth and glares at me. "Watch your mouth."

"Or what?"

"You don't want to find out."

"I'll tell you what I think. I think your pal Monahan had something to do with that crash. Wasn't he a pilot or something in Vietnam? I bet he could fuck up a plane real easy."

That hit home. Now they're both glaring at me.

Pristera's hands, still at his sides, are balled into tight fists. "Talk like that can get a scumbag like you in real trouble."

"Why, because it's true?"

"Do yourself a huge favor. Forget you ever met Rivette or even heard of Neil Monahan. Next time we see you we won't be so polite."

"What's it to you whether or not I had anything to do with Rivette?"

Raines, who's been pretty quiet up to now, glares at me and says, "Keep doing what you're doing and you'll find out."

They leave and don't even bother to close the door. They head for a big blue Plymouth Fury.

Me and the cops, we never got along. Back in my long-haired hippie days, they'd hassle me and my friends all the time, looking for drugs. We never had any on us, always got high in the house before we went out. I'm pretty sure they knew it but they rousted us anyway, for their own amusement. After a while I turned the tables on them. I'd give them the Eddie G. routine from *Little Caesar* or the Jimmy Cagney from *White Heat*—"You got nuttin' on me, coppah. I'm clean . . . see . . . I'm clean."

My friends would all crack up and the cops got really pissed. They hate it when they can't intimidate you. But what could they do, arrest me for bad gangster impressions?

I'm about to slam the door when Moish pulls up and bounds out of the car with a big smile. He glances back as the two feds pull away. "Friends of yours?"

I shake my head. "Not likely."

"They're either gangsters or cops," he says as he walks past me and goes to the kitchen. He grabs a bottle of iced tea from the refrigerator and makes a beeline for his chair. "Gotta be cops," he declares. "Gangsters drive better cars." He takes a swig, then gives me his patented smirk. "What happened, you kill somebody else?"

"They're FBI. But never mind that. Where were you all night?"

"Who the hell are you to give me the third degree?" he yells back. "I don't hear from you for two weeks. No phone call, nothing. I coulda had a heart attack for all you know. Then you show up and interrogate me like I'm the criminal in the family. You're the one they arrested, not me."

"I was never arrested, they just brought me in for questioning."

"The paper said you're a murderer."

I'm about to get into a screaming match with him, which I realize is just what he wants. The sneaky old bastard got me totally off track. I take a breath and say, "This isn't about me. I know you weren't at Ruthie's. I called her. She said she hasn't seen you since Mom's funeral. What the hell's going on?"

He screams, "How dare you check up on me, you little pisher!" He shakes the bottle at me, getting iced tea all over himself, me and the chair. "Where I go and what I do is none of your goddamn business." He bangs the bottle on the table, spilling what's left.

I grab my duffle bag. "I gotta go."

"Good! Go!" he shouts at my back as I storm out. "Don't hurry back. And don't bother to call."

I get to the door, turn around, and shout, "Don't worry. I won't." And slam it behind me.

PART TWO

The Eastern Tip of Long Island

CHAPTER THIRTY-FIVE

About a dozen people get off at the East Hampton Long Island Rail Road station with me. Most walk over to the parking lot, a couple jump into the waiting taxis. No sign of Glennum. I head for the lot. It's pretty empty. A few beat-up jalopies are scattered around. Station cars. Then I see a yellow VW Vanagon with flowers stenciled randomly on the door, the hood, the side panels, even the roof. A small magnetic sign, "East Hampton Eagle," is attached to the side door. I walk over and there's Glennum, sprawled out on the front seat, hopefully asleep and not dead. (Lately, people seem to have a way of dying after they talk to me.) I open the unlocked door and tap him on the shoulder.

He bolts up. "Stew, glad you could make it. Sorry I wasn't there to meet you but I gotta catch my *Z*s anytime I can."

"Are you okay?"

"Oh yeah. I'm training myself to sleep in fifteen-minute increments. I should be fine for a few hours." He gets out, grabs my duffle bag, and throws it in the back of the van.

I gesture up at the van. "Is this a remnant from your hippie days?"

He shakes his head. "Nah. I picked it up a couple of years ago."

"The flowers are a cute touch."

"Not my doing. It used to be a florist's delivery truck."

"Back in the day I thought it would be cool to get one of these, stick a mattress in the back, pick up chicks, and go on adventures."

"How'd that work out for you?"

"Never got the car. Never got the chicks. And most of my adventures wound up with me passed out on a floor somewhere in a pool of my own vomit."

"Maybe you'll have better luck this time around, 'cause while you're here this is your ride." He tosses me the keys.

"I'll sure intimidate the hell out of anyone I interview, pulling up in my flower child chariot."

"You're not supposed to intimidate them. You're supposed to make them feel comfortable, put them at ease."

"All I need is a couple of doobies and a lava lamp."

He smiles. "Whatever works. But right now we gotta go."

"Go? After three-plus hours on a rickety train, a man builds up a thirst. The only place I wanna go is for a drink."

"It'll have to wait till later. Right now we gotta get to the airport. There's a press conference scheduled for five thirty." He looks at his watch. "It probably already started."

"I thought there were only two newspapers in town. Why the hell do they need a press conference?"

"The plane crash is a huge story. We got TV, radio and newspaper reporters from all over. Ed Rivette's been in the public eye for twenty years, well before he ever thought of running for governor of Connecticut."

"Do you really think this is gonna be that big?"

"We'll be lucky if we can find a place to park."

East Hampton Airport is at the end of a long one-lane road. The terminal looks like a railroad station, except there's a runway where the tracks should be. I don't see a tower anywhere. All you'd need is a couple of cows on the big grassy field behind it and you'd think you were in Iowa. With all these billionaires flying in and out you'd think they could have built something a little bit more splashy.

The tiny parking lot is jammed. There are cars and news vans parked ten deep on the grass. We find a spot way in the back under some trees. As we're getting out, Glennum hands me a laminated card.

"What's this?"

"Your press pass."

I turn it over and in big block letters it says, "EAST HAMPTON EAGLE—OFFICIAL PRESS," then my name, the date and a picture of me that makes my driver's license photo look like it was done by Scavullo.

"Sorry about your photo. I got it off the newswire. It's when you went to the police station."

"Whatever. What does it entitle me to?"

He gives me a big smile. "Absolutely nothing."

"So what's the point?"

"It might get a couple of people to talk to you instead of telling you to drop dead."

"Does it work with women?"

"Not in my experience. But it's worth a try."

There's a makeshift podium in front of the terminal with microphones jutting out every which way, like snakes from Medusa's head. Eight rows of folding chairs, ten to a row, are on the infield facing it and there's a heinie in every seat. Me and Glennum, along with a dozen other latecomers, stand in back.

Five people in various stages of obesity are squeezed onto the small platform: Three older guys in dark suits and sour expressions, looking like they just came from an undertakers' convention, and a middle-aged woman who's the spitting image of Mrs. Murphy, my anti-Semitic fourth grade history teacher, same dull gray hair, severe eyes, and a mouth in a permanent frown.

Standing at the mics is a youngish, military-looking guy in a blue jumpsuit.

"Who are those people up there?" I whisper to Glennum.

"The guy in blue is from the NTSB."

"I probably coulda figured that out from the big yellow N-T-S-B letters plastered across his chest. What about the rest?"

"Local bigwigs. The town supervisor, the village administrator and the chief of police. They live for times like this."

We get a *shhhh* and a dirty look from the woman standing next to us who bears a striking resemblance to the Wicked Witch of the West.

We shut up and try to catch some of what the NTSB guy is saying.

"As we are still in the early phases of our investigation, we can't rule anything out; however, at this time there is no indication of foul play. This particular aircraft has a history of rudder malfunction, which is consistent with the eyewitness accounts of the crash trajectory. The airplane broke apart on impact. There were two passengers listed on the manifest, Edward Rivette and Urban Sangster, along with the pilot, Steven Carberry. No survivors have been located as of yet, but rescue and recovery efforts continue at the crash site on Long Island Sound." He looks out at the crowd. "Now, if there are any questions."

Dozens of hands shoot up. He smiles and points to a pretty young thing in the front row.

She stands. "Beth DiGiorno, *Newsday*. Was there any radio contact before the crash?"

Before he can answer, the blare of a siren cuts him off and a green-and-white ambulance rumbles down the infield and skids to a stop next to the podium. A couple of town cops who were dozing behind us jump up and start running toward it. Everyone's looking around, talking, shouting. Then, as if somebody pulled a switch—silence—as Ed Rivette steps out of the passenger door and walks slowly up to the podium.

There's a collective gasp.

He shakes his head sadly and leans into the mic. "I'm very sorry to have made this melodramatic entrance but it seemed like the most effective way to set the record straight." He looks out at the audience and sighs deeply. "Shortly before I was scheduled to take off for Connecticut this morning I was overcome with severe chest pains. I thought I was having a heart attack. My assistant, Ms. Lepro, drove me to the hospital where I have been undergoing tests all day. Turns out it was an unusually severe asthma attack. It wasn't until half an hour ago that I learned about the terrible crash and about this news conference. I asked to be brought here immediately."

Someone shouts, "If you weren't in the plane, who was?"

"I'm devastated to report that two of my closest and dearest friends were onboard. Urban Sangster, my cousin, my best friend and the marketing director of my company and my campaign, whom I have known since we both frolicked on these Hampton beaches as young children, and Harvey Nielsen, who was my fraternity brother at Princeton and has been in charge of all my marketing efforts since I started in business. They are two of the finest men I have ever known. Their untimely deaths are a horrendous tragedy."

"Do you suspect foul play?"

"Absolutely not!" he says emphatically. "I'm sure it was nothing more than a terrible accident." He glances over at the NTSB guy. "Unless, of course, the investigation discovers something to the contrary."

There's a cacophony of bellowed questions, all pretty much unintelligible. Then, above the din, a female voice shouts, "What about your campaign?"

"I realize that it should have been me on that plane." Rivette looks up at the sky. "I believe the good Lord spared me because he has other plans for me. And I believe that part of his plan is for me to provide a better future for the men and women of Connecticut. So yes, I will continue my campaign with renewed vigor. I will win the governorship and dedicate the victory to Urban Sangster and Harvey Nielsen, so that their sacrifice will not have been in vain."

There's another flurry of shouted questions. Rivette waves his hand and says, "Please. As a member of the fourth estate myself, I try never to be short with the press. But I beg your indulgence this one time." He looks mournfully out at the crowd. "This has been a very tragic, very sad and very exhausting day for me. I need time to try to make some sense out of everything that has happened and grieve for these two men whom I loved like brothers." He pulls a monogrammed, powder-blue silk handkerchief out of his pocket and dabs at his eyes. "The next time I meet with you, I promise no question will go unanswered." He gives a half-hearted wave. "Thank you." He walks off the podium and climbs into a gorgeous cream-colored vintage convertible, which I found out later is a 1933 Duesenberg Model J Convertible Coupe. Sharon Lepro is at the wheel.

I turn to Glennum. "That crash was no fucking accident! Monahan sabotaged that plane. The only accident was that Nielsen went down with it and not Rivette."

He smiles at me. "So prove it. This is your chance. The NTSB is going to declare it to be a case of rudder malfunction. You'll get no help from law enforcement. Monahan's a federal prosecutor and a former FBI bigwig. Those people take care of their own."

"What about some of those other reporters? If Monahan's guilty, it's a huge story."

"Right now it's a one-day story. 'Asthma Attack Saves Candidate.'"

"What about those death threats?"

"Nobody knows about them but you, Sangster and Rivette. Sangster's dead and you said Rivette refuses to say anything."

"Maybe after this he'll change his mind."

"One way to find out. Talk to him."

"Now?"

He shakes his head. "You can go see him tomorrow."

"Where to now?"

"I'll buy you that drink then show you to your new digs."

CHAPTER THIRTY-SIX

"I have a collect call for anyone from Stewart Grivens."

"What? Who?" Nicky sounds confused. "You mean Stew Gribnitz?"

"Just say yes," I yell into the phone.

The operator scolds me, "Please, sir."

"Yeah, I'll take it." There's a click when the operator hangs up and Nicky yells, "Whaddaya doin' calling me collect? Where the hell are you?"

"I'm in a motel lobby in East Hampton."

"It's almost midnight. What the hell are you doing there?"

"I came out here to work with Glennum. This is where I'm staying. You're the one who told me to call him. Remember?"

"That's why I'm shocked. You never do anything I tell you."

"There's always a first time."

"Look at you. In a big fancy hotel like James Bond. Did you check the room for bugs?"

"The only bugs here are roaches."

"Seriously?"

"I haven't seen one yet but I wouldn't be surprised. The place is pretty grungy. The paint's peeling off the walls and the bed's a little lumpy. But the shower's nice and hot and it's only fifty bucks a week so I'm not complaining."

"Do they have room service?"

"They don't even have a phone in the room. That's why I'm calling from the lobby."

"Oh." He sounds disappointed.

"Listen, I have news. Did you hear about Rivette?"

"Some reporter you are. That's an old story. I'm the one who told you that he and Sangster died in that plane crash."

"Wrong. Rivette's alive. It was Nielsen in the plane with Sangster."

"What? Nielsen?" he screams. "No fucking way!"

I tell him the whole story. Getting rousted by the FBI. The crazy press conference. Even my stupid confrontation with Moish before I left.

"Holy crap! What are you gonna do?"

"I'm through with that old bastard. I'm sick of being my father's parent. I'm not gonna waste any more time worrying about him."

"Not Moish. What are you gonna do out there?"

"Try to figure out a way to prove that Monahan sabotaged that plane."

"How the hell are you gonna do that?"

"I saw *All the President's Men*. I'll do what Woodward and Bernstein did."

"They had Deep Throat. All you got is deep doo-doo. Besides, they were real newsmen. You're an adman. What do you know about being a reporter?"

"I'll have you know I'm officially a card-carrying journalist. I have a card to prove it. What else do I need?"

"How about a fucking clue?"

"I'm hoping that comes later."

He doesn't say anything for a few seconds. Then he sighs and says, "You're really gonna do this?"

"Why not?"

"You'll be a gefilte fish out of water. You're a New York guy. What do you know about the Hamptons? You hate those rich phony bastards who live out there."

"They're only here in the summer. The only ones out here the rest of the year are the poor slobs who live and work here. I'll be right at home."

"Even so. Your life is in the city."

"What life? I have no job. No woman. I'm thirty-fucking-four years old and still living with my daddy. Out here there's a chance I might actually accomplish something."

"What are you talking about? We've accomplished a lot. Look at all the great ads we did."

"Great. We convinced a lot of people to buy a lot of crap they don't need. If I can prove that Monahan was behind that plane crash, that would be doing something important."

"That's a big if. You really think you can do it?"

"Probably not. But I didn't think I had a shot with Barbara and look how that turned out."

"Yeah. She ran back to Wisconsin after one night with you."

"But it was fun while it lasted."

"What? One night?"

"But it was a great night."

"This is serious. You really have to watch your ass. If this turns out to be the clusterfuck I think it's gonna be, you'll lose a lot more than a girl."

"I'm going with Bob Dylan. 'When you ain't got nothing, you got nothing to lose.'"

"How about your life? If it is murder, whoever killed Sangster and Nielsen won't think twice about killing you."

"Well, yeah, there is that."

The line goes silent for a few seconds. "If you're really gonna go through with this, what can I do to help?"

"Find out what you can about that Lepro creature. I don't trust her. I wouldn't be surprised if she's Monahan's spy."

"Anything else?"

"Maybe you can drive by Moish's house some night."

"You just said you were done with him."

"I am. But . . ."

"Yeah, I know. He's still your father. What should I say to him?"

"Don't say anything. Don't even stop. If he finds out I asked you, he wins."

"So what do you want me to do?"

"Just take a quick look. If there's no ambulance in front and the house didn't burn down that's all I need."

"I can do that. Meanwhile, try not to get yourself killed out there."

"I'll do my best."

CHAPTER THIRTY-SEVEN

It's after eleven. It took me a long time to fall asleep and an even longer time to wake up. I stopped at a luncheonette for some coffee and a muffin. Back home it would have been a bagel but nobody outside of New York City knows how to bake them. What they call bagels out in the sticks are just bready donuts.

I'm standing outside the *Eagle* building, which is on Main Street in East Hampton. I thought it would be a bustling thoroughfare with fancy, high-end shops like on Fifth Avenue or Rodeo Drive, but it's a quiet tree-lined street with a library on one side and an antique shop on the other. Both look like they were built during the Calvin Coolidge administration.

I walk in, slamming the heavy wooden door behind me, which rouses Glennum from deep slumber. Sprawled back on his chair with his mouth open and feet spread-eagle on his desk, he bolts up and shakes his head like a wet dog. "Who? Oh, Stew, it's you. I guess you were able to find the place."

"Between your directions and the Hagstrom's you left me in the van, I only got lost twice, which for me is a home run."

His desk has papers, pads, folders and assorted other paraphernalia strewn all over it. There's a Macintosh computer in the middle of the mess, the same kind as I had at UPAN. On a shelf over the desk is a big, old Underwood typewriter, like the one Cary Grant used in *His Girl Friday*. There are four other desks scattered haphazardly around the room.

"Which one is my desk?"

He waves a hand across the room. "Any one you like." He points to a storage cabinet in the back corner. "Pens, notepads and anything else you need are in there."

I go over to the desk closest to the front window. Might as well have a view, even if it's just of the Episcopal church across the street.

Once upon a time way back in the roaring twenties, I bet this building was some rich bon vivant's vacation home. On Saturday-night soirees, flappers probably danced the Charleston right where I'm sitting.

"Ready to go see Rivette?"

"Sure."

"Do you know what you're gonna ask him?"

"I figure I'll see what he says then play it by ear."

"Maybe you should write a couple of questions down, just to be on the safe side."

"No, I'm all right."

He doesn't look convinced. But all he says is, "You've been to his place before, right?"

"Yeah."

"Can you find it again?"

"I doubt it."

"The Hagstrom's should help. There's also a couple of pens and reporter's notebooks in the glove box."

"I never take notes."

"You have a photographic memory?"

I shake my head. "I can hardly remember where I park my car from one hour to the next. That is, when I had a car." I pull out my mini voice recorder with a flourish. "That's why I use this."

"Good. That should come in handy. Just remember to turn it on."

CHAPTER THIRTY-EIGHT

By the time I find Rivette's bungalow-slash-mansion, it's a little after twelve. He opens the door holding a drink in one hand and a cigar in the other. Last time I was here he fired me. Who knows what kind of greeting I'll get this time.

I'm pleasantly surprised when his face lights up in a big smile and he says, "Stew Gribnitz, so good to see you."

For a guy who's supposedly grieving at the grisly death of his two closest pals, he's in very good spirits. As opposed to the somber black suit I was expecting, he's wearing a blue plaid blazer, tan turtleneck cashmere sweater and brown corduroy pants.

He puts the cigar in his mouth and pumps my hand. "Come in, come in." He beckons me into the great room. There's loud music blaring on the stereo.

"You know how much I appreciate American traditions. Are you familiar with New Orleans jazz funerals?"

I shake my head.

"In New Orleans they celebrate the lives of the deceased with music, dancing and a brass band parade. I'm no hoofer and a one-person parade seems rather inane, but I do own a record of the Dirty Dozen Brass Band. And so I'm having my own truncated New Orleans sendoff for Harvey and Bitsie. I much prefer it to bleak mourning rituals. Don't you?"

"Uh, yeah."

"I'm glad you could join me to pay tribute to our fallen comrades."

"Me too." The poor guy is losing it. I guess coming so close to ending it all by plunging into a watery fireball would knock anyone for a loop.

"Let me get you a drink?"

"I'm driving, maybe I shouldn't."

"Can I tempt you with a twenty-five-year-old Laphroaig?"

"You just made me an offer I can't refuse."

He smiles, strides over to the bar and pours about four fingers of the 104-proof golden nectar into a crystal goblet. He hands me the drink then gestures toward the VW van. "When I saw you pull up in that thing, I thought we were being invaded by hippies."

"It's not mine. It belongs to Joe Glennum. I'm working for him now."

His smile dissipates. "He decided to shut down that rag of his and get into advertising? The first smart thing he's done in years."

"No, he's still a newsman. I'm working for him at the *Eagle*. As a reporter."

"Really? I had no idea you were also a journalist."

"Until yesterday, I wasn't."

He looks bemused. "Why the sudden career change? You're an outstanding ad writer."

I coulda said, "'Cause you were my last hope and you fired my ass." But I just grin sheepishly and say, "Thanks, Mr. Rivette."

"Call me Ed."

"I spoke to Urban the evening before the crash. He told me there was another death threat. The worst one yet. He was terrified."

"Odd. He never mentioned it to me."

"He knew you didn't take them seriously. He didn't want to let you down." I don't mention that he was ready to bolt before I talked him into going on the death flight.

He takes a long swig of his Scotch. "Bitsie was extraordinarily loyal."

"When your plane went down I called Glennum and told him about the death threats."

"Why tell Glennum? Why didn't you call the police?"

"No cop would take my word over Monahan's. And I have no credibility with the media. The only thing they know about me is in connection with Persons's murder. Glennum is the only reporter who wanted to hear my side of the story."

"That still doesn't explain why he hired you."

"He's too busy trying to keep the paper afloat to do it himself."

"What about one of the other reporters on his staff?"

"They all left. It was me or no one."

His frown melts into a self-satisfied smirk. "Seems they have more sense than I gave them credit for."

"I'm getting the feeling that you're not Glennum's biggest fan."

He clenches his teeth. "The man is a no-talent hack." He shakes his head. "No, he'd have to improve considerably to qualify as a hack. He's a sleazy gossipmonger. His so-called newspaper is good for only two things, lining birdcages and wrapping fish."

"So I guess now that I'm working with him I'm on your shit list too."

"What I think of Glennum has nothing to do with my feelings for you. I consider you a friend."

"I appreciate your saying that. I feel the same about you." I walk over and shake his hand. "Glennum wants me to follow up on the plane crash. I'm gonna keep digging until I prove Monahan did it. Is that a problem for you?"

"Absolutely not."

"But you said at the press conference that you were certain it was an accident."

"Of course I said that. I can't accuse my opponent of murder. Not without ironclad evidence. I'd be accused of slander. My campaign would be in ruins."

"So you're okay with me looking into this?"

"Of course. In fact, I'll assist you in any way I can. But as far as the public is concerned, I can have nothing to do with your investigation."

"Understood." I take a last big gulp of scotch, feel it warm my body and sooth my brain. "I appreciate having you onboard with this." I get up to leave.

I think he's gonna say "good luck" or "keep me posted" or something like that, but he looks at me real seriously and says, "Steven Keating."

"Who's Steven Keating?"

"Ask Glennum." He walks me to the front door.

On the way back to the *Eagle* I stop at a pay phone and call Nicky. Collect.

"Next time I'm not gonna accept. You just got paid $50,000, you can afford to make a fucking phone call."

"The phone company can't make change for fifty grand, besides, you're at work, you're not even paying for it."

"Are you kidding? Now that Terrance is in charge, he's checking the phone bills, office supplies. I'm waiting for him to limit us to two pieces of toilet paper per shit."

"Fine. I'll pay you back when I see you. And I'll buy you a roll of Charmin. By the way, I found my Deep Throat."

"Really? Who?"

"Rivette."

"You said he thought the crash was an accident."

"I was wrong."

"What happened?"

"After the crash he had second thoughts. He said to keep it hush-hush because if it came out that he was accusing Monahan of murder it would ruin his campaign."

"That's it, I'm coming out there. If you're gonna be Bernstein, I gotta be Woodward."

"Don't be ridiculous. You know less about being a reporter than me. And I don't know anything. Besides, you have a full-time job."

"Good point."

"Anything yet about Lepro?"

"Jeannie's still working on it."

"Jeannie? Why'd you get her involved?"

"I'm an art director. What do I know about research? She's an account exec. That's what they do."

"I hate it when you make sense. It throws me off kilter."

"You were never on kilter."

"Let me know what she finds out."

"No, I'm gonna keep it a secret."

"One last thing."

"Yeah?"

"Go fuck yourself."

"I'm one of the few men who can."

CHAPTER THIRTY-NINE

"How'd it go with Rivette?" Glennum says as I walk into the *Eagle* office.

"Not too bad."

"Really? I figured he'd throw you out on your ass once you told him you were working with me."

"He's not your biggest fan, that's for sure. How long has this feud gone on?"

"A very long time. The Rivettes, the Sangsters and a few other blue-blood families have been summering out here for generations. There was always a bit of a rift between the summer people and the year-rounders. We didn't appreciate being treated like the hired help. But it wasn't until Eddie Rivette and his pals came of age that the antipathy festered into major hatred."

"What did they do that was so bad?"

"At first it was just typical frat boy shit. They'd get drunk, ride around in their fancy Jags, Benzes and Porsches blasting their twelve-speaker car stereos. They peed on people's lawns, threw beer bottles in the street, pilfered stuff from local merchants daring them to do something about it—obnoxious, annoying, infuriating, but nothing to get really crazy about. Then things got worse."

"Sounds pretty bad already."

"They threw huge parties on the beach, invited a lot of the younger girls from town. Don't forget, these were rich college boys, Ivy Leaguers. The bastards slipped drugs into their drinks. Quaaludes. When they passed out, they raped them. Sometimes they took Polaroids. The poor girls were traumatized. Some are still messed up all these years later." He shakes his head in disgust. "Rivette was the ringleader."

"Are you sure?"

"You mean do I have proof? No. But it was him."

"What about the police?"

"Bought and paid for. Besides, the Hamptons needed the Rivettes and their ilk. Without them this place would be just another sleepy beach town. The mayor, the chief of police, the town council, they were all on Rivette's father's payroll."

"So nobody did anything?"

A subtle smile edges across his face, not joyous but proud. "My father. He was the only one who stood up to those bastards."

"Your old man was a cop?"

"Hell no!" He looks insulted. "He was a newspaperman. A better one than I'll ever be. He was the editor and publisher of the *Eagle*." He looks up at the old Underwood on the shelf above his desk. "That was his typewriter. I keep it there to remind me why I'm here. Maybe one day I'll be good enough to earn one of those." He points to a couple of dusty plaques on the wall.

I walk over. It looks like they've been hanging there for a long time. There's a layer of dust, the brass is tarnished and the frames are dull and chipped. They're from the National Newspaper Association. One is an award for leadership. The other for journalistic excellence. Both for Henry Glennum.

"Pretty impressive."

"He was the only one who ever held those bastards accountable. And he paid for it. With his life."

"They killed him?"

"Nothing that obvious."

"What happened?"

"One of the girls, Kathy Keating, killed herself after one of those parties. She walked into the ocean. Her body washed up a couple of miles up the beach."

"Any relation to Steven Keating?"

He jumps like he's been hit with a cattle prod. "How do you know about Steve Keating? Looks like you're a better reporter than I gave you credit for."

"Finish your story. Then I'll tell you."

"My dad wrote a series of editorials about the caste system here. How the summer Brahmins aren't subject to the same rules as the rest of us. How their entitled, delinquent sons break our laws, vandalize our property and take advantage of our young women without ever having to answer for or even apologize for their transgressions. He said if the police had any guts, they would arrest the whole lot of them for creating a public nuisance and disturbing the peace. Then, when they found Kathy's body on the beach, that was it. He turned up the heat, started running his editorials on the front page. He never went so far as to call Ed Rivette a murderer. But he did write that the actions of Rivette and his friends were what drove her to kill herself."

"Your dad had guts. What was the outcome?"

Glennum shakes his head sadly. "Not good. Rivette's lawyers dropped a libel suit on us. Five million dollars. They said they'd drop the suit if my dad sold the *Eagle*. That paper was his life. He loved it. He couldn't bear the thought of being responsible for its demise. A newspaper chain bought it."

"I'm no lawyer, but I looked into the libel law after the New York papers labeled me a mad-dog killer. According to what I read, as long as he didn't print it as fact, there's no case."

"It doesn't matter. We couldn't afford to defend the suit. The legal fees would have bankrupted the paper. After he sold it, my dad went into a severe depression. He hardly ate, didn't sleep, never left the house. Six months later, he had a stroke. He held on for over a year but he never recovered. As far as I'm concerned, Rivette killed Kathy Keating and my father."

"No wonder why you hate the guy."

"Like I said, this feud goes back a long time."

"How'd you wind up back with the paper?"

"The people who bought it either didn't know what they were doing, didn't care or both. They were hemorrhaging money. They were going to close it down. When I heard, I scraped up some money and made them an offer. It wasn't much but I guess they thought it was better than nothing. So here I am, editor, publisher, ad manager and delivery boy."

"Wow."

"Enough ancient history, tell me how you know about Steve Keating."

"Not much to tell. As I was leaving Rivette's house, saying I was going to prove that Monahan was behind the plane crash, he didn't say goodbye or good luck. All he said was Steven Keating. Why would he say that?"

"If there's anybody who hates Rivette more than I do, it's Keating. He was Kathy's older brother and he never believed she committed suicide. He always maintained that Rivette killed her."

"He actually accused Rivette of murder?"

"To anyone that would listen."

"Did anybody follow through?"

"My father checked it out. There wasn't anything there. If there was, he would have found it and put it on the front page."

"So that was it?"

"Not by a long shot. A couple of weeks later, Steve jumped Rivette right here on Main Street. He beat the living shit out of him, gave him a concussion and a few cracked ribs. It took five cops to pry him off."

"So his sister kills herself and now he's looking at jail time. What a fucking mess for the family!"

"The thing is, he didn't go to jail. Steve was first-team all-county linebacker. Had a few scholarship offers."

"What does that have to do with anything?"

"The police chief coached him in Pop Warner. He was also a Korean War vet. He gave Steve a choice. The army or jail. He joined the next day."

"The Rivettes went along with that?"

Glennum nods. "It smoothed over a lot of bad feelings in town. It's all up in the archives. Wanna take a look?"

"Yeah, I'd love to."

"Follow me."

He takes me to a room on the second floor. It's dark, dusty and has the musty smell of old books. He hits a switch and a bare lightbulb bathes the room in an amber haze. The walls are layered floor to ceiling with big black leather binders. Each has a year stamped on the spine. In the center of the room is a big wooden table and a few chairs.

"I thought you'd have them on microfilm or microfiche or something like that."

"My father thought it was sacrilegious to read the news on a piece of film. He'd say, it's okay for old movies to be preserved on film but newspapers should be preserved on newsprint. That's why they call it 'the paper' not 'the plastic.'"

He walks over and pulls out a volume. "Here it is, '67–'68." He carries it to one of the tables. "It was summer 1967. Have fun." He goes back downstairs.

I start reading about beach closings, petty thefts, car crashes. I go through all of July and nothing. Then the headline on the first August issue blares, "TRAGIC END TO WILD BEACH PARTY."

The first week's story calls it an accident. By the second week the scathing editorials begin. They end abruptly five weeks later. I check the masthead and Henry Glennum's name is gone. No mention of why he left. I never saw a story about Steve Keating's attack on Rivette. I keep leafing through the issues to see if there's anything else.

I'm well into 1968 and about ready to call it quits when I see: "FROM FOOTBALL HERO TO WAR HERO." Below the headline is a blurry photo of four young guys in olive drab standing in front of a Huey helicopter. I look at the caption and the first name I see is "Steve Keating, Crew Chief." Then another name jumps out at me. "Neil Monahan, Aircraft Commander."

I read how they rescued two squads of American GIs pinned down in some godforsaken Vietnam rice paddy. They took heavy fire but got all the men out alive. They were awarded the Bronze Star for their heroic efforts.

Steve Keating and Neil Monahan on the same flight crew. Holy shit!

CHAPTER FORTY

I run downstairs. Glennum's got the phone pinned to his ear.

I yell, "Keating and Monahan were in Vietnam together."

He glares at me, covers the phone. "Sshhhhhhh." Then I hear, "I don't know where you heard that the *Eagle* is closing. That couldn't be further from the truth. With all that's going on we expect circulation to increase. In fact, I brought an extra writer in from New York just to cover the plane crash." He pauses for a few seconds. "Trust me, those are just malicious rumors being spread by my competitors." Another pause. "You've been one of our most important advertisers for quite some time, and just to show our appreciation, for the next month we'll give you a full-page ad for the same price as your usual half page." He smiles contentedly. "Thank you." He hangs up.

"Nice line of bullshit."

He shrugs. "It's all part of the business. Now what about Keating?"

"He was in Vietnam with Monahan."

"A lot of guys were in Vietnam, that doesn't mean they knew each other."

"They were in the same helicopter crew. They got a medal together. It was in the paper."

His eyes bug open. "I thought Rivette was just blowing smoke up your ass. This could really be something."

"Keating was the crew chief. I bet he knows how to make a plane crash and have it look like an accident."

"I'm sure you're right."

"Do you know him?"

He shakes his head. "Not really. I haven't seen him in years."

"Should I go talk to him?"

"Of course. That's Journalism 101. Find out where he lives. There's a phone book lying around somewhere."

"First I gotta make a call."

"Go ahead."

I dial Nicky's number. I hear a quizzical "Hello."

"Yo, it's me."

"You didn't call collect."

"I'm calling from my desk in the newsroom." I give him the number.

"Look at you, an honest-to-goodness newspaperman."

"I got a desk and a phone, that doesn't make me a newsman. Wait till I write my first story."

"So, did Monahan crash the plane?"

"I can't prove it yet, but I'm getting close."

"No shit, you actually found something?"

"This local guy who hated Rivette was Monahan's helicopter crew chief in Vietnam."

"That doesn't mean he sabotaged the plane."

"He could have."

"Could have is a long way from did."

"I know that. That's why I'm gonna go talk to him."

"Be careful. Remember, you have no idea what you're doing."

"That never stopped me before."

"But you had me and Jeannie to clean up your messes."

"Speaking of messes, did Jeannie find anything out about Lepro?"

"Plenty."

"Well?"

"She's nobody to fuck with."

"What does that mean?"

"She's one badass bitch. She was in the Secret Service. That's where she met Rivette."

"Why does Rivette rate Secret Service protection?"

"He doesn't. Her job was to watch Vice President Mondale's daughter, Eleanor."

"I'm still not connecting the dots."

"Eleanor was a big party girl. Rivette threw a lot of parties at his Hamptons place. Eleanor was a regular. I think maybe they even went out for a little while. And wherever Eleanor went, Lepro went. She must have made an impression on Rivette 'cause after she got kicked out of the Secret Service, he hired her."

"She got kicked out of the Secret Service? Why?"

"Excessive violence."

"No shit?"

"According to Jeannie, she put a couple of guys in the hospital."

"Whoa. She looks like she's in pretty good shape, but not *that* good."

"She's a Muay Thai master."

"Muay Thai? I drank about five of those one night and threw my guts up."

"That's mai tai, you idiot. Muay Thai is a martial art."

"Like kung fu?"

"I think it's more like kickboxing, but I'm not really sure."

"I thought you knew all about that stuff. Don't you have some fancy karate belt?"

"I'm a brown belt in goju ryu karate."

"Sounds pretty impressive to me. What kind of belt does she have?"

"No clue. I don't even know if they have belts in Muay Thai."

"How do they keep their pants up?"

"You can joke around all you want, but Muay Thai is some serious shit. Don't do anything to piss her off."

CHAPTER FORTY-ONE

I'm in the VW hippie hot rod, trying to find Keating's house. The street sign says Accabonac Road but it should say Tobacco Road. It's like Scotty beamed me out of East Hampton and set me down in Appalachia. There are beat-up trucks in the driveways and all kinds of broken-down crap in the yards, from rusty lawnmowers to misshapen bicycles to dented refrigerators without any doors.

I'm lost. I pretty sure I followed Glennum's directions but there are no cars on the road and none of the street signs I'm seeing ring any bells.

I glance up at the mirror and there's a big blue car bearing down at me and he's in a big hurry. I slow down and pull over. As soon as he's past me he veers in front of me and screeches to a stop. This is getting fucking ridiculous. First we get run off the road in Nicky's car, now this.

Two guys in suits get out of the car. Big guys. A closer look and I realize I've seen them before. They're the FBI agents who hassled me at Moish's house. That's a relief. I thought they might be Red Monahan's hit men. I have no idea what they want but at least they're not going to kick the shit out of me. Or worse.

I crack the window. "You guys have nothing better to do than follow me around? You run out of dope dealers and illegal aliens to hassle?"

Pristera, the white one, says, "Step out of the vehicle."

I do.

"Lemme see some ID."

"Are you serious? You guys know who I am. This is harassment."

He sneers and holds out his hand. "ID, scumbag."

I pull my wallet out of my back pocket. Before I can get my license, he snatches it out of my hand, takes a twenty and sticks it in his pocket.

"Hey, you can't do . . ."

Then, out of nowhere, he gut-punches me. I hear myself make a sound, the sound you make right before you puke. I'm doubled over but I don't go down.

"We told you to stay the fuck out of it," Raines, the black one, snarls. Then Pristera hits me again. Same place. Harder.

The ground comes up and smacks me in the face. The next thing I know, they're peeling out, spraying gravel, sand and dirt on my head and I'm eating asphalt.

My wallet's lying on the floor next to me, twenty bucks lighter. I manage to pull myself upright and drag my sorry ass back into the van. I check my face out in the mirror. There are cuts and scratches over my eyes. My chin looks like a skinned knee. Not quite LaMotta after fifteen rounds with Sugar Ray, but not pretty. Time to have a heart-to-heart with the shmuck in the rearview mirror.

What the fuck are you doing? You're in way, way over your head, just like that time in Spinelli's. Remember how that turned out? Except this time you got a lot more to lose than two weeks' pay.

The shmuck in the mirror yells back: *You think I'm doing this for the thrill of it. Or because I think I'm some kind of crusader for justice. I'm doing it because it's my fault that Sangster is dead. He was scared shitless. He didn't want to go on that plane, and I talked him into it. Not because I thought it was the right thing to do. But, like the self-centered asshole that I am, I did it because I thought it would help me get back into Rivette's good graces. If I would have kept my big trap shut he'd still be alive. I can't bring him back. But maybe I can bring him some justice. I'll probably never be able to prove it was Monahan. But I won't be able to live with myself if I don't at least try.*

End of conversation.

CHAPTER FORTY-TWO

After driving around in circles for fifteen minutes, I finally find Keating's house. If by Hampton's standards Rivette's place is a bungalow, this is a broken-down lean-to.

I'm sore, nauseous and woozy. My clothes are ripped and dirty. I'm still tasting blood. Still, as bad as I look, I'm Prince Charming compared to this dump. The front lawn, if you could call it that, is a lovely mélange of dirt, weeds and assorted detritus. I walk up the warped wood ramp to the front door. There's no bell so I knock. No response. The dinged and rusted Econoline van parked in the gravel driveway has a thick layer of greasy dust on the windshield so I figure nobody's used it for a while. After half a minute I knock again, harder.

I'm about to leave when I hear, "Take it easy, I'm coming." After a few seconds the door creaks open. I'm staring down at a guy in a wheelchair. His hair is buzz-cut, his nose is flat and crooked, like when you press your face against a window. His arms are thick and sinewy, probably from pushing himself around all day. His faded, filthy dungarees are tied in knots at both knees.

"Steve Keating?"

"Yeah. Who the hell are you?"

"My name's Stew Gribnitz. I'm a reporter for the *Eagle*." He looks me up and down and grimaces. "You'll have to excuse the way I look," I say contritely. "I got into a little fender bender on the way over here." I figure that sounds better than telling him I got the shit kicked out of me by a couple of FBI gorillas.

"I read the *Eagle* all the time. I've never seen that name."

"I'm new." I hand him my bogus press pass.

He stares at it, looks up at me, then hands it back. "What do you want?"

"I'm looking into the plane crash. The one that happened the other day."

"What about it?"

"It was Ed Rivette's plane."

"Yeah, I heard. Too bad he wasn't on it." He pauses for a second. "Why are you talking to me?"

"You and Rivette have a history. You beat him up pretty bad. Accused him of killing your sister."

"That was a long time ago."

"You were a helicopter crew chief in Vietnam, right?"

He snarls, "Yeah, so what?"

"You know your way around an airplane."

"A helicopter ain't an airplane."

"Still, I bet someone with your training could screw up a plane like Rivette's and make it look like an accident."

"You accusing me of something?"

I shrug.

"It *was* an accident. Rudder malfunction. That's what they said on the news."

"That's the NTSB's preliminary finding. The investigation is still ongoing. We received information that there might be sabotage involved."

"What kind of information? From who?"

"A confidential informant." (Me.)

He pushes forward. "And what? You think I had something to do with it?"

"Did you?"

He looks down with disgust at his dead legs. "Not with these. How the hell am I supposed to get anywhere near the rudder?"

Since I have no clue where the rudder is or even what it does, I change the subject. "You were in Neil Monahan's flight crew."

"What does that have to do with anything?"

"With Rivette dead, your pal Monahan gets a free ride to the Connecticut governor's mansion."

"Except Rivette wasn't on the plane."

"You didn't know that."

His hands are squeezing the metal push rim so hard they're turning red. If he wasn't stuck in that chair I'd probably be kissing the dirt for the second time today. Instead, he just glowers and says, "Listen, asshole. I was nowhere near that plane."

"Can you prove it?"

"I don't have to prove anything to you."

"I have it on good authority that Neil Monahan, your old army buddy, was responsible for the crash."

"Good authority, my ass. He had nothing to do with it. No possible way."

"How can you be so sure?"

"I know Neil Monahan. He's no killer."

"What about strafing villages in Vietnam? Those weren't bouquets you were shooting."

"You don't know what the hell you're talking about."

"I read all about it in the *Eagle* archives. You flew Hueys. The Vietcong called them fire from the sky."

"Those were gunships. We were Dustoff."

"Dustoff? What the hell is that?"

"Medical evac. We were unarmed. We'd fly in, get the wounded and get the hell out. Most of the time under heavy fire." He looks back down at his legs. "That's how I got these. Coulda been a lot worse. Captain Monahan dragged me back to the chopper after I got hit. He took a bullet in the shoulder for his trouble. Then he somehow managed to fly us out of there. He's a fucking hero. Got the medals to prove it."

This isn't helping me prove my case. "What about Red Monahan, Neil's beloved half brother? You can't tell me he's not a killer."

"I don't know nothing about that, except what I read in the papers."

"What I read is he's been tried for murder three times and walked every time. Thanks to Neil."

He shakes his head vehemently and screams, "That's a lie! Neil hates Red."

"If he hates him so much, he had plenty of opportunity to say so. He never said a word against him."

"That doesn't mean he's protecting him. Red's still his brother."

"Half brother."

"Whatever." His eyes fill with hate. "I wouldn't need Neil Monahan or anyone else to convince me to kill Rivette. The sonuvabitch murdered my sister."

"I checked that out too. According to all the reports, she committed suicide."

"That's bullshit!" He's yelling again. "She was murdered. Rivette killed her."

"Then why wasn't he arrested?"

"'Cause his old man paid off the whole town—the police, the coroner, the DA. Everybody."

"What about the *Eagle*? Henry Glennum was no supporter of the Rivettes. If there was any evidence of murder, he would have published it."

"I don't know about that. I do know my sister. She would never kill herself. She loved life. I was with her the day she died. She was feeling great, looking forward to the rest of the summer and senior year. She was thinking of running for class president." He pauses for a minute, then says, "Besides, suicide is a mortal sin. She wouldn't risk going to hell."

"She was religious?"

He nods strenuously. "Oh yeah, she took after my mom. They went to church every Sunday."

"Even if your sister didn't kill herself, that doesn't mean it was murder. It could have been an accident, a riptide, she could have swum out too far."

"Not a chance. Kathy grew up swimming in these waters. She was number one backstroke on the high school team."

"Even if it was murder, how can you be sure it was Rivette? Summer in the Hamptons—a lot of young horny guys, a lot of beer, a lot of drugs, a lot of testosterone."

"It was him. The rest of his crowd were a bunch of gutless, rich-boy faggots. Except for that fat prick, Persons."

"James Persons?"

"You know him?"

I don't see any reason to go into my history with Persons. "I met him once." Which is actually true. I just neglected to mention that the only time I saw him we got into a huge fight and I wiped my ass with his tie. "How'd he wind up in Rivette's circle? I thought the townies and summer people didn't mix."

"We don't. They hate us. We hate them. Persons too, until he decided to become one of them."

"How'd he manage that?"

"Golf."

"Golf?"

"Persons's old man was a gardener at the golf course. The kid started playing when he was five. He was a fat, little shit but he could hit a golf ball. By the time he was twelve, he was beating most of the men around here. A couple of years later, he was hustling the rich kids when they came out for the summer. They couldn't believe that a chubby little dickweed from the other side of the tracks with ripped sneakers and second-hand equipment could be better than them with their fancy clubs and professional lessons. He took those assholes to the cleaners again and again and they kept coming back for more."

He pauses to allow himself a little smirk at this. "By the middle of the summer they finally caught on and kicked the shit out of him. Served him right too. After that, none of them would have anything to do with him. Except Rivette. He took the pudgy little prick under his wing. They started hustling at other courses all over the island. Next thing you know, summer's over and Persons gets a golf scholarship to some fancy prep school in New England. Old man Rivette arranged the whole thing."

"That doesn't make him a villain. Sounds to me like he did something nice for the kid."

"Nice, my ass. Persons was with Rivette the night my sister was killed. Him and that ghoul Sangster. They bought him off with that scholarship."

"So now Persons is dead. Sangster is dead. And if he wasn't in the ER that morning, Rivette would be dead too. All the people you blame for you sister's murder."

"Yeah." Keating grins malignantly. "But two out of three ain't bad."

CHAPTER FORTY-THREE

Back at the *Eagle*, Glennum is leaning way back in his chair, staring up at the ceiling. I don't know if he's dozing, meditating or deciding whether or not to spackle the cracks. When I walk in he bolts up. "What the hell happened to you? You and Keating have a fight? Looks like he won."

"I guess you haven't seen Keating in a while."

"Why? Does he look worse than you?"

"A lot worse. Or at least, a lot shorter. He got his legs blown off in Vietnam."

His mouth gapes open. "My God! I had no idea."

"For a newspaper guy you sure don't keep up with current events in your town."

"You think I keep tabs on everyone who lives in the Hamptons? I just assumed that he was keeping a low profile."

"It's hard to keep a high profile when you're stuck in a wheelchair."

"Did he tell you how it happened?"

"Yeah. Like we thought, he was in Monahan's Huey crew in Vietnam. They got ambushed."

"Does he still keep in touch with Monahan?"

"He didn't say. He did say Monahan saved his life over there and he would do anything for him."

"Like murder?"

"I didn't ask him. I didn't have to ask him about Rivette. He's still totally convinced Rivette murdered his sister. As much as he loves Monahan, he hates Rivette more."

Glennum jumps up, a big shit-eating grin on his face. "There's the link. We got him. Keating already wants Rivette dead. He could've sabotaged the plane and made it look like an accident." He gets up, walks over to my desk, and puts his hand up for a high five.

I leave him hanging. "You're right, he could have done it. But he'd have to get to the rudder. He'd need legs for that."

"How do you know? The rudder's all the way in the back of the plane. It might be possible."

"Without being seen? I doubt it."

"He could have shown someone else how to do it."

"Maybe, but I don't think so. I'm willing to bet that the rudder assembly of a plane, even an old plane, is pretty complicated. It's one thing to show somebody how to cut a cable; that's not the same as making it look like an accident and fooling the NTSB engineers. You have to really know what you're doing to pull that off."

He starts pacing back and forth. "Wait a minute. He was in a wheelchair when you saw him, right?"

"Yeah."

"That doesn't mean he's *always* in a wheelchair."

"That's crazy. Why would anyone choose to be in a wheelchair if they didn't have to be?"

"My grandfather had to have his leg amputated. Diabetes. He got fitted for a prosthetic limb. He hated it. He said it was awkward, clumsy, and it hurt like hell. He was much happier in his wheelchair. Could be the same for Keating."

"You want me to try to find out if he has prostheses?"

"I can do that. I have some contacts at the VA clinic in Riverhead. They'll know."

"So much for Keating. What's next?"

He holds up a hand. "Not so fast. What else did he say?"

"He said Sangster and Persons were with Rivette the night his sister died. Also that Monahan's Huey wasn't a gunship."

"What else could it be?"

"Medical evacuation. What did he call it . . . Dustoff."

"Never heard of it."

"Me neither. I thought it was some kind of furniture polish."

"So what is it?"

"Basically, it's an airship ambulance. They flew into hot zones under heavy fire and flew out the wounded. He said they went in unarmed."

"Do you believe him?"

"I don't know what to believe. Do you think the VA would have that information?"

"I'll ask." He stares at me for a few seconds. "What's the matter? You look upset."

"After talking to Keating I have twice as many questions and zero answers."

"That's why they call it investigative reporting. Sometimes the answers aren't what you expect. You having second thoughts about Monahan?"

"Nah. He did it. He was a combat pilot. He knows his way around an airplane. I doubt he fucked with the rudder himself, though he probably could have. More likely he got somebody else to do it. Keating? Could be. Maybe you're right and you don't need legs to sabotage a rudder."

"That makes Keating a suspect with or without Monahan. He said that he would kill Rivette if he could. Maybe he did."

"Or maybe it really was an accident."

"What about the death threats?"

"Maybe they had nothing to do with the crash. They were just to screw with Rivette's head. And then there's Persons."

"Persons? What the hell does he have to do with any of this?"

"Keating said that Persons was Rivette's protégé. That he was with Rivette and Sangster the night his sister got killed. How come you never mentioned that Persons grew up out here?"

I'm thinking this little tidbit will trigger some kind of reaction, but he just gives a noncommittal shrug. "I never knew Persons. I was in the navy when all that was going on. I never met him until he made all that trouble a couple of years ago."

"Wait a minute. You were in the navy? I thought you were an anti-war hippie like me."

"I was. I marched on Washington and everything. I didn't even like to play soldiers when I was a kid. All I ever wanted to be was a newspaperman like my old man."

"So what happened?"

"I graduated with a journalism degree. Was editor of the college newspaper. The whole bit. I thought I was going to set the world on fire. But the only thing that got burnt was my resume. I got rejected by every daily, weekly and penny saver between here and Muskegon. I was ready to give up, then my dad mentioned that the military always needs journalists. Every base has its own TV, radio and newspaper operation."

"Wasn't the war in Vietnam still going on?"

"It was just ending, but guys were still getting shipped home in body bags. Then it hit me—I never read about any navy guys getting killed, only army, air force and marines."

"Did the North Vietnamese even have a navy?"

"Not enough to worry about. I went to the navy recruiting office and told them I was interested in working on newspapers. They said no problem. I got through basic training more or less in one piece. The next thing I know I'm a journalist second class on the USS *Forrestal*. A lot of people around here will tell you I've been a second-class journalist ever since." He grins.

"What about Vietnam?"

"I never got within a thousand miles of the place."

"Pretty lucky."

"Enough of my life story. What the hell happened to you?"

I point to my face and my ripped clothes. "I thought the grunge look would work for me."

"Seriously."

I tell him about my run-ins with the FBI, both here and in Brooklyn.

"That doesn't sound right to me. Are you sure they were really FBI?"

"I'm not sure about anything. They flashed an ID. It said FBI in big letters with their pictures next to it."

He shakes his head. "That means as much as the press pass I gave you. I printed that right here. I could just as easily have made up a card that said FBI."

"If they're not FBI, who the hell are they? Monahan's men?"

"That would be my guess."

"That sucks."

"Not really. It means we're getting close."

"Close to what? The only thing I'm close to is getting my head bashed in or thrown in jail."

"The Keating link could be something."

"That's if he could have physically done it, which is a long shot."

"Monahan wouldn't have sent his goons to warn you off if he didn't think you were on the right track."

"Great. If I get any closer, I'll be on track for a bullet in my brain."

"If they wanted to kill you, you'd be dead already."

"Somehow that doesn't make me feel better."

He thinks for a couple of seconds. "Listen, if you wanna quit, that's okay. Can't say that I'd blame you."

I take a while to answer. "I'll see it through. I owe that much to Urban."

Big smile from Glennum. "Good. Here's your next assignment." He walks over and hands me a slip of paper. It says, "Spit-and-Polish Auto Detailing." Then it gives the address, phone number and hours of operation.

"Are you fucking kidding me?" I holler. "Urban's dead. The next governor of Connecticut did it. And all you're worried about is cleaning that piece-of-shit van of yours." I look out the front window and there's a half dozen people, all at least eighty, standing there, gaping at me. I guess they're not used to these kinds of outbursts out here in the demure and sophisticated Hamptons.

I turn back to Glennum to see his reaction. He's doubled over in laughter. Not the usual result of one of my temper tantrums.

"What the hell's so fucking funny?"

He gets himself under control . . . barely. "I don't want you to wash the van. While you were out I went down to the archives and dug a little more into the Kathy Keating incident. Earl Philips and Bart Talamini were the primary investigators on the case. A year or so later they both left the force. Talamini got a job working security for Rivette Publications and Philips opened up a car wash in Sag Harbor."

"And nobody thought that was fishy? One of the detectives suddenly has enough money to buy a business and the other one winds up working for the Rivettes."

Glennum shrugs. "Ed Rivette wasn't a suspect. Kathy's death was ruled a suicide. No one gave it a second thought. The only one who might have been suspicious was my father, and by that time he sold the *Eagle* and was in pretty bad shape."

"Both of the ex-cops still around?"

"I have no idea where Talamini is. Last I heard, Philips still owns the car wash. I thought you could drive over and talk to him."

"Are you sure he'll be there?"

He shakes his head. "I have no idea. But it's worth a fifteen-minute drive to find out. If anybody knows what happened that night, it's him."

"Why didn't you just say that in the first place?"

"I'm glad I didn't. I haven't laughed like that for a long time."

"Happy I could help." The phone on my desk rings and I jump. This brings another chuckle from Glennum. "Hello."

"It's me." Nicky's voice sounds a little shaky.

"Everything okay?"

"Maybe not."

"What's wrong?"

"I drove by your father's house like you asked. It didn't look right."

"What do you mean?"

"The mailbox was stuffed. The lights were off. There were some flyers and shit on the stoop. I don't think anyone's been there for a while. I got out and rang the bell. No answer. I tried the front door, it opened. I walked inside and the place was a total wreck."

"Fucking shit! They have my father."

"Who?"

"A couple of guys pulled me over out here and beat the crap out of me. They said they were from the FBI but we think they're lying."

"We?"

"Glennum and me."

"Who do you think they are?"

"Monahan's men."

"And you think they're the ones who have Moish?"

"Who else could it be?"

"You gonna call the police?"

"The police think I'm a criminal, and probably a murderer."

"What *are* you gonna do?"

"I dunno. There's really nothing I can do. Before I left we had a fight. He could have gone away just to spite me."

"And left the door open?"

"He's old. Maybe he forgot."

"And messed up the place too."

"Okay, I get it. Moish is probably in some kind of trouble."

"Suppose it is Monahan's men?"

"There's no reason for them to hurt him. It's me they're after. Maybe it was the bookie."

"I thought you said that was all cleared up."

"That's what I thought."

"What do you want me to do?"

"I can't think of anything."

"Call me if you need me." He hangs up.

Glennum says, "Everything okay?"

"My father's missing."

"Are you sure?"

"My friend Nicky went over to the house. The place was turned upside down. And it looked like nobody's been there for a while."

"And you think Monahan's men did it?"

"Could be."

"What are you gonna do about it?"

"Not much I can do. I'll keep digging out here. Once I get the proof that Monahan killed Sangster and Nielsen, everything else will sort itself out."

"You really think so?"

"Yeah. And I also believe in Santa Claus, the Easter Bunny and that all women want is a nice guy who treats them with respect."

CHAPTER FORTY-FOUR

There are five cars lined up outside of Spit-and-Polish Auto Detailing: two Benzes, a BMW, a Porsche and a vintage Jaguar XKE in British racing green. I decide not to drive the Vanagon to the end of the line; it would be like taking a sewer rat to the Westminster Dog Show.

The guy behind the counter is pushing sixty but looks like he can still handle himself. He's wearing a polyester Hawaiian shirt and a few gold chains around his neck. His hair is black and shiny, like he shampooed with shoe polish. He has a scar over his right eye and reeks of cloyingly sweet cologne. He looks vaguely familiar but I can't imagine where I might have seen him before.

He gives me a big phony smile. "Hello, sport, how can I help you?"

"Are you Earl Philips?"

"Who wants to know?"

"I'm a reporter with the *Eagle*. Would you mind talking to me for a couple of minutes?"

Still smiling, though through gritted teeth, he says, "What the matter? Joe getting to be too much of a big shot to write his own stories anymore?"

"You know Joe Glennum?"

"Sure. I knew his father Henry too."

"Actually, I'm here about a story Henry worked on years ago, Kathy Keating's suicide. I believe you were one of the investigating officers."

His smile is gone. "What's the matter, not enough news going on today? You have to dredge up shit from twenty years ago?"

"I'm doing background on the plane crash. It was Ed Rivette's plane that went down and Urban Sangster was onboard. The only other time those two names were in the paper was in connection with the Keating suicide. Joe thought it might give the current story some context if we mentioned what happened back then. He said you're the guy to talk to to get the facts right."

Philips shakes his head. "I don't know why anybody would be interested in that kinda ancient history, but Joe's the newsman. If he thinks so, I'm happy to tell you what I know." He walks out from behind the counter to a couple of upholstered chairs, the kind you see in dentists' waiting rooms. He sits down on one, I take the other. Over his shoulder is a display cabinet filled with car care items. Rags, shammies, Windex, Turtle Wax and those little pine tree–looking things that hang on the mirror that make the car smell like cleaning fluid. Another case has engine oil, transmission fluid, wiper blades and windshield washer. Does anybody really buy this kind of stuff at a car wash?

I put my hand in my pocket and flick on the voice recorder. "I spoke to Steve Keating. He's doesn't think his sister killed herself. He's sure it was murder. He says Rivette and his friends were responsible and you guys covered it up."

He starts slowly shaking his head. "I feel sorry for Stevie. He was a good kid. And a helluva football player. One of the best we ever had. His life turned to shit the night his sister died. He always saw himself as her protector. Then, when it really mattered, he was nowhere around. Probably drunk somewhere or with one of the local sluts. I figure he blamed himself for what happened then decided to take it out on Eddie Rivette. He coulda gone away for what he did but the Rivettes felt sorry for him. They knew he wasn't a bad kid, just all twisted up over what happened. So they let it slide. The army was the best place for him. Bad luck he got his legs blown off."

He stands up and straightens some of the packages in the display cases, even though they don't need straightening.

"All that happened a long time ago. I don't think picking at that scab will do anybody any good."

"Sounds to me, as far as Keating's concerned, the wound is still fresh."

"I checked all that out back then. We spoke to Steve, heard him out and checked into all his allegations. There's no way Rivette or any of his friends had anything to do with what happened to Kathy. As a matter of fact, they tried to help her."

"Help her? How?"

"According to a couple of her friends, she was depressed for a while and it all came to a head that night. Eddie, Urbie and Jimmy tried to cheer her up but there was nothing they could do. They were all going to a party over in Amagansett and they invited her to come. She said she just wanted to go home. They offered to drive her but she said that a walk on the beach might do her good. That was the last time anybody saw her alive."

"You're sure it was definitely suicide?"

"One hundred percent. We spoke to her classmates, her teachers, her neighbors. Her behavior had changed in the weeks before she died. She just moped around in a haze all the time. A lot of people thought she was on drugs."

Whoa! I didn't see that coming. "What kind of drugs? Grass? Acid? Coke? Where did she get it?"

He closes his eyes, trying to concentrate. "I'm pretty fuzzy on the details, it was a long time ago."

"And how come there wasn't anything about drugs in any of the newspaper stories about her?"

"Me and my partner kept it quiet. The girl was dead. The family was devastated. Why make matters worse by dragging her name through the mud? Believe me, it was suicide. There was never a doubt."

CHAPTER FORTY-FIVE

I'm heading back to the *Eagle* office on Lost at Sea Pike. I don't know where they come up with these street names but this one really fits. My head is swimming, more like drowning, trying to make sense out of what I just heard. Kathy Keating was either a morose, suicidal druggie or a happy-go-lucky, churchgoing optimist? She sure as hell couldn't have been both.

Everything points to Philips's story being legit except for Philips himself. He was just a little too slick. He seemed to have his answers rehearsed, like he knew what was coming.

Suppose Keating's right about Monahan. That he really is a decent guy. Maybe the plane crash was just a horrible accident like everyone says. But if those death threats didn't come from Monahan, who the hell did they come from? Were they for real or was somebody just fucking with Rivette? He admits he pissed off a lot of rich, powerful people after twenty years of muckraking with his high-finance scandal sheet. Any one of them could have hired someone to harass Rivette or maybe even wreck his plane.

But more importantly, at least for me, if Monahan didn't do it, what the hell is going on with Moish? Did he piss off some other bookies who are a little more badass than Shifty? Is he lying in a ditch somewhere in

Bumfuck, New Jersey? Maybe Moish and Ruthie really are together. My father's a very secretive guy. Maybe Ruth is too. If she is, she's a damn good actress. I really bought it that she hasn't seen Moish in years and was insulted that I thought they were together.

With all this ruminating, cogitating and mental masturbating, I never notice the flashing lights in my rearview mirror until they're right on top of me. I'm pretty sure it's not those phony FBI bastards; their car was unmarked. Either this is some kind of police vehicle, white with a blue stripe and a gumball machine on top, or a really bad Earl Scheib paint job. I know I'm under the speed limit. There was only one stoplight, and it was green when I went through it. Maybe the van's overdue for inspection.

I pull over. The cop car screeches to a stop behind me, lights still flashing. A uniform gets out and walks slowly toward me. He's holding his gun in front of him with both hands. (For a traffic stop?) I open my window to see what the problem is.

He points the pistol at my head and shouts, "Put your hands on the steering wheel."

What the fuck?

"Now!" he screams.

I do what he says.

"Lace your fingers behind your head and get out of the car."

This is fucking ridiculous. "I can't," I yell back at him.

He's getting agitated and shouts even louder, "Do it *now*!"

Obviously, the guy's a fucking idiot. "How am I supposed to open the door with my hands behind my head?"

He takes a step back. "All right, put your hands down, get out of the car, and lay on the ground, face down with your arms spread out."

I get out of the car but stay standing. I don't know if this guy's another bogus cop out to fuck with me or just a Hamptons version of Barney Fife, but either way, there's no way I'm gonna lay on the ground and let this asshole kick me in the ribs. One bogus cop beatdown is more than enough.

He takes a half step closer to me. There are beads of sweat on his forehead, which is odd because it's the middle of October, not that hot, and he's the one holding the gun.

He's a couple of years older than me, a good six inches shorter, and built like an accountant with a Twinkie addiction. I doubt this Weeble ever passed a police physical but I'm sure he couldn't pass one now.

He's holding the gun with two hands and it's shaking back and forth like a metronome.

"I said get down!" he screams.

"Show me some ID," I yell back.

"I don't have to show you anything. You're under arrest."

"What's the charge?"

"Murder."

"You're no fucking cop," I scream. "If you were you'd know I had nothing to do with Persons's death."

"Persons? I don't know about any Persons. What I know is you killed Joe Glennum."

"That's bullshit. Glennum's fine. I just saw him."

"Yeah, right before you bashed his head in."

Now he's right in my face. He's holding the gun in his trembling left hand and feeling for his handcuffs with his right while keeping his eyes trained on me. After a couple of unsuccessful tries, he looks down at his belt. This is my chance. I grab the wrist with the gun and twist. It drops to the ground. I slam him on the side of his face with my left hand and bury my right fist into his stomach.

He goes down like a sack of shit.

While he's lying on the ground, moaning, I pick up the gun and level it at him. I'm shaking more than he was. "Stand up."

He gets slowly to his feet. His face is translucent. "You don't want to kill me," he stammers. "Killing a cop, you'll get the chair for sure."

I never understood why a cop's life should be worth more than yours or mine, but now's not the time to have that discussion. "What's your name?" I bark.

"Timson. Ben Timson."

"Who sent you?"

He looks confused. "No one sent me. The whole force is looking for you."

"If you're really a cop, when was Glennum killed?"

"You know damn well when."

"Humor me."

"Less than an hour ago."

"And the police just happened to check the *Eagle* office right after it happened?"

The sweat is pouring out of him like a wet sponge being squeezed. "We got an anonymous tip. The caller heard a huge ruckus coming from inside the building—people yelling, cursing, fighting. Then there was a crash. Someone fitting your description ran out of the building and drove away in the *Eagle*'s van."

"What kind of crash?"

"Somebody smashed an old typewriter over Glennum's head. Crushed his skull."

I can feel myself grimacing as I picture how it might have happened. He's asleep at his desk. Somebody sneaks in. And boom! "That's awful news, but wasn't me. For the last hour, I was in Sag Harbor, talking to Earl Philips. If you're an East Hampton cop you should know him."

Timson smirks and shakes his head. "Try again, Gribnitz. Philips is dead. He died a long time ago. Car crash. I was at his funeral. The whole department was."

"That's crazy. I was just with him."

"Then you were with a ghost." He shakes his head. "What are you trying to do, build an insanity defense?"

I feel like somebody just cracked me in the skull with a two-by-four. My head's spinning. My legs are shaking. I'm gonna puke. If Timson really is a cop, that means Joe Glennum's really dead and so is Philips and my airtight alibi.

Philips must have died before Glennum bought the *Eagle*. That's why he didn't know he was dead.

I need time to think. I wave the gun around for effect. "Awright, Timson, pick up the cuffs." He does.

There's a yellow road sign about ten yards from where we're standing. I point to it. "Go over to that sign, put your arms around it, and cuff your hands together."

He glowers at me, trying to look tough, but I can see he's ready to piss himself. "You say you're not a murderer. Are you gonna shoot me in cold blood if I don't do what you say?"

"Are you willing to take that chance?"

He thinks about it for a few seconds then shuffles dejectedly over to the sign, circles his arms around the post, and cuffs his wrists together.

I head back to the van. As I'm climbing in I hear him shout, "You'll never get away, Gribnitz. Every cop on the East End is looking for you. Their orders are to shoot to kill."

With that happy thought I drive off. To where, I have no idea.

CHAPTER FORTY-SIX

I'm at the end. Of Long Island. Of ideas. And of my rope. I know it's the end because it says "Montauk. The End." on the bumper sticker of the old Ford Woody that's parked next to me. I'm in a vest-pocket parking lot looking out on the Atlantic Ocean. In addition to the Woody, there are a couple of Jeep Wranglers, a Volkswagen Beetle, a Suzuki motor scooter and a few nubby-tired bicycles.

The sign on the weathered wooden bulletin board says "Ditch Plains Beach. The East Coast's Number One Surf Spot." I don't see any ditches or any plains, but I do see a beach and about a dozen or so surfers. Lean young things in colorful skintight wetsuits and skullcaps, hanging ten, shooting the curl and doing all that other stuff the Beach Boys sing about.

The translucent turquoise waves rhythmically washing over the powdered sugar sand are hypnotically relaxing. But not for long. Every car engine, strange noise, or loud voice makes me jump and sends a shiver from the top of my head to my toes. I'm steeling myself for the barrage of bullets from a mob of trigger-happy East Hampton cowboy cops who want to live out their *Hill Street Blues* fantasies by filling a mad-dog killer and cop beater-upper full of holes.

How'd I get here? After I left Timson my brain was roiling with the fight or flight thing. I usually go with fight, which is what got me into this mess in the first place, so I figured I'd try flight. But where? When you're out in the Hamptons you have only two choices. East or west. South puts you in the ocean, north in the bay. Logic would say to go west. Back to the city, where I'm familiar with the terrain and have friends who could help me. I might stand half a chance of staying out of jail for at least a little while. Or go the other way, east, where I've never been in my life and nobody knows me.

Then it occurred to me that if I thought going back to the city was the smart move, so would the cops. So when I got back to Main Street I headed east, which turns out to be Montauk. Following my own instincts has got me into this mess. How much worse could it get doing the opposite? The whole ride I kept staring in the mirror looking for squad cars and SWAT trucks but all I saw was a couple of very unthreatening minivans and delivery trucks. There's a pay phone next to the bulletin board here so I try Nicky. I get his answering machine.

"Nicky, I need to talk to you. I'm in deep-shit trouble. Worse than anything ever. I'm someplace in Montauk. Don't ask me where. I'll call you when I figure it out."

CHAPTER FORTY-SEVEN

The sign outside says, "Welcome to Montauk, a quaint drinking village with a fishing problem." That's what drew me to BullShots Bar and Grill. I like a dive bar with a sense of humor.

Down the road there's a seafood shack, a couple of no-tell motels and a gift shop with a bunch of touristy crap. I bought myself an "I Heart Montauk" baseball cap and a pair of oversized aviator sunglasses. I know it's not much of a disguise, but Superman fooled everyone with a pair of Buddy Holly spectacles.

Game five of the World Series is on the TV over the bar. I'm sitting with a bunch of rowdy drunks in their forties and fifties with leathery skin, tobacco-stained fingers, beer bellies and multiple tattoos. And that's just the women. The Dodgers are up 4–1 in the bottom of the sixth. Hershiser's on the mound, mowing down the Oakland lineup like they were my summer camp softball team. You gotta hand it to the fucking guy; he's an equal opportunity assassin. He destroyed us. Now he's massacring the A's. At least the Mets took it to seven games. If the Dodgers win, and it sure looks like they will, it'll be over in five.

Montauk is as far east as you can go on Long Island. It's only fifteen miles up the coast from East Hampton but vibe-wise it's a thousand miles away. Where the Hamptons are Armani, Gucci and Ferrari

Montauk is Tommy Bahama, Sperry Top-siders and Suzuki. I'm sure the place gets a lot of tourists in the summer, but here in mid-October, I bet I'm the only one in the place who's not a local.

I ditched the Vanagon in Ditch Plains—kinda poetic, no? I left the keys in the ignition and took one of the bikes that was lying around. I left a note. "Borrowed your bike. Left the van as collateral."

I haven't eaten all day so I'm doing a pretty good job on the peanuts and pretzels in front of me.

The place is getting more and more crowded and more and more rowdy. Everybody seems to know each other. A lot of them are wearing BullShots T-shirts. Red with a bull's head with big horns sticking up like goalposts and a beer mug in between them. There's a dartboard on the wall and a quarter pool table in the back.

I'm the only one sitting in one place. Everyone else is going from one table to another, schmoozing like it's a bar mitzvah, watching the Series for a little while, checking out the dart games, kibitzing the pool players.

At the seventh-inning stretch the announcers break away from the game to a local news bulletin. The sound's very low so it's hard to hear. But the picture on the screen is unmistakable. It's the photo of me that Joe Glennum put on my press pass. I can make out the words "killer on the loose" and there's a TIPS number at the bottom of the screen. Thank God (and this coming from a confirmed atheist) nobody's paying too much attention. Just to be on the safe side I take a long, slow gulp of my Bass Ale, using the beer mug to hide my face.

A few minutes later, a cute little number sits down next to me. She's around thirty, with a tight body and short, spiky blond hair. She's wearing a loose-hanging sweatshirt with the arms cut off and a little bit of her midsection showing, tight jeans and flip-flops. She orders a pint of Guinness. She takes a sip and, with a dot of foam on her button nose, she says, "You're new."

"I'm actually slightly used. But the previous owner kept me in very good condition."

She starts laughing like it's the funniest thing she ever heard, dribbling some Guinness on her shirt. Instead of being mortified, like most of the women in the city I know, she wipes it off with the back of her hand. Then puts her hand on top of mine, which is resting on the bar, looks dreamily into my eyes, and says, "I'm Donna."

I'm about to say "I'm Stew" when I realize that along with my picture, they've probably been broadcasting my name all over the East End. So I say, "I'm Ed. Ed Norton."

She smiles. "Like *The Honeymooners* guy?"

"Yeah. My parents were big fans."

"That's so cool. I feel like I'm with a celebrity." Then she takes her hand off my hand and rests it on my thigh.

Great. Here's this sexy lady who's into me, which means the cops'll show up in five minutes and throw my ass in jail for the next twenty years. Something tells me she won't be waiting when I get out.

CHAPTER FORTY-EIGHT

The cops never showed up. Gibson hit another home run. The Dodgers won the Series. Hershiser was the MVP.

I tried Nicky again, told him what was going on.

For the last three hours Donna and I have been pounding beers, talking nonsense and exchanging bodily fluids.

Somewhere along the line I asked if the guys playing pool were butchers. She said no. Most of them work on the fishing fleet and a couple are in construction. "What makes you think they're butchers?"

I smile. "The way they're butchering their shots."

She grins, cocks her head, and says, "You think you can do better?"

"Are you kidding? With one hand. Even my left hand."

"You're full of shit," she says. "If you're so fucking good . . ." Did I mention she had a mouth like a longshoreman? "Why are you scared to play?"

I could have said I'm trying to keep a low profile, being on the lam for murder and all. But instead I say, "I don't want to show off."

She puts her hand between my legs and gives a little squeeze. "Well, I want to show you off."

She marches over to the pool table and slams a quarter down on the rail. "This is for my friend Eddie." Then she takes two dollars out of her pocket and slips them underneath the quarter. "And this is for anyone who thinks they can beat him. My two to your one." Then she turns to me. "C'mon, Ed. Show these bozos how it's done."

I spin around, looking to see who Ed is. Then I realize it's me.

I hop off the barstool and the room gets a little twirly. I guess downing half a dozen brewskis on an empty stomach will do that to you. I grab a cue stick off the wall, all the while convincing myself that becoming part of this crowd is the perfect plan. The police are looking for a lone fugitive on the run, not some pool-playing putz hanging out in a local bar.

The players are sitting next to the pool table, giving me the hairy eyeball. There are four of them, looking like they came in right from the harbor. Muddy work boots, soiled jeans, gnarled knuckles, weathered faces, stinking of fish. They huddle up. Then the youngest one stands up and grabs a cue. He's got a baby face but his hands look like they've been through a meat grinder. He's on the thin side but his muscles are ropes. His T-shirt says, "Montauk Princess Charters." He walks over, sticks a dollar bill under the quarter with Donna's two, extends his hand, and says, "Chuck."

I squeeze it hard and shake. "I'm St . . . Ed."

He gives me the Mike Tyson stare-down. "We play eight ball. You can break."

I give him a big smile. "Thanks, Chuck. Good luck."

The rules of eight ball are simple.

The fifteen object balls are divided into two groups. One through seven, the solids. And nine through fifteen, the stripes. Maybe you noticed there's one ball missing, the eight. That's because to win you have to call your shot on the eight. And sink it, of course. But you can't shoot at it until you pocket all the balls in your group. If the eight accidentally goes in before that, the guy who hit it loses. If you scratch on the eight, you lose.

I step up to the table and slam the cue ball into the pack. The balls scatter. The fourteen drops into the corner pocket. So I have stripes.

Remember, bar pool tables are two feet shorter and a foot narrower than the ones I played on with Urban, which is a huge difference. It's like lowering the basketball hoop from ten feet to eight. Suddenly I can jam like Dr. J.

I'm a little nervous and a little drunk so it takes me a couple of shots to find my stroke. I leave a few balls hanging and Chuck sinks them. He throws a smirk my way. That gets my juices flowing.

I can hear Donna talking me up in the bar area. People are turning their barstools around to check out the action. I hear a shout. "Show 'em, Chuck."

Chuck doesn't show 'em. He misses his next shot. By a lot. Some guys can't take the pressure.

There are three stripes left before I can shoot at the eight. All very makeable.

I look over at my opponent. The trash-talking Brooklyn schoolyard kid takes over. "Get comfortable, Chuckie," I say with a wink. "You're gonna be sitting for a while."

I run the three remaining stripes and leave myself a good look at the eight ball. I take my time, line it up, and send it toward the corner pocket. It kisses the rail and drops in.

Donna runs over, grabs the bills off the table, stuffs them in her T-shirt like a pole dancer at a titty bar, and gives me a big hug and a mouth full of tongue. She plants another two bucks on the rail and yells, "Who's next?"

After a short huddle, one of Chuck's pals grabs a stick. I rack 'em up and he breaks. Nothing goes in.

I'm feeling it now and sink three balls. This time I have solids.

He misses. I pocket two more. He finally makes a shot but leaves me a hanger after his next miss. I make quick work of it and play position for my final ball, the five. It goes in but I'm in crappy position for the eight. It's in the middle of the cushion and the only shot I have is a cross-side bank. I line it up and stroke it. It clips the point of the pocket, wobbles for what seems like a minute but is only about half a second, and falls in.

I hear a communal gasp. Then some scattered applause.

Donna struts up, grabs pile of dollars, and says, "That's my Fast Eddie. Anybody else wanna try?"

Now, as I remember from *The Hustler*, Fast Eddie got his thumbs broken in a place like this. I'm in enough trouble with a murder rap hanging over me. Getting involved in a barroom brawl would be a really bad thing.

Thankfully, no one else is interested and Donna leads her champion back to our barstools. The bartender puts two fresh pints in front of us.

"Nice shooting. This is on me."

I thank him and take a major swig.

Donna is now draped all over me, nibbling on my ear. Next thing I know her hand is making its way inside my pants.

I turn to say something but before I can get a word out, her mouth is locked on mine and her tongue is probing my tonsils.

When she finally comes up for air, I manage to say, "Do you live around here?"

"I have a room in a cottage a half mile down the road."

"Wanna show me?"

She gives my groin another squeeze. "Love to."

I pull two twenties out of my wallet and plop them on the bar.

The bartender says, "You got money coming back."

"Buy my pals at the pool table a beer and keep the rest."

CHAPTER FORTY-NINE

Donna has a little apartment on the top floor of a beach bungalow. Small living room, smaller bedroom. We're thrashing around on her couch like a couple of sumo wrestlers on crack. She's tearing at my shirt. My hands are exploring under her top. Our legs are knotted. Somewhere along the line my nose brushes my armpit. The stench—something like a skunk farting in a sewer—is puke inducing. Before she gets a whiff of eau de Gribnitz, I say, "I can really use a shower."

She sits up and grins. A tiny spit droplet glistens on the side of her mouth. Adorable. "Cleanliness is next to studliness." She points. "In there."

The bathroom's no bigger than a small walk-in closet, and the shower's the size of a stand-up coffin. I throw off what's left of my clothes and step in.

The soap shelf on the back wall is jammed up my butt crack and the shower head is hitting me between the eyes. I bend my knees, scrunch down, and turn the water on. I'm halfway soaped up when Donna yanks open the shower curtain and squeezes in. Her body is lean and lithe. She has the cutest upturned boobs with perky pink nipples the size and color of pencil erasers. A daisy tattoo sits halfway between her belly button and her pubes, which are shaved in a perfect little triangle.

We're working up a lather in every conceivable sense. Donna is either a dancer, a yoga instructor or a contortionist because she's getting into positions in that shower that would give an anaconda a cramp.

After about five minutes I say, "How about we take this into the bedroom?"

"Sounds great." She turns off the water and slithers out of the shower.

There's only one towel. She wraps it tightly around her body. She's sexier in terry cloth than most women are in silk. "Stay here. I'll get you something to dry yourself." She walks out, shaking that cute little butt, and closes the door behind her.

I don't know where she keeps the towels but she's taking a hell of a long time to come back. I'm just about to dry myself with a wad of toilet paper when she walks in wearing a policewoman's uniform. She's holding a pistol in one hand and a pair of handcuffs in the other. The gun is pointed right at my crotch.

I was never too big on sexual role-playing but I'm ready to give it a try. "What's this, the sex-crazed suspect and horny policewoman?"

She shoots me a sly smile. "Not quite. This is called 'Lady Cop Catches a Killer.' Are you ready to play, Eddie?" Her face turns deadly serious. "Or should I say Stewart?"

I've had some pretty major letdowns in my life but this one takes the fucking seven-layer cake. I'm ready for the ultimate thrill ride on the sexual roller coaster; instead it looks like a one-way ticket up the river— and I'm not talking about the Jungle Cruise at Disney World.

"You're not kidding, are you?"

She shakes her head. "Unh-unh."

"I don't understand. You could have arrested me anytime. In the bar. On the way here. Why did you wait? Don't get me wrong, I loved every minute of it. But it doesn't make sense. Are you really that big a cock tease?"

She smiles a little. "I didn't find out who you really were until just now. I checked my messages and there was one from the precinct saying be on the lookout for someone fitting your description. I called and they faxed me your photo. Just for the record, you're a lot better looking in person."

"So all that stuff in the bar and the shower, that was real?"

Her smile gets bigger. "Oh yeah. I'm really disappointed that it turned out this way."

"Not as much as I am."

"I guess not."

"Would it make any difference if I told you I was innocent?"

She sighs. "None at all."

"You really think I'm a murderer?"

"It doesn't matter what I think. I'm a police officer and you're wanted for murder. I have no choice."

"I guess a quickie for old time's sake is out of the question."

This actually makes her laugh. "You're a real fucking piece of work, Stewart Gribnitz, I'll say that much for you."

"What happens now?"

"I take you to the station where I book you."

With all this going on I actually forgot that I've been standing buck naked, dripping wet with my schwanz swinging in the breeze. I put my hands over my crotch to cover myself up. I don't know why, just a reflex, I guess.

I say, "I probably should get dressed."

She steps aside. "You first."

I go into the living room and gather up my clothes. She follows. While I'm getting dressed I say, "I know it doesn't make a difference but I really need you to believe that I didn't kill Joe Glennum. He was a friend. What possible reason would I have?"

"I have no idea. But like I said, it doesn't matter."

"I know it sounds like a cliché, but I was set up. Joe and I were getting close to proving that the plane crash last week was sabotage. Ed Rivette was the target. And Neil Monahan was behind it. With Joe dead and me accused of his murder, Monahan gets away with it."

She looks at me like I have three heads. "That's the wildest story I've ever heard. You know Neil Monahan was in the FBI. He's a sitting US attorney. And he's probably gonna be the next governor of Connecticut."

"We never thought it was going to be easy."

There's a knock at the door.

"Who's that, my police escort? You really thought I was that dangerous?"

She shakes her head. "I didn't call for that. Maybe they just decided to send someone to back me up."

She points the gun at me. "Don't move."

"Where am I going?"

She opens the door. Nicky's standing there. "Are you Donna?"

"Who the fuck are you?"

"I'm Nick, Stew's friend. The bartender at BullShots told me I'd find him here." He sees the gun she's holding at her side. "Hey," he yells. "What's going on?"

I scream, "Nicky, grab her. She's crazy. She's trying to kill me."

I've never seen Nicky do karate before, but I gotta say, I'm impressed. He spins around on one leg and kicks the gun out of her hand with the other. It skitters across the floor to me. He grabs her arm and twists it behind her back.

I pick up the gun. Point it at her. "All right, Nicky, you can let her go." He releases his grip. I gesture toward the couch. "Donna, go sit over there."

Nicky says, "They told me at the bar that this really cute girl picked you up and took you home. I knew there must be something else to it."

"Fuck you. She did pick me up and take me home."

"Yeah. So she could rip you off or kill you or something."

"No way. We were really attracted to each other."

"So what's up with the gun and the phony police outfit?"

"It's not phony. She's a cop. Tell him, Donna."

She's shaking her head in disgust. At me? At herself? At the situation? I'm guessing all of the above. "I'm officer Donna Bannon with the East Hampton Town Police Department, Montauk branch. Your friend Stewart is wanted for murder."

He starts to laugh. "Yeah, right. He's a cold-blooded killer. Machine Gun Gribnitz."

"It's true," I yell. "Somebody killed Joe Glennum and they think I did it."

His eyes bug out. "No way. Tell me you're kidding."

Donna glares at him. "He's not kidding and you're in a shitload of trouble. Right now, you assaulted a police officer and you're an accessory to murder. You'll rot in prison with your friend."

"C'mon. You guys are shitting me." Nicky looks at me, then at her, then back at me. We're not smiling. "You're serious?"

"I'm afraid so." I sigh. "I gotta get out of here. There could be squadrons of police on their way here right now. I could sure use your help, but I understand if you don't want to put yourself in any more jeopardy."

He thinks for a few seconds. "You're my partner and my best friend. I know you didn't commit any murder. Besides, you won't last five minutes out there without me."

"Great!" I hand him the gun. "Hold this." He takes the gun with both hands.

I get Donna's handcuffs and cuff her to an old cast-iron radiator in the corner. At this rate I'll have handcuffed the entire East Hampton police force before I'm through.

She looks up at me with concern. "You're making a gigantic mistake, Stewart. I like you. I might even believe you. But if you start running, nobody else will."

"Nobody will anyway."

"I don't want to see you get hurt."

"Me neither."

"Everybody on the force thinks you're a vicious killer. I know those guys. They're always trying to prove they're as tough as New York City cops. They'll shoot you just to prove a point. Let me take you in. At least you can tell your story."

"Once I'm in custody, you think they'll keep trying to find out who really killed Glennum? They're not even trying now. The only way I don't go to prison is if I can prove Monahan's behind all of it. Glennum, the plane crash, everything. I can't do that if I'm in jail."

"You can't do it at all. Every cop on Long Island is gunning for you. As soon as you show your face you'll either be arrested or shot." She looks over at Nicky. "And you're taking your buddy down with you."

"We'll see." I grab the gun from Nicky. "You still in?"

"Oh yeah."

"C'mon."

CHAPTER FIFTY

Nicky's behind he wheel. "Okay, Butch, what now?"

He always sees us as the stars of a buddy movie. Felix and Oscar. Hawkeye and Trapper. Woodward and Bernstein. Now, as two desperadoes on the run, we're Butch Cassidy and the Sundance Kid. I don't care if he needs us to be Abbott and Costello or Laverne and Shirley, I'm thrilled he's with me.

"I dunno. Just drive."

"Where? Back to the city?"

"I don't think so. Out here is where the answers are. We need a place to stay while we figure it out."

"You mean a motel or something?"

I shake my head. "That's the problem."

He rolls his eyes. "Oh, *that's* the problem. I thought you punching out a cop and handcuffing another one was the problem. Or being wanted for murder. Or having the FBI and Red Monahan's mob after us. Now you tell me that finding a place to stay is the problem."

"It's all part of the same problem. My face has been all over local TV, telling everybody I'm a combination of Charles Manson and Son of Sam. The people that run hotels, motels and B and B's, all they do is sit around all day glued to the tube while they wait for customers. They'll recognize me for sure."

"So what's the plan?"

"I'm thinking."

"You better think fast." His face is contorted, like he's in pain. "After I got your message I jumped in the car as soon as I hung up. You sounded really desperate."

"I was. Still am."

"Now I'm desperate. I didn't take any money. I don't have my meds. And I had a full stomach."

"I guess your irritable bowel is irritated."

"Oh yeah." He's grimacing. "I *really* gotta shit. And fast."

"No problem, we'll find a restaurant and you'll hightail it to the men's room."

"Don't you think I've been looking? It's the middle of the night. They're all closed. We're a long way from the city that never sleeps. This is the fucking town that never wakes up."

"Squeeze your cheeks. There's bound to be someplace open."

"Suppose not?"

"There's a lot of woods out here. You can shit au naturel."

He looks at me like I asked him to lick the toilet bowl. "How long have you known me?"

"You're right. Bad idea."

When Nicky and I first started working together, he was always running to the men's room. One day, I followed him in to see what the deal was. Nicky's a very private guy. He won't even pee if there's anybody else around, much less take a dump.

He was in the middle stall. I tiptoed into the one next to it and climbed up on the seat, which was tricky. They don't have lids, and those industrial-grade toilet seats can get pretty slimy. I looked over the top of the partition and there's Nicky with a pained look on his face. Germophobe that he is, the seat was totally covered with toilet paper. The floor tiles in front of him too.

I yelled, "Yo, Nick. Everything coming out all right down there?"

He looked up, horrified, and screamed, "Get the fuck out of here, you fucking psycho!"

I laughed so hard I almost fell into the bowl.

He kept screaming, "Get out! Get out! *Get out!*"

I didn't think he'd ever talk to me again. But somehow that brought us closer. We confided about our health issues, physical and mental. He told me about his Crohn's, lactose intolerance and manic-depressive acute anxiety syndrome. I told him about my anger issues, my impulse control disorder and my horrible marriage to the Orthodox Jewish Vampire Bride from Hell, which isn't technically a disease but close enough. Since then, whenever we had meetings or anything where we had to be out of the office, we always made contingency preparations for Nicky's unique toileting requirements.

We drive for another ten minutes, Nicky's breathing hard and fast, punctuated by the occasional groan. Beads of sweat are forming on his forehead. I'm thinking any minute there's gonna be an eruption. A Mount Vesuvius of shit. All of a sudden, we see a Mobil station lit up like a Las Vegas casino. He pulls in and screeches to a stop near the men's room way in the back. He jumps out and yanks on the door. It's locked. He runs to the office and comes out with a key on a slab of wood and a Baby Ruth candy bar. He throws me the candy, then dashes, doubled over, to the men's room.

He comes out a few minutes later, all smiles. "That was close."

"What's with the Baby Ruth?"

"Only customers can use the men's room."

"Why didn't you just buy gas?"

"All I have on me is a twenty and a couple of singles. The tank is half-full and I didn't want to waste the money or the time. The Baby Ruth was a buck. Enjoy."

"I'm not a big fan of sticky, gooey candy. You bought it. Why don't you eat it?"

He makes a face. "Those things are poison. They rot your teeth, clog your bowels, and raise your cholesterol."

Did I mention he's also a health nut?

"Why didn't you buy something else?"

"'Cause it was the first thing I saw. If there was shit on a stick up there, I woulda grabbed one of those."

We get back in the car. Nicky says, "Where to now?"

"I have no idea. Hotels, motels and B and B's are out. You don't by any chance have any camping equipment in the trunk, do you?"

He shoots me one of those looks. "You're kidding, right?"

"I'm sorry, Nicky. This really sucks. But it's my problem. No sense in me dragging you down with me. Just drop me off somewhere and head back to the city. I'll figure something out."

He slams on the brakes and glares at me. "Fuck you. I'm not bailing on you. We'll get out of this together."

"That's great to hear. But I'm all out of ideas."

"I have one. We can stay at Terrance's."

"Terrance has a co-op on Central Park West. That's not gonna do us much good out here."

He smiles slyly and shakes his head. "You've been out of the loop for a while. Things have been happening at the agency."

"I'm sure they have. But how does that help us?"

"Terrance bought a house in the Hamptons."

"Why didn't you say so?"

"I just did."

"Where?"

"I don't know. One of the Hamptons. What's the difference?"

"A lot. We gotta call him and find out."

There's a pay phone next to the bathroom. Nicky dials. I'm standing next to him so I can hear Terrance. After seven rings there's a groggy "Hello."

"Terrance. I'm here with Stew in the Hamptons. We need to stay in your new house."

"Have you any idea what time it is?" Grogginess makes way for testiness.

"I dunno. It's late. Whatever. We're in deep-shit trouble and we need your help."

"Tell me what's going on."

Nicky gives him a quick *Reader's Digest* of what's been happening. It takes a couple of minutes to convince him we're not on drugs and all this is for real. After that, he's all in. He gives us very explicit directions to his house in Amagansett, which is about ten miles from where we are.

Then he says, "It's a blue clapboard house. There's a red barberry bush to the right of the front steps. Next to the bush is a flat rock. The key will be under that rock. Jeannie will be there in the morning with your medicine and $500 in cash. Try not to get yourselves killed before we can find a way out of this mess."

I grab the phone from Nicky. "Thanks, Terrance, you're a lifesaver. I'm your slave for life."

"Just don't burn the house down."

CHAPTER FIFTY-ONE

I wake up staring at a strange ceiling. It has curlicues. Who the hell has a ceiling with curlicues? Oh yeah, Terrance. I'm in his Hamptons hideaway. I sit up and look around. It isn't quite as opulent as Rivette's place but it's still pretty spectacular. And, Terrance being Terrance, it's exquisitely furnished, like an old English country house. Imagine if Martha Stewart was the interior decorator for Emily Dickinson.

Terrance's directions were, of course, accurate and detailed. It took us a while to find the key. Neither one of us city boys had any idea what a barberry bush is and the fact that it's red doesn't help in the black of night. We finally found it, let ourselves in, and crashed in the living room. We wanted to be close to the front door so we could hear if anyone came nosing around.

There are two couches. We each took one. I had a hard time falling asleep. Not that the couch wasn't comfortable. It's a big leather job about the size of an Oldsmobile with huge, soft cushions. It's just that with every car that drove by or squirrel scurrying across the roof, I bolted up and grabbed Donna's gun from under the cushion where I hid it, looking for killer cops, mob hitmen, Freddy Krueger.

I must have fallen asleep eventually but I have no clue what time or for how long.

"Hey, Nicky, you awake?" I yell.

No answer.

I start yelling, "Nicky, Nicky, where the fuck are you?" I throw open the bathroom door. He's not there. Could someone have snatched him in the middle of the night? No, that's crazy. I run back to the living room, throw on my clothes, grab the pistol, park myself on a chair and wait.

The knob turns. I stand, gun in hand, ready for whoever comes charging through the door. It's Nicky. He throws his hands, which are holding two paper bags, in the air. "Don't shoot, Kemosabe." I guess now we're the Lone Ranger and Tonto.

I put the gun down, take a deep breath. "When I woke up and you weren't here I freaked out."

"I couldn't sleep so I went out to pick up some breakfast." He hands me a bag. "Coffee and a bagel. I didn't know if you wanted cream cheese or butter so I went with cream cheese. Is that all right?"

"It's perfect. What are you eating? A kelp omelet?"

"Very funny. It's actually an egg-white spinach omelet on whole wheat toast and ginger-mint tea."

"Same thing."

We sit on either end of the coffee table. I can't remember the last time I ate, not counting the pretzels at BullShots. I shove half the bagel into my mouth and chomp. It's better than filet mignon.

Nobody says anything while we stuff our faces.

I finish my last bite, take a swig of coffee and say, "Well, here's another fine mess I've gotten you into."

He gives me a vacant look.

"You don't know that line? It's Laurel and Hardy. They invented buddy movies."

A glimmer of recognition. "Oh yeah. *March of the Wooden Soldiers,*' right?"

"Yeah. Among others." Now's not the time to lecture him on one of the greatest comedy teams ever.

Still picking at his omelet, he looks at me and says, "What's the plan?"

"The plan is to make it through the day without getting shot or arrested."

"That's not a plan. It's a hope."

"Okay. The plan is to hope we can get through the day without getting shot or arrested."

"C'mon, Stew."

I stand up and start pacing. Sometimes that helps me think. Then it hits me. "You know, I've been approaching this all wrong."

"Yuh think? Monahan's thugs and every cop on Long Island are after you. You're wanted for murder. And your only alibi witness died a year and a half ago."

"Thanks for sugarcoating it."

"This isn't funny."

"Listen to me. I've been trying to think like an investigative reporter. Or maybe a detective."

"That sounds right. You're trying to solve a mystery."

I shake my head. "What the fuck do we know about solving mysteries?"

He shrugs. "Not much."

"Exactly. But there's something we do know."

"We know we're in deep shit."

"Aside from that. Think." His face is blank. I keep going. "We know advertising."

He shakes his head. "How does that help us? This isn't an ad campaign."

"Suppose it was. Let's look at this like it was a creative brief."

The light in his eyes is looking a little less dim. "Okaaay."

"I know this is usually where Terrance comes in, but we've sat through enough of his input meetings. We can do it without him. You still with me?"

"I think so."

I stand up super straight, like I got a pole up my ass, trying to imitate Terrance. "We'll start with the objective. Find the real killer or killers."

"Duh."

I ignore him. "Next step: current market conditions." I hold up four fingers. "There have been four murders."

"Four? I count three. Sangster, Nielsen and Glennum."

"You forgot about Persons."

"Oh yeah. What's he, the outfielder?"

"Outfielder? What the hell are you talking about? This isn't baseball." Then it hits me. Nicky's one of the most intelligent people I know, but he's also a functional illiterate. "You mean outlier."

"Yeah, that. And you think they're all connected? I don't see it."

"I'm the connection. I was accused of killing Persons and Glennum. And I'm investigating the deaths of Sangster and Nielsen."

"So far you're not helping your cause."

"I'm not finished. Rivette also knows all four."

"You think he's the killer? I thought you idolized the guy."

"Of course he's not the killer. He's the target."

"So who is it?"

"My money's still on the Monahans."

"You really think Neil Monahan murdered four people?"

"I don't think he did it himself. Red did Persons and Glennum. Keating did the plane."

"Maybe Keating did it on his own. You said he blames Rivette, Sangster and Persons for his sister's death. That's three out of four."

"Even if he sabotaged the plane, and somehow figured out a way to get in and out of Persons's apartment in his wheelchair without being seen, why should he want to kill Glennum?"

"Maybe he thinks the newspaper covered up his sister's murder."

"That's good. I didn't think of that. That ties them all together."

"My money's on Keating?"

I shake my head. "I can't get past the wheelchair."

"That could be a fake. I've seen movies where a guy stayed in a wheelchair for years while he went on a killing rampage."

"I talked about that with Glennum. He checked on Keating with the VA file. Those injuries are real."

"Records can be changed."

"You think Keating has the juice to alter government documents?"

"Monahan does."

"So even if Keating's in on it, Monahan's still the main guy."

"Why'd he kill Persons? As far as we know, Monahan didn't even know Persons."

"'As far as we know' is the operative phrase. I bet if we dig a little we'll find a connection. Or Monahan could have offed Persons as a payment to Keating for sabotaging the plane."

He shrugs. "Maybe. But even if you're right, how are we gonna prove any of this? You can't even show your face outside. But even if you could, nobody's going to talk to us."

"That's the brilliant part of my plan."

"I was hoping there was one."

"Rivette."

"Rivette's the brilliant part of your plan?"

"Exactly. We team up with him. He has the money, resources and contacts. Everything we don't have."

"Why should he hook up with us? He's running for governor. It's less than two weeks to the election. The last thing he needs is to be associated with a couple of mooks who are wanted for murder."

"You're wrong. The last thing he needs is to be murdered himself. Monahan already tried to kill him once. He's sure to try it again. Probably before Election Day. As a candidate, Rivette can't accuse his opponent of murder. And he certainly can't investigate. But we can. If we can prove that Monahan did it, Rivette becomes the governor. And we're off the hook. It's a win-win."

Nicky makes a face like he swallowed a bug. "What about Rivette's bodyguard, that Lepro woman? She's a fucking pit bull, only meaner and uglier. She'll never let us near him."

Before I can tell Nicky my scheme for getting past Lepro—it involves him seducing her—somebody starts banging on the door.

CHAPTER FIFTY-TWO

As Nicky turns the doorknob, my heart's pounding out of my chest. With my luck, the whole East Hampton police force is standing outside with machine guns and bazookas ready to shoot first and ask questions never. I know Nicky thinks of us as Butch and the Kid, but I'm not ready for that fiery finale. So I do what any other red-blooded ex-hippie dopester would do. I hide behind the couch.

He opens the door. It's Jeannie. He drops to his knees and says, "Thank God, thank God, thank God," while kissing her hand.

She pats him on the head. "It's good to see you too." She looks around. "Where's Stew?"

I jump up and yell, "Here."

She screams. "What's the matter with you? I almost peed in my pants."

I mumble, "Sorry."

Nicky's back on his feet. He wraps his arms around her and starts sucking on her face. It startles me for a second. This is the first time I've seen them together as a couple. She looks a little uncomfortable too, gives him a peck on the forehead and steps away. He smiles awkwardly and says, "The Three Amigos are back together."

Jeannie reaches into her Mary Poppins bag. Just like the magic bag that Mary pulled lamps and tables and trees out of, Jeannie schleps her giant black satchel around wherever she goes. It's filled with everything that we might possibly need for a meeting, presentation, road trip or voyage to outer space. Food, books, presentation boards, extra pairs of shoes. Once, when we pitched Modell's, she had a football, a softball and a pair of Nike high-tops in there. We didn't get the account but I got to keep the swag. Jeannie digs deep into it and pulls out a baggie with a bunch of pill bottles and hands it to Nicky. "Your drugs."

Nicky puts his hands together like he's praying and bows his head. "Thank you so much. You're my sweet angel."

She reaches back into her bag, comes out with a wad of bills, and tosses it on the couch next to me. "There's $500 there. Terrance thought you might need it. He wanted me to stress that it's just a loan."

I wink at her. "Who knew Terrance had a heart. I always thought he had a calculator beating in his chest."

"He does. That's why he expects to be paid back. With interest."

Nicky, who's standing around fidgeting, says, "None of that matters. You're here. That's what counts. Did you eat breakfast?"

"I'm not really that hungry."

"Of course you are. It's a long drive."

"No, really."

He grabs his jacket and scoops the keys off the coffee table. "Tea and a blueberry muffin, right?" He's out the door before she can answer. She walks over and punches me in the chest. Hard.

"Oww. That really hurt."

"What the hell's the matter with you, ya big dope?"

"What do you mean?"

"It's one thing being an out-of-control creative on Madison Avenue. That goes with the territory. But beating up cops, including a police-woman, that's going way too far."

"I didn't beat her up. All I did was handcuff her to a radiator."

"You think that makes it okay?"

"I had no choice."

"Stop it," she screams. "Of course you had a choice."

"They were gonna arrest me for murder."

"Did you do it?"

"Of course not."

She yells louder. "You're gonna have a helluva time convincing anybody after what you pulled. I bet every cop on Long Island is gunning for you. I had an uncle who was a cop. They don't like it when somebody attacks one of their own."

I wink. "I attacked two, does that get me off the hook?"

"I'm glad you think this is all a big joke. You're wanted for murder, assault and God knows what else. And you're dragging Nicky down with you."

"I never thought it would get this bad. And you're right. This is my mess, not yours or Nicky's. Why don't you guys go back to the city. I'll figure something out."

She shakes her head. "You know he won't leave you here. He'd follow you into the pit of hell if he thought you needed him. He said that whatever happens, you'll either get out of it together or go down in flames together."

"When did he tell you all this?"

"Last night, while you were asleep."

"He called you in the middle of the night?"

"We talk all the time, day and night. That's what couples do."

"I keep forgetting you two are a couple."

She shrugs.

"I never saw that coming, you and Nicky."

"Why not? Nicky's a terrific guy."

"Of course. He's the best. It's just that . . . I don't know. We were all . . . you know, pals. The Three Amigos and all that crap."

"We were. Then you left and we were the two amigos." She grins. "Then amigo led to *contigo*."

"I didn't leave, I was fired. Remember? And my good friend Terrance didn't do anything about it."

She glowers at me. "You really are clueless. You have no idea how good a friend Terrance is to you. Who the hell do you think arranged the deal with Rivette?"

"That was Boyce."

"Don't be naive. Boyce was getting ready to dump the agency. You were one less problem he had to deal with. When Terrance brought up the idea of you working with Rivette, Boyce went along with it. But it was Terrance's idea. You think it was easy getting Nielsen to let you cozy up to his key client after what happened with Persons?"

"You said Nielsen hated Persons."

"He did. But he's not your biggest fan either. The only time I ever heard him mention your name it was preceded by the words 'loud-mouth clown.'"

"All right. Terrance is a fucking saint. That still doesn't explain you and Nicky. I didn't think he was your type."

"You mean sweet, loyal, considerate, and good looking?"

"I just thought you went for the more . . . you know . . . he-man kinda guy."

"You mean, like Ari?" She cringes. "No thank you. What a self-centered sleaze."

"So at least I was right about something."

"Speaking of sleazes, Nicky mentioned that you were going to try to get Rivette to help you."

"That's the plan. Why? You think Rivette's a sleaze?"

"That's what I hear."

"From who?"

"Jackie."

"Who the hell is Jackie?"

"She was Nielsen's assistant. She worked with Rivette for years. He was a client of Nielsen's."

"What did she say?"

"Have you ever been to Rivette's office?"

"Yeah."

"Did you notice that all the women there were young, blond and busty."

"Now that you mention it, I knew that there was something I liked about that place."

She shakes her head in mock disgust. "Rivette screwed every one of them. It was one of the requirements of employment."

"I find that hard to believe. Rivette's rich, powerful and handsome . . . in a distinguished kinda way. He can get all the women he wants."

"Maybe what he wants is the thrill of having a woman who doesn't want him. A lot of men are like that. Ted Bundy, for instance. He was handsome too."

"So now Rivette's a serial killer?"

"That's not what I'm saying. Just that he's like a lot of men who use their power to take advantage of women."

"Even if you're right, lots of guys hit on women. That doesn't make him evil."

"I'm not saying it does. All I'm saying is be careful. He might not be the hero you think he is."

"Rivette's a good man. I don't trust his assistant slash bodyguard slash, I dunno, procurer. That beast Lepro. I wouldn't be surprised if she was knee deep in this shit pile."

Her eyes light up. "You know Terrance is a research freak. When we got the Rivette account I did a background check on all his top people, including Lepro, and found something very interesting . . ."

Before she can finish, we hear the sound of keys jangling outside. The front doorknob starts to slowly turn.

"Must be Nicky with your breakfast."

"Good. I'm starving."

"I thought you weren't hungry."

"I wasn't. Now I am."

The door opens but it's not Nicky. It's Mr. Clean, if Mr. Clean had a feminine side. About six feet tall with zero hair on his face, head or anywhere else I can see. His shoulders are boulders. He's wearing a pink-and-white-check short-sleeve shirt with a matching pink bow tie. His biceps are straining out of his sleeves. His pants are a light pinkish beige. No socks, which is weird, considering this is October and it's chilly, and two-tone brown-and-tan loafers, I'm guessing Gucci. In a voice that would make Liberace sound like Barry White, he says, "Who are you and what are you doing here?"

I have to stop myself from laughing at hearing this Minnie Mouse squeak coming out of Skull Murphy's doppelgänger.

Jeannie says, "We're friends of Terrance Asiago. He's letting us stay here for a couple of days. Who are you?"

"Kevin Uhlmann, real estate agent. I sold Terrance this house. He asked me to keep an eye on it when he's not around."

I say, "Thanks, Kevin. We'll make sure we leave everything in one piece."

Looking skeptical, he stares intently at me, glances over at Jeannie, then glares back at me. He points a manicured finger at me. "You look very familiar. Where have I seen you?"

"Maybe at one of Terrance's parties."

Still eyeballing me, he says, "No, that's not it." His eyes widen. "I know. On the TV news. You're that murderer." He starts waving his arms back and forth spastically and screams, "Help! Police!" and heads for the door.

I make a mad dash for him, grab his shirt, spin him around, slap him hard in the face and yell, "Shut the fuck up!"

He turns to face me, his chest heaving. I'm cringing, ready for this brick shithouse to land on top of me and crush me into dust. But he just stands there whimpering, his arms dangling at his side. A red welt is forming on his cheek where I slapped him, and there's a tear at the corner of his eye.

I straighten myself up. "Calm down, Kevin. I'm sorry I hit you."

He sniffs. Then in a Truman Capote drawl says, "Don't mention it."

"For what it's worth, I didn't do those things I'm accused of. And I'm not gonna hurt you." I pick the gun up off the table. "Unless you give me no choice."

Where are the handcuffs when I need them? I guess I'll have to improvise. I look over at Jeannie. "Can you go to the kitchen and see if there's any rope or string?"

She rolls her eyes but goes. A minute later she's back, holding a couple of zip ties. "This is all I could find."

"Even better. Tying knots was never my strong point. One of the reasons I got booted from the Boy Scouts." I hand her the gun. "Hang on to this."

She cradles it reluctantly in both hands like it's a wounded bird.

"All right, Kevin. Turn around and put your hands behind your back." The zip tie barely fits around his wrists. He winces as I pull it taut. I walk over to the closet and open the door. "In here."

He shuffles in.

I slam the door shut and lean a chair against it.

Jeannie says, "What now?"

"We better get the hell out of here. It won't take the cops long to figure out where we are."

"What about Nicky? We have to let him know where we're going."

"How can I let him know? I don't have any idea myself."

"You better think of something. We can't just drive around in circles."

"We'll go to Rivette's house. He's the only person within a hundred miles of here who's on our side."

"Should we leave Nicky a note?"

I shake my head. "If the police get here first, it'll lead them right to us."

"We can't just leave him hanging."

"Of course not."

"So what do we do?"

I stand there like a mook not saying anything. In the immortal words of Curly, my favorite Stooge, "I'm trying to think but nothing happens." Then I get a brain flash. "You got any of those magazines that Rivette publishes in that bag of yours?"

"Yeah, a couple."

"Good. We'll spread them on the coffee table. Hopefully, when Nicky gets here he'll see them and know where we are."

She's shaking her head, looking pretty skeptical. "I don't know."

"He'll figure it out. I'm telling you."

She's doesn't look convinced. "All right, I guess."

I grab her arm and we run out the door. There's a BMW and a Toyota Corolla in the driveway.

"Which one is yours?"

She smirks. "Guess."

I head for the Toyota.

Jeannie throws me the keys. "My hands are shaking. You better drive."

CHAPTER FIFTY-THREE

"You have no idea where we are, do you?"

"I know exactly where we are." I look up at a street sign. "Harbor Hog Road. Who thinks of these names anyway?"

"Who cares? I thought we were going to Rivette's house."

"We are."

"In that case, you're going the wrong way."

"Why didn't you say so?"

"Because I thought you knew how to get there."

"With my sense of direction, I'm lucky if I can find my ass with toilet paper."

She cringes. "There's an image I didn't need." She reaches into her Mary Poppins bag, pulls out a dog-eared spiral-bound notebook and starts flipping through the pages. "Here it is, 703 Briar Patch Lane."

"Oh yeah. Last time we were here I remember wondering if we'd run into Brer Rabbit."

"What are you talking about?"

"It's an old Disney movie, *Song of the South*." I get a blank stare so I keep going. "Brer Rabbit's always getting into trouble with Brer Fox and Brer Bear but he's too smart for them. It's like if Bugs Bunny lived on a plantation in the Deep South." She looks at me like I have three heads, none housing a brain. "Never mind. You wouldn't by any chance know how to get there, would you?"

She grabs another sheet out of her bag. "I have directions." She looks down for a few seconds. "It's right off Montauk Highway."

"Where's that?"

"We were just on it. Make a U-turn."

"You're okay with going to Rivette's?"

"I still think he's a sleaze but I can't think of anywhere else."

"He's all right, you'll see. It's that fucking lizard-breath Lepro who gives me the creeps."

"She should. Nicky told me he gave you some background."

"Yeah. She's some kinda martial arts maven. Mai tai, Nicky said."

"Close. It's Muay Thai. Mai tai is a drink they put umbrellas in."

"Yeah, he said that too."

"She also gets her kicks beating people up, especially men. Put a few in the hospital. That's what got her kicked out of the Secret Service."

"I heard that."

"But what you haven't heard is that before she transferred to the Secret Service she was a US marshal in the Judicial Security division."

"And this matters how?"

"It puts her and Monahan in the same place at the same time. She worked a couple of his high-profile trials."

"I knew it." I bang my fists on the steering wheel. The car swerves.

"Careful!" she screams. "Crashing into a tree isn't going to help our situation."

"Sorry. I got excited. This is it. The connection. She's his inside man."

"Not so fast. First of all, she's a woman. Secondly, all we know is that they were in the same room a couple of times along with hundreds of other people. There's no proof that they ever said one word to each other."

"I don't care. I know they're in cahoots. It's the only thing that makes sense. I wouldn't be surprised if she was the one who sabotaged the plane."

"There's nothing aviation-related in her background."

"She could have worked with Keating."

"It's a long shot but suppose you're right. Maybe we shouldn't go to Rivette's."

"As long as she doesn't know we know, we have the upper hand."

Ten minutes later, we're at Rivette's door. His Duesenberg isn't in the driveway but I knock anyway. Nobody answers. I'm standing there with Jeannie trying to think of a plan B. I got nothing. So like the rational, level-headed guy that I am, I yell "*Fuck!*" at the top of my lungs and start pounding the door with both fists.

Jeannie, who's used to this moronic behavior from me, stands there patiently with her hands on her hips, shaking her head. All of a sudden, the door opens and there's Lepro, wearing a sleeveless T-shirt and workout pants, dripping with sweat. I can't help staring enviously at her biceps.

"We didn't disturb you, did we?" I say, sort of sheepishly.

She gives me a Medusa stare. "What do you want?" she says in her guttural man-voice.

"We're here to see Mr. Rivette."

"He's not here," she grunts. She would have made a great Klingon on *Star Trek*.

"When's he coming back?"

"Why?"

She's not much for conversation.

"We need to see him."

Still staring at me like I was a turd she's having a hard time scraping off her shoe, she says, "No." And starts to shut the door in my face.

I stick my foot in the threshold to keep it open. "Whaddaya mean, no?" Now I'm yelling. "It's very, very important. A matter of life and death."

Jeannie, who's been standing behind me, looks up at Lepro with pleading eyes and quietly says, "Please. Can't we just wait for Mr. Rivette inside. We really do have something extremely vital to talk to him about."

She folds her formidable arms across her chest, shakes her head and says, "Sorry."

"Unacceptable!" I scream, and push the door with both hands and storm past her.

"Stop!" she yells at my back.

I head for the great room.

A husky guy in a Hawaiian shirt with gold chains and greasy hair comes lumbering at me. It's the shmuck from the car wash. The one who said he was the dead cop, Philips. He's crouches down in what looks like a sumo wrestler's position.

I slam on the brakes. I have no desire to be tackled by this human dump truck. "How's the detailing business?"

He clenches his fists and says, "How about I detail your fucking face?"

"I'm looking for Mr. Rivette. Where is he?"

"None of your fucking business."

"You killed him, didn't you? You and that ape-woman out there. You're Monahan's hit squad."

Next thing I know I'm on the floor curled up in a fetal ball. I feel like Darryl Strawberry just took his home run cut and connected with my kidney. I roll over slowly, look up, and there's Lepro standing over me like Muhammad Ali after he KO'd Sonny Liston.

I must have been out for a couple of seconds 'cause Jeannie's sitting on the couch next to the fake Philips. He's got a vice grip on her arm and she's grimacing.

"Get up," Lepro growls. "Or I'll kick you again."

I turn over, struggle up to my hands and knees and slowly unfold myself into a close approximation of an upright position.

"Over there." She points to the couch next to Jeannie.

I shuffle over slowly and lower myself next to Jeannie. "Is Rivette dead?"

Bogus Philips leans over, punches me in the side of the head and says, "Shut the fuck up. You don't get to ask no questions." He looks over at Lepro. "What do we do with these two?"

"Nothing till we hear from the boss. Put them in the vault for now."

Bogus Philips pulls out an ugly little black pistol. His sausage fingers can barely fit into the trigger guard. He waves it at us. "Let's go."

We get up slowly, me more slowly than Jeannie. I don't know what hurts more, my back, my head or what's left of my self-respect. He marches us to the other end of the house. He opens a regular looking door and there's what looks like a bank vault door behind it. Thick steel with a big combination lock. He shoves us in and slams it behind us.

We're in a large room. There are no windows, just two vents near the ceiling. The walls are concrete. Stacked against them are dozens of paintings, some in frames, some just canvases. They vary in size from maybe a foot square to one or two that take up most of the wall.

Jeannie takes a few of the unframed canvases, piles them on the floor and sits down on top of them, staring straight ahead.

I'm pacing back and forth. "I'm sorry."

She shrugs. "Whatever."

"Are you okay?"

She glares at me. "Of course I'm not okay. We're locked up in this steel-plated crypt while those two psychos decide how to dispose of our bodies after they kill us."

"Nicky's still out there."

"And what? When he gets back to Terrance's house, either he'll find Uhlmann locked in the closet or the police waiting for him. Either way, it doesn't help us."

"You're not giving him enough credit. He'll figure it out. He'll realize that Rivette's is the only place we could possibly go. Then he'll come get us."

She sighs and shakes her head. "I love Nicky. He's kind, smart and talented. But if you think he's gonna come charging in here like some kind of Dirty Harry, you're delusional."

"I hope you're wrong. 'Cause he's our only hope."

CHAPTER FIFTY-FOUR

We've been locked in here for about an hour. There's a brochure about this bunker lying around. Nothing much else to do so I read it. This place is soundproof, bombproof, fireproof, waterproof. There's a sprinkler system and a closed-circuit TV camera. The cops could come, arrest Lepro and that other thug and nobody would ever know we're down here.

I look over and tears are trickling down Jeannie's cheeks. I gotta cheer her up. With the way I feel right now, it's like Nicky working the suicide hotline.

I walk over to her and put on the strongest face I can. "What's the matter?"

"You know what's the matter. I'm scared, Stew. I'm scared out of my mind. I don't want to die."

"Me neither. And we're not going to." I wish I could come up with a viable reason that would convince her (and me) that I'm not just blowing smoke, but I got nothing, so I change the subject. "You think you and me ever had a chance?"

She looks confused, which is better than despondent. "What do you mean?"

"You know, as a couple."

A little anger is creeping in. "You never gave it a chance."

"I know. I was afraid."

"Of what? Being happy?"

"Of fucking everything up. Like I did with every other woman I've ever been with."

She looks skeptical.

"I'm serious. Every relationship I've ever had was a total clusterfuck. My marriage to the Orthodox Jewish Vampire Bride from Hell wasn't my first horror show, it was the climax in a long line of catastrophes. There was bipolar Linda who every time I walked in the door I wasn't sure if she was gonna throw dishes at me or get down on her knees and treat my shvantz like a creamsicle. Jo-Ann, the out-of-body sojourner who disappeared for a month because she couldn't find her way back into her body. How about Carol, the prim and proper librarian who had a closet full of whips, handcuffs and dog collars that she couldn't wait to try out on me. Beth, the sex-obsessed converted Catholic who made me drive her to confession every time we had sex—sometimes three times in one night. After a while I was on a first-name basis with the priest. But wait, there's more."

"All right, all right, I've heard enough." She pauses for a second. "You think I'm like them?"

"Of course not. But there's a pattern here. Every time I get serious with a woman it turns into a huge, reeking pile of crap. I didn't want that to happen with us. I love what we have. You're the one woman I've ever known that I can talk to about anything. Who likes me for the shithead I am. No games. No bullshit. A real friend. I'm good with friendships. It's relationships I suck at."

"I don't have the greatest track record either. My ex-husband cheated on me on our honeymoon. And my other long-term boyfriend was a meth head."

"Maybe that's why we're both so fond of Nicky. He may be a total nutball but he's a terrific guy, a great partner, and the most honest, loyal, no-bullshit, nonjudgmental person I've ever met."

"He's also a great . . ."

I cut her off, wave my arms in the air, and shout, "I don't want to hear it. I know you guys are dating and you're consenting adults but I don't need to know the intimate details."

"I was gonna say 'cook.'"

"Oh."

She looks up at me with hopeful eyes. "Do you really think there's a chance Nicky might be able to get us out of here?"

"I really do." How much of a chance I don't go into.

I guess we're all talked out 'cause nobody says anything for a couple of minutes when the handle on the inside of the door starts to turn slowly. The in walks Ed Rivette followed by Sharon Lepro.

Jeannie jumps off her makeshift seat. I stand there with my mouth open. "Mr. Rivette, you're all right. Thank God. I thought they killed you."

"To quote the great Mark Twain, 'The report of my death was an exaggeration.'" He's standing in front of us, smiling benignly. His hands are behind his back, probably handcuffed. Lepro comes in behind him. I figure she's gonna lock him in here with us until Monahan tells them what to do.

Rivette takes his hands from behind his back. One is holding a gun. It looks like a prop from a Halloween cowboy costume and the handle is yellow with what looks like a bull embossed on it, but that's not what I'm concentrating on. It's the fact that it's pointed directly at my chest.

Still smiling, he says, "Stewart, you know how greatly I appreciate Americana. It may please you to know that you will meet your end by the actual sidearm that Bat Masterson used. It cost me $88,000 at auction and hasn't been fired in anger since he shot A. J. Peacock with it in Dodge City in 1881. But rest assured, it's in perfect working order."

I know I just heard it but I still don't believe it. "Why?" It comes out more like a croak than a word.

"I think it was to settle a dispute between Peacock and Masterson's brother about either a gambling debt or a woman. The record is unclear."

"Not that!" I scream. "Why us? Why do you want to kill us? We're on your side."

"You really haven't guessed, Stewart? I'm surprised. I thought you were more perceptive."

An M-80 just exploded in my brainpan. "You mean it was you? It was you all along? You sabotaged your own plane?"

"It really wasn't difficult. I've been tinkering with it for years. There are very few men on the planet who know the inner workings of a P-51 Mustang better than I."

Jeannie screams, "What kind of a monster are you? Don't you feel anything?"

"Of course I do. I really loved that old aeroplane, but one has to make sacrifices to attain the ultimate prize."

I'm still trying to make sense of what I just heard. "And Persons and Glennum? You killed them too?"

"Technically, that was Miss Lepro. There's a woman who really enjoys her work. Dispatching of Glennum with his father's antique typewriter was a particularly inspired touch."

I'm shocked, angry, confused, terrified and disappointed all at the same time. "You have everything. Money. Power. Prestige. Respect. Why murder all those people?"

He clears his throat and puffs out his chest like he's about to make a major speech. Egotistical bastard that he is, it must have been killing him to have his most brilliant scheme go unnoticed and unappreciated. Now he can pontificate to us and bask in his evil glory reflected in our stunned faces. At least until he puts a bullet in our brains.

"Throughout history the great dynasties have been built on bloodshed. The Caesars, the Medicis, the Plantagenets. I follow in their footsteps."

"You mean Congressman Whittaker dying in that car crash, that was you too?"

He nods and throws up a smug, self-satisfied grin. "Those things don't just happen."

"And Persons was with you when you killed Kathy Keating. So he had to go."

"No one meant to kill that girl. It was an accident, really. We were young, wild, drunk. We lost count of how many drugs we had given her. After she stopped breathing, what could we do, tell the world that we were drugging high school girls to sodomize them? We had to make it look like suicide."

"Then Persons starting blackmailing you?"

"Oh no. After that night we became closer, like brothers. Committing murder together gives men a powerful bond."

I blurt out, "Sounds like a Hallmark card."

Jeannie asks, "Urban too? That's hard to believe."

He smirks. "Bitsie? He never participated. Like Chauncey Gardner, he liked to watch."

I'm still trying to take this all in. "You mean he just stood there while you and Persons raped those girls?"

He gives a little shrug and says, "*Suum cuique pulchrum est.*"

I have no idea what that means and don't really care.

Jeannie says, "Why kill them now? All this happened more than twenty years ago and they were implicated with you."

"Once I decided to become the governor of Connecticut and eventually president, the stakes were raised enormously. Persons showed himself to be a weasel and an extortionist. He couldn't be left to his own devices."

"I thought you said he never blackmailed you."

"Not me, Nielsen. He was fleecing the poor man down to his socks. How did you think a poor slob like James Persons could afford his house in East Hampton. I knew it would only be a matter of time until he turned on me. I was all set to make it appear that Nielsen was responsible for Persons's untimely demise. Lord knows, he's had ample reason." He nods at me approvingly. "But then you conveniently had your very public confrontation, where you threatened and actually assaulted him, albeit with his own haberdashery. I loved hearing that story, by the way. I wish I could have been there to witness it."

"I'm glad you enjoyed it."

"Be that as it may, it positioned you perfectly. Couple that performance with your well-established hair-trigger temper and history of violence, and it provided me with an opportunity too good to pass up."

"That posse of news hacks who ambushed me at the police station, that was your doing too?"

The fucking psycho actually took a little bow. "The better to implicate you with."

I glance over at Jeannie. She's on the stack of paintings, quivering with dread. I give her a wink. It brings the faintest of smiles.

As long as I can keep Rivette talking, he's not shooting. "Whittaker, Persons and even Urban, I can see. But Nielsen and Glennum? Killing them makes no sense to me."

"Glennum was a third-rate journalist and a first-rate nuisance. His father wasn't much better. That rag of a newspaper of theirs should have been put out of its misery decades ago. The Keating matter was the best thing that could have happened for that scandal sheet. Of course they had no real proof of culpability, but their constant and irritating drip, drip, drip of rumor and innuendo was affecting my family and had to stop. A $100,000 bundle dropped in their laps fixed the leak better than any plumber could have."

"I don't get it. If he had no proof, why did he have to die?"

"He had proof of the payoff. My father enforced an agreement with the elder Glennum not to pursue the Keating issue. The son had a copy. It could have been extremely damaging."

"Okay. Why Nielsen?"

Rivette smiles and shrugs. "That was unplanned but not unwelcome. Harvey Nielsen was an insufferable bore. Pompous, arrogant, self-important. He insisted on accompanying Bitsie on the flight, and I did nothing to dissuade him."

I can't think of any more questions so it's time for plan B, whatever that is. Rivette's gun is hanging at his side. He's only a couple of feet in front of me. I could jump him, grab the gun, then shoot Lepro. Piece of cake . . . if I were James Bond. I might just try it anyway. It's a thousand-to-one shot but it beats just standing here quietly, letting him shoot us.

I'm still thinking about it when the vault door opens. Nicky strides in.

A split second of hope turns immediately to despair as pseudo-Philips lumbers in behind him, shoving a gun in his back.

Rivette smiles expansively. "So pleased you could join us, Mr. Coletti."

Jeannie runs over and hugs Nicky. Then she turns to Rivette. Tears running down her cheeks, she pleads, "Please! Please don't kill us."

"Not at the moment. I have precise plans for you three."

Phony Philips walks over to Lepro, puts his hand over his mouth, and whispers something. She nods and looks over at us like a vulture salivating over a dead dog.

Rivette turns toward them. "Did anyone see you come in?"

Phony Philips shakes his head. "Nobody was anywhere near the place."

Rivette says, "That's excellent." Then he lifts Bat Masterson's old six-shooter. I'm about to leap at him when he fires two shots. At them.

Lepro falls silently to the ground, blood oozing from her chest. The other guy utters a gurgled, "What the f . . ." and crumples.

Rivette smiles and says, "As I said, perfect working order." Then he walks out and slams the vault door behind him.

CHAPTER FIFTY-FIVE

The three of us are standing, mouths open, gaping at each other. Jeannie runs over to the two bodies. She gently puts two fingers to their throats.

"Are they dead?" Nicky asks.

Jeannie nods glumly.

Nicky says, "What's going on? Why'd Rivette lock us up?"

"He probably intends to kill us."

I get a blank stare. "I thought Monahan was the bad guy and Rivette was on our side."

Jeannie says, "We thought so too, but we were wrong."

"So, if he's the bad guy and those two . . ." he points to the bodies, "are also bad guys, why'd he shoot them?"

She says, "Good question. Maybe he's tying up loose ends."

I say, "If they're loose ends, what the hell are we?"

"Whatever we are, we still have a chance," says Nicky.

I turn to him. "Sorry I got you into this mess."

He gives me a little smile. "I didn't have anything else to do today anyway."

Jeannie hops off her seat and goes over next to Nicky. She takes his hand. "I can't believe how brave you are."

"I was never afraid to die. It's living that scares the hell out of me."

They look lovingly at each other. They're really good together. Hopefully they'll be good for longer than the next few minutes.

"Were the police there when you got back to Terrance's? Maybe they followed you here, figuring they'd find me." All of a sudden, facing a murder rap seems a hell of a lot better than eating a bullet from the six-gun that tamed Dodge City.

Nicky shakes his head. "The place was empty when I went in. Or, at least, I thought it was. Then I heard this banging and yelling coming from the closet. When I opened it, this crazy, bald-headed guy jumps out screaming his head off about murder, assault and all kinds of crap. His hands were tied up with one of those plastic thingies. As soon as I cut it off him he ran outta there like the place was on fire."

"That was Kevin Uhlmann, Terrance's realtor."

"Realtor? What the hell were you doing? Buying a house?"

"It's a long story. We had to lock him in the closet."

Jeannie shoots me a dirty look. "No coming-out-of-the-closet jokes, okay?"

"Who, me?" I wink, then turn back to Nicky. "What happened next?"

"I figured something came up and you guys had to leave. Rivette's house is the only other place in the Hamptons that you know, so that's where I went." He points to the dead guy on the floor. "He answered the door, stuck a gun in my face, and you know the rest."

No one says anything. Thirty awkward seconds later Nicky asks, "Anybody got any ideas?"

I shake my head.

Jeannie is back on her art pile, quietly sobbing.

"What the fuck?" Nicky reaches into his jacket pocket, pulls out a pack of Marlboros and a sleek black-and-silver lighter.

Jeannie sits up and yells at him, "What are you doing? I thought you quit smoking."

"I did. I haven't touched a cigarette in almost a year."

She points to the Marlboros. "So what's that?"

"I keep those just in case."

"In case of what?"

Before he can answer, I say, "Wait a minute. That might be our ticket out of here."

Nicky looks at me cross-eyed. "You think I should smoke our way out?"

I point up to the ceiling. "The sprinklers. If we hold the lighter up to them it'll turn the water on."

Jeannie says, "So we'll be all wet before Rivette shoots us?"

"No. It said in the little booklet that the sprinkler system is linked to the local fire department. Once the police and firemen come down here, we're home free."

"That's not bad," Nicky says.

I turn to Jeannie. "You're the lightest. I'll boost you up."

I squat down, cup my hands. She hops on. I lift her as high as I can. Nicky keeps her steady as she puts the lighter up to the sprinkler head.

After about a minute my arms are killing me. I shout, "What's happening?"

"Nothing."

"Are you keeping the flame close to it?"

"Yeah. It's right on it."

Nicky says, "Maybe that one's broken. Let's try the other one."

We repeat the process.

After a few minutes Jeannie says, "It's not working. Let me down."

As I'm squatting down I hear a scratchy voice. "Sorry to disappoint you. I had the sprinkler system disabled. I wouldn't want a mishap to ruin more than a hundred million dollars worth of American masterpieces."

I look up. There's a small video camera mounted on the ceiling. There's obviously an intercom too.

"Rivette, you sick sonuvabitch," I yell. "You're fucking finished. Nicky spoke to the cops before he came here. They're on their way."

There's some static, then a snicker. "I very much doubt that or they would be here already. But if the police do arrive, they'll arrest you and your friends for shooting Ms. Lepro and Mr. Talamini, which will be added to your other charges."

Nicky looks up at the camera and yells, "Stop torturing us. If you're gonna kill us, do it already."

"All in good time, Mr. Coletti. I have a very dramatic mise-en-scène planned for you but I'll need the cover of night to do it justice."

I take off my jacket and throw it over the camera. "Lights out, asshole."

I go back to my buddies and whisper. "He said he has a hundred million dollars worth of paintings down here. What do you think he'll do if we start the world's most expensive bonfire with that fancy lighter of yours?" I head for a stack of canvases. "C'mon, Nicky. Let's get some kindling."

I grab a painting of cowboys and horses and hold it up.

Nicky shakes his head and says, "Not that one."

"Why not?"

"That's a Frederic Remington. He's an immortal."

"Okay. Get another one."

Nicky makes his way through the stack, shaking his head after each one. "This is unbelievable! I grew up idolizing these guys. Winslow Homer, Mary Cassatt, another Remington, Charles Russell, Thomas Moran. He goes to another pile. "Here's a whole bunch from the Hudson River School. I feel like I died and went to art heaven."

"If we can't figure out a way to get outta here it's a good bet you will die. As far as you getting into art heaven, I'm going with the under."

He stands in front of them, shaking his head with his arms folded. "I'm sorry, Stew."

I scream, "What's the matter with you? If we don't burn these paintings, we're dead."

He shakes his head vigorously. "Destroying these masterpieces would be worse than killing myself. I'd be annihilating my artistic soul."

I've seen that look before. There's no way to change his mind. I get another idea. I go rummaging from stack to stack until I finally find what I'm looking for. I hold up a canvas. "Look. It's abstract."

He walks over, takes a look, then shakes his head. "That's a de Kooning. Can't do it."

"You always said you couldn't stand abstracts. You called this kinda stuff paint vomit."

"It is. But it's historic."

I grab another painting. "How about this?"

"Rothko. Same deal."

One more. "What about this one? It's a fucking comic strip."

"Roy Lichtenstein. No way."

"Goddamn it!" I scream. "We don't have time for you to be the fucking savior of the art world." I grab him by his collar and drag him over to some other canvases. "If you don't find some fucking paintings we can burn, that psycho is going to kill us."

He grabs one and hands it to me. It looks like the nightmare I had after I flunked my high school geometry regents—all concentric circles and triangles in vibrant colors smashing into each other.

"I hate Frank Stella," he says. "You can set anything of his on fire."

I go to another wall. There are some huge canvases that look like my bathroom wall the last time I painted it. Complete with the drips and splotches. "How about these?"

He looks over, flinches, and gives them a thumbs-down. "That's not art. Incinerate them. We'll be doing the world a favor."

I'm holding the lighter up to one of the canvases but I can't get it to catch. I figured they were oil so they'd go right up. "How come this thing doesn't burn?"

"How should I know? I never tried to set any of my paintings on fire."

He goes over to a storage cabinet tucked in the corner. Inside are bottles of turpentine, linseed oil and other stuff I imagine they use to clean the paintings. He grabs a bottle of turpentine. "This should do the trick." He walks over and pours some on the canvas. "Try it now."

I light it and the flames shoot up. "That's more like it," I yell.

Once it's burning pretty good we drag it to the middle of the floor and pile some of the others on top of it. I yell, "Hey, Rivette, it's a little cold in here. We built a fire to keep us warm." Then I yank my jacket off the video camera. "This is your multimillion-dollar art collection going up in smoke."

Over the loudspeaker we hear, "Bastards!"

Nicky whispers, "I thought we were only going to set fire to the bad paintings."

"We are. But he doesn't know that."

CHAPTER FIFTY-SIX

We have a pretty good blaze going. Close to a dozen canvases. It never occurred to me that the smoke from these old canvases would be toxic. But it's occurring now. My eyes are burning and I'm coughing and wheezing from the foul-smelling fumes. My head is pounding and I'm trying not to puke. I can hear that Nicky and Jeannie are suffering too. We're huddled on all fours close to the floor. Nicky saw on some show that if you're in a fire you should crawl around on the ground 'cause the air is fresher there. Good thing we came up with a plan before we started this bonfire 'cause right now it's hard to see and impossible to talk. The idea is for me to jump Rivette when he comes into the vault to save his precious paintings and keep him busy while Jeannie and Nicky get the hell out.

If I manage not to get shot or pass out from smoke inhalation, I'll get to the street, find a pay phone, and call them at Terrance's house. They'll pick me up and we'll go to the police. It'll still be our word against Rivette's but at least we'll be alive. It's not a great plan but it's all we got.

Nicky wanted to stay and fight but I convinced him that it's more important for him to make sure that Jeannie gets out safely.

It's been five minutes and still no Rivette. Maybe he doesn't give a shit about his paintings and figures he'll just let us die of smoke inhalation and save himself the trouble of shooting us.

The vault handle is starting to turn. I signal for Nicky and Jeannie to get ready. The door opens and Rivette's standing there holding a gun in one hand and a fire extinguisher in the other. The smoke hits him and he starts to cough. He drops the extinguisher and rubs his eyes.

This is my chance. I launch myself at him and execute a tackle that Sam Kornhauser, my old Erasmus football coach, would be proud of. If I could tackle like that in high school maybe he wouldn't have cut me after the third scrimmage.

We both hit the ground hard. The gun goes flying. I scream, "Nicky. Jeannie. Run." I can see them feeling their way through the smoke and scattered debris, toward the door. In the meantime, Rivette is kicking, punching, gouging me like his life depended on it—and it does. But not as much as mine does.

I feel like I'm wrestling a manatee on crack. He's a big sonuvabitch, maybe an inch taller than me and at least twenty pounds heavier. He's flailing away with those ham-hocky fists of his, connecting every once in a while. I'm starting to feel faint, nauseous, out of breath. I'm hoping he feels just as bad.

We're rolling around on the floor when my arm hits something hard and metallic. It's the fire extinguisher. With as much strength as I have left, I punch him in the balls. He squeals like a lobster in a steam pot and rolls off me. I get on my knees, grab the extinguisher, lift it over my head and drop it on him.

He howls. I don't know if I hit him full or just grazed him, and I'm not gonna wait to find out. I struggle to my feet and haul ass out of there.

CHAPTER FIFTY-SEVEN

So far, so good. I'm out in the street gulping fresh air. Oxygen never tasted so good. Nicky, Jeannie and the car are gone. I'm totally spent but I will myself to keep moving. I stagger-limp down the driveway and come to a road. There are no cars and no people, just trees and thick shrubs on both sides. These rich bastards love their privacy. My clothes are ripped, my face is cut and bloody and I'm walking like Quasimodo after a three-day drunk. To say that in this neighborhood I stand out like a Watusi at a Ku Klux Klan meeting would be a huge understatement. Every time I hear a car I duck behind a bush.

After about an hour I spot a pay phone. I dial Terrance's number collect. Jeannie answers. "Stew, are you all right?"

"I'm fine." If fine means dizzy, nauseous and hurting in places I never knew you could hurt in.

"Where are you?"

I look up at the street sign and tell her.

"Can I speak to Nicky?"

"Nicky's not here. He's supposed to be with you."

"When you didn't show up he went back to help you."

"Fuck! Now I have to go back and get him."

"Don't be ridiculous. I'll pick you up. Nicky'll probably be here waiting for us when we get back."

Twenty minutes later I'm at Terrance's, sprawled out on the couch, fading in and out of consciousness, waiting for the six Advils to kick in.

Still no sign of Nicky. Jeannie's pacing around the house twirling the hair by her ear and straightening things out that don't need straightening.

The phone rings. She runs to answer it.

"That's Nicky," I say. "Find out where he is and I'll go get him."

Jeannie yells, "Nicky?" into the phone. After that, she's dead silent. She starts shaking. Her face contorts like either she's gonna scream or cry. She hangs up and tears are streaming down her face. She gasps for air.

"What happened? Was it Nicky? Where is he?"

She sits down and takes a deep breath. In the five seconds it takes her to start talking I'm thinking he's either dead or in the ER on life support.

Finally she says, "It was Rivette. He has Nicky. He said he has no desire to hurt him and he'll let him go if you go back there and take his place."

I stand. "That's it. I'm going."

She screams, "No." She runs over and grabs me in a bear hug. "You can't. He'll kill you."

"I can't let Nicky die for me."

"Rivette's gonna kill Nicky no matter what you do. He can't let either of you live. We have to call the police."

"We can't call the police. They won't listen to me. I'm number one on their 'Most Wanted' list, with a bullet . . . aimed at my head."

"Okay, no police. But there must be something else. I'll call Terrance."

"What's he gonna do, send a strong memo?" She has no answer for this so I say, "I have to go. I took Rivette once, I can do it again." I try to look braver than I feel. "Where's the gun?"

She gets the gun out of the TV credenza, hands it to me, and says, "I'm going with you."

"Absolutely not! You need to be here. If we're not back in an hour, then it's time to call the police."

CHAPTER FIFTY-EIGHT

I'm driving back to Rivette's house and weighing the possible outcomes of my showdown with him. If I manage to kill him, the best I could hope for is life in prison. If he kills me, that's it, for both me and Nicky. The only outcome that doesn't end with me either dead or in jail for life is for me to somehow disarm him and take him prisoner or shoot him in the leg or somewhere that doesn't kill him. And after I miraculously accomplish both of these feats, I'll still need to somehow convince the police that an esteemed publisher and politician is a mass murderer. As Barney Boyce once said at a meeting, looks like I'm stuck between a rock and a hot plate.

I'm almost at Rivette's when I see a big, blue Plymouth Fury in the rearview mirror. It looks like those fucking FBI assholes. This is the last thing I need. If they really are FBI, they'll arrest me. If they're working for Rivette, they'll shoot me. Either way, if they stop me, Nicky's dead meat and I'm screwed. I floor it.

Unfortunately, flooring it in Jeannie's five-year-old Corolla is about second gear in most cars. It takes them all of two minutes to run me off the road.

They get out of their car and walk toward me. I grab the gun off the passenger seat. If I'm going down, at least I can take one of them with me. I level the gun at them and in my best Dirty Harry impression I say, "All right, assholes, this bullshit stops right here."

I think I'm doing pretty good. I sound tough. I'm holding the gun with two hands, the way they do on TV. All in all, I figure I'm looking like a serious badass.

That's why it's so disappointing that they don't stop walking. They don't even pull out their guns. They just start shaking their heads and chuckling.

"Stop right there," I yell. "I mean it." My hands are shaking but maybe they can't see it.

Pristera, the older white one, walks right up to me. He grabs the gun by the barrel, yanks it out of my hands and says, "Careful with that, Gribnitz. You'll hurt yourself."

I'm all out of options so I might as well try the truth, always a last resort, at least in the ad business. "I know this sounds crazy, but I'm not the killer. It's Rivette. If you really are in the FBI you gotta believe me."

Pristera says, "We know."

I'm not sure I heard right so I keep going. "He killed Whittaker and Sangster and Glennum . . ." Then it sinks in. "You know?"

"Yeah," Raines chimes in. "We've been on to Rivette for months. Since Whittaker."

"So why didn't you arrest him?"

"You can't just pick up a guy like Ed Rivette, drag him in and interrogate him like he's some bum off the street."

"You mean like you guys did to me."

"That wasn't us. That was the NYPD."

"That's right. All you did was beat the shit out of me."

Pristera says, "We wanted to scare you off."

"Why? What were you afraid of?"

"We thought either you'd get killed or get in the way. That you'd make a tough investigation even tougher. And that's exactly what you did."

"Let me get this straight. You couldn't get rid of me the first time so you thought you might as well kick the crap out of me on the highway, just for shits and giggles."

"Not exactly. When we saw you wouldn't quit, we decided to use you."

"Use me? How?"

"We put a tracking device in your wallet."

"Bullshit! When?"

"When we took the twenty dollars out of it."

"So if you had me on radar, where the hell were you when that bastard was about to kill us?"

They look a little embarrassed.

Raines says, "We don't monitor it 24/7. We were looking into what happened to your friend Glennum."

"Do you know Rivette has Nicky?"

"Yeah. We have somebody watching the place."

"Why don't you arrest him?"

Pristera says, "For what? Having somebody at his house?"

"There are two dead bodies in there. You can arrest him for that."

"What bodies?"

"Lepro and his other stooge."

Their eyes bug out and their mouths jut open. Raines says, "They're dead? Since when?"

"When he had us locked up in his vault room. They came in and he just shot them with that antique six-shooter of his. I'm guessing he was gonna try to make it look like we all killed each other."

Pristera says, "That's enough to go on. You stay here. We'll have someone pick you up."

"No way! My friend Nicky's still there. I'm seeing it through to the end."

Raines shakes his head. "Can't. Too dangerous."

"I've already been beat up, shot at and run into a ditch. How much more dangerous can this be?"

He shouts, "No!"

"The bodies are in the vault room. You'll never find it on your own. And Rivette sure as hell won't show it to you. Without that, you have no evidence."

They look at each other for a couple of seconds. Then Pristera says, "Okay, you can come. But you gotta stay in the car."

"Deal. I just want to see Rivette's smug face when you drag him out in handcuffs."

CHAPTER FIFTY-NINE

We're parked at the end of Rivette's long driveway. Pristera wags a finger at me. "Stay in the car."

"Of course." I wink.

"I'm serious. I don't want to have to handcuff you to the steering wheel."

"Yeah. Whatever."

They're almost at the front door when there's a huge explosion. The door flies off its hinges. Projectiles of metal, glass and God knows what else rain down. Through the haze I can see that Pristera and Raines are on the ground. They look like they're in pretty bad shape.

I dive into the front seat, grab the two-way radio and scream, "Mayday! Mayday!" I don't know what the hell Mayday means but it always gets a lot of action when they do it in the movies.

There's a staticky buzz. Then, "Agent Raines?"

"No. I'm at Rivette's house. There's been an explosion. Raines and Pristera are hurt. Send help."

"Who is this?"

I drop the radio and scramble out of the car. I'm thinking of Nicky. He's in there somewhere.

I head for the house. Then I see someone running toward the beach. It's fucking Rivette. He's limping a little.

I chase after him. He has about thirty yards on me. But I'm gaining. I have two good legs and I'm fifteen years younger.

We're on the beach. He's ten yards in front of me and still running. The scumbag is in better shape than I thought. My lungs are burning, but rage and adrenaline keep me going.

Rivette stops. Turns. We're face-to-face. We're both breathing hard and loud, like two old queens in a gay porno movie.

He's smiling. I don't get it. He looks at me like he was my professor and I just aced the final. "I'm very proud of you, Stewart. I never dreamed that of all the highly competent people standing in my way, you would be the one to stop me."

I scream, "You're fucking crazy!"

"That could be. A sane person would have disposed of you a while ago but for some reason I had a soft spot for you." He reaches into his pocket. "I can rectify that now."

He pulls out a tiny gun. Some kind of ancient derringer. Another one of his fucking antiques. He points it at my chest, pulls back on the hammer and squeezes. There's a click but no shot. "Damn!" he yells. He eyes it disdainfully then chucks it at my head. It clips me over my eye. Now I'm really pissed.

I leap at him and we both go down. We thrash around on the sand. I remember from his bio that he was a wrestling champ in college. He's still got some of his old moves. The next thing I know I'm on my back and he has his hands around my throat.

The only thing I know about wresting is from watching the WWF guys on TV. Hulk Hogan, Bruno Sammartino, George "the Animal" Steele. I ask myself, what would they do? Fight dirty, of course.

There are no wooden chairs or metal stanchions to use as weapons but there's plenty of sand. I grab a handful, throw it in Rivette's face, and follow it up by jabbing the heel of my hand into his nose (I think I saw the Iron Sheik do that one). He falls back. I throw him off and scramble on top of him. My knees are on his shoulders, pinning him to the sand. He's yowling like a caged animal, rubbing his eyes, squirming and shaking, trying to throw me off. I can feel his strength ebbing. All that running and fighting has finally taken its toll.

My left hand is wrapped around his throat. I raise up my right and smash it down on his face. He bellows like a gored bull. I hit him again. This time on the side of the head. He goes limp. I keep punching with both fists. I can feel his face getting mushy. My knuckles are raw. My arms are aching but I keep swinging. Pictures of Nicky and Glennum and Urban, all lying dead, are swirling in my head.

Hands grip my arms and shoulders and yank me off him.

Now I'm flat on my back in the sand, looking up into the hazy sun. There's a bunch of blurry blue figures standing over me.

I try to stand up but it's not going so good. I fall back down. I feel like one of those little wooden dolls where you push a button on the bottom and it flops over. The best I can do is to sit up. I'm dizzy and I feel like any second I'm gonna puke.

One of them grabs my arm. My eyes begin to clear. It's Timson, the cop I beat up. He's grinning and glowering down at me. "You're under arrest."

"For what?"

"Murder. Assault. Resisting arrest. That's just for starters."

CHAPTER SIXTY

I'm flat on my back, looking up into the nostrils of half a dozen cops from three different East Hampton law enforcement agencies. They're arguing with each other about who gets the first chance to slam my ass in jail. The town police say it should be them because I coldcocked their boy Timson. The village police want me for when I handcuffed Donna to the radiator. And the marine patrol are claiming first dibs because my WrestleMania bout with Rivette happened in their jurisdiction, which is anything wet or sandy. They all want to arrest me for Glennum's murder. Who knows why a dipshit little beach resort needs three different police departments. The only thing I'm sure of is no matter who wins, I lose.

A couple of EMS guys are carting Rivette out on a stretcher. I'm screaming that he's the real murderer. At the same time, half a dozen cops are shouting questions at me. And nobody's paying attention to anybody.

Then it gets quiet.

Pristera and Raines come limping across the sand, scratched and bloody, holding their IDs in the air. Pristera shouts, "FBI. We'll take it from here."

All the vitriol that was echoing back and forth among the three

Hamptons police departments is now aimed squarely at my former tormentors. Now, hopefully, my saviors.

It takes several minutes and a lot of yelling, cursing and whining for them to sort it out. Finally, the local cops give way when Raines tells them that Rivette really *is* wanted for six murders and I'm a confidential informant working undercover for them.

While all this is happening the place is getting more and more crowded. Reporters, photographers and a couple of news vans with satellite dishes on top.

My head is spinning like I'm on a bad acid trip. Now I really think I'm hallucinating. 'Cause here comes Nicky hobbling toward me.

I struggle to my feet. We stagger toward each other in slow motion like a Special Olympics version of *Chariots of Fire*.

"Nicky, you're alive!" We man-hug. "When I heard that explosion, I thought you were dead."

"I wish." He gives me a half-assed grin. "Rivette locked me in that vault room. It's a fucking fortress. You coulda dropped an atom bomb on the rest of the house and nothing woulda happened to me as long as I was inside there."

A couple of minutes later, Jeannie shows up, escorted by some more FBI types. Another group hug.

Pristera and Raines do a pretty good job of keeping the newshounds at bay. A couple of agents take statements from Nicky and Jeannie. After an hour things start to quiet down. The reporters and bystanders get bored and the local cops stomp away in a pissy huff. Nicky and Jeannie want to stay with me. I tell them it's not necessary but they don't budge.

Nicky says, "The Three Amigos stick together through thick and thin."

Then Pristera tells them they have to debrief me and it might be several more hours.

Jeannie whispers something to Nicky, who nods glumly.

Nicky says, "Stew, we're gonna go." We do another group hug and they leave.

Now the beach is pretty much deserted. Me and my two FBI

buddies drive about a mile down the road. The sign says, "Georgica Beach, Open to the Public." We park ourselves at a picnic table.

Even though they know a lot of what happened, they want it from the beginning. So I give them the whole saga from wiping my ass with Persons's tie to my WrestleMania special with Rivette.

They're both taking notes at a furious pace, stopping me every once in a while to ask a question.

After I'm done, Pristera says, "Put your story together with what we got and it's a lot. But it might not be enough. Rivette's a fucking blue blood with a lot of money and powerful friends. I wouldn't be surprised if he has relatives on the Supreme Court. And you know he'll have the best lawyers in the country. They'll claim that the whole thing is a political hatchet job. That you're the killer and you made everything up just to save your ass. When you're on the stand they'll twist everything you say. It'll be your word against his."

Raines says, "Are you sure you want to do this?"

"Fuck yeah!" I shout. "That fucking scumbag tried to ruin my life. Now I'm gonna ruin his." I look from one to the other. "I notice that you guys take a lot of notes. I bet you have to do a lot of that in your line of work."

Raines says, "Yeah. Every time we interrogate someone." Then he gives me a look like I lost my last screw. "What the hell does that have to do with anything?"

"I'm supposed to take notes whenever I go to a meeting, but I suck at it. I usually just don't bother, but even when I do, I can't read my own writing. Jeannie, on the other hand, is great at it. She's like one of those courtroom stenographers. Whenever we have an important meeting she knows to make me a copy of her notes. The problem is, she doesn't come to all my meetings. And Nicky's useless. He doesn't write at all; he draws pictures. So I got myself this." I pull the voice recorder out of my pocket and lay it on the table. "It's a Sony. Does a great job. I bet you guys could use something like it. Listen to how good it sounds." I click it on and Rivette's voice, as clear as if he's sitting next to us, starts pontificating. "Throughout history the great dynasties have been built on bloodshed. The Caesars, the Medicis, the Plantagenets. I follow in their footsteps . . ."

They listen to Rivette's whole speech then break into the two biggest shit-eating grins I ever saw.

Raines jumps up, thrusts his fist in the air and shouts, "We got the sonuvabitch."

I hand him the recorder. "You might want to make a few copies of that tape, just for safekeeping."

Pristera says, "We owe you. If there's anything we can do."

"As a matter of fact, there is. Can you guys put out an APB or a BOLO or whatever the hell you call it when you want to find someone who's missing?"

Raines says, "Who are you looking for?"

"My father. Nicky checked the house in Canarsie and he said it looked like nobody's been there for a while. I'm worried."

They both look embarrassed.

Raines says, "We've been meaning to tell you."

"Tell me what?" I get that clammy feeling in the pit of my stomach. "He's dead, isn't he?"

"No. He's fine."

"What's going on?"

Pristera says, "We thought he might be in danger. That Rivette would use him to leverage you."

Then Raines says, "We figured it would be best to get him out of the house until everything was settled."

"So where the hell is he?"

"We arranged for him to have a free week in Atlantic City. We know a judge there who helped us with the arrangements. We made it so he thought he won some sorta contest. He was ecstatic. Said now he could get married in style." He smiles at me. "Looks like you're gonna have a new mama."

My brain is rattling. I mean, thank God he's all right. But married? I guess Ruth was lying after all when she told me she hadn't seen Moish since my mother's funeral. Maybe I could learn to like her. But I'll never think of her as my new mama.

PART THREE

Back Home

The lights are on so I guess he's . . . I mean they're home. After everything that's gone on, I shouldn't be nervous meeting my father's new wife, especially since I've known her since I was a kid.

I'm not sure how to greet her. A hug? A handshake? A kiss on the cheek? I won't mention our telephone conversation when she said she hadn't spoken to Moish since my mother's funeral. For some reason they wanted to keep it a secret and I'll respect that.

I can hear music playing inside. Already an improvement. Except if it's opera. I can't stand opera. Ruth seems like the kind of person who would like opera. Or at least pretend to.

But no, it's Harry Belafonte. Cool. I haven't heard that since Dolly was around.

I still have my keys, but before I open the door I compose myself and paste a phony smile on my face. I walk inside. The house smells like food. Good food. As opposed to Moish's cheap cigars. Another improvement. This might work out better than I thought.

There's someone on the other side of the living room. Her back is to me. Funny, I remember Ruth being shorter and dumpier.

"Hello," I say, not too loud. I don't want to scare her.

She turns around. It's not Ruth. It's Dolly. It's maybe fifteen years since I've seen her and she looks exactly the same. Almost. She flashes that big, broad smile of hers and shouts, "Steeeew-heart." Then runs over, throws her arms around me and gives me a bear hug. "It's a blessing to see you." She takes a step back. "Let me look at you." She cracks another huge smile. "Last time I saw you, you were a boy. A big boy but still a boy. You're a man now. And a handsome one."

"Dolly. I can't believe you're here. That's so great. I had no idea you'd be here."

"Your father wanted it to be a surprise."

"Yeah. He's full of surprises. Where is he anyway?"

"He went out to the store to get some things. You know we just got back earlier today."

I look around. What the hell is going on? No sign of Ruth. Could Raines and Pristera be kidding me about Moish getting married? And why is Dolly here? I know Ruth always had a cleaning lady. Could they have hired Dolly as a live-in maid?

The door opens. There's Moish, holding a bag of groceries.

"Stewboy," he bellows. "I didn't know you'd be here."

"Hi, Dad. I didn't know, myself, until a little while ago."

"Did Dolly tell you?"

"Tell me what?"

"The news."

"You tell me."

"I won this trip for two to Atlantic City. I couldn't even remember entering the contest. But at my age the memory isn't what it used to be. A full week at Harrah's. What a place! First class all the way. I've never been in a room like that. The bed was huge. And the sheets, soft like butter. We saw the Buddy Hackett show. I pissed in my pants from laughing so hard. Then I got this idea. We're here already, why not get married and make it a honeymoon. We're gonna do it sooner or later. Why not sooner? I'm not getting any younger, you know."

"Wow."

"Yeah. I wish you coulda been there. But it was a spur-of-the-moment thing. And those guys you were working with, they said I shouldn't call. That you'd be out of touch."

"What guys?"

"Those two cops. The FBI guys. They came here the day after you left. They said you were working on some kinda undercover operation. That's what that murder business in the paper was all about. What'd they say . . . establishing your cover story."

"Forget about that." I run over and give him a hug. "Congratulations!"

He looks relieved. "You're good with it?"

"Yeah. I think it's great. Where's Ruthie?"

He scrunches his face. "Ruthie? How the hell should I know?"

"Isn't that who you married? You said you were seeing her."

He shudders. "Ruth Bernstein, ugh. That was to throw you off the track." He breaks into a self-satisfied grin. "And it worked. I could never stand that woman. She was as big a phony as that husband of hers. I don't know what your mother ever saw in her."

"So who . . ."

Dolly, who was taking it all in from the other side of the room, roars with laughter. She walks over and tenderly takes Moish's hand.

"Dolly?" It's starting to sink in. "You and Moish? Married?"

Moish looks glum. He turns to her. "You see. I told you he wouldn't like it."

I frown. "Of course I don't like it." They both look dejected. Then I run over, throw my arms around them. "I love it!"

We're all in a clinch, hugging, kissing and carrying on like drunken Hasidim dancing the hora.

When we finally break I ask Moish, "Why didn't you want to tell me? You know I love Dolly. She was practically my second mother."

He shuffles uncomfortably. "I know. I was afraid maybe you'd think that Dolly and me, that we were doing something behind your mother's back."

Dolly says, "I told him that was nonsense. But you know your father, he's a stubborn old mule."

"I know Dolly would never do anything like that." I turn to Moish. "You, I'm not so sure."

Dolly smiles. "He's too stuck in his ways to be carrying on with strange women. It took me and your mother twenty years to train him. We're the only two women on Earth who could put up with him." She starts laughing that rich laugh of hers. Me and Moish, we crack up too.

Moish says, "What about you? First you're a murderer. Then you're some kind of undercover spy. How did all this happen? I thought you wrote want ads."

"C'mon, Dad, we've been all through this. Not want ads, magazine and newspaper ads. And TV commercials. Radio too."

"Okay. So when did you become, what did those FBI boys call it, a confidential information operator?"

"It's a long story. I'll tell you what. Since I never got a chance to go to your wedding, let me take you both out. We'll celebrate you and Dolly getting married and I'll tell you all about me and the FBI."

His face lights up. "There's a new Chinese place that opened up not too far from here. It's supposed to be pretty good." He turns to his bride. "Whaddaya say?"

"Sounds fine to me."

CHAPTER SIXTY-TWO

It's three in the morning. I'm lying in my old bed in my old room, counting the cracks in the ceiling. Superman had his fortress of solitude. This is my bunker of ineptitude.

I was already out of the house when my parents moved here but my mother fixed up this room in the basement. "We'll always have a place for you, Stewie, no matter where we live. And no matter where you live."

I kissed her, thanked her, and told her I was a big advertising hotshot and she didn't need to keep a room for me. That soon I'd be buying them their dream house out on Long Island.

Then I got fired the first time and wound up here with a suitcase in my hand and a hangdog look on my face like Felix at Oscar's door during the opening credits of *The Odd Couple*. In a few months I hooked up with another agency and got a studio in a fourth-floor walk-up in Gramercy Park.

I lasted two years there until they got a new creative director who said I didn't fit with his new vision. That vision was giving his gay boyfriend my job. I'm sure that wasn't the only kind of job he gave him. So back to Canarsie I went.

Two more firings and one abysmal marriage later and here I am again. It coulda been worse. A couple of days ago, with several murder convictions hanging over my head, I thought my next address was gonna be Cell 23, C Block, Attica.

Dinner with Moish and Dolly was great. After five minutes it was like them being married was the most natural thing in the world.

I gave them the whole story and they were very impressed. Moish said he was even prouder of me than when he thought I was the second coming of Murder Incorporated. Dolly said she always knew I had big things in my future. They told me I should make a movie. Then there was a heated discussion about who should play me: Harrison Ford, Clint Eastwood or Sylvester Stallone.

I was feeling pretty pleased with myself until I got home. Then it hit me. Not only isn't there going to be a movie, there's not going to be a job either. Ari, who is now the half owner of UPAN, hates my guts. And my chances of hooking up with another agency after being bad-mouthed up and down Madison Avenue by Harvey Nielsen is somewhere between slim and go fuck yourself.

Just 'cause my reputation is shit in New York, it's not the end of the world. There are ad agencies all over the country. I could try a different city. I still have most of the $50,000 that Rivette gave me. That should keep me going for a while. Maybe I'll go to Green Bay. At least I know one person there. With my luck, I'll get there and she'll be married . . . to Ray Nitschke.

When I got home there was a message from Nicky saying I should show up at UPAN tomorrow at ten o'clock. Terrance has a severance check for me. He said I shouldn't worry about running into Ari, he's out of town.

Do I really want to go there and face everyone? Having them all feel sorry for me? I could call Terrance and ask him to mail me the check.

So what am I gonna do? Stay here all day and gape at Dolly and Moish?

I'll go. I know I'll keep in touch with Nicky and Jeannie, but there are a lot of people I really like at the agency who I might never see again. It'll be good to be with them one more time.

CHAPTER SIXTY-THREE

The clock over Helen's desk says 10:10. I get a little twinge, that old feeling that Terrance is gonna ream me out for being late. Then I realize I don't work here anymore.

As soon as Helen sees me she jumps out from behind her desk, grabs me, pulls me up against her and plants a big, juicy kiss on my cheek. I swear to God, if she were fifteen years younger I'd marry her tomorrow.

"They're all in the conference room."

"They? Who's they? I thought Terrance wanted to meet with me about my severance."

"I don't know anything about that. Just go ahead in."

The corridor is deserted. It's been less than two weeks since I've been here and it already looks different. All the walls have been painted. There's new carpeting and new furniture. Our ads are back hanging on the wall but in nicer frames. That brings a smile to my face.

The conference room door is closed. I ease it open and shuffle softly inside. The room is filled front to back with rows of folding chairs and almost every one is occupied. I can see Nicky and Jeannie in the front row along with some other familiar faces.

The conference table is off to the side with a huge breakfast spread.

Coffee urns. Trays of bagels, donuts and fruit. Napkins, paper plates, all that kinda stuff.

I spot an empty chair in the back and sit down, trying to be as unobtrusive as possible.

Terrance is at a lectern in front of the room. He points at me. "Stewart, I'm glad you could make it."

Everyone turns to look at me. So much for unobtrusive.

He clears his throat. "I was just informing the staff that as of today, UPAN is officially under new management. There will be some modest changes, hopefully for the better, but by and large it will be business as usual. Since you played such a big part in making UPAN the agency it is today, I'm pleased you could be here to witness the day that we enter a new phase in our growth."

He beams a self-satisfied smile. "I was just about to mention that I have personally spoken to all our clients and they are looking forward to continuing their work with us. All except Rivette Publications, who I don't think will be working with any agency for the foreseeable future." This gets a laugh. "Now as my grandmamma Angelina used to say . . . *Mangia!*"

There's a stampede to the breakfast table. I'm still sitting, trying to decide whether I should be upset, jealous or pissed off. I know Terrance offered me my old job back and I told him to shove it, but that doesn't mean he has to call me in here to show off how well he and everyone else is doing. He could have sent me the goddamn severance check in the mail. Fuck it. I'm here. I might as well eat.

I'm looking around for Nicky when Terrance grabs my arm and starts dragging me out of the room. "What? You're throwing me out?"

"Don't be an ass. There's something I want to show you."

"I've seen enough. Now let's talk about my severance so I can get the hell out of here."

"In good time." He puts an arm around me and leads me down the executive corridor. "First come with me."

We're at Boyce's old office. There's a new door with a gold plaque. Etched on it in big, bold letters is "Terrance Asiago, Chairman & CEO."

"Very impressive. Does Ari have a door just like it?"

Terrance gives me one of his fake surprise expressions, the same one that I've seen him pull on clients dozens of times, usually after he hits them with a bill they didn't expect.

"Oh, didn't you know? Ari's not with the agency anymore."

Talk about your proverbial ton of bricks. "What? The last I heard he was co-owner."

"That was before he was arrested."

"Arrested? You mean they finally made being an arrogant asshole a crime?"

I get the classic over-the-glasses stink eye. "You haven't lost your perverse sense of humor. In fact, he was charged with espionage."

"He's a spy? That doesn't make sense. He's Israeli. They're our allies. Who the hell did he spy on, the Oriental rug place down the block?"

"You're close. He was charged with industrial espionage. Many of his clients were companies doing business with Israel. Some were defense contractors. He was caught stealing proprietary information, including classified military data."

"So? He's in jail?"

He shakes his head. "He's in Tel Aviv. An arrangement between the Israeli embassy and the FBI. Very hush-hush."

"So it's just you? You're the head honcho? The big kahuna? The grand high exalted mystic ruler?"

"Enough!" he shouts. Then he starts pulling me down the hall. "There are still some things I'd like to show you."

"I hope my check is one of them."

He ignores me. A couple of doors down we're in front of one that says, "Nick Coletti, Creative Director, Art."

I'm smiling so hard my face is gonna break. "It's about fucking time. Good job, Terrance, Nicky's the best."

"Of course he is."

I wag my finger at him. "One thing. You can't turn him into being just a supervisor. That'll kill him. He'll be great mentoring the younger art directors, but he needs to work on his own stuff too. He'll go crazy if you turn him into another do-nothing suit. No offense."

He rolls his eyes. "None taken. As far as Nicky having his own accounts to work on, of course he will. He's one of the best art directors in the city. It would be foolish not to utilize one of our most valuable assets."

"Good. But be careful who you team him up with. He's quirky. It took me weeks to break him in. The wrong partner will be a disaster."

"We found someone we think will be perfect."

"Oh really? Who is this mastermind?"

"I'll let you meet him. Here's his office. Right next to Nicky's."

The letters on the door say, "Stewart Gribnitz, Creative Director, Copy."

It takes a few seconds to sink in. "Does this mean I don't get a severance check?"

"I'm afraid so." He gives me a huge hug, almost breaks a rib. I forgot how strong he is. "Congratulations!"

I kiss him on the cheek. Then in my best Bogie voice I say, "Terrance, this could be the start of a beautiful friendship. Strictly platonic, though. Don't expect me to be kissing you on a daily basis."

He grimaces. "Heaven forbid."